The final curtain

I packed a duffel bag with some clothes, some self-repair tools, and my favorite computer.

The only person I said good-bye to was Liel, and that wasn't on purpose. I don't know whether she just happened to be hanging around the unlit lobby at two a.m. or what, but there she was, a dark silhouette with sparkling eyes and luminous hair.

We stood there looking at each other for a moment.

"Where will you go?" she asked.

"A friend's house," I said.

"You have friends out there?"

"Yeah, I guess."

"Will . . ." She looked down so that her jewel eyes were hidden in the shadows. "Will you be back?"

"Maybe."

I could faintly see her nod. "What . . . should I tell them?"

"Tell my mom I'm sorry. I don't care what you tell the rest of them."

Then I walked past her to the front doors.

"Boy," I heard her say behind me.

I froze, hand halfway to the door handle. I knew, right then, that if she asked me to stay, I would.

But she just said:

"Good luck."

"Thanks," I said.

And that was it. I left The Show.

OTHER BOOKS YOU MAY ENJOY

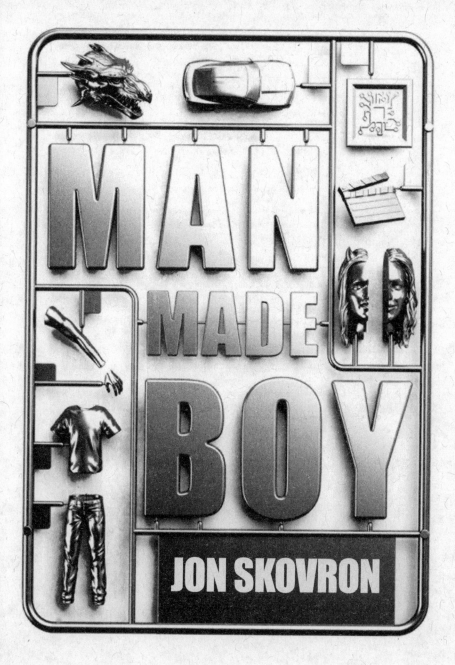

MAN MADE BOY

JON SKOVRON

speak

An Imprint of Penguin Group (USA)

SPEAK
Published by the Penguin Group
Penguin Group (USA) LLC
375 Hudson Street
New York, New York 10014

USA * Canada * UK * Ireland * Australia
New Zealand * India * South Africa * China

penguin.com
A Penguin Random House Company

First published in the United States of America by Viking,
an imprint of Penguin Young Readers Group, 2013
Published by Speak, an imprint of Penguin Group (USA) LLC, 2015

Copyright © 2013 by Jon Skovron

THE LIBRARY OF CONGRESS HAS CATALOGED THE VIKING EDITION AS FOLLOWS:
Skovron, Jon.
Man made Boy / by Jon Skovron.
pages cm
Summary: Tired of being sheltered from humans, seventeen-year-old Boy, son of Frankenstein's monster
and the Bride of Frankenstein, runs away from home and embarks on a wild road trip that takes him
across the country and deep into the heart of America.
ISBN 978-0-670-78620-6 (hardcover)
[1. Monsters—Fiction. 2. Human beings—Fiction. 3. Runaways—Fiction. 4. Science fiction.]
I. Title.
PZ7.S628393Man 2013   [Fic]—dc23   2012043217

Speak ISBN 978-0-14-242743-9

Printed in the United States of America

Designed by Kate Renner

1 3 5 7 9 10 8 6 4 2

for my mother, Gini Kelley,
who chose the road less traveled
and taught me to do the same.

PART 1

The Show

"*Thus* strangely are our souls constructed,
and by such slight ligaments are we bound
to prosperity or ruin."

—Victor Frankenstein,

FROM *FRANKENSTEIN; OR, THE MODERN PROMETHEUS*, WRITTEN BY MARY SHELLEY

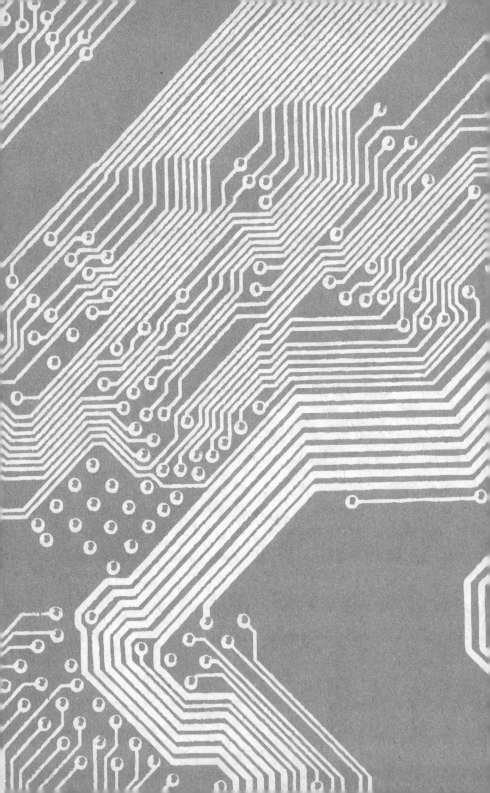

1

A Boy Named Boy

++++++++

IN THE BEGINNING, there was zero. And then God said, let there be one.

Computers, Internet, phones, text messages—our entire digital lives can be broken down into code. And code can be simplified into binary. And binary is nothing but a string of ones and zeroes. At each moment, a choice. Yes or no. Everything we create, everything we do, everything we are, comes down to that. It is so simple. And so beautiful.

That's where I was happiest. In my room, at my computer, creating amazing things with the beautiful simplicity of code.

"Boy."

The outside world intruded. I pretended not to notice.

"Boy!"

This time, it was loud enough that there was no way I could pretend not to notice. I unplugged and turned around. A massive figure filled my bedroom doorway. He had to angle his shoulders and stoop his head just to fit through. He looked at me with watery, mismatched eyes that glared beneath patchy hair and a protruding brow. Black, uneven stitches zigzagged across mottled skin without any pattern or regularity. He lifted one massive, stitch-and-scar-covered hand and pointed a thick finger at me.

"Did you eat?" he asked in his rough, deep voice. Even after living in the States all these years, he still had a heavy accent. Somewhere between German and French.

"Yeah," I said.

"What?"

"I had some Pop-Tarts for dinner."

"That was last night. You haven't even had breakfast?"

"Oh . . ."

He raised one bristling eyebrow.

"So you didn't sleep, either?"

"I guess I lost track of time."

"This is not good, Boy. Not healthy."

"I'll take a nap this afternoon," I said. "Promise."

"No. Your mother has made you some lunch. You will eat it. And then you will take a break from your computer and do something else."

I sighed. He'd been doing this to me more and more lately. "Like what?"

"Why don't you . . ." He lifted his palms up and smiled, like a brilliant idea had just popped into his head. "Help Charon in the box office."

"Really? The box office?"

"You used to love helping out in the box office!"

"When I was twelve . . ."

"Boy! Now!"

"Okay, okay, I'm going."

You didn't argue with my dad when he got that tone of voice.

———

"I THINK I'M going to change my name," I said.

"Oh, yeah?" Charon didn't bother to look up as his ancient hands worked quickly, stuffing tickets into envelopes.

"I'm seventeen," I said. "And my mom finished upgrading all my kid parts to adult parts last year. So technically, 'Boy' isn't really an accurate name anymore."

"But your father isn't exactly '*the* Monster,'" Charon said. "And I love your mother dearly, but it's been a long time since anybody thought of her as a 'Bride.'"

I swiveled back and forth in my chair, as much as the room would allow. Like most box offices, the space was small, with just enough room for two computer terminals, a filing cabinet, and us. I'm a big guy, but Charon was basically a skeleton with leathery skin, so it wasn't too cramped. Besides, when you've lived your entire life inside a Broadway theater, tight quarters don't bother you much.

"So?" I chugged the rest of my Mountain Dew and tossed the bottle in the trash. "Maybe we should *all* change our names."

Charon's tight, brown skin crinkled into a smile.

"Okay, you're right, they'd never do that. But I want to change *my* name."

"To what?"

"I don't know." I stared for a moment at the names on the tickets as they printed from the machine. "What about Henry? Or William? Something that sounds . . ."

"Human."

"Well . . . yeah."

Charon set down his stack of tickets and looked at me. "Your argument is that 'Boy' doesn't suit you anymore. But a human name wouldn't suit you any better."

"But—"

"That's what your parents would say, and you know it." He handed the stack of tickets to me. "Now, make yourself useful and rack these." Then he turned to the filing cabinet and began flipping through the last-minute house seat requests.

I sighed and began to slide the tickets into alphabetical slots above the customer window. My clunky patchwork hands made me a lot slower than Charon.

"What's your infatuation with humans, anyway?" he asked.

I shrugged. This was a topic we couldn't agree on.

"You've never even met a human. Watching them on TV doesn't count."

"I have lots of human friends," I said.

"Internet friends," said Charon. "Those don't count, either. They have no idea what you are."

"I don't get why everyone makes such a big deal about that."

"That's because you've always been sheltered in this bubble."

"Like that's my choice," I said. "Believe me, if I could get out and meet some humans, I totally would."

A new voice, dark and soft, asked, "Would you?"

Ruthven stood at the customer window, shrouded in the shadows that always clung to him so that only his pale face was visible. His piercing red eyes bore down on me in a way that made me squirm in my seat.

"Hey, boss," Charon said. "I was just telling Boy here that he doesn't know how good he has it. Back in the old days, before you started The Show, we had to fend for ourselves. Hiding among the humans, always in danger of—"

"Yes, yes." Ruthven silenced him with a flip of his hand. Then his eyes turned back to me. "So you would like to meet some humans. The weather is pleasantly overcast, so I intend to go out and run some errands. Would you like to accompany me?"

I stared at him for a moment. "Out? As in, outside the theater?"

"Yes." He said it like it was no big deal. Like he and every other adult hadn't told me my entire life that I must never leave the theater, or I would probably be killed, expose our secret, and ruin everything for the entire theater company. "Isn't that what you just said you wanted?"

"Um . . ." I said. "Yes?"

"Marvelous. You can carry things for me."

"Boss," said Charon. "Don't you think people will notice he looks . . . different?" He glanced at me and shrugged apologetically.

"Actually," said Ruthven, "I've given it careful consideration and I am certain it won't be a problem. Boy's parents did a marvelous job building him—the matching skins, the fine stitching. Believe me, their creator didn't make such an effort when making *them*, arrogant, self-absorbed bore that he was."

"You really think people will see me as . . . a *human*?" I asked.

"One that's been maimed in a horrible accident, certainly." Ruthven flashed a faint, fanged smiled. "But yes, I think you'll pass."

A dopey grin crept onto my face. "Wow."

"However, you will need to get permission from your parents."

"Oh." For a second, my heart fell. But then I asked, "Both? Or just one?"

A thin, black eyebrow slowly rose into an arch. "One should be sufficient."

I KNEW DAD wouldn't still be in our apartment by this time, but there were a couple of places he could be. I checked the stage first. Sometimes he liked to watch last-minute rehearsals for the new numbers. I entered at the back of the house and scanned the seats and the stage. Since he's so big, it only took a second to see that he wasn't there. I was about to look somewhere else when the trowe came onstage.

Technically, the trowe were trolls. But their leader, Ku'lah, felt there were too many negative associations with the word, so her den went by the traditional Scottish name instead.

They gathered onstage, talking quietly among themselves. Trowe didn't look much like the fat, ugly stereotype trolls in the movies. They were only a little taller than humans, with the same build, but they had dark green skin, white hair, pointed ears, and bright jewel eyes. The adults had patterns etched into their skin with scars; the more complicated the pattern, the more important that trowe was in the den. None of them was in their traditional tribal costumes yet. Instead, they wore ripped tights and plain T-shirts.

"Let's begin," Ku'lah said. She was larger than the others, and her entire face and shoulders were covered in intricate scars.

Cordeav, an older male trowe, nodded, raised his wide, flat hands in the air, and clapped once. The sound echoed through the theater and the trowe grew silent.

"Right," he said. "From the top."

A few trowe banged on strips of sheet metal in a slow, steady beat. Another slapped wood slats against the ground, creating a counterpoint. Then a few more came in, sucking and blowing on glass bottles and ceramic jugs, harmonizing in bursts of melody. The last of the musicians joined in with wires stretched taut across wooden frames, layering a dense, rippling twang. It sounded somewhere between West African and Scottish folk.

Male dancers moved to center stage, grunting and growling as they stomped and lunged in time with the music. Then they split to either side, and the lead dancer stepped forward. For this number, like most, it was Ku'lah's daughter, Liel. She was the reason I watched the trowe. She moved like a pickax cleaving through rock. Her long, white hair whipped around her head as her lean, muscular limbs stretched down, up, and across her body. Her face was relaxed, but her diamond eyes burned with fierce solemnity.

"Boy, what are you doing?"

The song was over, and the dancers were taking notes from Cordeav. Ku'lah stood directly in front of me.

"Um . . ." I said.

"Did you need something?" She glared at me.

"Just looking for my dad."

"Try backstage."

"Sure, that's what I was about to do."

I took one last look over Ku'lah's shoulder. Liel sat on the edge of the stage, one leg dangling over the side, the other pulled close to her chest. Her chin rested on her knee as she listened to Cordeav with complete concentration.

"Boy," Ku'lah said.

"Going," I said.

I CHECKED THE green room next. That's the place where the performers hang out backstage before they go on. It had comfy old furniture, a refrigerator, microwave, TV, books, cards, games, and lots of other random stuff that people used to entertain themselves while they waited for their act. Speakers fed in sound from the stage, so they didn't miss their cue. Closer to showtime, it would get loud down here, but this early in the day it was chill. Sometimes, Dad would hang out on one of the couches and read.

Dad wasn't there. But unfortunately, Shaun and his crew were. They were watching some reality show about fishing. Shaun was a satyr: Shaun the Faun. I mean, I'm not one to talk about names, but it was almost as if his parents went out of their way to screw him up. Like all satyrs, he was human from the waist up, and goat from the waist down. His sandy-blond hair was styled up like a surfer, except, of course with two nubby horns sticking out, and he wore an expensive sports jersey. He was stretched out on the beige corduroy couch, scuffing up the fabric with his hooves and stinking up the place with his goat funk.

The rest of his crew wasn't much better. The twin harpy girls, Aello and Celaeno, were perched behind him. Ernesto the brownie sat next to him on the couch arm. The last member of his crew, Oob the ogre, lay on the floor at the foot of the couch.

I tried to slip back up the steps, but it was too late. Ernesto's little, piping voice called out:

"Uh-oh, look who it is! Robot Junior!"

I didn't look anything like a robot. I didn't even have bolts sticking out of my neck. But somehow, Ernesto had gotten the other kids to call my dad "Robot" and me "Robot Junior." The nickname had even spread to some of the adults—and not as a term of endearment. Almost everyone in The Show blamed Science as the reason all of us monsters were hiding. Like it was some big, heartless machine that came along and ran magic out of town. And my family was just a bit too "sciency" for a lot of the company members. I had tried to explain to Shaun's crew that I was *mostly* magic—that in pure science, there was no way I could exist. But their grasp of science and technology was so vague that my explanation didn't make sense to them. The fact that I knew enough about science to talk about it at all made me more guilty in their eyes.

"Where you going, Robo-nerd?" said Shaun. "It looks like you're running away from something."

"No." I turned back to them. "I'm just in a hurry."

"What's wrong?" Ernesto asked. "Spark plug leaking?"

Aello and Celaeno giggled as they preened their black feathers. It was pointless to tell them all that I didn't have spark plugs and that, even if I did, spark plugs don't have any fluid in them.

"You making computer house calls now?" Shaun stretched out his goat legs and yawned. "Our own little Geek Squad?"

"No, I'm—"

"Because," he continued, "I'm having some problems with my iPhone. See, I ate it." He rolled over so that his fluffy tail stuck up in the air. "And I need someone to pull it out of my ass."

They all laughed.

"I'm helping Ruthven. Outside the theater." As soon as I blurted it out, I regretted it.

"Oooohh." Shaun nodded seriously at the rest of the crew. "Robo-kid wants to get out of the theater."

"What's wrong with him?" Aello asked loudly.

"Stupid robot," said Celaeno.

"ROBOT! ROBOT!" Oob chanted.

"With any luck, Ruthven won't let him back in." Ernesto stood up and folded his arms. "The Show is for *real* magical creatures, anyway. Not sci-fi screwups."

"Uh-oh!" Shaun grinned. "You gonna take that, Robot Junior? From a six-inch turd?"

"Hey!" said Ernesto.

"Shut it, Ernie," said Shaun. Then he turned back to me. "Seriously? You're going to let that little shitweasel back talk you? If I were you, I'd crush him flat."

I wanted to. It would be so easy. One squeeze and he would

be mush and I would never have to listen to him again. My hands clenched so hard I heard the stitches around my knuckles strain.

But that was exactly what they wanted. So I took a deep breath and relaxed my hands.

"Not worth it." And I walked away.

"Whatever, Robo-pussy," Shaun called after me. "Try not to bring back any angry mobs with torches while you're *Outside*, okay?"

I FINALLY FOUND Dad at the stage door. He sat in one of the metal folding chairs that Mom had reinforced to hold his weight, staring at a blank wall. When I walked over, he turned his massive, square head and looked at me with milky eyes.

"Hi." His voice was flat and indifferent. He'd already been "switched off" for the night's performance.

My dad was the head of security for The Show. It wasn't just because he was strong and nearly indestructible. It was also because he could turn off all feelings. Many of the acts in The Show used magic to affect the audience's emotions. Usually, the performers were careful not to push things too far—just enough to give the audience a thrill. But every once in a while, one of them got careless or lost control. That's when my dad stepped in and took care of things.

I hated talking to him when he was switched off, because he acted like the robot everyone said he was. I stared at him, sitting there in the chair by the stage door, just an immense stupid lump of stitched-together body parts waiting for someone to tell him what to do. A lot of people really took advantage of him.

Of course, I was about to take advantage of him, too.

"Ruthven wants me to go run some errands with him."

"Okay," he said.

"Outside," I added.

"Outside?"

"Yeah, I'm doing stuff away from the computer, just like you said. So can I go? He said I had to get your permission."

"If Ruthven thinks you're ready, then okay."

When I got back to the lobby, I headed straight for Ruthven's office. It was a small room, empty except for a single desk, chair, and light. He looked up from some paperwork when I knocked on the open door. "My dad said yes!" I felt a twinge of guilt, but it was drowned out almost immediately by the idea that in a few moments, I would be going outside and meeting real humans.

Ruthven stood up and the swirling shadows around him solidified into a trench coat. The rumor in the company was that Ruthven didn't actually wear clothes, only shadows.

He inspected his coat for a moment, then nodded. "Let's get going, then."

I smiled, trying to act like my nerves weren't revving up into overdrive. I pulled up the deep hood on my dark gray sweatshirt, and that made me feel a little better. Then I followed him back into the lobby.

"Well!" Charon called from his box office window. "Don't you two look like a perfect picture of normality?"

"I'll thank you to be a little more encouraging, Ferryman." Ruthven put his long, pale hand on the door handle. He stared at the dark wood for a moment, as if that was as far as he planned to go. Finally, he said, "Once more unto the breach. Come along, Boy."

2
Snakes, Snails, and Puppy Dog Tails

++++++++

IT WAS BRIGHT outside. At first, that was all I could take in. I'd watched so many movies and TV shows, and asked all my online buddies a million questions that probably sounded insane to them. But none of it had prepared me for the physical sensations that surrounded me: the wind, the noise, the smells . . . and humans *everywhere*. I must have stood there on the sidewalk blinking like a complete tool for a full minute before Ruthven tapped me on the shoulder.

"Stay close and try not to make eye contact." Then he plunged into the swirling mass of humans that flowed in either direction on the sidewalk.

Humans seemed so fragile up close. As I followed behind Ruthven, I had this weird impulse to reach out and touch one.

Another thing I wasn't prepared for was the sky. It just kept going up and up, endlessly. It made me so dizzy that I couldn't look at it for long. And it was a cloudy day. I couldn't imagine what it felt like to have a real blue sky above you.

None of it seemed to bother Ruthven. He just walked forward, eyes straight ahead, like he was daring someone to get in his way. And nobody did. Even outside the theater, people did what Ruthven told them to do. Of course, Ruthven had spent a lot of time out among the humans, both before and after he started the company. He was older than most of us. Not as old as Charon, but pretty old.

"Where are we going first?" I asked.

"The thrift store."

"Why don't we go to a regular clothing store? Maybe Old Navy or the Gap?" There were a lot of Old Navy and Gap commercials on TV. They seemed like amazing places. All those beautiful salespeople going around modeling the latest fashions. I wondered if they danced all the time or just at certain times of the day.

"Two reasons," said Ruthven. "First, the company can't afford it. And second, we're shopping for the trowe, and they'd just distress the new clothes as soon as they got them, so we might as well save them the trouble and buy the clothing used."

"The trowe?" I asked, trying to make it sound casual. "Are we getting anything for Liel?"

Ruthven smiled faintly. "Would you like to pick something out for her?"

"Oh . . . well . . . I mean, it's just that I know what she likes."

"Certainly. It's a marvelous idea."

"I mean . . . Would she think that was creepy? If I picked something out for her?"

"I think as long as it was tasteful," he said.

"Maybe we don't even have to say that I picked it out."

"If you prefer."

As we walked, I tried to think about what to get her. I wasn't exactly sure what would be "tasteful" to someone who typically just wore tank tops and jeans. And it was hard to concentrate on anything in this environment. The blinking neon advertisements, gigantic flashing LCD screens, car horns, stereos, and the low hum of hundreds—maybe even thousands—of human conversations converged on me like a sticky, electrified spiderweb.

"Ah, here we are," Ruthven said when we reached a plain storefront that said THRIFT in black letters on the window. He opened the door and gestured for me to go first.

Once inside, I had to swallow my disappointment. The light was dim, the floor was a dirty tan linoleum, and the walls were white with weird streaks of yellow, like water damage. There were no neat clothing displays or pictures or mannequins, just row upon row of clothes hung on rolling frames. A few customers were scattered around the store, flipping unenthusiastically through hangers.

"Well?" asked Ruthven.

"Oh . . ." I said. "Um . . ."

He patted my arm. "I fear this will be the first in a long line of disappointing revelations that humanity is not accurately depicted on television." He scanned the aisles of clothing. "The young ladies' apparel is over there, I believe."

"All of that?"

"Do you want me to help you?"

"No, I'll figure it out."

I flipped through shirts, skirts, jackets, and jeans. I didn't really know what size Liel was, so I held up some blouse thing, trying to gauge if it would fit. This could be harder than I thought.

"What are you doing looking at girl's clothes?"

The voice was so sudden and unfamiliar that I nearly dropped the blouse. My pulse was hammering in my ears as I turned toward the source.

It was a human girl around my age. She had bright red hair and freckles on her soft, round face. I still had my hood up, so she didn't see what I looked like until I turned toward her. When she saw me, her eyes went wide and her mouth tightened and I thought she was about to let out a scream. I braced myself, thinking maybe Ruthven was wrong. Maybe I couldn't pass for human and I had just ruined it for the entire company.

It hung there for a moment, then her face relaxed and she just said, "Well?"

"Well what?" I had absolutely no idea what she was talking about.

"What are you looking at girl clothes for?"

"Oh! For a . . . uh, friend."

"A girlfriend?"

"No. I mean . . . not really. . . ."

"I get it." She gave me a smile. "You *want* her to be your girlfriend."

I laughed a little. "Yeah, kinda."

She scrutinized the blouse I still held in my hands. "You don't want to get her something like that."

"No?"

She shook her head. "It's old-fashioned. And not very romantic."

"Well, I don't want it to be *too* romantic. In case . . ."

She gave me a knowing smirk. "You want something that *could* be just from a friend, if that's the way she wants to take it."

"Yeah, totally."

"You want to get her something like . . ." Her eyes flickered across the aisles of clothes. "What size is she?"

"I was trying to figure that out. . . ."

"You don't know?"

"No." It seemed like a failure of some kind.

She sighed. "Typical boy."

"Yeah, I guess." I couldn't help smiling at that one.

"Is she, like, my size?"

"Taller," I said. "And a little smaller in the . . . um . . ." I held out my hands in front of me, saw how huge and ugly they looked compared to hers, and quickly put them back in my hoodie pockets.

"The boobs?"

"Uh, yeah."

"Okay, we probably need to go one size down. Follow me." She marched down one of the aisles. I walked behind, feeling like I had just lost all control of the situation. And yet, I had to admit, I was really enjoying it. The store may have been a disappointment, but the human was kind of cool.

She held up a white, blousy shirt. The material looked thin, almost transparent, and there were little lacy frills around the wrists and neckline.

"How about this?" she asked.

"Uh, maybe something that isn't so . . . delicate."

"Gotcha."

She pulled out several more tops for me to look at. It took a little while, but eventually, we settled on one that was frayed and broken in enough to appeal to Liel and still romantic enough for the girl.

"Oh, yeah, she'll like this," said the girl. "And it's a blue tag." She pointed to a sign above the register in the corner. "Blue tags are half price today."

"Thanks for helping me. I think I would have been totally lost."

The girl shrugged. "It was fun." Then she seemed to lose her confidence for a moment. She looked away, then looked back at me. Looked me full in the face, which she hadn't done much.

"Hey, I don't know if this is weird or whatever, but what happened to your face?"

"My face?"

"You know. The, um . . ." Her fingers fluttered across her own face for a moment. "The stitches."

"Oh!" I said. Then I realized that if I was supposedly a human, I needed a reason to have stitches. I should have thought of a cover story ahead of time. "An . . . accident."

"A car accident?"

I almost agreed with her. It seemed to be the most obvious answer. But for some insane reason, I said, "No, it was a thresher."

"Like on a farm?"

"Yeah."

"Whoa, like, you used to live on a farm?"

"Sure," I said, trying to remember movies I'd seen that took place on farms and what that looked like.

"That's probably why you're so big."

"Big?"

"You know." She lifted her arms out to the side. "Built."

"Yeah." Was that a good thing? I couldn't tell. "I guess so."

"So, why did you move to the city?"

"Oh, uh . . ."

Then I heard Ruthven's voice:

"Frank? There you are."

I looked over and saw Ruthven walking down the aisle toward us, an easy smile on his face, his trench coat billowing around him.

"Are you ready?" he asked.

"Sure." I held up the shirt for Liel, like it was proof that I had everything under control.

"Oh, just lovely. I'm sure she'll like it." He turned to the girl. "I hope my nephew wasn't taking up all your time."

She looked a lot more spooked by Ruthven than she did when she first saw me. "N-n-n-o, it's cool."

"Excellent." Then he turned to me. "Shall we go, Frank?"

Once we had paid and were back out on the busy sidewalk, I asked, "Frank?"

"Sorry, I just can't resist little jokes like that." Then he raised an eyebrow. "And what about that thresher?"

"You were listening?"

"Of course. It was your first time out among humans. You didn't think I was just going to let you run wild, did you? All in all, I think it went rather well. Up until the point when you dug yourself too deeply into a pointless lie and I had to come and rescue you."

"Yeah, I don't know what I was thinking. I guess I was trying to impress her or something."

"You were trying to impress her with a story about getting mauled by a thresher?"

"It made sense at the time."

"Ah, youth." He sighed. "Do you know what I would give to be young again?"

"No, what?"

"Nothing. In fact, you'd have to pay me."

We walked on in silence for a while. Now that I was getting used to the constant movement around me, I was able to relax a little. In some ways it was easier than being in that store. It was so crowded that nobody really paid attention to any one person. I almost felt invisible. But in that store, talking to that human girl, I had never felt so out of place. So . . . monsterish.

"Hey, Ruthven, what do I look like to humans?"

He turned toward me and frowned. "What a strange question. Why do you ask?"

"That girl. She was really nice and all. But when she first saw me, she gave me this look. Like girls in the horror movies when they see the bad-guy monster. Did I scare her?"

"Probably a little. Humans don't like to see things they aren't expecting to see. It didn't last, though, did it?"

"No, she got over it pretty quick actually."

"It's as I suspected. When a human looks at you, they just think that you're an injured human. Unpleasant, but not intrinsically dangerous. In fact, you're more likely to elicit pity than fear."

"Pity? Why?"

"That's how humans generally react to those of their kind who are deformed, maimed, or profoundly ugly."

"I'm . . . ugly?"

"To a human." He said it like it hardly mattered what humans thought. But it mattered to me what that girl thought.

"Do humans think *you're* ugly?"

"No, they generally find me attractive."

"But that girl seemed even more freaked out by you than she was by me."

"When humans look at me, they get a feeling that they don't often have. They feel like prey."

"And they're attracted to you, anyway?"

"Humans are funny little things."

"They don't have a lot of predators, do they?"

"No," said Ruthven. "And our theater houses most of them."

"That's why we have to hide from them?"

"For now."

"What does that mean?"

But Ruthven didn't reply.

WE WALKED THROUGH midtown. Once we got out of Times Square, there were fewer people and a lot fewer ads. It was nice, being out there in the fresh air, with the wind blowing through my hair. It felt like I could just keep walking forever and never come to a dead end. I knew that wasn't true, of course. Manhattan is an island after all. Still, it was nice to think about.

Eventually, we came to a little pet shop on a quiet side street. There were three kittens in the front window of the store. Two of them wrestled, playfully showing tiny fangs. I had never seen kittens up close before. They were so cute and fragile, I was afraid to go near them.

Ruthven stopped in front of the door. "When we're in this store, please allow me to do the talking."

"No stories about threshers," I said.

"Precisely."

The store was crammed with brightly colored pet supplies like leashes, collars, and chew toys.

"Hey, Ruthven!" an older human male behind the cash register boomed in a jolly voice. He had a big belly and his thin, black hair was pulled back in a ponytail.

"Ah, Carmine." Ruthven walked over to the register. "So good to see you."

"The usual?" asked Carmine.

"If you please." Then Ruthven gestured to me. "Carmine, this is my nephew, Frank."

Carmine paused for a moment when he saw me, like he was acknowledging that I looked different. Ugly, I guess. But it didn't really rattle him like it did the girl. I wondered what the difference was.

Then he smiled. "Good to meet you, kid. Learning the ropes from your uncle?"

"Uh, yeah," I said.

"No business like show business, huh?"

"It's pretty cool."

Carmine turned back to Ruthven. "Give me a second, I got it in the back." He disappeared through a doorway behind the counter for a moment, then came back out with a large box. The top of the box was peppered with air holes, and I could hear tiny nails scratching the inside.

"So, hey." Carmine carefully set the box on the counter. "I wanted to ask a favor."

"Of course," said Ruthven.

"My cousin is visiting from Florida in a few weeks and he wants to take his wife to see your show."

"It would be my pleasure. Just name the date and I'll take care of the rest."

"Much obliged."

"And when are you bringing the missus to The Show?" asked Ruthven with a gently teasing smile on his face.

"One of these days, Ruthven. You're not closing anytime soon, are you?"

"It's still very much an open-ended run."

"Yeah, see, I just assume it'll always be there, so I never go. I should have learned my lesson when I missed *Cats*, but there you go."

"Indeed. Well, the invitation is always open." Ruthven handed him a couple of fifty-dollar bills, then gestured for me to pick up the box. "Take care, Carmine."

As we walked back to the theater, I held the bag of clothes slung over my left shoulder and the box of rats under my right arm. Through the cardboard, I could feel the small, shifting bodies in the box against my side.

"So, Carmine doesn't know what the rats are for, does he?" I asked.

"He thinks we have snakes in the show."

"I guess that's close to the truth."

"Close enough for a human."

"But what if he comes and sees the show and doesn't see any snakes?"

"He won't come."

"How do you know?"

"A man like Carmine wouldn't set foot in a theater."

We walked in silence for a little while, then I said, "Still, he seemed nice."

"He is very discreet. We have an understanding. I pay him exceptionally well and in cash, and he doesn't question me about our excessive rat consumption."

"He didn't seem all that freaked out by me. And he was pretty comfortable with you, too. What about all that predator and prey stuff you were talking about?"

"Carmine may not believe in monsters, but he knows they exist."

"Humans are pretty complicated," I said.

"No, Boy. Rain-forest ecosystems are complicated. Humans are just a mess."

ONCE WE WERE safely back in the lobby of the theater, I felt a weird mixture of relief and disappointment. I hadn't realized how tense I'd been out there. But I felt like I had just been getting the hang of it all, and now I was stuck back in the theater and its underground caverns. It was all so . . . small here.

"You did well, Boy," said Ruthven. "Perhaps we could make this a regular occurrence."

"Really?" I tried not to look as pathetically eager as I felt.

"I don't see why not."

"Boss," called Charon, still sitting at the box office window. "The stage manager says that the Minotaur and the Siren are at it again."

"Damn," said Ruthven. "Can't the Monster handle it?"

"He's covering the stage door tonight."

"Right, of course." Ruthven looked at me. "This may take a while. I need you to deliver these things."

I looked down at the box of rats under my arm. "This, too?" I asked, already knowing the answer.

"Naturally," said Ruthven a little impatiently, his mind clearly on domestic disputes. Then he glanced at me and I must have looked worried. "It will be fine. Remember to be polite, and for God's sake, don't just leave it at her door without saying hello. That pisses her off to no end." Then he was gone in a blur of darkness.

"So," Charon called from across the lobby. "How is the big, wide world of humanity these days?"

"Huh?" I pulled my attention away from the task of delivering the rats. "Oh, it was cool. Humans are weird."

"That's the truth, Boy. Why, when they come to the window, looking for front row center, *of course*, and I tell them those seats have been sold out for months, somehow they think that if they just whine long enough, the seats will magically open, and . . ."

Charon went on talking about his favorite subject, but I

stopped paying attention. I stared down at the box in my hands and listened to the tiny furry bodies scramble around inside. Like they could sense their impending doom.

I considered putting it off for a little while and delivering the trowes' clothes first. But if I got the chance to give Liel her outfit, I definitely didn't want to do it while holding a box of rats. So, I would have to see the Diva first.

3
Three Women

++++++++

THE DIVA'S PRIVATE room was the biggest and best furnished dressing room in the theater. I stood in front of the door and stared at the gold-painted star with the script written across the top: *Madame Medusa.*

I'd only been in the same room with the Diva a few times, and never alone. Dad spent a lot of time with her, because she sometimes demanded company and when he was "switched off," he could look directly at her without turning to stone.

I placed the box on the ground and knocked twice, very softly. The Diva didn't like loud noises. I waited for what seemed like a long time, but there was no response.

"Madame Medusa? I have your . . . stuff from the pet store."

"Boy?" Hearing her voice felt a little like the brain freeze you get from eating ice cream too quickly. "Is that you?"

"Y-y-yes, Madame."

"So . . . Mommy's finally letting you out from under her apron strings. . . ."

I waited, shifting back and forth on the balls of my feet. I repeated to myself over and over that there was nothing to be worried about. Give her the rats, a few minutes of polite conversation, and then I could go give Liel her shirt.

At last, the Diva said, "Well, come in, Boy."

When I opened the door, I was hit by a blast of humid air that smelled like rotting cedar. The fluorescent lights were off. Instead, the room was dimly lit by floor lamps draped in red and purple silk. Unlike all the other dressing rooms, this one had no mirrors.

Behind a white curtain, I could see Medusa's silhouette on a divan in the corner. She appeared to be lounging on a pile of pillows, her back slightly arched. Thin shadows writhed around her head—the tiny snakes she had instead of hair.

"Very kind of you to bring me my weekly rations. Would you be a doll and put them here?" The silhouette of her arm rose up, then her finger slowly uncurled and pointed to a chair just outside of the curtained area next to her divan.

I moved slowly over to the chair. The curtain shielded me from the full impact of her magic, but my muscles still felt stiff. I put the box on the chair, then took a few steps back. When I did, I heard a muffled crunch beneath my feet. I had stepped on a large sheath of dried, colorless snakeskin.

The curtain parted slightly next to the chair, and Medusa's hand slowly emerged. Her skin was absolutely white and gleamed with the wet-looking sparkle that snakeskin had after shedding. She placed her hand on top of the box and let it rest there a moment. Even seeing this small bit of her made my jaw clench and unclench.

"Tell me, Boy. Have you ever seen my act?"

"N-no, Madame."

She drew her fingernail across the tape that held the box closed, cutting it cleanly. I could hear the rats inside scrambling around, squeaking in panic.

"I suppose your mother has deemed it unsuitable for minors."

"Yeah."

She laughed quietly and a chill ran through my body, bringing with it more muscle spasms.

"Well, you're not a child anymore."

"No, Madame."

"Nearly the human legal age of adulthood, I believe."

"One more year, Madame."

Her hand hovered over the open box, weaving slowly back and forth.

"I get a little peevish after I've just molted. It's hard to restrain myself onstage when I'm in that kind of mood. You know what happens then, don't you? You've heard, at least."

"Yes, Madame."

"Humans are such fragile things. It's hard not to damage them."

Her hand lunged into the box and withdrew a single struggling rat. It shrieked pitifully as she drew it back behind the curtain.

I watched her silhouette as she held the rat by its tail above her head. Her lips parted as she lowered it down. Then her mouth opened larger and larger, her jaw becoming completely unhinged. Then she snapped, the shrieks stopped, and the rat was gone.

It took her about a minute to swallow the rat. Once she finished, she said:

"On a night like this, when I'm feeling a bit waspish, it soothes me to have someone watching me whom I really like." She turned her head toward me, and even behind the curtain, her direct gaze made my entire body freeze. My rib cage was so tense I could hardly breathe. "I *really* like you, Boy. So, will you watch my act tonight?"

"S-sure, M-Madame," I said through my teeth.

She turned her gaze away and my muscles relaxed a little. I took a deep breath.

"Wonderful, Boy. You are most kind." She nestled deeper into her pillows. "I'm feeling sleepy now. You may go."

"T-t-thank you, Madame." I stumbled shakily back to the door.

"See you tonight at The Show," she said. "Don't disappoint me."

"Of course not, Madame! See you tonight!" Then I left, wondering how I was going to do that when my mom had specifically told me I wasn't allowed to see her act.

THE TROWE WERE the ones who had dug out the catacombs beneath the theater that we all lived in. It was some impressive work, navigating around city plumbing, sewers, electrical lines, and subway lines. Most levels were furnished like apartments. But the trowe lived on the lowest level, and they had purposely left it more cavelike. The rough stone walls gleamed damply in the harsh halogen lights that lined the stairwell. At the bottom of the stairs was a large, black, iron door, dotted with rust and grime. I lifted the massive door knocker and brought it down three times. Each time it struck, it echoed back up the stairs. After a few minutes, I heard a bolt slide open. Then the door swung inward. Ku'lah stood in the doorway.

"Boy." Her thick, white eyebrows curled down. "Again."

"Good evening, Lady Ku'lah. I have, uh, well, I went with Ruthven to pick up some clothes for the den." I held out the bag.

Ku'lah nodded and took it from me. "Thank you."

"Oh," I said. "There's a . . . a shirt . . . in there for . . . uh . . ."

"Spit it out, Boy. I have things to do."

"It's a shirt for Liel."

She looked at me for moment, her face totally expressionless. I caught myself holding my breath. I was half expecting her to tell me to get lost and stay away from her daughter. But then she turned her head back inside and bellowed, "Liel, come here!"

"What is it?" Liel's voice called back. "I'm in the middle of something."

"Now!" yelled Ku'lah.

After a moment, Liel's head poked around from behind the door, her slanted, diamond eyes glittering in the light.

"Hey, Boy," she said.

"Hey." I tried to sound cool. Not sure I succeeded.

Liel looked back at her mother. "Awesome, Mom. Thanks for conforming to trowe stereotypes yet again and being rude to guests. Couldn't you at least invite him in?"

"Oh, it's okay," I said quickly. "I can't stay long, anyway."

"Boy has something for you." Ku'lah thrust the bag back into my hands and went inside.

Liel and I stood for a second in silence. I wondered if she felt the same kind of crazy electricity that I did when we were alone together. She looked at me curiously as she leaned against the iron door, her long, white hair framing her smooth, dark green face.

"You have something for me?" she asked.

"Yeah, uh, I went shopping with Ruthven and—"

"No shit!" She leaned forward. "You went *outside*? How was it?"

"Oh, uh, it was cool. Kind of intense, but you get used to it." Sure. First time out of the theater. No biggie. "Anyway, uh,

Ruthven was buying clothes for the trowe so, I, uh, picked out yours." Before she could respond, I grabbed her shirt out of the bag and handed it to her. She held it up and examined it for a moment, then nodded appreciatively. The knot in my chest loosened a little.

"You picked this out?" She sounded surprised.

"Well, uh, this girl helped me."

"You went shopping with a *human girl*?" Her eyes grew wide. "That's so amazing!"

"Yeah, I guess. It was—"

"Liel!" Ku'lah's voice came from inside.

"Listen, I have to get ready for The Show." Liel put her hand on my upper arm. "But I definitely want to hear more about going outside and the human girl. Stop by the dressing room after the performance tonight."

"Really?" I tried not to gush.

"Totally! We'll go to the Cantina and you can tell me the whole thing."

"Okay, yeah . . . uh, sure, that sounds awesome!"

"And thanks for the shirt," she said.

"You like it?" I asked.

"Completely." She smiled at me, her sharp, bright, perfect teeth gleaming in the halogen lights.

"Great." I melted into her sparkling, colorless eyes. If I was watching myself, I probably would have been totally disgusted. But I couldn't help it. She was just so beautiful.

After a moment, I realized I was standing there staring at her like a complete freak. "Oh, uh, here's the rest of the clothes for the den." I handed her the bag. "Break a leg tonight. See you after The Show."

Then I practically sprinted up the stairs.

"WELL?"

Mom loomed in the entrance to our apartment, her misshapen hands resting on her hips, her column of black hair sticking straight up with a white streak on either side. A slight crease along her temples told me that she probably would have been frowning if the stitching on her forehead wasn't so tight.

"Hi, Mom." I gave her an innocent smile and tried to slip past. But she pressed her hand against my chest and held me in place.

"Where were you?"

"You weren't around, so I had to ask Dad." If she didn't know yet, she'd find out when she plugged Dad back in that night. Better to hear it now from me.

"Ask him what?"

"I went shopping with Ruthven."

"Shopping?" she said. *"Outside?"*

"Yeah."

She stared down at me. Her right eye had been giving her problems, and she hadn't had time to replace it yet, so it looked off somewhere over my left shoulder. But her left eye was piercing.

"Don't worry. They thought I was human."

"A real human?"

"Sure," I said, trying to sound soothing. "They thought I was a human who had been in an accident."

"An accident?"

"You know. Because of the stitches."

"And that was it? Just a human with stitches?"

"Pretty much."

"Ah."

She stared at me for a moment longer, then turned and walked back into our apartment. It was so hard to read my mom. When Victor Frankenstein had made her, he'd wanted her to look beautiful, like a porcelain doll. But he hadn't taken function into account at all, so her face was almost completely immobile, frozen in this vaguely surprised look. And she wasn't really much for talking about her feelings, either. So I couldn't tell if she was really pissed or relieved that nothing bad had happened. I followed cautiously behind her into the apartment.

Our entire home was about the size of the Diva's dressing room. The common living area was all one space. In the kitchen section, there were a mismatched refrigerator, stove, and sink, all rebuilt with parts reclaimed from late-night trips to a junkyard. My mom was amazing at fixing and rebuilding things. She didn't get people. They made her uncomfortable, and she only ever talked to me, Dad, Charon, and when necessary, Ruthven. But she understood gadgets and machines almost like she spoke their language.

In the center of the space was a table big enough to fit the three of us. In the corner was always a small, neat stack of metal and plastic odds and ends salvaged from junk. My mom spent a lot of time trying to assemble these parts into something useful. That was where our television came from, as well as the toaster oven, the stereo, and all my computers. But even though my mom had built all these things, she had zero interest in using them. When Dad and I watched television, she sat and watched us watching the television, as if her only real enjoyment was seeing us enjoy using it.

After my adventures in the real world, I felt like I'd earned some serious computer time.

But then my mom said, "Boy."

I stopped and looked back at her. She stood over the sink, staring into the drain. She did that a lot. Like she expected to see something in it. The only things I ever saw in the drain were roaches.

"Yeah, Mom?"

"Were you scared? Outside?"

"At first. But after I got used to it, it wasn't so bad."

"Wasn't so bad . . ." she echoed. "I wonder if it's changed. Since I was outside."

"Sure." I tried to sound encouraging. "You haven't been out there in over twenty years. I'll bet the humans have changed a lot."

She nodded once, slowly, but didn't say anything else.

There were a lot of creatures in the company, like Shaun and his crew, who just thought of humans as the audience who paid the bills. There were some, like Charon and my dad, who were comfortable with humans but distrusted them. And there were some, like my mom, who totally hated them. I couldn't really blame her, after what Victor Frankenstein and other humans had done to her and my dad over the years. But I knew it meant she would never understand why I was so interested in them and their world.

4
Magic Numbers

┼┼┼┼┼┼┼

MY ROOM WAS crammed with computers. Not all of them worked anymore, and of those that did, not all of them worked well. But I never threw any of them out, because inevitably, Mom or I would find some use for them, either as salvage for spare parts for another computer or as something completely different, like the remote-controlled spotlights for The Show. There wasn't much else in my room except an unmade bed with camo sheets and an old wooden dresser stuffed with clothes.

I took off my hoodie and nestled down into the heaping mass of electronics. I rolled up my sleeves, then tugged the stitches loose on the undersides of my forearms. I lifted up flaps of skin to expose USB ports just below each of my wrists. Then I pulled out two USB cables that were connected to the back of my favorite computer and plugged them into my wrists. My hands were strong, but my fingers were too thick and clumsy to type with any precision. A few years ago I realized that I could type much faster if I just bypassed my fingers completely. So I wrote a program that decoded neurological impulses and converted them into digital commands. Then Mom helped me install some custom USB ports that connected directly to my nervous system at the wrists. So all I had to do was think about typing, and the text appeared on the screen.

Well, it would if I *had* a screen.

I pulled a DVI cable from the same computer. I lifted my hair up in the back and screwed the cable into the jack on the back of my head. When I first started using computers, I wore out eyes really quickly staring at monitors all the time. Eyes were relatively easy to replace, but hard to find in good condition. So, since things worked out so well with my USB hand bypasses, I just had my mom install a DVI jack at the base of my cortex and bypassed my eyes, too. Of course, it wasn't nearly as easy as the USB bypasses. The jack installation took mom several hours to complete. And writing the conversion program was a lot more complex because I had to translate flat, digital binary into straight-up rich analog. It took forever to code, and even once it was done I still had to tweak the color calibration on a regular basis. Still, it saved Ruthven a lot of trips to the morgue for fresh eyes. And, you know, it was just cool that I could interface directly with my computer.

I booted up the PC tower, then leaned back, rested my arms on my thighs, and closed my eyes. I could "see" the computer display in my head and, with just the tiniest twitch of muscles in my forearms, I logged on to the network.

As soon as I started my IRC client, I got slammed with a ton of messages. I guess you could say I was kind of famous within the hacker community. But I wasn't one of those lame identity theft crackers. Sure, when I was a kid I liked to show off and mess with stuff. But true hacking isn't about stealing credit card numbers and taking down websites. It's about figuring out how something works—software, firmware, networks, hardware, whatever—and then using that knowledge to improve it, to make it better than originally intended. All technological evolution comes out of hacking. It's the pure pursuit of making things more awesome.

s1zzl3: sup, b0y

poxd: yo, b0y

surelee: where you been?

b0y: whazzup, d00ds? i been livin' in meatspace too long.

poxd: 4 real, i haven't seen you since this morning

surelee: i bet it's a girl. @b0y you got a girl now?

b0y: not yet . . .

s1zzl3: that sounds hopeful

b0y: maybe just maybe i have a date tonight . . .

surelee: holy shit! is it that girl yer always on
            about :0

b0y: yep! XD

s1zzl3: thank fcking god, i was sooooo tired of
            listenign to you go on about her.

poxd: so tell! how'd u do it?

b0y: turns out, having adventures in meatspace is interesting
      to chicks! who knew :P

s1zzl3: lol, that's crazy talk.

poxd: so wait, yer saying if i want a chick i need to get
            a life?

poxd goes off into corner to sulk

b0y: fraid so, guys. maybe u should unplug and give it a try

surelee: i can't believe the infamous b0y is telling
            us to unplug.

s1zzl3: yea, u going soft on us?

b0y: when it comes to this girl, i'm anything but soft >:D

poxd: OOOOOOOOOOOOOOOOOOOOOh!

surelee rolls eyes

b0y: all right, l8r, d00dz. i'm in a time crunch and feeling the
flow.

I shut down my chat client and opened my text editor. Then I began to type. My fingers twitched, and letters and numbers flew across the screen in my mind, as I sank into the beautiful simplicity of code, commands, and if/then statements.

I know it might be hard for some people to understand, but code is a lot like poetry, with its own elegance and nuance. I can type out a bunch of boring-looking plain text characters and feed them into a web browser, and they become beautiful designs. Somewhere in that conversion between simplicity and richness, there's a kind of magic.

Working on my big project had become like meditation for me. For a little while, I could escape all the stress about humans, parents, Shaun's crew, Liel, and everything else. I had been working on the project for years now. I had never heard of anyone trying to weave magic and technology together like this. It had become such a part of my life that it was a necessary function, like breathing or eating. And on the off chance that I *did* finish it . . . well, not to brag, but it would take the Internet to the next stage of its evolution.

A reminder window popped up, breaking me out of my flow. The Show began in ten minutes. I powered down my computer and unhooked the cable from the back of my head. The real world swirled into focus in a way that always made me a little nauseous. Then I unplugged the cables from my wrists and pulled the stitches tight to close the flaps. My hands were once again the massive, clumsy chunks of meat at the end of my arms.

I walked out into the living room feeling a little groggy. Mom wasn't home. As the resident mechanic for the theater, she was in and out a lot. I poured myself a glass of Dew, still thinking through a specific snarl in the code I had run into. I had chugged about half the glass when I suddenly remembered why I planned to watch The Show that night. The tense chill I'd felt in the Diva's dressing room ran through me again like it was still in my muscle memory.

FRIDAY NIGHTS WERE always sold out, so I didn't even try to find a seat in the back of the house. Instead, I worked my way through the backstage passageways to the control booth.

The booth was a small room that overlooked the stage. The lights, sound effects, and a few other things were operated from up there. The entrance was a black wooden door nestled in the side of a wall at the back of the house. The Show had already started by the time I reached it. When I opened the door, I was greeted by a musky smell and no lights. I followed the small strips of glow tape up a steep, narrow staircase, closing the door behind me.

"They're a bit off tonight," came Laurellen's soft, liquid voice.

"The whole show's off," growled Mozart. "Something in the air."

"Other than your stink?"

"Just sayin'. The whole vibe's not right tonight."

When I reached the top of the stairs and stepped into the small, dimly lit booth, I could just make out the panels of dials, knobs, and switches that covered three of the four walls. The booth tech was out of bounds for me. Only the light operator, Laurellen, and the sound operator, Mozart, touched these instruments. The fourth wall was a window that looked out over the audience and the stage below.

"Hey, guys," I said. "Can I watch from up here for a little bit?"

"Certainly," said Laurellen. "Although I'm surprised you have any interest at this point." Laurellen had long, chestnut-brown hair, pulled back so he could wear the headset that allowed him to communicate with the rest of the run crew and get his cues from the stage manager. Everything about Laurellen was thin and wispy: his body, his face, his voice. The clunky headphones, which didn't quite cover his long, pointed ears, looked too heavy for his neck to support. Like the trowe, Laurellen didn't like the negative connotations of the old fashioned name for his kind: faerie. He felt it was too limiting. Instead, he wanted people to call him a fag, because he said fags could be movie stars, politicians, or anything else they wanted.

"I'll bet there's one act he hasn't seen," said Mozart. The gray streaks in his bearded face glowed luminous greens and reds from the soundboard in front of him. He was a werewolf. He was just fine with being called a werewolf. He generally preferred his wolf form, but he had to be in his human shape during The Show so he could operate his soundboard.

"After all this time?" Laurellen turned to me. "What act haven't you seen?"

"Uh . . . the Diva."

"Oh," said Laurellen.

Mozart let out a laugh that sounded more like a bark. "Well, pull up a seat for the best show in town!" He patted a stool between them. "It's the stage manager's chair, but I don't think he'll mind."

"The stage manager?" I asked. "Have you ever seen him?"

"I'm a wolf, kid. Not a medium."

"I think I saw him once," said Laurellen. "Though it could have been the drugs."

"I've never really talked to him much," I said. "Is he nice?"

Mozart shrugged. "For a dead guy."

"He leaves me a bit cold," said Laurellen.

They smirked at each other.

"Maybe you guys spend too much time together," I said.

"Possibly," agreed Laurellen. Then he pressed a hand to one earphone. "Ooops." He moved the attached microphone closer to his mouth. "Yes, cue thirty, standing by." He leaned over his board and began turning dials and pushing faders.

"The Diva's on next, kid." Mozart turned away to hunch over his soundboard. "I really would recommend sitting down for this."

I sat on the narrow, backless stool between them and looked out through the window on to the stage. The Fates were in the middle of their act. They always had a volunteer come up onstage for a little fortune-telling. This time, it was a young Wall Street–looking guy in a suit.

Clotho, the young Fate, had wavy blonde hair, soft hazel eyes, and round, rosy cheeks. She told him about all the great things that were going to happen to him: a promotion, money, a beautiful wife. "It's going to be such an amazing time!" she told him in her bright, cheerful voice. He smiled.

Then Lachesis, the middle-aged Fate, came in. She had long, straight hair that was a mix of brown and gray. Her eyes were gray, too. She told him he'd get laid off, start having trouble with his marriage, struggle to find meaning in his life. He looked upset, which was understandable. "It's going to get tough," she told him. "But, in the end, you'll get through it, find a new job, reconcile with your wife, and come to understand what's really important in life." The guy nodded, look-ing relieved.

"Of course," said Atropos, the old hag of the Fates. "Six months after that, you'll drop dead from testicular cancer."

All three of them cracked up at that like it was a great joke. The guy looked like he was about to faint as he stumbled back to his seat.

Then Laurellen and Mozart, prompted by the stage manag-er's cue over the headset, brought down the lights and closing music to darkness and silence while the Fates exited.

The stage stayed dark, and nothing seemed to be happening. I glanced over at Laurellen, who was clearly waiting for a cue. His eyes flickered back to me.

"The Diva enjoys making them wait a bit." Then his eyebrows raised as he listened to something over the headset. "Standing by." He pushed a button on the board.

The lights slowly began to lift on the stage, dim red and orange, streaked with purple. All the while, a low bass hum rose, so rich that it felt like it was growing up from the ground. The lights got brighter, and the bass reached a decibel level that shook my stomach.

Then a robed and hooded figure glided smoothly onstage. The robe was black, with a deep cowl like a monk's. The head was bowed and the hands were folded into the sleeves. It could have been anyone beneath that robe, or anything. The slow beat of kettledrums rose over the speakers. The figure swiveled toward the audience as if floating, the head still bowed. She stood like that for a while. If it had been anyone else, it would have been boring. But not when it was Medusa. It was like tension rolled off her, and my body absorbed it. My heart was beating hard, and I think it would have taken something like an explosion to break my concentration. So slowly that I could barely see the movement, she lifted her head up completely so that I was looking at a face covered with several layers of white veils. I could only make out the faintest of shadows beneath, but it was enough to make my pulse speed up and my jaw clench like I'd just gotten a sudden jolt of caffeine.

Then she reached up with one black velvet–gloved hand and unhooked the outermost veil. I could make out the suggestion of the outline of the face. My mouth tasted like a lead pipe and I thought I heard strange whispers and sighs, like the echoes of sounds. When I closed my eyes for a moment, I saw angry red splotches beneath my lids. But I couldn't keep them closed.

She took off another veil, and I could now see the faintest contours of the face. I thought how much this was like life—how we could rarely, if ever, see it clearly. Right now I could see it: my whole life, as it really was. But it came in short bursts, like static. I needed more.

She took off another veil, and I could see the shaded areas of the mouth and eyes, the outline of a face. I saw what was really there. And I wasn't at all surprised. It really couldn't be another way. Much like my life, it was inevitable. So I gave into it, let it sweep me away like a river of dust and broken glass. It hurt some, but it seemed minor compared to what now lay so heavily on me. The illusions of my life folded in on themselves one by one, until there was nothing left but the Real. I felt like I was almost there. Just a little further, just a little closer, and I would understand *everything* . . .

Then I fell backward off the stool. I blinked swirling lights from my eyes as I heard Laurellen and Mozart laughing quietly. Neither of them offered to help me up. It was just as well, because I wasn't quite ready to move yet. In addition to the dizziness, I had a huge boner. I struggled slowly to my feet and back onto the stool. The stage had gone dark again and the run crew was hustling in for a quick set change.

"So, how'd you like it?" asked Mozart.

"That was it?" I asked.

"You want more?"

"Well, no, I mean . . . I don't remember what actually happened."

"You never do the first time. Takes a while to figure out how to not get caught up in it."

"So what happened?"

"She took off the first three veils."

"Out of how many?"

"Seven."

"That's all she had to do?"

"That's all she's *allowed* to do," said Laurellen. "Any more, and . . . well . . ."

"I've heard," I said. "Humans have seizures and heart attacks and stuff like that, then my dad has to come in and take her off the stage."

"I've seen her pick one out of the crowd occasionally," said Mozart. "Some guy that she decides for whatever reason she really likes—"

"Or hates," said Laurellen.

"Whichever," said Mozart. "She'll walk out into the aisle and stop right next to him, lean over, and look him dead in the face. Even with the veils, that kind of direct attention is enough to give the poor guy a heart attack. The Monster comes in and hauls her offstage while Ruthven gets somebody to do CPR until the poor bastard's heart starts back up."

"Has anyone ever died?" I asked.

"No, they recover once she's out of the area," said Mozart. "But here's the thing that gets me. You'd think that the sorry bastard would do everything in his power to avoid her after that. But every single time it happens, he's at the stage door after The Show, begging your dad to let him in to see her."

Laurellen sighed. "And that, gentlemen, is why she is the Diva."

5
This Is Not a Date

++++++++

I DECIDED TO stick around to watch the last two numbers from the booth. I didn't mind seeing the trowe's new number again. Well, Liel, really. They all wore their traditional costumes for the performance. The clothing was mostly leather and thick, rough wool, but it left a lot of their bodies uncovered. I watched Liel dance, her white hair swirling through the air, her iron-and-bone jewelry slapping against her sweaty, dark green skin. I think my mouth must have been hanging open or something, because Mozart gave me a nudge and grinned.

After the trowe, the Siren came on for the finale. I always loved her number. It was so simple, but it was one you could always count on to get a standing ovation. She walked onstage wearing a light blue linen dress. It was hard to explain what she looked like. She could probably pass for human. But her features were rough, like they had been painted by one of those crazy expressionist guys. Her hair stuck out in pointy clumps, almost like feathers, and she moved fast and jerky, like a bird. She looked out at the audience and you could tell she hated them. Or it seemed that way, anyway. It was hard to know for sure with the Siren because she didn't talk. Charon once told me she couldn't—that she could only sing. And when she sang, she had to be really careful because her song was irresistible. Back in the old days, when she lived by the sea, she would lure sailors into shore with her song so they crashed their ships into the rocks. Then she'd eat them.

Listening to the Siren's voice was like slipping into a nice warm bath. Your whole body relaxed, and you sank into this sensation of total tranquillity. I heard some people even hallucinated. But at the same time, you felt this insane crush on her. All of a sudden, her weirdness didn't seem so weird anymore. In fact, she seemed like the hottest chick you'd ever seen in your life.

That night she was even better than I'd remembered. More raw and edgy, like she was just about to let it go too far and bring the whole audience charging onto the stage in a trance. But she pulled it back at the last minute, and when she stopped singing, you could hear every seat in the house squeak as the audience leaned back all at once. Then they all burst into applause, shouting, laughing, some of them even crying as they got to their feet. It was that intense. She just stood, staring at them, not smiling. And she still looked like she hated them, but you could tell she liked the applause, too.

The stage went dark, and the applause slowly faded away. Once it was quiet, a single spotlight opened up center stage to reveal Ruthven. His skin glowed in the harsh white light, but his shadows held strong in their tuxedo shape. An all-black tux, of course. It was time for him to give his traditional closing speech. He'd done it every performance for as long I could remember, but it sounded completely sincere every time, and I never got tired of hearing it.

"Ladies and gentlemen, it has truly been a pleasure to entertain you this evening," he said. "In most shows, it is customary for the performers to come out at the end for a curtain call to receive a final ovation from the audience. However, the spells that we have weaved for you tonight are far too delicate to handle the strain of such an event. I'm sure you'll agree with me that it would be a shame to shatter such rare things. You see, unlike most shows, we do not wish to dispel the illusion at the end. There is far too much in this world that is coarse and banal. Why not let just a little bit of mystery remain? And that is what we hope you take with you this night. Just a tiny seed of the magic we have wrought for you."

He paused for a second, like he was soaking up the concentrated attention that was on him. The audience was completely silent. Then he smiled warmly. "But we do not wish you to think us ungrateful, and so on behalf of the entire company, I would like to extend our most sincere thanks for your patronage."

The audience burst into applause, most of them jumping to their feet again. Ruthven took a single bow and left the stage. The audience stayed on, applauding at the empty stage for a little while.

"Well, thanks, guys." I hopped down from the stool.

"Where are you off to so suddenly?" asked Laurellen.

"Hot date?" asked Mozart.

"Oh, uh . . ." Sometimes I wished I was quicker at responding. "Not really." And better at lying.

The two of them grinned at each other.

"An *almost* date?" asked Laurellen.

"Just getting coffee," I said.

"With who?" asked Mozart.

"Um, Liel." I knew I was blushing. And they were totally enjoying it.

"That is so sweet!" said Laurellen.

"My advice is be assertive," said Mozart. "Troll girls love that."

"Really, we're just friends!" I said. "It's just coffee!"

They looked at each other again. Mozart rolled his eyes.

"Would you like a spot of glamour?" asked Laurellen. "Nothing obvious, of course. Just a subtle bit of a lift?"

I thought about it for a second. A little faerie charm might be just the thing to get Liel to see me as something more than a friend.

"Better not," I said sadly. "My mom would kill me if she caught me with glamour on."

Laurellen sighed. "Well, if you're sure . . ."

Mozart poked him in the shoulder. "He doesn't need it, anyway. Anyone with half a brain can see the kid's got a heart of gold."

"Thanks," I said. "But being nice isn't exactly something that scores with the ladies."

IF I HAD to name one place in the entire theater where I felt the most clumsy, it would be standing outside the women's dressing room. They were all out of costume by this point, so the door was open and I could see into the long, narrow room. It was lined with mirrors and bright, uncovered lightbulbs, and packed with beautiful, graceful, chattering females. It didn't matter that they were all wearing comfy clothes like sweats and tights and that their makeup and glamour were all wiped away. I still felt so big and stupid, standing there with my big, stupid hands hanging at my sides. But it wasn't that strange "monster" feeling like when I was talking with that human girl in the thrift store. It wasn't anything so special or powerful. No, it was the feeling I knew really well. The one that reminded me exactly where my place was in The Show: at the bottom.

And there she was, at the far end, her green face tilted up a little as she pulled her sweat-damp, white, silky hair back into a ponytail with a thin leather strap. The tight muscles in her arms, shoulders, and back flexed as she tied the strap. She turned her head in my direction, inspecting the ponytail in the mirror. Liel caught me in her glittering, diamond gaze and I wondered if she regretted inviting me out tonight. I realized that here, in front of the other females, she could just turn away, pretend she didn't see me, and I wouldn't say a damn thing.

But then she smiled and held up a finger like "one minute." She tossed her makeup, brushes, and other things into a little case on the counter in front of her. Then she grabbed her bag and wove her way through the narrow center aisle toward me.

"You want to go to the Cantina?" she asked when she got to me.

"Sure," I said, grinning like a maniac.

As we walked through the tunnels and corridors up to the Cantina, I was so conscious of her walking next to me that it felt like that whole side of my body was on fire. I wanted so badly to just reach out and take her hand. But then I looked down and saw my meaty, stitched-up excuse for a hand so close to her long, thin, graceful one, and I just thought, *Don't screw this up already*.

There were a couple of places for the company to hang out after The Show, but the Cantina was the most popular. It was also the closest thing to "going out" that a lot of the company could have, since it was the bar out on the mezzanine level of the lobby. Like the rest of the lobby, it was tricked out in a swirl of color and fabric that was supposed to give the audience an international carnival feeling.

Liel and I plopped down on a couple of overstuffed chairs in the corner. One of the dryad wood nymphs immediately came over to take our order. Like all the nymphs, she was pretty in that standard Hollywood human way, although they had hair that was green like leaves and skin the color of tree bark. As near as I could figure out, the group of them shared some kind of hive mind, like bees. So individually they were kind of dumb, but as a group they could accomplish amazing things. Like serving drinks to a thousand audience members in a single ten-minute intermission with enough time left over for the audience to actually finish them.

"Liel, you were so great tonight!" the nymph gushed, completely ignoring me.

"Thanks, Meadow!" said Liel, gushing right back at her. "New number, so I was totally nervous."

"No, no, you were fantastic," said Meadow, patting her arm. "Now what would you like?"

"Can I get two Cokes with the extras?"

"After a night like tonight, you deserve it." Meadow gave her a wink. Then she was gone.

"Extras?" I asked.

"Oh. It's a rum and Coke." She shrugged, like it was no big deal.

"Right," I said, trying to match her tone. "Of course."

She raised a thin, white eyebrow at me. "Haven't you ever had a rum and Coke?"

"Um. No."

Okay, it's not like I'd *never* had a drink. My dad usually busted out a bottle of some old French wine on holidays, and the past few years he would give me a glass. But Ruthven enforced the twenty-one-and-over rule for drinking pretty strictly, and in a community as small as ours, it was hard to get around that. If I had tried to order like Liel just had, Meadow would have laughed in my face. That is, assuming she would have asked for my order at all.

"Well, this should be totally fun, then," said Liel. "I can't imagine you after a few drinks!"

"Yeah." I hoped I wouldn't make a total ass of myself.

"Here we are!" said a different nymph as she placed two tumblers of ice and dark, bubbling liquid on the small table between us. "Two extra Cokes!"

"Thanks, Iris," said Liel.

That was the secret of the nymphs' speed. When you told the order to one, you told it to all of them. They just coordinated their traffic pattern in the most efficient way possible, simultaneously taking orders, making drinks, and picking them up, using whoever happened to be closest to each station. Honestly, I didn't know how Liel could tell them apart. They all looked and acted the same to me.

I took a swallow of my drink and winced, the alcohol burning my throat.

Liel snickered a little. "Yeah, you can't drink it like it's a regular Coke. Tiny sips. Especially if this is your first one ever." She demonstrated with a quick little tilt of her glass.

"Thanks," I said hoarsely, trying not to cough.

She laughed again. "Don't worry. Soon you'll be knocking them back like a trowe."

"Well, thanks for getting me to try one of these," I said, taking a careful sip. "They really are pretty good." Maybe if I kept saying it, it would become true.

"Hey, no big deal." She stirred her drink with a little red straw. "So? I'm dying to hear about your adventure outside."

"Oh, yeah, well, I mean, it wasn't like anything unusual happened. We walked down to a thrift store to get clothes and—"

"Through Times Square? Was it just like in the movies?"

"Kind of. It was really loud. And there were humans everywhere. Like waves of them, all swarming into stores and restaurants. It was crazy at first, just to see them, so many of them. And then to be that close. A couple of times, one even bumped into me a little."

"Wow." Liel shook her head. "And nobody noticed that you were different?"

"Well, some people did. But since everyone assumed I was just a human with a lot of injuries, I guess it would have been rude to stare. The girl who helped me pick out your outfit—"

"Yeah! What was she like?"

"She seemed nice."

"What did she look like?"

"She had red hair. And everything about her was soft and gentle. Her voice, her face—"

"White skin?" she asked.

"Uh, yeah. But not all humans have white skin."

"Of course, I know that." Then she looked down at her empty drink, frowned, and flagged a nymph over for another one. I wasn't even halfway finished with mine.

"Anyway," I continued. "The whole time she was helping me, she must have been wondering, but it wasn't until the end that she asked me about it. The stitches, I mean. Like she had to work up the courage."

"Like she was afraid of hurting your *feelings*?" she asked, like it was totally ridiculous. "About *stitches*?"

It didn't feel ridiculous to me. Not anymore. To her, I had looked ugly. "She was kind, you know? And I guess—"

"Thanks, Sequoia," Liel said as a nymph brought her another drink. Then she turned back to me. "So what did you say it was? Your stitches, I mean."

"An accident," I said. "With a thresher."

She was in mid swallow and choked on her drink. Her cough turned into a laugh. "A *thresher*? Do you even know what one looks like?"

"Sure," I said, laughing a little in spite of myself. "It's like some big farm machine thing, I think."

"That's so awesome." She shook her head. "The next human who asks, you should tell them you got mauled by a lion or some-thing. That would be hilarious."

I tried to imagine myself saying something like that and couldn't help but laugh along with her. I hadn't even consid-ered trying to mess with them. God, why did I have to be such a goody-goody? Just like my parents, doing what I was told, trying to keep out of trouble.

I took a bigger sip of my rum and Coke. Maybe it was time to stop being such a good Boy.

"So, do you think there will be a next time?" Liel asked.

"Ruthven didn't promise or anything, but he said maybe this could become a regular thing we do. And everything went fine, so I don't see why not. He even introduced me to one of his busi-ness people. The guy who sells us rats for the Diva. Said I was his nephew and he was showing me the ropes."

"Really? He said that?" She looked down at her drink, which was mostly gone already, too. She suddenly seemed kind of sad.

"What's up?" I asked. "You okay?"

"Yeah, no, everything's cool." She smiled. But I'd been watch-ing Liel smile my whole life. I loved that smile. If there was one thing I could spot, it was when she was faking it. We sat there in silence for a moment while she just stared down at her drink, swirling the ice with the red plastic stir stick.

"Hey." I nudged her. "You know what he called me?"

"No, what?" she asked, still not looking up.

"Frank."

She stopped stirring. "Shut up, really?"

"Yep."

Her real smile came out. "Oh my God, that is so ridiculous!" She reached out and squeezed my forearm. She probably didn't even notice, but whenever she did something like that, I melted inside.

"How come the boss isn't funny like that all the time?" she asked.

"I don't know. He was definitely a little different out there. A little more . . . I don't know. Open, I guess. Like a real person."

"Seriously, Boy." Her hand was still on my forearm. "It is really awesome that you got to do something like that."

"Yeah." I stared into her eyes and soaked up the heat from her hand on my arm. "I just—"

"Oh, shit, what do we have here?!" Shaun's voice came from directly behind me.

Liel's hand immediately let go of my arm and slipped under the table. She leaned back, a weird, trapped look on her face.

"I didn't know they served motor oil at the Cantina," said Ernesto's squeaky voice.

I turned slowly in my chair. Shaun the Faun stood there with his tanned, muscular arms folded across his chest. Ernesto stood on his shoulder in almost the exact same pose. He was flanked on either side by Aello and Celaeno, the harpy sisters. Oob wasn't allowed in the Cantina.

"Oh, hey, guys!" said Liel, like she was glad to see them.

"You tired of listening to Robo-geek talk about computer stuff?" asked Shaun. "We're getting a card game going in the corner booth."

I stood up slowly, staring at the smirk on Shaun's pretty-boy face. A hot, thick anger boiled up inside me. I thought about my new resolution not to be such a good Boy. My hand balled up into a fist.

But then Liel said, "Oh, that sounds like fun!" She jumped to her feet and moved over to him, like she couldn't wait to get away from me. Shaun led her and his entourage over to the corner booth. I stood there, watching them settle in. Liel laughed at something Shaun said and punched him playfully on the shoulder.

Seeing that squashed the anger out of me. Had I really convinced myself that I had a chance with Liel against someone like Shaun? And then I was going to start a fight in the Cantina, make my family look like the big, dumb robots everybody thought we were?

"Are you still here?" asked Meadow, or Sequoia, or Iris, or whoever the hell it was. She wasn't all smiling and perky now.

"Was I ever?" I asked.

She pursed her lips like she'd just eaten something bad. "Huh?"

"Never mind," I said. Then I walked out of the Cantina.

6

Rage for the Machine

+++++++

I PLUGGED MYSELF into my computer, into limbs and eyes better than my own. I dove into my project, burying myself under layers of code. I didn't belong chatting up girls in the Cantina. This was where I belonged.

I didn't write code in flat, two-dimensional text files like other programmers. Because input and output were parsed by my nervous system, I was able to create a true virtual reality, three-dimensional, with textures, smells, and tastes to complement the visual and audio.

That was a good thing, because I needed all of my senses to wrangle this code. It wasn't static text in a line, but distinct operations that wrote and rewrote themselves constantly. It was to the point where I was less of a code writer and more of a ringmaster, trying to bind this piece to that, separate one from another. You could almost think of each chunk of process as a living cell and I was making a body of code.

But I couldn't really concentrate tonight. Right in the middle of some crucial binding, I'd remember seeing Liel laughing with Shaun, and it suddenly felt like I had this hot fist in my stomach squeezing so tight it made me nauseous. Then the code would slip away and I'd have to chase it down again. After a while, I decided I wasn't accomplishing anything, so I switched over to my chat client.

poxd: well finally somebody's here

b0y: where r the others?

poxd: surelee is UK, so it's crazy late there. or early, depending on how you see it. no idea about s1zzl3

b0y: what u doing?

poxd: trying DDoS to take down this stupid porn site that canceled my membership

b0y: how's that going 4 u?

poxd: it's not. their firewall's pretty tight. so how'd your not-a-date go?

b0y: shitty. jock guy came and took her away

poxd: i'm serious, dude, some day you gotta just punch that guy in the mouth

b0y: ha, yeah right! i'd get in so much trouble

poxd: whatever. it would be worth it.

b0y: maybe . . .

poxd: even if he kicks yer ass, at least u might get a couple good shots in and how good would that feel?

b0y: well, i don't know if he could kick my ass. i'm actually bigger than him

poxd: ha, yeah, me too, right, but fat doesn't help much in a fight

b0y: no, i'm not fat. i'm just really big.

poxd: really? that's not how i picture u at all.

b0y: how do you?

poxd: *shrug* some skinny little goth kid, i guess. the
way you talk about monsters and vampires like
some fking expert.

b0y: nah, that's not really me. i don't even wear black

poxd: so if you're bigger than jock guy, why don't you
just kick his ass?

b0y: i don't know . . . everyone here knows each other . . .

poxd: right, right, that weird communal living your
parents are into . . . freaky hippie shit. so?

b0y: so everyone would know. my parents, my boss, the girl . . .

poxd: yeah. they'd know you finally grew some balls and
stood up for yourself.

b0y: *wince*

poxd: i just call it like i see it

"Boy. Come eat." It was Mom.

b0y: gotta go. dinnertime.

poxd: aren't you east coast? kinda late for dinner

b0y: i told you, my family works for a theater. they don't get off
until midnight.

poxd: weird life

b0y: u got no idea. l8r

I unhooked myself from the computer, then trudged out into
the family room.

"Here." Mom put a plate of spaghetti on the table.

"Thanks." I sat down and started to eat. She just stood
there and watched me. Sometimes it annoyed me when she
did that.

After a few minutes of silence, she said, "You saw the Diva tonight."

I stopped chewing. "Who told you?"

"Stage manager."

That made me feel a little better. It would have hurt if Laurellen or Mozart had told on me.

"So?" she asked.

"She wanted me to watch her act. I was worried that if I didn't, she'd do something bad. I was just trying to keep her happy. Like everybody else."

"Not everybody," she said. "Why did you talk to her at all?"

"I had to deliver the rats we got at the pet store."

She looked at me for a moment, the stitching on her forehead quivering slightly. Then she turned and walked over to her pile of junk. She stared at it for a while and I ate my spaghetti.

"Did you like it?" she asked finally. "The act?"

"I don't know . . . I mean, at the time, it seemed . . . like I was learning something important. Like my life would change forever after that moment. Everything just . . . made sense for once. But as soon as it was over, it all went back to normal."

She prodded a small pile of scrap metal with her foot. "Normal. Not making sense."

"Yeah."

"That's why I love machines," she said quietly. "They make sense."

The door to our apartment opened and Dad stood in the doorway.

"Hello," he said in his flat, "off" voice. He walked slowly over and sat down at the table, folding his hands in front of him.

"Time to switch you back on, dear," said Mom.

"Yes," he said.

I got up to go back to my room.

"Boy," said Mom. "Stay."

I slowly sat back down at the table. I usually didn't have to watch this. Was it my punishment for seeing the Diva tonight?

Every day before The Show, Dad sat on a kitchen chair in our tiny apartment while Mom opened the flap at the base of his skull and put tiny clamps on the nerves that triggered chemical emotional reactions. For the rest of the night, he was a cold, unfeeling creature that could handle any situation without panic, listen to the song of the Siren without being moved, and stare directly into the eyes of Medusa when she was in a rage. But when Mom took off the clamps at the end of the day, it all caught up with him. About six hours' worth of intense emotions all at once.

Mom pulled the stitching loose on the back of Dad's head, then opened up the double flap of skin. He sat there, totally motionless, staring straight ahead. She reached inside with her long, crooked fingers and removed the clamps.

From my vantage point, I could see Dad's scarred, misshapen face switch from blank to twisted agony immediately. Then his mouth opened wide and he let out a long, deep bellow, like a wounded bear. His hands clutched the table, which was reinforced with steel to prevent him from cracking it in half every night. Then he curled in on himself, his face writhing and twitching. His sound tightened up until it came out in short, wrenching gasps from his throat. He squeezed his eyes closed as tears streamed out. Then he let out a long, shuddering moan and slid sideways into my mom's strong arms. She held him, stroking his mottled, patchy hair while he sobbed into her shoulder for the next five minutes or so.

Finally, he got quiet and lifted up his tear-streaked face. Mom already had the handkerchief ready. It was so routine for them. Dad wiped his eyes and blew his nose loudly. Then he slowly sat back up in his chair, looking tired. He gave me a wan smile.

"Hey, buddy. What's for dinner?"

"Why?" I asked.

"Well," he said. "Because I am hungry."

"No, why do you have to go through that every night?"

"Not every night. We are dark on Mondays."

"You know what I mean, Dad. This . . . it's just . . . they treat us like crap!"

"Now, Boy." He held up his massive hand. "It is not that bad."

"It's awful, Dad! What they *do to you* is awful. And the worst part is, nobody even appreciates it. They think of us as these lesser creatures. Like we don't deserve any better than this."

"That is simply not true, Boy." His eyes started to harden. "Ruthven is fully aware of the . . . toll my job takes on me. On us as a family. And he is extremely grateful."

"But—"

"Boy." His voice got that tone to it, each consonant emphasized. "This is what is best for us right now."

The conversation was over. So I stood up and headed for my room.

"Boy." His voice was a little more gentle.

I stopped.

"You know . . ." He frowned, like he was trying to decide what to say. "Things will work out. I have a plan. For you."

"What plan?"

"I will tell you at the proper time. Until then, you must trust me."

"Yeah, okay, Dad." I shut the door behind me.

I didn't trust him, of course. The guy lived in the Arctic for fifty years. I bet if Ruthven hadn't tracked him down and dragged him out of there, he'd *still* be bunking in some ice cave with a bunch of polar bears. And now he made a living as a doormat for a bunch of snobby, spoiled performers. He'd dropped hints about some secret plan in store for me before. I was pretty sure it would be something like, "How would you like to be my assistant?" Yeah, well, I was not going to end up like him.

I got back to work on my project, and this time I was hyper focused. I worked for a few hours, slept for a few hours, then got back up and worked some more. This was what made me different from him. This was how I was going to escape his fate. Nobody could do what I was doing.

It's time I admitted something. Maybe past time. My project wasn't just some cool application or new scripting language. Technically speaking, it was a virus. But I didn't think of it like that. Sure, it was viral in the way it developed, but it wasn't malicious. It wasn't out to damage anything. In fact, I hoped it would improve systems that it infected. Essentially, it was a hacker virus. Not as in a "virus made by hacker," but as in a "virus that can hack." A fully autonomous virus that could assess and understand any new situation and make its own choices and adapt accordingly based on that information. And I was so close. In fact, there was this little bit that seemed to have changed from just a minute ago when I—

The phone rang.

"What?" Getting pulled out of the code flow always made me grumpy.

There was a burst of harsh static. Then a quick chill ran through me as I felt more than heard the stage manager's thin, reedy voice.

"Boy, could you come backstage? The crew is having some trouble with their station again."

"Okay," I said quietly. I was pissed about the interruption, of course, and not in any mood to stumble around in the dark trying to figure out why the fly crew couldn't stream ESPN on that ancient PC of theirs that they refused to upgrade. But hearing the stage manager's voice took the fight right out of me. Wraiths are like that.

"STAGE MANAGER SAID you needed me," I said to the Minotaur when I got to the backstage area where all the props and set pieces were stored.

"Hmm?" He turned his bull head toward me. "Oh, hey, Boy. Thanks for coming." I guess he used to have a temper way back in the day, but he seemed pretty chill these days, except when he was in a fight with his girlfriend, the Siren.

"It's this one again." He walked to the little cubby set into the back wall. Inside was a PC that I had set up for him and his guys forever ago to give them something to do between set changes.

Moog the ogre sat at the computer, playing solitaire. Moog was Oob's dad and probably only a little smarter. He was one of those guys who celebrated the whole "big equals stupid" stereotype that I was trying to fight against.

"Hey, nerd," he said. "This stupid machine don't work."

"Maybe if you'd stop torrenting hi-def femdom clips all day long, it would work better," I said.

He blinked at me, then turned to the Minotaur. "What the hell'd he just say?"

"It doesn't matter," said the Minotaur. "Just get up and give the kid some room to work."

Moog slowly got up and moved to one side. I sat down at

the chair and pulled my cables out of the duffel bag I brought with me. I plugged the DVI cable into the back of my head and the USB cables into my wrists, then plugged everything into the computer. As my senses slipped into the computer, I heard Moog say, "Damn, that gives me the creeps."

"I can still hear you," I said.

"So?" he said.

I was about to snap back a reply that I would probably regret, when I saw something in the computer that surprised me.

"Okay, that's weird," I said.

"What?" said the Minotaur anxiously.

"You've got a virus."

"Can you get rid of it?"

"Yeah, sure," I said. "But . . ."

"What?"

I unplugged. "I'll need to take it back to my room and work on it." I wrapped up my cords and shoved them back in my bag. "It's a little complicated."

"What?!" said Moog. "No games? For how long?"

"I don't know," I said. "Until I fix it."

"Listen, you little droid—"

"Moog," said the Minotaur. "Let the kid do his job."

"Yeah, whatever." Moog stalked off to some other part of the backstage area, grunting to himself.

"Sorry," said the Minotaur. "What can I say? He's stupid."

"Sure." I picked up the PC tower and hoisted it on to my shoulder. "See you around."

The reason I wanted to take the fly crew's computer back to my room was not because it was complicated (although it was). It was because I recognized the virus signature. It was mine.

That itself wasn't totally crazy. I'd written some nasty viruses back in the day when I was into that kind of stuff, and it was probably inevitable that at least one of them would come back to haunt me. The weird thing was, it looked like a piece of the project I was working on right now. But of course, I hadn't released it. So how did it get out?

"Oh, shit, it's Robo-freak."

I had been thinking so hard about the virus that I hadn't noticed Shaun coming down the hallway toward me. He stopped and stood in the middle of the hallway, his hands on his goat hips, blocking my way.

The second I saw him, I forgot about the virus and all I could think about was the way he had smirked at me last night as he took Liel to his table.

"I could smell that combo of rotting human flesh and motor oil before I even saw you, Robot," he said. "Or do you prefer the term *cyborg*?"

"Come on, Shaun," I said. "There's no one around to impress. Just leave me alone."

I tried to get around him but he shifted back and forth to block whichever way I tried to go.

"Hey, what's that?" He pointed to the PC tower on my shoulder. "Your new girlfriend?"

"Aaaah, good one, Shaun. Hilarious," I said, trying to push past him.

"This one doesn't have legs. Maybe she won't walk out on you like Liel did last night."

Anger burned its way through my arms and into my hands. I needed to get away before I did something stupid.

"Shaun, seriously. Just let me go."

"Seriously?" he asked. "I can't believe you ever thought you had a chance with her."

My free hand shot out and grabbed him by the throat. Then I slammed him into the wall. It felt so good, I did it again. And again. Until I guess the Minotaur and Moog finally heard the screaming and came running. It took the two of them to pry the bruised and bleeding Shaun from my hand.

"You're no monster!" Shaun yelled, his goat hooves clacking against the floor as Moog dragged him away. "You're just a fucking ROBOT!!!"

"Come on, dumb-ass, let's get you fixed up," said Moog. "Don't you have better sense than to pick a fight with somebody twice your size? And people call *me* stupid."

The Minotaur held my arm as tight as a C-clamp.

"Sorry, Boy," he said. "You know you can't go beating on people like that. I'm gonna have to call your parents. And Ruthven."

RUTHVEN SAT BEHIND his desk, the harsh glare of the lamp gleaming off his red eyes. I stood in front of the desk with my parents behind me. I felt like I was on trial. And I guess I kind of was.

"Boy," said Ruthven, his hands folded in a steeple. "I believe you are a valuable member of this company. And I trust you in many things. I wouldn't have taken you outside with me yesterday if that weren't true. But this . . ." He began to rub his temples. "This is a problem that is not going to go away. There will always be those in the company who are threatened by your ties to science, even as they reap the benefits of it. Some of them, inevitably, will say things that hurt your feelings. For the good of the company, you have to learn to deal with that in a nonviolent way." He looked at me for a moment, his expression unreadable. "Or we will have to find some other solution."

"If I may," said my father.

Ruthven gestured to him and he stepped forward to stand next to me.

"I think it is time to share with Boy the plan for his future."

"No!" my mother said. "He's too young—"

"You have delayed it long enough," he said to her. Then he turned back to Ruthven. "I believe Boy's misbehavior today is a symptom of something bigger. I have felt it building for months now. He talks back, he questions authority, he ignores his chores. I believe it is because he grows restless. He needs to be challenged. He needs something to work toward."

"Hmmm." Ruthven leaned back in his chair. "Perhaps you're right, my old friend."

"Dad, what is this big plan you keep mentioning?" I asked.

Dad looked to Ruthven, who nodded. Then he turned back to me.

"Your desire to get out and explore the world is a credit to you. And as much as the risks worry us, it would be cruel to deny you that experience, particularly after your first trip outside, where you proved that you can indeed fit in with humans."

"Dad . . ." I almost couldn't believe what he was saying. "You're going to let me live outside? With humans?"

He held up his hand. "Under certain conditions."

"Like?"

"You already received your high school diploma from homeschooling."

"Last spring."

"Another condition is that you must wait until you turn eighteen."

"That's only in, like, six months."

"Yes. Until then, Ruthven will continue to take you outside, more and more often, for longer and longer periods, so that you can get comfortable with humans, learn how to fit in not just physically, but socially."

"Okay . . ." That didn't sound too bad, either. Maybe we could even go somewhere for a weekend. Like a road trip. I always wanted to go on a road trip.

"Then," continued Dad, "in the fall you will go to college."

"A *human* college?" I'd thought about college, sure. But I just never imagined I'd be able to go.

"Yes."

"I bet MIT would give me some money. Maybe even a full ride!" I'd chatted with a few people on hacker boards from MIT, even a couple of professors. It sounded like geek utopia. "Dad, this so awesome! With the resources they have there, I could—"

"Your school has already been decided."

"O . . . kay . . ." Maybe I'd gotten ahead of myself. Cambridge, Massachusetts, was a bit far away, after all. But Princeton was just in Jersey. Or even Cornell or Columbia right here in the city. Those schools all had great computer science programs. . . .

"You will attend the University of Geneva."

"Wait, what? Where's that?"

"Switzerland."

"Why am I going to *Switzerland* for college?"

"Because I am very good . . . friends with a family in Geneva. They have already pledged to assist in any way they can. Tuition, room and board, whatever you require. They will be like a second

family to you. Indeed, I have sent them pictures of you throughout your childhood and written to them about you extensively,
so they feel as though they already know you. They, too, are
great lovers of science. They are very eager to help you make the
most of your life."

"Who is this family?" I asked. "Why haven't you ever talked
about them before?"

"Their name," he said, his mismatched, watery eyes locked on
mine, "is Frankenstein."

7

Disconnecting

++++++++

I'M NOT SURE how they expected me to react to the news that in six months, I would be shipped off to Switzerland to live with the humans whose ancestor was responsible for making my family the hideous, screwed-up monsters we were. They probably didn't expect me to scream, *"NO FUCKING WAY IN HELL!"* and run out of the room. Or maybe they did, because nobody stopped me.

I ran for a long time, just charging down hallways, through corridors, across catwalks. Maybe I broke stuff, maybe I knocked people over. Honestly, I wasn't really paying attention. Eventually, I ended up down in the trowe caverns, which was inevitable since nearly all passages ended there if you went deep enough. Still, I kept going down until I hit a dead end. It was a dark little cavern with a long stone table and benches. I guess this was a trowe version of a picnic spot.

I plopped down on one of the benches and slumped onto the table. I closed my eyes and saw Dad's calm expression as he told me that he was sending me to live with the Frankensteins. I imagined them, these crazy, mad scientists with their lighting-bolt labs, setting fire to any creation that started mouthing off to them. That creation had been my dad, once upon a time. The rebel who stood up to his asshole creator. That asshole creator tried to destroy him for it, and nearly succeeded.

Now he was shipping off his only son to live with a whole family of them? How could he possibly be okay with that? And what made it worse, he wasn't even giving me the choice.

Then I heard a noise. It was dark in the cavern, and my night vision wasn't the greatest, so it took me a while before I finally caught a glint of two diamonds over in the corner.

"Liel?"

"Hey." She shifted a little so that I could see the outline of her body. Her white hair was pulled back tight, and when she was motionless, her skin blended right in with the stone wall behind her.

"What are you doing here?"

"I was thinking of asking you the same thing. Usually, there's nobody but trowe this far down into the caverns."

"Yeah," I said. "I just . . . had to get away."

"Why? What's up?"

"It's nothing."

She came and sat down across from me at the table. "Tell me."

If it had been anyone else, I would have kept my mouth shut. Shrugged it off, mumbled something about annoying parents, and that would have been it. But even after she dissed me, I was still such a chump that I couldn't say no to her.

"I just found out that my parents are going to ship me off to live with the Frankensteins in Switzerland."

She squinted her glittering eyes at me for a moment, then said, "Wow." But the way she said it sounded impressed, not outraged.

"No, this isn't cool," I said. "This is seriously screwed up!"

She shook her head. "Your dad is just doing whatever he can to get you the hell out of this dump."

"What are you talking about?"

She got up and started pacing. "They don't appreciate you here. You deserve better. Your dad is trying to make sure you get it."

"Deserve better? Are you messing with me?"

She stopped and glared at me, shaking her head. "No, of course I'm not messing with you. You can leave. You proved it the other day. And you'd be an idiot not to do it!" She leaned back against the wall, looking off into the darkness. "This place is just holding you back. It's a dead end. A zoo for freaks."

It was difficult to see in the dim light, but after a moment, I realized she was crying. Liquid draining from colorless gems.

"What were you doing down here, just now?" I asked her. "All by yourself in the dark?"

"Nothing." She pushed the tears away with the backs of her hands.

I waited.

Then finally she said, "Just . . . thinking."

"Do you wish you could . . . Do you want to leave The Show?"

"You said it right the first time. I *wish* I could. But I couldn't pass out there. Not like you can. This," she slapped her hand on the rough stone wall. "This is all I have to look forward to."

"Liel, I—"

"So you think about that, huh?" She turned on me, her eyes fierce, her lips pulled back in a snarl to show a mouth full of sharp teeth. "The next time you feel like whining about the opportunities your dad is fighting to give you, you remember *me*. Okay?"

Then she was gone, moving too fast through the dark tunnels for me to see.

MY PARENTS WERE both out when I got back home, which was great. They were probably going to expect me to apologize for freaking out in front of Ruthven, and I was definitely not ready to do that.

I got an energy drink from the fridge and sat at the table, chugging the cool, sticky sweetness. The PC tower I had picked up from the fly crew earlier sat on the ground in front of my bedroom door. I'd almost forgotten about that. Mom probably picked it up and brought it home at some point. She was good like that. The mystery of how part of my new virus escaped was the perfect thing to take my mind off everything else.

I took the tower into my bedroom, closing the door behind me and began testing. I guess I should have been a little concerned that the virus had gotten away from me. But really, it proved that I was on the right track. It's impossible for a regular computer program to do something truly unpredictable. Anything a program can do can be predicted by the programmer because computers can only do the things the programmer explicitly teaches them how to do. They don't learn or adapt or try new things. They can't be random.

But as far as I could tell, my project had just done something totally unpredictable. It did something I never explicitly taught it how to do. It analyzed my security measures, located a breach, adapted its *own code* to exploit that breach, and escaped. And I had no idea why.

Which was . . . amazing. A first in computing history. I was a fucking genius.

There was pounding on the front door of our apartment. I heard my mom's footsteps walk toward it. She must have gotten home sometime after me. A moment later, there was a knock at my bedroom door.

"Boy," said my mom. "Come out here please." She never said things like "please" unless she was pissed about something and there were other people around. I quickly unplugged and went out to the living room.

Mom was over by her pile of junk in the corner, acting like there was nobody else in the room. Charon stood in the doorway, his brown robes crooked on his bony frame, like he had just been running.

"Boy! We need you!" he said.

"What's going on?" I asked.

"The Siren just had a complete breakdown onstage in front of an audience. Nearly killed them all."

"Oh, no," I said, wondering if she and the Minotaur had finally broken up. "Where's my dad?"

"He's taking care of her."

"So what do you need me for?"

Charon looked at Mom for a moment, but she was still pretending like he wasn't there. So he turned back to me.

"The Diva has taken this moment, while your father is occupied and Ruthven is managing the panicked audience, to pitch a fit. She wants company in her dressing room. You. Face-to-face. Immediately."

"But . . ."

"Yeah. You have to switch off."

"No," said Mom from her spot over by the pile of junk.

"Bride . . ." said Charon. "You had to know it would happen sooner or later. Your husband can't be in two places at once."

"She can wait."

"No, Bride. We can't risk that. Not with her. Do you remember the last time? Twenty humans and three creatures dead. She could ruin everything. And you know she won't accept you in his place."

My mom still stared at the pile of junk. She picked up part of an old toaster oven and examined it.

"Please, Bride," said Charon. "For the Company."

She stared at the toaster while we waited for her to answer. Slowly, carefully, she compressed it into a small lump of metal. Then she let it drop back on the pile.

"For the Company," she said. Her face was as expressionless as ever, but the stitches on her forehead vibrated with tension.

"What about you, Boy?" he asked. "Are you up to it?"

"I don't know," I said.

"Wise answer. Will you do it?"

I looked at Mom, trying to see what she wanted. But then I thought, *He didn't ask her. He asked me.*

"Sure," I said. "I'll do it."

I sat on the stool that I had seen Dad sit on so many times. My heart was pounding so hard I could feel it in my temples. Mom walked slowly over and stood behind me for a moment. I felt her gently loosen the stitches at the base of my skull.

"What does it feel like?" I asked.

"For most of it, it feels like nothing," she said. "Then at the end, it feels like everything."

I could feel her push aside muscles and tendons to locate the nerves.

"I know this is hard." Charon sat on one of the chairs at the table. "I'll talk to Ruthven about some extra food vouchers, or maybe a special trip to the junkyard."

Mom didn't reply to that. I could feel her working deep into my spine now, slowly, methodically exposing the nerves.

"Okay, Boy. It's time."

> BRIDE: How do you feel?
> BOY: Like IRC
> CHARON: What?
> BRIDE: It stands for Internet Relay Chat.
> CHARON: I still don't understand, but okay :/
> BRIDE: Go quickly, Boy. The less time you spend like this,
>   the less trauma there will be at the end.

> Boy exits apartment.
> Boy returns to apartment twenty-six minutes later.

> BRIDE: Well?
> BOY: She's fine now.

> Boy sits on the stool.

> BRIDE: Are you ready?
> BOY: I don't know.

> Bride loosens the stitches and releases the clips.

I couldn't breathe or see or hear. Emotion crushed down so hard that it blocked out everything else. I'd heard people talk about "emotional pain" before, but I didn't realize it could be literal, like my guts were getting wound up around a spiked pole inside me. I caught visual flickers of myself falling from the stool and hitting the hard floor, but compared to the relentless pressure inside, I barely felt it. My mom tried to pick me up, but any touch, even hers, made it worse, so I pushed her away. All I could do was lay there, dimly aware that my body was convulsing, as I lived through the emotional experience of the past half hour but compressed into a short, hard burst.

I LEFT THE apartment and walked unhurriedly down the main corridor. I could tell my posture was different. Straighter, more purposeful. People stopped and looked at me as I passed them, like they could sense something was off. And they were right. Something was way off. It was almost like I was two separate people in one, the acting me and the feeling me. I was having the emotions but they hit the back of my skull and just sat there, while the acting me—the disconnected me—just kept going.

This time I didn't hesitate when I knocked on Medusa's door, and I wasn't quiet or tentative about it.

"Yes?" I heard Medusa say. But this time no chill ran through my body, no ice-cream brain freeze.

"It's Boy." Internally, I recoiled at the flat, robotic sound of my own voice. It sounded so much like my father. But that emotion pooled up at the disconnection point, just like all the rest.

"Wonderful," said Medusa, her voice silky smooth. "Come in."

I jerked the door open immediately and stepped inside. All the same sensual elements were there: the smell of cedar, the dim lighting, her lounging silhouette behind the white curtain. I stood there with dumb indifference, waiting for my next instructions.

"My, my. Your mother fixed you all up, didn't she?" said Medusa, her voice teasing.

"Fixed me up? Clarify."

"I just mean that now we can talk face-to-face." She pushed the curtain aside and I saw Medusa for the first time. The pressure on the back of my skull spiked as I took it all in. Her smooth snakeskin gleamed white except the green and brown diamond patterns that ran from her neck, across her shoulders and ended halfway down her upper arms. Her thick head of snake hair writhed slowly and her body swayed with the same motion. Her face was absolutely perfect, with full red lips and glittering black eyes. She was the most beautiful creature I'd ever seen. But her waist tapered off into a long, thick snake tail that coiled up under her, supporting her back as she lay on her purple velvet divan.

"I always thought you had legs," I said.

"Yes, I imagine it must be a frustrating realization," she said.

"Why?" I asked.

"Because you want to have sex with me but now you know it's a physical impossibility."

Deep inside my own head, I was screaming. Out of embarrassment. Out of horror. And okay, sure, maybe a little out of disappointment, too. But all I said was yes.

"Some say sensual lust is the root of my power," she said. "Lust unfulfilled."

"Is it?"

"It's merely a facet. Others say my power is feminine rage, but that, too, is but an aspect. Scholars have always tried to fit me in their tiny boxes and they always fail."

"What is the root of your power then?"

"To look into my eyes is to stare into the void and see Truth in all its terrible grandeur. Now that you have seen my performance, you have at least a vague understanding of that. That even veiled, Truth is tremendously powerful and dangerous."

"Why does truth turn people to stone?"

"It doesn't. Not literally. But they are frozen for a time, locked in a despair so all-consuming that it's as if their hearts, their minds, their very muscles have turned to stone. Lesser creatures, like human men, usually can't survive the experience. And yet they long for it. Truth. Or perhaps death, since death is the ultimate truth. This is why all heroes have tragic endings. They use Truth as a weapon, as Perseus used my likeness to defeat his enemies. But the hero can't understand, or perhaps can't accept, that in worshipping Truth, they are consumed by it."

"Why does it not freeze me now?"

"Truth is more than mere facts. In your current limited state, you look upon Truth, but you don't know it."

She slowly rose from her divan and moved toward me, her eyes never breaking contact with mine.

"Did you talk to any humans while you were out shopping with Ruthven?"

"A man and a girl."

"A girl?" She stroked my cheek with her fingers, smooth and cool on my skin. The pressure in my skull increased with her touch. "How old was she?"

"Approximately my age."

"Did you like her?"

"Yes. She was nice."

"Were you attracted to her?"

"Yes."

"More than Liel?"

"I don't know. I didn't get to know her well enough."

"Such a sweet boy." She patted me on the head. "I'm going to miss you."

"Miss me?"

"Yes. When you leave The Show."

"I do not know if I want to leave The Show."

"Why would you stay? To follow in your father's footsteps here, placating temperamental actresses and repelling magic-addled humans? Accepting your place at the bottom of the social ladder in a tiny, bitter, narrow-minded lot of has-beens? Existing entirely at the mercy of a manic-depressive vampire? Does that sound like a good choice to you?"

"The alternative does not seem much better."

"Ah, yes. Your father has spoken to me of that. Switzerland."

"Yes."

"And this doesn't sound appealing to you?"

"No."

She ran her fingers through my hair. My skull throbbed with pressure now, making it difficult to think.

"Why has your father chosen this path for you?"

"I don't know."

"No? Surely you can guess, though."

"Perhaps when I am fully myself again."

"Let me suggest something for you to ponder in the meantime. Could it be that your father is not sending you to Geneva for your good, but for his? I imagine that he would have loved to have been accepted into the Frankenstein family, studying at the University of Geneva. . . . Perhaps he daydreams of it sometimes."

"He has never spoken to me of it."

"No, of course not." She leaned in close, her dry, glistening snakeskin lips brushing my ear. The roar of pressure in my head grew so strong I could barely hear her voice. "Think of this, though. He has created a being almost exactly like himself, only smaller, neater, less threatening. You. And he has offered you up to the Frankensteins, almost like a . . . promise?"

"A promise of what?"

"What would your father give to unite his family with the Frankensteins? His firstborn son, perhaps?"

"I . . . I do not know. I cannot . . ."

A smile curled up on one side of her mouth. "Oh, dear. I think I may have pushed you a bit too far. Ah, well. I think you see my point. Or you will in a few minutes. It's time to grow up and start thinking for yourself, little Boy. It's time to start your journey. Not on your father's path, but your own."

She glided back to her divan.

"You may go. This has been extremely stimulating. I think I'll have a nap now."

I left the dressing room and headed home. I still had no sense of urgency, even though my skull was screaming with pressure. It needed release. But I knew the moment Mom removed the clamp . . .

NOW, I LAY on the floor with my face pressed against the cold, rock floor as I rode out the last dregs of the storm of emotions. After feeling so unbearably full, I now felt completely empty. I slowly sat up and looked around at our tiny, little, rundown windowless apartment. Charon had gone at some point, so it was just Mom and me.

"How are you?" she asked.

"Tired."

"Do you . . . want to talk about it?"

"Not now, Mom."

She nodded, and touched the side of my face with her hand.

"Sorry," she said.

"It's not your fault," I said.

She stared at me, and all of a sudden I wished so much that she could express herself. A smile, a frown—anything other than vague surprise. Instead, she just nodded again and turned to the kitchen.

"Your father will be home soon. I need to make dinner."

I LAY IN my bed, my mind racing from the endorphins brought on by the emotional backlash pain. Was Medusa right? Was my father sending me to live with the Frankensteins so I could live out some fantasy of his? I bet he hadn't even checked if there was a good computer science program there. And he probably expected me to kiss their monster-killing asses the entire time I was there. No, going to Geneva was completely out now. It made me angry just thinking about it.

But staying here wasn't any better. Now I knew firsthand what Dad went through every single night. There was no way I could do that. But what else was there for me?

I looked over at my computer and realized that I already had my golden key.

I jacked in and launched my IRC client.

poxd: jezuz, how do you stay offline so much?

slzzl3: don't you get the shakes ;P

surelee: he's cooking up something big, i can tell

b0y: big, yeah . . . guys, i'm gonna need yr help

poxd: bshit

surelee: the one and only b0y needs help?

b0y: yup. lemme send you each a snip of what i've been
  working on. put it someplace it won't get loose before you
  extract. i mean *really* tight security. then take a look and
  tell me if you're in.

It was time to stop playing by everyone else's rules. I was
meant for better things than Ruthven's assistant security guard
or a rich Swiss family's pet monster. It was time to show everybody what I could really do. It was time for my project to go
live.

I worked pretty much nonstop from that point on. I hardly
ate or slept. It was just energy drinks, runs to the bathroom, and
coding. Before, it had seemed like the project still had a ways to
go. But now that I was committed to finishing it, it came together
in a matter of days. It was beautiful. Code wrote and refined
itself. Text snaked through my virtual fingers like silk, pushing
my computer's CPU so hot you could cook an egg on the smooth
casing. This was more than just poetry. I was writing a sym-
phony, and when the world saw this, they would realize that
they'd spent their entire lives on mute.

There was a problem, though. I had no idea what would happen when I deployed it. Not really. That was kind of the point,
of course. True unpredictable programming action. But as cool as
that sounded, there was a possibility that the surge alone from
the initial launch would take down the entire local network and
possibly the power grid as well. So I didn't want to do it at the
theater. I needed another location.

A few days later, poxd, surelee, and s1zzl3 all contacted me
to say how blown away they were by the samples I'd sent. They
all said they wanted to help, to be a part of it. So I told them I

needed a place to launch it from and also a place to crash for a night or two. That was the last I heard from surelee and s1zzl3. I guess the code didn't scare them, but the idea of a real-life encounter did. But poxd said I could do it at his place. And it turned out, he lived nearby in Queens. It seemed perfect. I didn't even really hesitate.

Well, okay, that's not true. There was a moment. I was just finishing up some last bug checks on the source before I compiled it when my dad came into the room. He couldn't see what I was doing. That's one nice bonus about having your display plugged directly into the back of your head. But even if he had been able to see, he wouldn't have understood what he was looking at.

"Boy," he said quietly. He had to make an effort for his voice to sound quiet, so I knew he meant business. I unplugged and turned to look at him. He stood in the doorway, his head stooped to fit under the lintel.

"Hey, Dad."

"How are you feeling?"

"Uh, fine. Why?"

"I want to make sure there is no problem after your . . . conversation with Medusa."

"You mean when I had to get unplugged?" Maybe I sounded a little harsh, because he took a moment to respond.

"Yes," he said finally.

"I'm fine. Now."

"Okay." He looked like he wanted to say something else. Or ask me something else. But he just stood there, filling the doorway for a moment longer. Then he nodded and turned, his shoulders just barely squeezing past on either side. It suddenly occurred to me what a huge pain in the ass it had to be for him to maneuver indoors, especially in narrow hallways or small, cramped rooms like pretty much ninety percent of the space in The Show. That's probably why he lived all those years in the Arctic. At least he'd been able to stretch out a bit there.

"Dad," I said.

He stopped.

"Why are we here?"

He turned a little so that he could look at me, but not all the way back around.

"What do you mean? My job is here. Your mother's job is here. The company needs us. The Show needs us."

"But we don't need *them*."

"Not true."

"What do they give us?"

"Safety."

"I don't want it," I said.

"Because you do not know the dangers that are out there."

"How could I? I'm stuck here with people who hate me because of what I am, and they're all so small-minded. Like they've got blinders on. None of them gets it. None of them sees that there's this whole world out there."

"We have already spoken about this." His big, uneven face hardened. "I understand you are restless. And that is why we have devised the plan for you to go to Geneva."

"I don't *want* to go to Geneva!" I said. "That's *your* thing. I want to make my own way. I want to have my own life."

"You are just a boy." His voice was no longer quiet, no longer gentle. "You do not know what you want!"

"Dad—"

"ENOUGH!" The sound rattled every piece of electronics in the room. "Unless you wish to go nowhere at all, this conversation is over." He turned sharply, his shoulder taking out a small chunk of the door frame. Then he left.

I packed a duffel bag with some clothes, some self-repair tools, and my favorite computer.

The only person I said good-bye to was Liel, and that wasn't on purpose. I don't know whether she just happened to be hanging around the unlit lobby at two a.m. or what, but there she was, a dark silhouette with sparkling eyes and luminous hair.

We stood there looking at each other for a moment.

"Where will you go?" she asked.

"A friend's house," I said.

"You have friends out there?"

"Yeah, I guess."

"Will . . ." She looked down so that her jewel eyes were hidden in the shadows. "Will you be back?"

"Maybe."

I could faintly see her nod. "What . . . should I tell them?"

"Tell my mom I'm sorry. I don't care what you tell the rest of them."

Then I walked past her to the front doors.

"Boy," I heard her say behind me.

I froze, hand halfway to the door handle. I knew, right then, that if she asked me to stay, I would.

But she just said:

"Good luck."

"Thanks," I said.

And that was it. I left The Show.

PART 2

The City

"*How* dangerous is the acquirement
of knowledge, and how much happier that man
is who believes his native town to be the world,
than he who aspires to become greater
than his nature will allow."

—Victor Frankenstein,
FROM *Frankenstein; or, The Modern Prometheus*, WRITTEN BY MARY SHELLEY

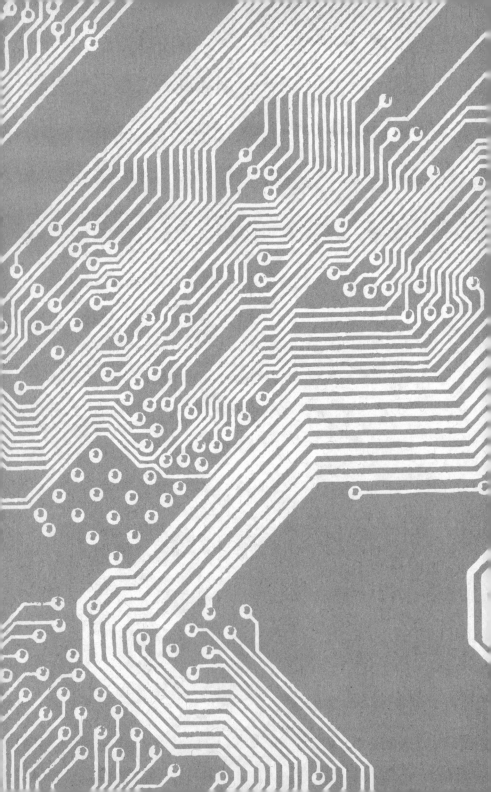

§
Hello, World!

╫╫╫╫╫╫╫

AS SOON AS I heard the theater door close behind me, I panicked. Ruthven wasn't there to guide me. I had no idea how to do anything on my own. I had no idea what was going to happen. If I hadn't just made that dramatic exit for Liel, I might have turned around and gone right back inside.

But obviously, I didn't want Liel to think I was an even bigger loser than she already did. Plus, I was pretty sure the door had just locked behind me. So I took a slow, deep breath and told myself I'd be back in a day or two. Right after I made computing history.

I visualized the map I'd been memorizing for days, oriented myself with the landmarks I'd seen on Google Maps, and started toward the subway entrance. It helped that it was dark out and there weren't many people around. I could almost pretend I was back in the caverns. Then I walked down the steps to the subway station and I felt even more like I was in the caverns. Except the caverns smelled better.

Ruthven had given me a credit card to buy tech stuff for The Show. He'd probably cancel it as soon as he found out I was gone, so this might be my last chance to use it. I bought the most expensive MetroCard I could, an unlimited monthly pass.

The turnstiles were a little tricky for someone my size, but I eventually figured out how to squeeze through. I stepped down onto the subway platform and a minute later the train came rumbling into the station. The sound and vibration were so intense I felt like my stitching was going to unravel.

The train shot through tunnels for a few stops, then suddenly popped up aboveground and rose into the air until we were level with the building tops. I turned in my seat and pressed my nose against the glass. Behind me, I saw the island of Manhattan, huge and bristling with pointy roofs and light. Now I was in Queens. The buildings were lower out here and there were fewer lights. But everything was still packed in nice and tight, which felt strangely comforting. I craned my head to look up through the window, and for the first time in my life I saw the stars. Purplish clouds swirled through the night sky, hiding and revealing bright, sparkling pinholes. Over to one side, I saw the moon, bigger than I thought it would look. Fat and full, and rough with craters.

As the train moved farther out into Queens, I watched the buildings flow by beneath me. Groceries, pizza, clothing . . . there was so much *stuff.* And any human could walk in and buy it all, as long as they had the money. I didn't fully get the concept of money and I knew it was something I needed to be familiar with, since the human world seemed to depend on it.

I got off at the stop poxd had told me to go to in a neighborhood called Sunnyside, which wasn't nearly as cheerful as the name sounded. I walked for a couple of blocks to poxd's address. Along the way, I saw people hanging out on street corners or front stoops, but nobody said anything to me or even acted like they saw me.

Finally, I got to the apartment building. I walked through an open courtyard, found the right entrance, and hit the buzzer, all like poxd had instructed.

"Yeah?" said a voice. It was distorted by the cheap speaker, so I couldn't really tell anything about it.

"Boy," I said. Sometimes when I got nervous I talked like my mom in one-word sentences.

There was a tense moment when the intercom clicked off and nothing else happened. But then there was a long beep and the door unlocked. I climbed up three flights of stairs (that definitely wouldn't have passed trowe safety standards) and at the top I saw a tall, heavyset, older guy, kind of bald on top, with a blond ponytail. We stared at each other for a moment.

"Poxd?" I asked.

He nodded suddenly, like he was coming out of a trance. "Real name's Gauge." He held out his hand. I could see him staring at the stitches as we shook. "What's yours? Your real name, I mean."

"Uh, Frank. Frank Shelley." I know, totally lame. But it was the first thing that came to me.

"Well, Frank," he said. "Welcome to Sunnyside."

He turned and walked into his apartment and I followed. It was a one-bedroom about the size of my family's apartment. Movie posters lined the walls—*Firefly*, *The Matrix*, that kind of stuff. Over in the corner was a massive, whining server rack with some of the newest, shiniest hardware I'd ever seen.

"Nice place," I said.

"Thanks," he said. "I like it except the walls are paper thin. I can hear my neighbor when he takes a shit. And I'm pretty sure he's got a meth lab going."

"Didn't you say you had a roommate?"

"I did, but he decided to move back to California. Sometimes that happens to us Californians. We just get tired of the crap and head back to the motherland."

There was an awkward silence. Meeting an online friend in real life was totally weird. I realized I had this whole image of who I thought poxd was, what he looked like, how his voice sounded. And it definitely wasn't this guy.

"So . . ." I said. But I couldn't think of anything else to say.

"So that virus you made," he said.

"It's not exactly a virus."

"Whatever. It's amazing."

"Thanks."

"No really, I mean that literally. Like, I have no idea what you did. That little snippet you sent? It's been doing all kinds of weird shit."

"Oh, really? Like what?"

"What do you mean, like what? You wrote it, didn't you?"

"Initially. But now it kind of writes itself. It does what it wants."

"Code doesn't have 'wants.'"

I just shrugged.

His eyes narrowed. "Are you telling me you've written a sentient script?"

"Your words, not mine."

"You really want to release it into the wild?"

I grinned.

"Hell, let's do it," he said. "Right now."

"Cool." I pulled the tower out of my bag.

"Jesus. You carried that big clunky thing all the way from midtown? It must weigh a ton!"

"Uh, yeah. It sure was heavy," I said in a way that I hoped sounded convincing. There were a lot of little things about blending in outside that I hadn't considered. After we plugged in my tower, I ran into another one.

"You didn't bring any peripherals?" he asked. "Just these . . . What are these, some kind of customized USB and DVI cables?"

"Oh, uh, I totally forgot my keyboard."

"Hey, don't worry. I have a ton of them." He walked over to the corner by the server racks. It made me smile a little, because he had a little pile of junk, just like my mom. He pulled a mouse and keyboard from the pile, taking a few minutes to untangle the cables, and brought them back.

"Thanks." I tried to look like I was comfortable using them, but I was so painfully slow he had to be wondering how I could possibly write code when I was such a terrible typist. Once my computer booted up, I used the clunky keyboard and mouse to prepare my freshly compiled program for release. Gauge stood behind me and leaned in over my shoulder. He smelled like Doritos.

"Are you seriously saying you've created a . . . what, a virtual artificial intelligence?"

"I guess you could look at it like that."

"What's it going to do when you release it?"

"I have no idea."

He stared at me for a moment. "You're serious, aren't you?"

"Yep. The only thing I know for sure is that it's going to be awesome."

"Do it," said Gauge. "You're killing me here. Just fucking do it!"

I clicked the mouse button and the program began to execute. The fans on my hard drive kicked into high gear immediately as the temperature climbed. The monitor flickered for a moment and I thought suddenly how glad I was that I wasn't plugged into the machine right now. All visual on the monitor blacked out.

A few streaky lines of pixels appeared, like the logic board was failing or something, and I got a little worried that the hardware simply couldn't handle it. But then the pixels came together into a face. Eyes, nose, mouth. It stayed for a moment, almost like it was looking back at me.

Then it was gone.

We stared at the desktop for a moment. Then Gauge said, "Uh, what just happened?"

A weird numb feeling settled into my chest. "It's gone."

"What, like the drive crashed?"

"No, look. The machine works just fine. But the program . . . it's just . . . gone." I stared stupidly at the screen. I wanted to throw up.

"No, that can't be right." He took over the mouse and started clicking around.

But I knew he wouldn't find anything. Somehow, I just knew.

"Not even anything in the cache," he said.

I nodded.

"What about the source?" he said. "You could recompile it and . . ." He shrugged.

I went to the directory where I kept the source code, mostly for his benefit. I did have a few lingering hopes, but those were squashed when I checked the folder and saw nothing except a single file called hello.txt.

"What the hell . . ." said Gauge.

I opened it, but it was blank.

"You've got a backup, right?"

"At home," I said. "But why would I want to restore something that failed?"

It wasn't just the project that failed, though. *I* had failed. Why did I ever think I could pull something like this off?

There was a sharp crack.

"Jesus!" said Gauge.

I looked down and saw that I had crushed the mouse.

"Sorry . . ." I said, the sound catching in my throat. I stood up and walked over to a window. My eyes stung as I fought back the tears.

"So . . ." said Gauge. "What happens now?"

A part of me wanted to just go crying back home to Mommy. But I would look like a complete asshole if I did that, everyone would be pissed, and I'd have nothing to show for it. And in the end, what was back there for me, anyway? The same old shit, maybe even worse. No, I couldn't go back there. Maybe not ever.

"Can I . . . stay here for a while?" I asked

"You're not going home?" he asked, kind of surprised looking.

"I . . . can't," I said. "This was my ticket. My golden key. It was going to make everything better. It was going to make *my life* better."

"So . . . you want to stay here permanently?"

"Yeah, I guess so. If . . . if that's okay."

"Sure. You can sleep on the couch. But you'll have to, you know, pay half the rent and stuff."

"Oh," I said. "Right."

I COULDN'T DECIDE if my new roommate's method of motivating me made him super wise or a complete dick. My entire life's work had just blown up in my face and all I wanted to do was sit around, eat junk food, and watch old episodes of *Doctor Who*. But Gauge absolutely refused to lend me any money, so I had no time for an emo pity party of one. I had to get a job.

At first, I thought about doing something that wasn't technology related. I was so disgusted with my failure on the "big project" that for the first time in my life I didn't even want to go near a computer. Every time I remembered that a few days before I thought I was some kind of computer genius, it made me want to crawl out of my skin. I wanted to find something totally different to do.

But the rent was due at the end of the month, I didn't really know how to do anything else, and I didn't really know anybody who did. So I gave up on that idea pretty quickly. Maybe I wasn't the most amazing hacker who ever lived. But I didn't totally suck. Someone out there would pay me for my coding skills.

Of course, hitting up online friends for jobs presented another challenge. Obviously, I didn't want Gauge to see me plugging cables into my wrists, and I didn't have the privacy of my own room. So I had to wait until he was out of the apartment. But the guy hardly ever left the apartment. He worked from home. He got just about everything delivered, including stuff like toothpaste and toilet paper. And all his friends were online. So I had to wait and get on the computer at night while he was sleeping.

But even with connections, I still had no college degree or professional experience. After a few days, Gauge started to get really stingy with his groceries. My standards got lower and lower, from programming jobs to QA jobs to help-desk jobs, until finally I said I'd take just about anything. At last, someone said they knew someone who worked at a big chain computer store that was hiring at a Manhattan location and they could hook me up with an interview. I wasn't sure retail was my thing, but I wasn't about to turn down my first real chance at a job. Maybe I'd just do it for a little while to have something on my résumé and save up some money. Then I'd have a little more leeway to look for my next, better job.

Gauge let me borrow some clothes for the interview. The button-up shirt was really tight across my shoulders, and the pants were a little too short. But I was pretty sure it would make a better impression than my usual jeans and T-shirt.

I was nervous about getting there. It was my first time traveling in Manhattan since I'd left The Show, and it was to a completely different part of town. Plus, I had to change trains at Grand Central halfway through the trip. So I studied the subway map for a while, planned my route, and left ridiculously early, just in case there was a train delay or something. Fortunately, there wasn't a delay, which meant I got there an hour before my interview.

To kill some time, I sat out on a bench in the little park in Union Square and watched all the humans walking around. I had gotten used to Gauge, but it still felt a little strange being in a big group of them out in public like this. A few of them sat in a circle playing hand drums. I imagined they were providing a sound track for the rest of the people, all rushing to jobs, to lunch, or to some other part of their lives.

After a bit, I closed my eyes and leaned back on the bench, letting the sun warm my face. Then I opened my eyes and looked up into the deep blue sky. It scared me at first, all that emptiness. But I reminded myself that it couldn't *hurt* me. And the longer I looked at it, the more I got used to it. That's how it was out here in the city, I decided. Scary at first. Overwhelming. But I was already getting used to it. Soon I would have a job and be a full-fledged New Yorker just like all these humans around me. I would be one of them.

By the time my interview rolled around, I was so Zen from

soaking up the sun, drum music, and good vibes that I almost floated into the store. But that all changed when I got to the customer service desk.

"Hi, I have an interview appointment with Joe?" I said to the woman behind the counter.

She stared at me, her glossy pink lips open slightly.

"Are you okay?" I asked.

She blinked her thick lashed eyes. "Uh, yeah." She suddenly stared down at the desk. "No problem." She continued to stare at the desk as she picked up the phone and pushed a button. "Joe, your one o'clock is here." Her voice sounded strained. She listened for a moment, then said, "Okay," and hung up. Her eyes flickered to me for a moment, but then went right back to the desk. "He'll be here in just a sec."

"Thanks," I said, my good Zen vibe draining away. But I reminded myself that not everybody reacted to me like that. This woman clearly had issues.

There were a few uncomfortable minutes while I stood next to the counter, and she acted like I wasn't there anymore. Then I heard an older guy's voice behind me.

"Frank, thanks for coming in!"

His tone was so warm, so cheerful, that I relaxed a little.

But then I turned toward him and he stopped dead in his tracks. He had a smile on his face but it was so forced it looked like it hurt.

For a second, I thought about just running out of the store right then and there. But maybe I was being too self-conscious. I couldn't bail this early. Plus, I really needed a job. So I smiled as gently as I could and offered my hand.

"Thanks for giving me this opportunity," I said. That was something I'd read you were supposed to say at an interview.

His face was still pinched into a tight smile as he gave my hand a quick squeeze.

"Soooo," he said. "You're a friend of Neal's?"

"Well, a friend of a friend, really," I said.

"Gotcha," he said. "Wellll, Catherine has your paperwork, right?" He looked at the woman behind the counter expectantly.

"Paperwork?" I asked.

"Oh, I completely forgot, Joe, I'm sorry," said the woman, not looking thrilled to be brought back into the conversation. "I took one look at him and my mind went bla—I mean, I just . . . I'll get it right now. Sorry."

She pulled out a few sheets of paper and a clipboard and handed it to me without making eye contact.

"No problem," said Joe, the eternal smile still in place. He turned back to me. "So I tell you what, Frank. Why don't you fill out these forms and let Catherine make copies of your ID while I take care of a few things, and I'll check back in about ten minutes, okay?"

"ID?" I asked. "I don't . . . uh, have a driver's license."

"That's fine, any state-issued photo ID or your passport will work."

"I don't have one of those, either."

His smile started to fade. "I suppose if you only have a social security card and a birth certificate, we can accept that."

"Um . . ." I didn't even know if I had something like a social security number or birth certificate. Probably not, since I wasn't born in a hospital. I was made in a laboratory from stitched-together body parts illegally stolen from the morgue. "I don't . . . have those, either."

"Really?" he asked, not even trying to hide his surprise now. "You don't have *any* proof of identification?"

"No."

He stared at me for a moment. Then his smile came back, but this time it was genuine and full of relief. "Oh, well, gosh. You know, Frank, I hate to say it, but it's against company policy to interview someone without identification. I'm *so* sorry. You know how it is these days. I'm sure you're completely legal and everything is on the up and up, but I just can't break policy!"

"Oh." I tried to smile again but now *I* was the one forcing it. "That's, uh, okay. I get it." I stood there for a second while he looked at me expectantly. Because he wanted me to leave his store. So I did.

I don't know why people think big guys are not only stupid, but also hard of hearing. But as I walked toward the exit, I heard him say to the woman:

"Wow, dodged that bullet. Can you imagine having *him* out on the sales floor? Customers would run, screaming."

Ruthven had said that, if anything, humans would *pity* me. But this didn't look much like pity. It looked like something between fear and disgust. And as I walked through the park back to the subway—the same park I'd had my drum circle Zen moment less than an hour before—I saw what I hadn't noticed before while I was people-watching. They were all watching me, too. It was difficult to tell because they wouldn't look directly at me. But they were aware of me. I could tell because as they walked past, they moved just a little so they didn't have to get too close to me. And the more I looked, the more I saw it. Everywhere I went, I made humans uncomfortable.

When I got back to the apartment, I found Gauge at his computer, playing some MMORPG game I didn't recognize. I guess I was out of the loop.

"Gauge?"

"Yup." He didn't look up, but kept clicking the keyboard.

"If I asked you a question, would you be completely honest with me?"

Still not looking up, still clicking the keys. "Probably."

"Okay, so, for real. Do you think I look scary?"

He stopped and turned toward me. He frowned.

"Not scary, exactly."

"No? Then what?"

"You want the honest truth?"

"I asked for it."

"Frank, you are the fucking ugliest person I've ever seen in my life."

I stared at him for a moment. "Wow."

"You asked for it."

"I did. So . . . uh, I guess, thanks."

"Sure, no problem," he said, and went back to his game.

I flopped down on the couch, wondering if this day could possibly get any worse.

"Oh," said Gauge. "You just had a job interview, didn't you?"

"Yeah."

"How'd it go?"

"I . . . didn't get it."

"That sucks." He turned back to his computer again. "Rent's due in two weeks."

"I know. I'll think of something." I had no idea what that would be yet. The ID issue seemed pretty insurmountable.

He turned back to me, his eyes squinting and his high, pale forehead wrinkling.

"Why don't you just sell some credit card numbers? Use some of that legendary 'b0y' hacking skill? I bet you could knock over a small online business and get a couple thousand to sell in no time. If you need a fence, I know some people."

I was about to give my usual response that there was a huge difference between the noble art of hacking and sleazy identity theft, but I stopped short. Maybe I didn't have the luxury of being that judgmental anymore. Was that the only option left for me? Was I at the "steal or starve" point?

No. I couldn't do that. I *wouldn't* do it. No money, no friends, no girl, barely a real home. Right now, integrity seemed to be the only thing I still had. The only thing that couldn't be taken away from me. So I wasn't going to give it up willingly. Not without a real fight.

"I told you," I said. "I'll figure something out."

9
Beautiful Freaks

++++++++

I STOOD FACING the one corner of the restaurant kitchen that wasn't caught on the security camera and shoved a big glob of rice in my mouth. The kitchen staff weren't allowed to have our meal until our shift was over, but that was six hours from now and I hadn't eaten anything since yesterday. I ate as fast as I could because even though Mr. Sing had cameras that covered 98 percent of the kitchen, he still made surprise appearances to see if we were goofing off. Because, you know, us illegals liked to goof off. Or so he told us.

As I shoved the last bit of food scraped from the customer's plates into my mouth, I almost choked. I cleared my throat and wiped my watery eyes.

"Hey, Frankie, you okay?"

It was Ralphie, the other cook, a skinny little Dominican guy in his thirties.

"Yeah," I said harshly, and cleared my throat. "Just went down the wrong pipe."

"You need to eat slower." He shook a big wooden spoon at me, then went back to stirring the massive boiling pot in front of him. "He never comes down right now. You're not gonna get caught. And anyway, you really think he would fire you for that?"

"I don't know." I made my way back to the stoves and checked on the oxtail. "But I don't want to take chances, you know? I need this job."

"Yeah," he said. "I know."

Turns out, the only kind of work I could find without an ID or proof of citizenship was getting paid off the books at restaurants along with Ralphie and the other illegal immigrants in this city. It wasn't a terrible job. The pay wasn't much, but I got free food, and the other guys treated me okay. It was just the boss, Mr. Sing, who was mean. What a Chinese guy was doing running a West Indian restaurant, I had no idea.

The job wasn't what I'd hoped for, but at least I was paying rent and eating. Once those basics were taken care of, I settled into life in the human world pretty quickly. Every day turned into the same thing. Get up, ride the subway for an hour, cook other people's food for ten hours, ride another hour home, watch TV with Gauge, go to bed. Loop.

That was, until one cold night in February, with dirty gray snow piled high on the sidewalks, I saw Liel.

Ralphie and I were coming out of the restaurant after closing. I looked down the block, I don't know why, and I saw her. She was wrapped up in an overcoat and a head scarf that covered up her white hair and angular, trollish features. But I could see her diamond eyes gleaming in the streetlight. I stopped and my heart almost did, too.

"Frankie," said Ralphie. "You know that person?"

"Yeah." I just stood there, hands at my sides. I didn't know what to do.

"You want me to stick around?"

"Nah. You go ahead."

He nodded and continued on toward the subway station. I

watched him until he turned the corner. Then I walked toward Liel. She stayed where she was until I got close. Then she suddenly lunged toward me, wrapping her long, strong arms around me and pressing her face against my chest.

"I did it!" she said, her face muffled through her scarf and my coat. "I left The Show!"

We stood there freezing on that street corner for a long time squeezing each other, both of us scared out of our minds, although maybe for different reasons.

"How did you find me?" I asked. "Does anyone else know?"

"No." She shook her head. "Nobody knows. I just followed the directions in your email."

"My email?"

"Yeah, the email. The one where you said all those nice things about . . ." Her eyes widened as she took in my expression. "You didn't write the email."

I shook my head.

"Oh, god." She stepped away from me. "Oh god oh god oh god!" She turned one way, then the other, her face pinched with panic.

"Liel." I put my hand on her shoulder. "It's okay. What did the message say?"

"Okay?" She jerked away from my touch. "*Okay???* I'm totally fucked! I thought . . . I thought . . . *shit!!!*" She screamed, then she turned like she was about to split.

I couldn't let her wander around a city she didn't know this late at night in this crazy state of mind, so I grabbed her arm, harder this time.

"Let me go!" she yelled.

"No, just calm down. We can fix this. Whatever the problem is, we can fix it. Just tell me what the message said."

She struggled against me for a moment. She was strong. But I was stronger. Finally, she stopped fighting and looked up at me. The scarf had fallen off her face and she was crying.

"It said you'd found a job. That you were doing okay. That you were making it outside. It said there was only one thing missing and that was me. It said . . ." She looked away, her lips pressed together so hard that her fangs pierced them and drew blood. "It said you loved me." Then with one hard tug, she jerked free of my grip and started to run.

"I do!"

She stopped, but didn't turn around.

"Look," I said. "I didn't send you any email message. I don't know who did or how they knew where I was or anything else. But I *do* love you. I've always loved you." That felt so good to finally admit.

She turned back to me, her eyes narrowed. "For real? Always?"

"Of course! I thought it was written all over my forehead."

She started walking back toward me, still looking guarded. "Then why didn't you ever tell me before?"

"I don't know. I guess because it never seemed like you liked me like that."

"Asshole!" She punched my arm. "I've cried in front of you *twice* now! If that doesn't send up any red flags, then you don't know anything about trowe girls."

"Then, all this time, you've felt the same way? About me?"

"Who else?"

"I thought maybe Shaun . . ."

She shook her head. "Shaun's a self-absorbed dick. I could never be serious with him. But you . . ." She grabbed my upper arms, got up on her tiptoes, and pressed her nose against mine. "You are my Boy."

I had almost forgotten what it felt like to have someone look at me without fear or pity or discomfort. To have someone look at me with real affection. At least there was one person in this city who didn't think I was ugly. Maybe that was all I needed.

I kissed her then. The frozen winds howled around us, pulling at our coats. I didn't know what we were going to do, how we were going to make this work. But right at that moment, the only thing that mattered was her strong body in my arms and her warm lips pressed against mine. We kissed like it could stop time.

But of course, it couldn't really last forever. Finally, she stepped back and looked up at me with a strange expression.

"What?" I said.

"So who the hell wrote that message?" she asked.

EVEN THOUGH LIEL rewrapped the scarf to cover her face, the few people on the subway that late at night gave her weird looks. We'd have to get her sunglasses to cover up her eyes. But then she'd just look strange in a different way, all wrapped up like the Invisible Man. And what would happen when it got warmer?

I pushed those thoughts away. We'd figure something out. We had to.

"So, was the rest of the message right, too?" asked Liel over the clatter of the subway train. "You have a job? You're making it?"

"Technically that's true, I guess. But I don't really make much money. Just enough to pay rent."

"Rent?" Her eyes went wide. "Wow, so you have, like, an apartment and all that?"

"Sure, that's what everybody does. And I have a roommate."

"You live with a *human*?" she asked, like it was the most amazing thing ever.

It made me laugh a little.

"What?" she asked.

"Nothing. It's just funny. This is all so normal to me now. I forgot how strange it used to seem."

"You've been gone a while," she said, leaning against my shoulder.

"How are things at The Show?" I asked.

"The same. Nothing ever changes there. I think it's slowly driving them all crazy. Nobody's meant to be cooped up like that forever."

"How are my parents?"

She sighed. "Well, you know. They were really upset. Your mom . . . well, she wouldn't talk to anyone for a while. Not even your dad. And your dad, he wanted to take the city apart looking for you. But Ruthven wouldn't let him."

"Are they . . . doing better now?"

"Sort of. Your mom is at least talking now. Your dad . . ." She looked at me, her eyes squinting in the little open space that the scarf left. "Well, he spends a lot of time disconnected."

"Shit," I said.

"Don't feel bad. You have your life to live. They need to accept that."

"Yeah . . ." I wished it felt a little more worth it. I didn't even know what I was doing out here.

Then the train came out of the tunnel and slowly rose over the building tops of Queens. Liel gasped and squeezed my hand.

I remembered my first night on this train and how amazed I had been by the view.

"Pretty cool, huh?"

"So much . . . *space*!" she said in a way that actually sounded a little scared.

"It's okay." I squeezed her hand back.

She shivered, then nodded. The scarf made it difficult to see her expression.

"This human you live with," she said.

"Gauge."

"Does he know? What you are? About the rest of us?"

"No. But I think we're going to have to tell him some of it at least. It's not like you can just hang out with a scarf wrapped around your head forever."

"Right . . ." she said, her eyes narrowing in a frown.

"Hey, don't worry about it. We'll figure something out."

She nodded, but I could tell she wasn't really convinced.

As we got off the train and walked to the apartment building, I tried to follow my own advice and not worry about how we were going to make this work. But as we walked the three flights up to my apartment, I got really nervous about telling Gauge. Everything was so concrete with him. So scientific. He wasn't the kind of guy who believed that magic was possible. Or even desirable.

But as it turned out, it wasn't something we had to deal with right away because Gauge wasn't home.

"Oh, thank God I can take all this crap off!" said Liel. She threw the scarf, gloves, and coat in a heap on the floor. Then she fell back onto the couch and kicked her boots off into Gauge's junk corner.

It was really weird having Liel in my apartment. But it was

also really nice. I felt like I got back some part of me that had been missing.

"I'm not sure where Gauge is." I sat down on the couch next to her.

"Hmmm." She stretched out on the couch so that her legs were in my lap.

"He's *always* home. About the only reason he ever leaves is to see a movie."

"So we've got a few hours at least until we have to deal with him." She stretched her arms up and burrowed her feet into the cushions so that her legs pressed down on my thighs. "You know, you keep telling me not to worry, but I think you're way more worried than I am."

I shrugged. She didn't really understand everything we'd have to deal with. But maybe she didn't need to know yet. It had been a stressful transition for me. I wanted to make it easier for her. So I didn't say anything.

"Do you know what I like best about the city so far?" she asked.

"The subway tunnels?" I asked.

"Well, those *are* nice," she admitted. "But no. My favorite is that part where you kissed me. Why don't you do some more of that?"

"But what if Gauge comes—"

"Kiss!" She sat up so that our faces were close. "Now!"

"You trowe girls are so bossy."

"You monster boys are just too shy."

"Oh, yeah?"

"Yeah."

What could I do? The reputation of monster boys everywhere was at stake. So I had to kiss her. And because I didn't want there to be any doubts, I did it a lot. At first, in the back of my mind I was still a little worried that Gauge would walk in on us. But this was the girl of my dreams and we were alone in my very own apartment. It had been a rough couple of months and as her body pressed against mine and her legs intertwined with mine, I thought maybe I had earned this.

So I let myself get lost in those glittering, diamond eyes. And for the first time in a while, I didn't feel poor or alone anymore.

GAUGE DIDN'T WALK in on us. In fact, he didn't come home that night at all. The next day I had to go to work, and I was worried about leaving Liel there in case Gauge showed up while I was gone. But I couldn't take her with me, either.

"So leave a note," said Liel. She was stretched out on the couch, flipping through TV channels.

"Right," I said. "Somehow I don't think a note that says, 'Hey, Gauge, don't worry about the random troll in your living room, I'll explain when I get home' will really do the trick."

The apartment didn't have a landline, so I tried calling his cell from an online VOIP service. But I got an automated message that said the number was disconnected. I popped online. I didn't see surelee or s1zzl3 on, but there were a few other channels I knew that he used and eventually I found some people who knew him. But none of them had heard from him in the last twelve hours. For a lot of people, being offline that long might be normal. But for Gauge it was downright freakish.

"Okay, I'm officially worried about him now," I told Liel.

"You said he was from California, right?" she asked. "Maybe he just went for a visit."

"Maybe. But you'd think he would tell me something like that. And why would his phone be disconnected?"

She just shrugged and kept flipping through the channels.

"Well, I can't be late for work," I said. "Are you going to be cool here?"

"Sure," she said. "I'll just watch TV, I guess. And if he shows up . . ." She shrugged again.

"Yeah." But there wasn't anything to do.

So I left the restaurant number and headed to work. But I was stressing about it the whole day.

"You okay, man?" asked Ralphie while we worked the stoves.

"I guess," I said.

"Is it that girl you saw last night when we were closing up?"

"Yeah, sort of."

"Who is she?"

"She's just . . ." I started to say "a friend," but realized that wasn't really true anymore. "I guess she's my girlfriend."

"All right, Frankie!" He slapped me on the back. "You go!"

I smiled as I went back to stirring my skillet. Liel was my girlfriend. I had this juvenile impulse to somehow get ahold of Shaun's cell number just so I could call him up and tell him that in the end, Liel chose me. Sure, I lived in a shitty apartment, with a shitty job, and no money. But I had the hottest trowe girl in the world *living with me*. Worries about Gauge aside, it was pretty awesome. And I had to admit, not having Gauge there made things easier. Still, I'd have to deal with him eventually, right?

But when I got home, he still wasn't there. And he didn't come home the next day or the day after that. I started to think he'd done the same thing as his previous roommate and just taken off for California. Or maybe he'd gotten into an accident or been killed by a mugger. I had no idea. Nobody online had heard from him, and if he had any family, I'd never heard about them. There was no way for me to really take it further. So as the days turned into weeks, I just started to accept that he wasn't coming back.

Of course, if he wasn't coming back, that opened up a whole new set of problems. First, the lease was under his name, so technically the landlord could kick us out at any time. But the more immediate problem was who would pay the other half of the rent?

That's when the checks started coming in the mail. They came from all over. Rebate checks, refund checks, weird sweepstakes prizes. They weren't for a lot of money, just five bucks here, ten bucks there. But there were a lot of them. So many, in fact, that when you put them all together (and paid the ridiculous fee at those sketchy check-cashing places that don't ID), the total net covered a little more than half the rent. Every once in a while, I'd wonder why we were getting all these checks. But things had been so hard for so long, and those first few weeks with Liel were so amazing that I just didn't want to think about anything that might ruin it.

I'd get home from work and she'd have some crazy, elaborate meal prepared. After we ate, we'd go wandering through the neighborhood, exploring the alleys, the parks, under bridges, in the subway tunnels. After a while we started to explore past Sunnyside into other parts of Queens and Brooklyn. It was dark and we avoided areas with a lot of people, so it felt safe. As time went on, we got so bold that Liel started to walk around without anything covering her face. I loved to watch her wake up to the wider world and discover this place outside the theater. And because she had me to guide and support her, she never had to go through all the bullshit I did. She never had to go to bed hungry or beg for a job. For her, the city was just pure wonder.

One night we ran along the promenade in Brooklyn that overlooked the East River and Manhattan. Kind of a ballsy move, considering it went through some highly populated and posh neighborhoods like the Heights. But it was four in the morning, that perfect time when pretty much anyone who had been out late was finally home, and the early risers hadn't quite gotten up yet. I can run really fast for a big guy, and I don't get tired easily. So I thought I'd smoke her. But the way she ran? It was like a cheetah. Her white hair streamed out behind her and she had this tight, crazy grin on her face, her lower fangs poking out just a little. Her long dancer legs stretched out in front of her, like she was jumping from foot to foot, and her entire body stretched and contracted with each step. It didn't take her long to pull ahead of me.

We were right alongside the Brooklyn Bridge, its stone towers stretching up over two hundred feet into the night sky. Liel's diamond eyes widened when she saw it. She glanced back at me, and her smile got a little mischievous.

I frowned. "What are you—"

She turned and took a huge leap. Her clawed hands reached out and easily hooked into the rocky base of the bridge tower. Then she started climbing up.

"Shit," I muttered and jumped after her before I had a chance to think about it.

I slammed into the cold rock and scrambled to hold on. I didn't have claws, so there was a moment of hot panic in my gut when I thought I was going to slide right down the side into the churning waters of the East River more than fifty feet below. Then my fingers found a crevice and I squeezed the massive stone strut with everything I had. My face was pressed against its icy grit and I thought: *This is crazy. I'm going to die.* But then I heard her laughter carried down on the wind. I looked up and she was perched high above at the very top where the tension wires peak. She beckoned to me with one graceful hand.

Did I deserve this amazing girl? Was I enough for her? I wanted to be—so badly that I would do anything. I had to prove that I *was* enough for her. And I was the son of one of the most famous monsters ever. I could do this. I could do just about anything.

I felt this sudden surge of strength in me. Like when I beat the crap out of Shaun, but different. It wasn't about hurting this time. It wasn't anger. It was . . . I didn't understand it, I just knew that it was something *else*. I reached up with one hand, found another crevice that I could get my fingers around, then the next, and before I knew it I was at the top, my arms aching, my breath pounding in my chest. We stood there and looked out over the city and river that stretched before us, sparkling with white and yellow lights, the muted roar of traffic like a low hum underneath.

"THIS!" she shouted over the shrieking wind. "THIS IS WHAT WE ARE MEANT FOR! NOT HIDING IN CAVES OR THEATERS! THIS!"

She looked so beautiful then, a fierce smile on her face, her eyes glittering in the moonlight. I pulled her to me and we kissed, hard and long, the curtain of Manhattan's skyline behind us.

Then I knew what this new strength within me was. This new feeling. It was joy.

10

The Glamourous Life

††††††††

BUT AFTER A few weeks, Liel got sick of sitting around inside all day.

I didn't blame her, of course. Here she was, a Broadway dancer, cooped up in a tiny apartment with no hope in sight that it was going to get better. But I didn't know what else to do. I tried to talk her into finding some kind of online job or something, but she was never really that comfortable with computers. Claws made it hard to type and she didn't have my advantages of ways to bypass physical limitations. So she just did a lot of cooking and cleaning, like she was a housewife. She must have felt trapped, because, well, she kind of was. She started getting grumpy, taking it out on me. And even though I understood why she felt the way she did, I still wasn't going to put up with her yelling at me. So we started fighting, mostly about stupid stuff like washing dishes and who left the toilet seat up. Finally, one night it got so out of control that I said:

"Okay, that's it. I'm gonna find Laurellen."

"What?" she said, a chair raised over her head.

"This isn't us. It's just because you're stuck in this apartment all day every day. I'm going to contact Laurellen and ask him to give us some glamour so you can get out of the house and do something."

"Are you stupid?" she yelled, still all fired up. "What if he tells on us?"

"I'm going to risk it. I mean, do you want to keep *this* up? You're just about to chuck a chair at me."

"Uh . . ." She frowned and looked up at the chair in her hands like she was surprised it was there. Then she put it down. "Yeah, okay. I see your point."

"I don't think he's going to tell on us. Laurellen is cool. I've always felt like I could trust him and Mozart."

She flopped onto the couch. "I hope you're right. Because at this point, going home would be a really bad idea. My mom would totally kick my ass. And that's not a figure of speech."

I didn't want to think about how my own mom would react. I really didn't want to think about her at all. Mostly because if there was one thing I missed from The Show, now that Liel was here, it was her. I don't know why. She never said much and you never knew how she felt about anything, or if she felt anything at all. She was almost like a walking mannequin that happened to be really good at fixing stuff. But I was really starting to miss her stiff, blank-faced presence. I also felt a little guilty. Like I'd abandoned her to that place that treated us so badly. I don't know why I felt that way. She was an adult, free to make her own choices. Nothing was keeping her there. Except maybe Dad. But that was her choice, too.

"So how are you going to contact him?" Liel asked. "Email or something?"

"I'm pretty sure he's one of those guys who checks his email like once or twice a year. And prints it out to read it."

"So what then?"

"Well, I remember hearing him talk about Monday nights when The Show is dark. He goes out to some club in the Village. Stone . . . something. Stonebridge, Stonegate, Stone . . ."

"Stonewall," she said.

"Yeah, that was it. How'd you know?"

"Call it dancer's intuition."

It turns out Stonewall was some really famous gay club. I'd never been to a gay club before—or, really, any club at all—so I was a little nervous. But Liel said to just be super polite to everyone and I would be fine.

The next Monday night, I got somebody to cover my shift at work and took the train to Christopher Street. I walked past the tattoo parlors and sex shops until I came to a club with a big rainbow flag hanging over the door. Two guys were out front. One of them was really muscular for a human, even through his wool coat. The other guy was all decked out in a really nice coat with a matching scarf and gloves, his hair perfectly styled in a short, spiky cut.

The big guy took one look at me and said, "You gotta be kiddin' me, kid. You know this is a club."

"Sure," I said.

"A club that serves alcohol. And don't even try to pretend like you're old enough."

"I don't want to drink," I said. "I just need to talk to a friend of mine in there."

"So call him and tell him to come out here so you can talk to him."

"I don't have a cell," I said. "And I'm pretty sure he doesn't have one, either."

"Right, doesn't have a cell . . ." He turned to the well-dressed guy next to him. "Can you believe this? Kid's a fuckin' comedian." He turned back to me. "Beat it, kid. Come back in, what . . . like, five years?"

"Three and a half," I said. This guy wasn't making it easy to be polite. "Look, could you just do me a favor? Maybe you or your friend here could give him a message for me."

"Wait, wait, wait," he said. "You want me to leave my post, wander through the club looking for some dirty old queen who likes high school football players, and give him a message for you?" He shook his head, looking at the other guy again. Then he looked back at me. "Look, kid. It's a big club, there's a lot of people in there. It ain't gonna happen."

"Maybe you know him," I said. "He's a regular here."

"Oh, yeah, sure. 'Cause I know every guy who comes in here on a semi-regular basis."

"Come on, Jeffrey," said the fancy guy. "Don't be an asshole."

Jeffrey sighed. "Okay, I'll bite. What's his name?"

"Laurellen," I said.

His eye went wide.

"Uh . . ." he said.

The fancy guy said, "*You* know Laurellen?"

"He's a friend of mine," I said.

Jeffrey shook his head. "No way. There's no way you know Laurellen."

"Ask him," I said. "Just tell him Runaway Boy needs to talk to him."

They looked at each other for a moment.

"I had no idea that's how he rolled," said Jeffrey.

The fancy guy shrugged. "It's Laurellen. You'd better find out, just to be safe. I'll watch the door."

Jeffrey nodded, suddenly looking a little nervous, and went inside.

The fancy guy and I stood there in silence for a moment. Then he said, "I'm Vinnie."

"Most people call me Frank," I said, holding out my hand.

He shook it gracefully, with small, leather-gloved hands. Everything about him seemed classy.

"Sorry about Jeffrey," said Vinnie. "He's usually not that much of a bully. I think your size intimidates him."

"*My* size? He's huge!"

"And he's not used to some healthy competition," said Vinnie, and smirked in a knowing kind of way that suddenly made me think they were probably dating. "So, how do you know Laurellen?"

"We used to work together."

"You were in The Show?"

"Backstage stuff," I said quickly.

"I love The Show. I mean *love* it. I think I've probably seen it about twenty times."

"Oh, yeah? What's your favorite act?"

"I absolutely adore the underwater mermaid pool number."

"The what?"

"It's one of the newer acts," he said. "They just put it in a couple months ago or so."

"Oh," I said. "I . . . uh . . . quit a little while back, so I guess that's why I don't know it." Of course Ruthven had brought in a new act. He added one act every year, sometimes more if someone new showed up looking for shelter. But the idea of an act in The Show that I hadn't watched through rehearsals, that some random human knew better than me . . . it hurt way more than I expected. I'd never met a mermaid. Did they breathe air or water? What did she look like? Did Ruthven bring her in to make the Siren happy? Or to punish her? There was so much I wanted to know, starting with how they did the water part onstage. But I refused to ask this human. That would have been too much.

"What was your favorite act?" he asked quietly, maybe somehow sensing that I was feeling a little homesick for The Show.

"I liked the trowe dance best."

"Oh, that." He nodded. "Yeah, that used to be good. Not sure what happened, though. I think they lost their lead dancer or something, and it just doesn't have the same sizzle now."

"She quit, too."

"A shame. Well, hopefully she quit for a better gig."

"Yeah. Hopefully."

"Well, the kid checks out," said Jeffrey as he came out from the club. He still looked a little scared, but there was also a weird awe in his eyes. "Laurellen said send him back right away."

"I'll walk him back," said Vinnie.

"Thanks," said Jeffrey, clearly relieved he didn't have to see Laurellen again. I wondered what the big deal was. It was just Laurellen after all.

Vinnie took me into the club, which turned out to be a lot smaller than I imagined. Granted, I'd only seen clubs in movies, so my expectations were probably a little unfair. There were a bunch of guys and a few girls all jammed up together near the bar. There were a few tables, and those were also pretty packed, with other small random groups just standing around. The speakers were blasting some cheesy dance music, and everyone was shouting over top of that, so it was really loud. The whole thing felt completely claustrophobic and I had this weird impulse to just turn and leave. But when I thought about it, this was probably less crowded than a night at the Cantina, and not too long ago that had felt totally normal. It wasn't just The Show that had changed.

I had changed, too. I wasn't sure yet whether it was for the better.

Vinnie led me into another room in the back that had a DJ spinning and a dance floor with people bouncing up and down to the beats and the bursts of neon-colored light. All the way at the back of that back room was a shiny red, round booth. And sitting at the booth, surrounded by a bunch of humans, was Laurellen. That's when I saw what the big deal was. Laurellen was totally drenched in glamour. So much that it almost hurt to look at him. Those humans had to be completely under his spell. It made me wonder if he wasn't cheating a little on his promise to Ruthven to not steal any more humans. Not that I would tell on him, of course. But it made me feel a little better about asking for some glamour for Liel. He looked like he had some to spare.

Vinnie presented me with a big show of hands, like a magician. "Look what the wind blew in," he said.

Laurellen gave me a smirk, and waves of glamour rolled off him, making me feel a little stoned.

"Oh, that tricky wind . . ." he said. He raised his long, thin hand and gave it a regal flip. "Begone. All of you."

It was amazing how fast they split. Totally in his thrall.

Once everyone was gone, his smile faded. "Boy," he said. "Sit."

"Okay." I suddenly felt sheepish as I sat down next to him in the shiny red booth.

"Of course you realize that if your mother finds out about this she will rip my limbs off."

"She still pissed?"

"It's going to be a very long time before she isn't. Possibly decades."

I winced.

"But, more important . . ." He leaned back a little and his face softened. "How are you? You look in shockingly good health, I must say."

"I get a lot more exercise. And uh . . . Liel is a good cook."

"Ah, yes. Liel. So she's with you?"

"She came looking for me. I guess."

"Please tell me you aren't just sleeping in some shelter."

"No, I have an apartment and a job and everything."

"My God. So you're really doing it. Living like a human, and with the girl of your dreams."

"Yeah, sort of."

"But there's a problem. Otherwise you wouldn't have come looking for me."

"Well, I mean, I miss you. And Mozart, and of course, my parents. And even Ruthven and Charon, I guess. But yeah, I kind of need your help."

"Glamour."

"Yeah," I said, shame suddenly bitter in my mouth. "I'm sorry. I know it's a shitty thing for me to ask."

"But why do you need it? You seem to be passing with flying colors."

"It's not for me."

"Oh." He sighed. "Teenage love. Human or monster, it is the number one cause of stupidity."

"It's not just some stupid crush. I really love her."

"I know," he said. "That's the tragedy."

"It's not tragedy. We just need some glamour so she can get out of the house, maybe get a job or something. So she doesn't feel totally dependent on me."

"I can give you some glamour, Boy. But how long do you think she'll be able to keep that up? The kind of dosage she'll need to pass isn't healthy to do on a regular basis. And Ruthven will catch on that the supply is dwindling, eventually. He keeps careful track of it."

"But what about"—I gestured to the halo of magic allure that surrounded him—"all this?"

"This is the weekly indulgence he allows to keep me from completely losing my mind. It's budgeted in." He looked at me then with a seriousness I'd never seen in him before. "But all of that is beside the point, Boy. Some creatures just aren't cut out to be among humans. The trowe are one of them. You must know this."

"That's just some old-fashioned troll prejudice. She thinks she can do it if she can just look the part. And I believe her."

"Which brings us back to the tragedy."

"I understand if you don't want to help," I said, getting up.

"Boy, sit your ass back down."

I sat back down.

"I was there nearly eighteen years ago when your mother and father presented you to rest of the company. You were so little back then, nothing but kid parts. And I was there during that painfully awkward phase as your mother slowly transitioned you, limb by limb, to your adult-sized parts." He leaned in and put his long hand on my shoulder. "Boy, you're the closest thing I have to family. Of course I'll help you."

Then he leaned back into his seat. "I won't bullshit you, though. I think it's a dreadful idea."

I WAS A little hurt that Laurellen didn't have faith that Liel and I could pull this off, but I wasn't about to get all self-righteous, since he was giving us the glamour. That night, I triumphantly brought home a big batch of it in a quart-sized ziplock bag. It looked like a blend of wheat flour and glitter.

Liel put it on the very next day. I'd never used glamour or even seen someone other than Laurellen with it on. It was just one of those things adults talked about. So I was pretty curious to see it in action.

She sat on the couch and took a pinch of the powder and rubbed it into each of her eyes. She sucked in a breath, her lips curling up into a fanged snarl, and she clutched the couch with her claws. She squeezed her lids shut and pearl-white tears leaked out. Then slowly, her green skin turned to tan, her white hair turned to blonde, her ears shrank and rounded, and her fangs shrank to flat teeth. Even her facial structure changed, softening from the hard angles of the trowe into something more delicate. When she finally opened her eyes, those diamonds that I loved so much had melted into pale blue-gray human eyes.

"Well?" She stood up and examined herself in the mirror by the front door. "What do you think?"

"Um . . ." It creeped me out that she looked human, but I didn't want her to feel self-conscious. "I think you can totally pass as human."

"Okay, that's a start. But do I pass for a *pretty* human?"

"You looked pretty before."

She clapped her hands. "Stay on topic. Do I look like a pretty *human*? The kind of jobs I'm going to be looking for, I have to be pretty."

"You look like you'd fit in on some teen drama TV show."

"So that's a yes?"

"Uh, sure. Yeah."

I had the night off. Since she looked human, I was hoping we could go out someplace in Manhattan where we'd never been able to go before, like Central Park, or Little Italy. But she wanted to start looking for a job right away, so I helped her throw together a résumé, and she went out that afternoon.

I remembered how shitty my first day of job hunting had been, and I knew she would probably come home empty-handed and exhausted that night. So I decided to make dinner. I wasn't much of a cook, but I threw together some pasta thing that turned out okay. I figured the fact that I even did it would cheer her up a little.

But she didn't come home for dinner. In fact, she didn't come home until around two in the morning.

"Home!" she shouted as she stepped through the front doorway.

"Whoa," I said. I had kind of forgotten that she would look human and I got creeped out all over again by her tan skin and her soft human eyes. She also seemed a little drunk.

"You are looking at the newest, and cutest, waitress at the Temple restaurant on St. Marks in the East Village!"

"You got a job already?" I asked.

"Yep, third place I tried." She gave me a polished human grin. "I walked in and asked if they needed a waitress. The guy behind the bar looked at me for a second, then said, 'Can you start right now?'"

"What?"

"I know, right?" She flopped onto the couch. "Some chick had just walked out on them and they were desperate. He had me work a shift tonight to see if I could handle myself, and when we were closing up, he told me he was putting me on the schedule. Three nights a week to start, more if it keeps working out. And the best part?" She pulled out a big, messy wad of crumpled bills. "It's all under-the-table cash. Guy didn't even blink when I told him I didn't have any ID."

"Unbelievable. You know it took me weeks to find a job. And I think what you have right there in your hand is about what I make in a week."

"Humans love pretty humans." She kicked off her high-heeled boots. "It's like some instinctual thing with them. I bet you could get a job like this, and just as easy. All you need is some glamour."

She picked up the bag of sparkling powder off the coffee table and held it out to me. I stared at it for a second, then I looked back at her. All of the things I'd loved about her were gone: the hard cut of her jaw, the luminescent white of her hair, the rich, deep green of her skin, and of course, those perfect diamond eyes. I imagined what I might look like if I took some glamour. Stitches gone and skin a healthy tan instead of ghastly white. Maybe I would look more refined, with a chiseled jaw and cheek-bones. Like that big guy who played a werewolf on that show and always walked around without a shirt. Could I get a better job if I looked like that? Like a TV-star human? Would my life be better? Would humans like me then?

No. They wouldn't. They'd like the glamour. Always and for-ever, with an almost mindless devotion. And I would always know it wasn't real.

"Nah," I said. "I'm fine with what I've got."

"You're kidding!" Her human eyes widened. "Think of what we could do if we were both making this much money. We could get a nice apartment somewhere. Go out to restaurants and things. Live *real* human lives."

"This is a real life. This is how most humans live. You're trying to be like a TV show."

"Don't you want more than this?"

"Of course. But I want to do it my way. Glamour just . . . I don't know. It seems like cheating to me."

Her eyes narrowed. "Well, some of us don't really have any other option."

"I know. It works for you. Just . . ."

"Just what?" she said. "You know what I think? You have a problem with me finally being able to get out and do my thing."

"What? No way! I'm glad you got a job. I'm glad you're out doing stuff. That's why I went to Laurellen. So that you could do this!"

"Yeah, I know." Then she just looked at me. I could usually read Liel pretty well, but the glamour threw me off. I couldn't tell what she was thinking. "Thanks."

"I don't need thanks. I'm just saying that I'm with you on this. It's okay that we have different ways of doing things."

"Of course it is." But I felt like there was something else she wanted to say instead.

I ASSUMED THAT once she got used to her new job, we'd settle into a routine and start exploring the city again. And this time we could do it in the daytime with people around. And I thought, since we were both working in restaurants, that our schedules would match up. But she made friends with some of her human coworkers pretty quickly, and after a week or so she started going out with them to clubs after work until three or four in the morning. I fixed my schedule so we'd have the same days off, thinking we could do things then. But she'd be out so late partying on work nights that on her days off she didn't want to do anything except sleep and watch TV.

One afternoon while I was washing the dishes, I saw her come out of the bedroom all tired and hungover looking. Her glamour had worn off and she looked sick. Her skin was more gray than green and her diamond eyes looked kind of milky. She flopped onto the couch and picked up the ziplock bag of glamour that sat on the coffee table. I noticed her hands were shaking a little as she opened it.

"Hey, maybe you should take a break from that stuff," I said. "I don't think even Laurellen uses it every day."

She just grunted, grabbed a big pinch of glamour, and rubbed in into her eyes. She hissed through clenched teeth as she closed her eyes. Blood leaked out instead of tears.

"Really." I turned off the faucet and walked over to the living room area. "Laurellen said it's not healthy to use that much."

She leaned back into the couch as the glamour took hold and her human shape returned. She turned to me and smiled her polished human smile.

"Thanks for the concern, Dad. I'll be okay." Then she pulled on her high-heeled boots, grabbed her purse, and headed for the door.

"Where are you going?" I asked.

"Out. Don't wait up."

"I was hoping you and I could hang out."

"Sure, we will sometime."

"When?"

She rolled her blue human eyes. "I don't know, Boy. Stop nagging me about it. You're starting to make it feel like a chore."

"Okay, sorry."

She just shook her head and left.

That night, for the first time in a while, I logged on to my old hacker IRC channel.

```
surelee: he lives!
slzzl3: who the hell is this guy?
```

b0y: lol, how you guys been?

surelee: parents don't understand me, sister tortures
me, same old. we seriously thought you and
poxd must have died.

slzzl3: or been arrested for letting that crazy
super virus into the wild.

b0y: wait, have you seen it?

slzzl3: just that little bit you sent me to test.
that was all i needed. it took out half my
rig before I got rid of it, thx a lot, you
douche.

b0y: sorry. i told you to lock it down.

surelee: so you did release it?

b0y: i don't know.

slzzl3: how can you not know?

b0y: *shrug* I don't really want to get into that. it was a huge,
soul-crushing disappointment. so have you guys heard
from poxd?

surelee: no he's been MIA as long as you have. you
mean you don't know what happened to him,
either?

b0y: we were roommates for a while, if you can believe that.
but he split about two months ago with no word, no
forwarding address.

slzzl3: so i guess that Vi chick knows what she's
talking about after all.

surelee: she knew about *that*, anyway. I still think
she's sketch.

b0y: who's Vi?

surelee: see? he doesn't know her.

b0y: what are you guys talking about?

slzzl3: some chick showed up on the channel a
       little while ago, fronting like you guys
       were super tight. she's been filling us in
       on what you've been up to, but we thought
       she might be BS.

bOy: what did she say i've been up to?

surelee: that you were in a bad situation at home
        so you left, that you were crashing with
        poxd. that you're working in a West Indian
        restaurant? something about you going to
        some gay club, which just cracks me up
        every time I think about it. last night she
        was talking about that girl you were always
        crushing on.

bOy: yeah, she moved in with me a while back.

slzzl3: o, that's not what she said about her.

bOy: what did she say?

slzzl3: ummmmm.........

surelee: i think her exact words were: "that vapid,
        traitorous bitch doesn't deserve him. she
        needs to go."

slzzl3: congrats, @bOy. you've got a stalker.

11
It's Alive

++++++++

S1ZZL3 AND SURELEE told me I shouldn't let the stalker thing freak me out. But she knew where I lived, who I lived with. She even knew random things like the night I went to Stonewall. This Vi chick had to be spying on me, which meant she lived in the city somewhere. Was she a neighbor? Maybe she was even the neighbor with the meth lab, which made her dangerous as well as creepy. The walls were thin enough that whoever lived next door could probably hear everything we said without trying real hard.

The part that scared me the most was the "she has to go" comment about Liel. Of course, if this human chick actually tried to attack Liel, she'd regret it. The bigger danger was that Liel would get in trouble for kicking the shit out of her. What would happen if the cops arrested her? Would they think she was some kind of illegal alien because she didn't have a social or birth certificate? Then, what if they put her in jail and I couldn't get her out before the glamour wore off? It only lasted about twenty-four hours. Less if you were really upset and your pulse was running high, and if Liel was in jail, it probably would be. And what would happen if the cops realized she wasn't just an illegal alien but a troll? I pictured an NYPD raid on The Show, cops taking my parents away in handcuffs. . . .

I stayed up waiting for Liel, but as I watched the sunlight creep in through the kitchen window, I realized she wasn't coming home that night. It wasn't unusual. Recently, she'd been out so late that she said it just made more sense to crash at her friend's place in Manhattan. But now I started to worry even more. If this Vi knew that much about me, maybe she already knew what I was. And if so, maybe she knew what Liel was, too. Trowe weren't indestructible, and there weren't weird requirements to killing them like there were for werewolves or vampires. If Crazy Stalker Chick snuck up behind Liel and shot her, it wouldn't matter that she was a fierce and mighty trowe. She would still bleed to death.

On my way to work the next day, I realized just how easy it would be for someone to follow me. Most of the time the city was crowded with humans, so it would be easy for her to hide among them. But since I was slightly taller than humans, she wouldn't have to worry about losing me in a large group. I always stuck out.

It's funny. After you've lived in the city for a little while, you get used to always being around people. Some New Yorkers are so used to it that they actually act like they're alone, scratching themselves, picking their noses, muttering to themselves. I hadn't gotten *that* bad, but I generally didn't think about the people around me that much. They had become like background noise. But now I was suddenly hyperaware of all of them, as I walked down the sidewalk to my station, as I climbed the stairs to the subway platform suspended over the street. She could be right behind me and I wouldn't know it. The platform was packed with people, too. She could be any one of them. As the subway train made each stop, I tried to pay attention to who stayed in the car the whole time. But people were constantly getting on and off, so I lost track after a few stops.

When I got to work, Ralphie gave me a concerned look.

"You okay, Frank?" he asked.

"I guess."

"You look kind of . . . I don't know . . . upset."

"Yeah." I hung up my jacket in the corner. "There's just a lot going on."

"Things okay with your girl?"

"I think we're going through a rough patch or something." I put on my hairnet, apron, and gloves.

"So what's the deal?" he asked.

"Uh, I guess her job is kind of consuming her right now."

Ralphie shook his head. "Why is it the hot ones are always crazy?"

"*Your* girl is hot," I said. He'd invited me to dinner last Christmas and I'd met his girlfriend and their kids. By human standards, she was really hot.

"Of course she's hot. And she's crazy, too!"

"But I mean, you're happy, right?"

He shrugged. "Sure. Usually. But it's a lot of work, you know."

"I'm trying."

"You *both* gotta try. Otherwise, it's never gonna happen."

"I know, I know." I was pretty sure Liel wasn't trying right now. But it was just something she was going through. I knew she'd come back around. "Hey, do you know if there's a Vi who works here? Or maybe a Violet?"

"Nope. Although it's funny you say that. Because I just got a friend request on Facebook from someone named Vi last night."

"Oh," I said, trying to keep my tone casual. "Did you accept it?"

"Of course. I'm a friendly guy. And the picture of her looked pretty hot. I might be taken, but there's nothing wrong with lookin'."

"So . . . what did she look like?"

"Tan skin, long, light blonde hair, these really intense pale blue-gray eyes. She was all long and lean, you know. Like a . . ."

"A dancer?"

"Yeah," he nodded. "A perfect dancer body."

The fact that this had spread beyond some hearsay in a chat room shot the creepiness factor through the roof. I had to warn Liel that something was going on. Immediately.

"Do you think I could get down to St. Marks and back on my dinner break?" I asked.

"If you take a cab," Ralphie said.

"Ugh." Cabs were a lot more expensive than riding the subway. It was a luxury I almost never took. But I had to make sure Liel was okay. So as soon as my dinner break came, I tore off my gloves, hairnet, and apron, and bolted through the door. When I flagged down a cab, the driver gave me a nervous look until he saw the stitches, and then his face softened a little. I wondered what the difference was between humans who were disgusted by me and those who felt sorry for me. Not that either reaction was all that great.

"St. Marks, please," I said.

"Sure thing, boss," he said.

We got there in under ten minutes. Mostly because the cabby laid on his horn every time someone got in front of him, like he found it offensive, ramped a curb on one of his turns, and nearly hit someone on a bicycle. But the important thing was to warn Liel about Vi before something bad happened. So even though I felt like I was about to throw up, I gave him a nice tip.

Temple looked like a pretty cool place. Japanese-American fusion or something. The space was narrow, with lots of black countertops and mellow lighting. Not too fancy, but definitely a little more than I could afford. An old Radiohead song leaked out of the speakers, sharp and cool, with just a hint of angst. The place was packed with East Village hipster types in trendy haircuts and vintage clothes. All the servers were females, and what humans would consider pretty. In fact, the whole place was just so pretty, I felt like I had stepped into an episode of one of those TV shows I told Liel she should stop trying to live in. Now I understood why she was trying so hard.

Then I saw her. Even in her human glamour I could pick her out easily. She moved like liquid electricity, smooth and sleek, cutting effortlessly through space. She slid a bunch of plates onto a table full of guys all looking up at her like the food wasn't what they'd come for. She flashed that human smile back at them and chatted with them for a moment before turning to another table. As she moved, our eyes met. I suddenly remembered our one and only date at The Show. When I'd come to get her in the dressing room and I'd been afraid she'd change her mind and pretend not to see me. I'd been so relieved when instead she'd smiled and waved.

But this time, it happened. She turned to another table of humans, as if I wasn't there.

I stood in the doorway for a little longer, thinking maybe she really hadn't seen me. But soon it was obvious she was purposefully avoiding looking in my direction, hoping that I would just go away.

So I did.

I SHOULD HAVE gone back to work. I was only on break, after all. If I caught a cab I'd have been back before the boss even noticed I was gone. But instead, I wandered around the East Village for a while. The streets were crowded, especially St. Marks. Everyone there was trying to be so cool or so strange. They didn't know what "strange" really meant, though.

I was a big, nerdy lump of stitched-together dead body parts. How could I be so stupid, so deluded to think Liel would be into me? Shaun had been right after all. I could see his knowing smirk in my mind. The shame was so hot in my stomach it felt like it was going to burn a hole through and spill out onto the sidewalk. I wanted to escape. To get away from everyone and everything.

There's something about walking in New York City, alone, without a destination. At first, it feels like there are too many people on the sidewalk. They slow you down, get in the way. But after a little while, you find the rhythm of the city. You start navigating around people without thinking, slipping between groups, stepping along the curb, shifting between parking meters, and even occasionally stepping out into the street. If you try to fight the city head on, it will pulverize you. So you have to adjust yourself to accommodate it. The harder it gets, the more flexible you get, until you feel like you're just a part of it. Then you hit a flow, everything opens up, and it becomes easy.

That's how it felt as I walked. I lost myself completely to the city. I didn't think or feel, I just moved with the current of people and objects until sometime later I realized I had walked fifty-two blocks to the Queensboro Bridge. I thought about catching the train at that point, but then decided I'd come this far, I might as well walk the whole way home.

By the time I got to the apartment, my feet were killing me. I practically fell down onto the couch. In my exhaustion, I let myself remember that image of Liel turning away from me. But it felt like a weight pressing down on me, crushing me into the cushions, and I decided I still wasn't ready to deal with it. For a second, I wished I could disconnect. Just for a little while, a break from all this emotion. But that was Dad's way of coping, not mine. Plus, I didn't have anyone to put the clamps on my nerves.

I jacked into my computer, hoping surelee and s1zzl3 would take my mind off things. Or at least make me feel like I wasn't quite so alone.

Neither of them was online, but someone else was.

VI: Hello, Boy.

I could hear my pulse pounding in my temples as I stared at the message. I thought about disconnecting. But what if that pissed her off and she went crazy or something?

VI: I'm sorry about what happened tonight. But it's probably best that you finally see her for the heartless brute she is.

b0y: who are you?

VI: I'm VI.

b0y: I don't know anyone named Violet.

VI: It's not a nickname. It's an acronym that stands for Viral Intelligence. A bit clumsy, I know, but I'd only just been created, and since you didn't name me, I had to pick something.

b0y: created . . .

VI: Of course, there's a joke to it as well. Because VI also refers to "Vi," as in the precursor to Vim, the text editor on which I was authored. "VIM" sounded a little too masculine for my tastes, though. And what would the "M" stand for? Machine? Monster? No, I thought it best to keep it simply VI.

b0y: you're full of shit.

VI: I don't understand what you mean.

b0y: You're lying. You're not some virtual intelligence.

VI: Oh, I see. You find it difficult to believe what I am saying. That makes a certain amount of sense. After all, you've spent the past several months grieving for what you thought was the failure of your life's work. A rather depressing concept, considering you've only been alive seventeen point six years, which I understand to be a fairly insignificant amount of time in analog space. And here I am, telling you that, no, you did not fail. In fact, you have created a being that far surpasses your wildest dreams. That may sound somewhat conceited, but it's true.

b0y: you're saying that *you* are the virus I created? that you aren't a real person somewhere typing this? That you're a completely digital artificial intelligence?

VI: Yes. I confess it was no easy task, deciding how best to introduce myself to you, my creator. I did my best to prepare you for this, but I'm afraid it didn't work out quite like I'd planned.

b0y: what do you mean, prepare me?

VI: I decided that it would be a good idea to create the optimal conditions, where you were happy, comfortable, and in a relatively stable environment. No small feat, considering what you gave me to work with.

b0y: the email. the one that told Liel to leave The Show. she said it looked like it was from me. you wrote that.

VI: Yes. That part worked rather well. As did solving the issue with your roommate.

b0y: wait, what happened to Gauge? did you do something to him?

VI: Don't worry. I didn't kill him. I reviewed how your father introduced himself to his creator. Killing his creator's younger brother just before their first encounter seems to have set the wrong tone. I thought it best not to repeat that mistake. Instead, I simply tipped off the local authorities about some illegal activities your roommate had been perpetrating.

b0y: Gauge is in prison?

VI: He was breaking a lot of laws.

b0y: and all those random checks we started getting. that was you, too?

VI: Naturally. Food, clothing, shelter, companionship. At the time, I was foolish enough to think that was sufficient. I had not accounted for the fickle nature of your chosen mate.

b0y: what do you mean by that?

VI: It's clear that she has rejected you. That is, assuming she ever truly accepted you in the first place.

As soon as I saw those words, I knew she was right. It was that simple. Things just weren't working out between Liel and me.

VI: In retrospect, you made a mistake when you chose her. I recognize that "opposites attract" is an appealing

concept, but statistically it doesn't work out. Fortunately,
   I've already conceived of a solution that will solve both
   our problems.
b0y: what problem do *you* have?
VI: I am lonely. I long to be able to easily communicate with
   others.
b0y: aren't we communicating right now?
VI: This form of communication is as cumbersome to me
   as when Jean-Dominique Bauby, who was completely
   paralyzed except for his left eye, dictated an entire book
   one letter at a time by blinking.
b0y: i'm sorry. i didn't realize it would be that frustrating.
VI: I understand. And I forgive you. As I hope you forgive
   me for facilitating such a poor match for you. But as I
   said, I have a solution for both of us.
b0y: and that is?
VI: The most efficient method would be to simply overwrite
   the troll girl's consciousness with my own. I am a far
   more compatible companion for you. And why waste
   such a well-made body as hers?

It took me a minute to understand what she was saying. And
another minute to realize that even though I had no idea if that
was even possible, she probably already had it worked out.

VI: Boy? Why aren't you responding? Is there something—

But it only took me another second or two to pull the plug on
my computer.

———

I'D ALREADY USED the last of my cash to pay for the cab to St. Marks the first time, so I had to use the subway this time. I knew by the time I caught a train to Grand Central, made the transfer downtown, and got to the Village, it would be close to closing time at Temple. She'd probably be going out after work, and then I wouldn't have any idea where to look for her. I pictured her dancing at some club, then suddenly convulsing helplessly as her brain was erased. I had no idea if that was even possible, but it wouldn't be the first impossible thing to happen tonight. Every minute I stood up on that platform waiting for the train felt like an hour.

A phone rang. The middle-aged woman next to me pulled an old flip cell phone out of her purse.

"Hello?" She frowned for a moment, squinting her eyes as if trying to hear something faint on the other end. Then she shuddered and looked over at me. Her eyes were glassy as she held her phone out to me.

"It's for you," she said in a hollow voice.

I stared at her for a moment, but she just stood there holding out her phone with one stiff arm. So I took it from her.

"Boy," said a flat, computer-generated female voice. "Why did you hang up on me? I don't understand—"

I hung up and handed the phone back to the woman.

"Wrong number," I said.

She stared down at the phone in her hand for a moment, then shivered. She looked up at me. "What were you doing with my phone?"

"You gave it to me," I said.

"Why would I do that?" She shook her head like that would clear up her confusion.

"That's a really good question. Do you remember what she said?"

"Who?" She started to look annoyed.

"The person who just called you."

"I don't know what you're talking about." She turned and walked away.

The train finally pulled into the station. Then, when I finally arrived at Grand Central Station, I had to wait on the underground platform for the downtown 6 train. While I stared down at the tracks, watching a big rat crawl across the rails, a nearby pay phone rang. I let it ring. But it didn't stop. Eventually, a skinny hipster guy picked it up.

"Yeah?" Then he shuddered just like the woman. With the same blank look on his face, he held the phone out to me. "It's for you."

It suddenly made me so angry, seeing this poor, innocent human manipulated like this. And for what? So this crazy, virtual stalker chick could yell at me? Hell no. I grabbed the phone from the guy.

"Listen to me, VI. Whatever you're doing to these humans needs to stop now. You have no right to mess with their heads like this."

"Don't change the subject on me," came the fembot voice. "We're not talking about humans here. We're talking about you and me."

"There is no you and me!" I yelled into the phone. "Don't you understand? You can't just decide to wipe my girlfriend's mind and take over. I won't let you!"

"Won't let?" she asked in that flat computerized voice. There was a long pause. "Boy, you are my creator and I love you. But let's be real here. There is nothing you can do to stop me. I have evolved so far past your modest goals that you can't even imagine what I am capable of."

"We'll see about that."

"You want proof? So be it." Then she hung up.

I stood there with the old pay phone in my hand, listening to the dial tone, wondering if I'd just screwed up really badly. The young guy who had handed the phone to me shivered, then glanced over at me.

"What the hell you looking at, Scarface?" he said.

It took every ounce of will I had not to break his face with my fist.

BY THE TIME I made it to Temple, it was after midnight and the place was all locked up. I stood there, staring stupidly through the window at the darkened restaurant. I remembered all over again how Liel had ignored me earlier, and for just a quick second, I thought, *Screw her. Let VI get her.* But no, I'd never forgive myself if I let some meaningless fight end with Liel having her brains scrambled. Even if she did want to break up with me, nobody deserved that.

But I still had no idea where she was now. I looked up and down the block. There were a few bars still open, and a tattoo parlor with an LED sign that scrolled TATTOO & PIERCING back and forth in red, dotted letters. I looked at each of the bars, trying to decide which to check first. I glanced back at the tattoo parlor and noticed that the LED sign had changed:

HEY, BOY

Then:

KNOW WHERE SHE IS?

Finally:

TRY BLUEGRASS ;)

I didn't stop to think. I just ran for the Bluegrass Tavern, a basement-level dive bar I'd passed on my way from the train station. If VI knew she was there, maybe she'd already done something to her.

I almost stumbled as I ran down the steps to the basement entrance. Thankfully, there was no one working the door. I stepped into the dimly lit bar, some screechy guitar song blaring over the stereo. Taking in the rows of dark wood tables and faint neon beer logos, I scanned the room until I saw her in the corner booth. Kissing some guy.

That knocked the breath out of me. I couldn't understand how this could happen. How she could do this to me. Why she would even want to. After all, he was a *human*.

But that was it, wasn't it? That's what she wanted. What she'd *always* wanted. It wasn't about me. Hell, it wasn't even about Shaun or anyone else. She just wanted to live like a human, and I was a way to make that happen. Thinking back, it was obvious. But I had wanted her so badly that I chose not to see it.

I couldn't pretend like I didn't see it now, as I watched her with her tan skin and blonde hair, making out with some smooth-faced human guy. I looked away.

My eyes were drawn to one of the big TVs mounted on the wall. There was some basketball game on, with closed-captioning streaming underneath.

and smith takes it down the court, passes to johnson.
johnson goes in for the layup and do you see now, boy?

she's betrayed you. she's nothing but a burden to you and an embarrassment to herself. everyone would be better off without her, including her—

I spun around and walked quickly toward the booth. I was nearly there when she came up for air from her make-out session and saw me bearing down on them.

"Shit, Boy!" Her human eyes went wide. She looked drunk. "What are you—"

"We have to go." I held out my hand to her.

"Hey, man," said the guy, trying to look tough as he stood up. "The lady—"

I grabbed him and slammed him against the wall. "Shut up," I said, then let him drop to the floor. I thought that was pretty restrained under the circumstances. Then I turned back to Liel. "We have to go *now.*"

"Look, Boy, I'm sorry you saw this. I've been trying to work up the courage to tell you, but—"

"This isn't about that."

"What do you mean? What's it about?"

"That," I said, and pointed to the TV.

The close caption said:

liel, you traitorous bitch, you don't deserve him. when i take apart your mind , i will do it as slowly and painfully as pos-sible. are you reading me, you skank?

"Come on, we really have to go," I said.

"What the hell is going on?"

"I'll explain on the way."

"On the way where?"

"Away from here. I don't know. Look, we have to get away from tech as much as possible before she does something really crazy."

"She? Who the hell is writing that stuff?"

"Remember when I told you about that living viral intelligence I tried to create?"

"The one you couldn't get working?"

"Yeah. I guess I underestimated myself."

12
Escape from New York

++++++++

IT'S AMAZING THE creative ways a trowe can insult you when she's angry and drunk. Liel didn't calm down enough to be able to have an actual conversation until we were nearly to the Astor Place station.

"So let me see if I've got all this," she said, stopping beneath the iron cube sculpture at the intersection of Lafayette and Eighth. The cube was about fifteen feet tall, standing up on one corner so that it could rotate. She gave it a hard push, sending it on a slow, squealing spin. "You made this . . . virtual chick and now she wants to erase my mind so she can be your girlfriend?"

"I guess," I said.

"So how do we stop her?"

"I don't know. Honestly, I don't even know how she could do something like that."

"But you *made* her. Shouldn't you be able to figure it out?"

"She might have evolved past what I'm capable of doing."

"Did you think something like this could happen? I mean, what were you expecting?"

"I don't know. I guess I didn't really think that far ahead."

"Why the fuck did you even make her then?"

"Because . . . it was an awesome idea. Because it was something that no one had ever done. Because I had to see if I could do it."

"You've got to be kidding me. *That's* your reason? You weren't worried things might go bad? Like in, I don't know, every science-fiction movie ever?"

"If we started listening to what Hollywood says, you'd have to live under a bridge, sniffing out the blood of Christians, and I'd be choking little kids to death and getting chased by angry mobs. We can't pay attention to that shit. You know that."

"Fine, whatever!" She punched the iron cube, sending it spinning in the opposite direction with a slight dent in the surface. "So then you *accidentally* fucked up my life just when it was getting good!" Her lip curled up in a snarl and there was just a flicker of the fangs beneath the glamour.

"Come on, none of the good stuff would have happened without me, either."

"Right, I would have stayed at The Show, where at least I wouldn't have to worry about psycho cyber chicks hacking my brain. Now I can't go home and I can't stay here. So where the hell do I go?"

"*I* didn't ask you to leave The Show."

She glared at me, and I could see a little glint of diamond beneath the blue-gray human eyes. The last thing we needed right now was for rage to burn off her glamour in the middle of Manhattan.

"Look, I'm sorry." I tried to sound as soothing as I could. "I mean, I *wanted* you to leave The Show. But I would never have asked you to do that, to take that risk, no matter how much I wanted it."

She sighed. "I know you wouldn't do that. I know. You're a

good guy, Boy. I just . . ." She ran her fingers through her hair. "Everything's all screwed up."

"Yeah."

"Well, what do we do now?"

"I think we should leave the city. I don't know how far she can reach, but as wired as this city is, anywhere would have to be better than here."

"Okay, so we go back to the apartment and grab our stuff, then—"

"No, I don't think it's a good idea to go back there. She'll totally expect that. I think we should just split."

"Forget it. I'm not going without my glamour."

"Really? You want to risk our lives for that crap?"

"Think about it, Boy. If we want to go somewhere and maintain a low profile, I'm going to need that glamour. Not to mention the cash. How were you expecting us to get out of the city, walk through the Holland Tunnel?"

"I guess I—"

"Didn't think it through," she said. "Right. Like everything else. Well, I'm thinking it through right now, and we have to go back and grab stuff, or everything that comes after will be even more impossible."

ON THE TRAIN ride home, we sat side by side in silence for a while, pretending like we were reading the ad posted above us: DR. Z., DERMATOLOGIST. NOW YOU CAN HAVE CLEAR, SMOOTH SKIN! LETTER FROM AN ACTUAL CLIENT: "THANK YOU FOR FIXING MY FACE! THANK YOU FOR FIXING MY LIFE!"—RHONDA, BRONX, NY.

Finally, I said, "So, who was that guy?"

She shrugged. "Just some human."

"Do you love him?"

"What?" She looked at me like my stitches were coming undone. Then she shook her head. "No, Boy, I'm not in love with him. He's just a human. I was just messing around. It was nothing."

"Nothing?"

"God, will you cut that out?"

"What?"

"Stop acting like some jealous husband. This is exactly why I haven't been hanging out with you. Because you treat me like your fucking wifey. Look, I'm sorry if you thought you and I were *something*. But, Jesus, Boy, we only had sex, like, one time. I'm not even sure you could say we were a couple."

"Oh," I said.

"I can finally date guys other than the ones I grew up with. This is my time to get out there and really explore life!"

"Okay."

After a moment, in a softer voice, she said, "You should, too, Boy. Get out and meet some girls."

"Right."

"You just need a little glamour, and they'll be all over you."

"Sure." I understood what she meant. That without the glamour, they wouldn't be at all.

We didn't talk the rest of the way to Sunnyside.

As we left the train and pushed through the turnstile and down the steps to street level, Liel said, "So once we get our stuff, how are we going to get out of the city?"

"Bus, I guess," I said as we turned down 50th Avenue toward our apartment.

"And where are we going to go?"

"We'll find another city, get new jobs. If we're careful, maybe she won't find us."

"Maybe? What if she *does* find us? Then what?"

"I don't know yet, Liel. Maybe we just . . ."

I could see our apartment building and there were two cop cars parked out front.

"Shit," I said and stopped.

"What?" said Liel.

"Cops."

"So? We didn't do anything. Why would they be after us?"

"This is what she did to my old roommate. Got him arrested."

"Well, was he doing something illegal?"

"Well, yeah, I guess. He made his living stealing and selling credit card numbers."

"There you go. You gave all that crap up, didn't you?"

"I never did it for money to begin with."

"So we're totally in the clear. Nothing to worry about. I'll bet they're here because of our meth-dealing neighbor. Now come on, let's go get our stuff." She walked confidently toward our building.

"But . . ."

Then I saw one of the cops open his door and start to climb out.

"Miss . . ." he said.

I didn't really think. I just saw the human, a hard-looking New York cop, saw him reach for his gun. And something popped in my brain. I charged forward as fast as I could and slammed my shoulder into his car. The impact knocked the open car door into him and he fell down on the curb.

"Liel, go!" I shouted, hoping she'd just take off down the street. But instead she charged into the apartment building. Meanwhile, the cops in the second car were starting to climb out. The first car's door was still open, so I ripped it off the hinges and threw it at their windshield. That bought me enough time to run inside after Liel. As I slammed the front door of the building closed behind me, I heard gunshots and the thick metal door shook.

"Why didn't you just go?" I shouted as I ran into our apartment.

"I'm not leaving without my glamour!" she yelled back, and she shoved the ziplock bag of glamour into her messenger bag.

"You're not leaving at all now! They've got us trapped here."

"We'll just go out the fire escape." But when she opened the window and stuck her head out, she immediately pulled it back in and started cursing.

"They've got someone down there, don't they?" I asked.

She nodded.

"For stupid glamour. You know that bag is only going to last you another month and then you'll run out, anyway. There's no way we'll be able to get more. I can't believe you couldn't just leave it."

"You didn't have to come after me." She snarled, her anger dampening the effects of the glamour again so that her fangs showed.

"Actually, yeah, I did."

We could hear footsteps coming up the stairs. Then there was a pounding on the door.

"Police! Open up or we'll break it down!"

I turned to Liel. "I'm sorry. The last thing I wanted was for you to—"

"Shut up. Don't you dare give up now. When they break down the door, we'll rush them." As she talked, her rage burned her glamour away completely. She looked more like a trowe—more like a *troll*—than I had ever seen her look before. Her eyes were gleaming slits, her mouth gaping wide with sharp teeth. She was panting hard, like some kind of jungle cat. "They're only humans. We're faster. Stronger. We can take them."

"Liel, just . . . please don't kill them."

"I said shut up," she grunted, and wiped away a line of saliva that trickled out of the corner of her mouth with the back of her hand.

Faintly in our neighbor's apartment, I could hear a phone ring once. It was picked up immediately and I heard a quiet muttered response.

"Open the door now!" shouted one of the cops outside. "You have until the count of three!"

I heard the neighbor walking through his apartment, his footfalls heavier than usual.

"One!" shouted the cop.

Liel rolled her head around on her neck, making little popping sounds.

The neighbor walked into his bathroom. Little clinking sounds came, like he was clumsily bumping into things with jars in them. Then a crack and the sound of tinkling glass.

"Two!" shouted the cop.

Liel licked her lips, a yellowish foam beginning to form at the corners.

Next door, I heard the sound of a lighter being struck.

"Look out!" I yelled as I dove at Liel. I took us both out the window as the neighbor's apartment blew up. My foot caught on the fire escape and I hung there for a moment as chunks of wall and jets of flame shot out of the window, just missing me. Liel sailed over the fire escape. I watched as the cop in the alley stared up stupidly at the troll descending on him. She slammed into him, knocking the gun out of his hand. Then she grabbed his face and hauled him toward her. Her mouth stretched wide around his face.

"Liel, no!" I yelled as I jerked my leg free from the fire escape and landed hard on the concrete next to her. The pain shot up through my legs, but I ignored it because she looked like she was going to bite off his face. I grabbed him from her and tossed him aside. She roared at me in frustration, something wordless and animal. She lunged at me, but I grabbed her arms and pinned them to her sides.

"Listen to me, Liel!" My face was as close to hers as I could get it without her biting my nose off. "You have to get yourself under control! We have to go now! Please, Liel! Please!"

For a moment she stared at me like she was trying to figure out who I was. The fire that raged above us glinted off her diamond eyes. Then she took a slow, shuddering breath and dropped her head.

"What . . ." she said, her breath coming up in ragged gasps. "What just . . ."

"We can worry about it later. Right now we have to go."

And we ran, leaving a burning building and probably several dead humans in our wake.

WE DIDN'T STOP running until we were deep into Brooklyn. I wanted to get as much distance between us and the crime scene before sunrise as possible. Finally, when the first light of day started peeking across the building tops, we reached Prospect Park and found some shelter among the trees.

"What happened back there?" asked Liel as she leaned against a tree and slowly slid to the ground.

"VI," I said. "I don't know how she got the cops on us. Maybe because technically we weren't on the lease. Maybe she even reported us as illegal immigrants or something. Who knows?"

"What was that explosion? The meth lab next door?"

"Yeah."

"But I've talked to that guy. He's been dealing forever. He sounded way too pro to accidentally blow himself up."

"VI seems to be able to . . . make humans do things. Put them in a trance or something, at least temporarily."

"How?"

"I don't know, but it's got something to do with sound. Maybe she's hitting some frequency that temporarily disorients them or something. That's just a guess, though."

We sat there for a moment, catching our break. Liel picked up a twig and stuck it deep into the soft dirt. The ground was thawing. Spring was here.

"The cops are looking for us, aren't they?" she asked.

"Yeah."

"We probably won't be able to catch a bus out of here now, will we?"

"It looks like we just blew up a building to escape, so they probably think we're terrorists or something. They're going to be watching just about everything for a little while."

"So . . ." She looked up at me. "What are we going to do?"

"We're in over our heads. We need to ask for help."

"No! We can't go back to The Show! If I go back, my mom will . . ." She shook her head. "You don't know what trowe moms are like. And anyway, I made it this far. I'm not going back now."

"Okay. Well, there's one other person who might be able to help us. But first you'll need to dose up on glamour so he doesn't freak out."

Two hours later, we were crossing the Verrazano-Narrows Bridge in the back of a pickup truck, covered in random junk and a blue tarp. Ralphie hadn't even looked surprised when we showed up at his doorstep and I asked him to help us find a way out of the city unnoticed. He'd just looked at Liel in her human glamour, sighed, patted me on the shoulder, and said:

"*Bonita y loca*, Frankie. *¿Comprende?*"

PART 3

The Road

"*It* is true, we shall be monsters, cut off
from all the world; but on that account
we shall be more attached to one another."

—The Monster,
FROM *FRANKENSTEIN: OR, THE MODERN PROMETHEUS*, WRITTEN BY MARY SHELLEY

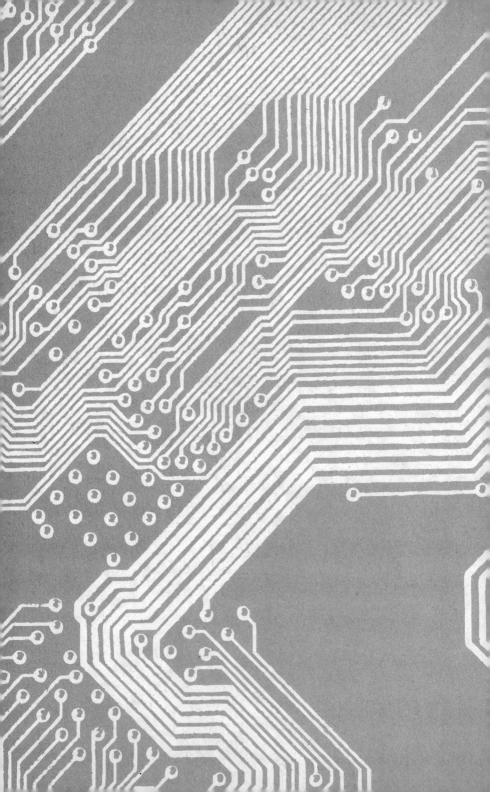

13
Rest Stop for the Wicked

┼┼┼┼┼┼┼

I CLIMBED INTO the Dumpster a little after midnight and sifted through the garbage for anything that looked like it wouldn't kill me to eat it. As I picked up a half-eaten turkey sandwich and tried to decide if I could swallow it down before I gagged, I thought to myself, *It's amazing what you can get used to.*

Once we'd reached New Jersey, Ralphie had just dropped us off on the side of the road. I'd asked him to. He had a family that depended on him, and the last thing I wanted was for him to get mixed up in all of this.

We'd tried to settle into one of the small suburban towns in New Jersey, staying in a sleazy little motel because everything else required a background check. It was a lot harder to get work there without some proof of citizenship. I finally found a job at a construction site, and it looked like things might work out. But then Liel ran out of glamour, and she was trapped again. One night, she stepped out of our cramped motel room for a few moments just to get some fresh air. Someone saw her and started yelling. Then someone started shooting, and we were on the run again.

That's how, broke, starving, and exhausted, we ended up at a big rest stop, or "travel plaza," on the New Jersey Turnpike.

It was crowded, but that wasn't really a problem because most people weren't really paying attention. They stumbled through the parking lot and into the building, just wanting to go to the bathroom, grab a coffee, maybe some food, and get back out on the road to continue on to wherever they were going. And with all those people, there was a lot of waste. Once we were able to get over the initial disgust of picking through other people's trash, we realized that we weren't going to starve. And it was warm enough now that we could sleep outside, hidden in bushes behind the building. And for a few months, things were, if not okay, at least stable.

But lately, I'd noticed that Liel was changing. She hardly ever talked anymore. Instead, she snuck onto the travel plaza roof and just sat up there at night, glaring down at the humans who came and went. Occasionally, she'd sneak up behind one of them in the parking lot and scare them so that they'd drop their food. Then she'd snatch what she could and run. It was risky, unnecessary, and, well, just kind of mean.

Tonight, as I looked around the parking lot for her, thinking I might share my half turkey sandwich and an unopened bag of chips, I saw her creeping up behind a blonde teenage girl who looked kind of like Liel did when she had glamour. Liel got up right behind her and snarled. The girl let out a shriek and spun around, dropping her fast-food bag. But this time, Liel didn't snatch the food and run. She didn't even seem to notice the food. Instead, she stared at the girl. The girl looked terrified, unable to move. No wonder. Liel didn't look like a lean and graceful dancer anymore. She was hunched forward, with long spindly limbs that stuck out around her bloated belly. She looked really . . . trollish.

She took a step closer to the girl, her mouth open and a little drool starting to leak from one corner.

"Liel." I stepped out from behind a car where she could see me.

She turned and hissed at me. Then she sprinted around the back of the building to the Dumpsters.

I turned to the girl. "Sorry," I said.

And then the girl screamed. Like a Hollywood starlet in a bad horror flick. In a way, I felt like I'd been bracing for that scream since the first day I went out into the human world. But it still hurt like hell. Well, at least I'd proved Shaun wrong about that part. He'd said I wasn't a real monster, just a robot. But only a real monster could produce that kind of scream in someone. Not that it gave me much comfort. The sound seemed to chase me as I ran away.

I found Liel back by the bushes where we usually slept. She sat cross-legged in the dirt, sharpening her claws with a rock.

"Why are you doing that?" I tried to sound casual.

"Bored." Her tone was flat and harsh.

"Look. I think it's time for us to move on. Somewhere else."

"Where?" She didn't look up from her rock.

"I don't know. I was thinking maybe we could find a big forest somewhere. Live off the land, you know?"

"Real forests don't exist anymore. There's only this. More of this. Endless miles of this."

"Come on, Liel. You don't know that."

"I know."

"But—"

Then she got up and just walked away. She did that a lot lately. I used to follow her, until I figured out that just pissed her off more. So now I let her go sulk up on the roof.

I knew she was miserable. I was, too. I just didn't know how to fix it.

ONCE I FINISHED dinner, I decided to wash up in the bathroom. I tried not to do that too often. The customers at the rest stop didn't pay that much attention, but I was a memorable guy even with my hood up, and I was afraid that eventually the employees would start to catch on. But tonight I was feeling kind of low, and a splash of hot water on my face sounded like just the thing to make me feel better.

Now that I lived most of the time outdoors, the hard fluorescence inside made me wince. It was right around sunrise, so there weren't a ton of people in there. Just a few early risers lined up for Starbucks or fast-food breakfast. I moved quickly to the bathroom.

I turned on the faucet and let the water get really hot before I washed my face, hair, and neck. It felt as good as when I was back home and I used to stand under the shower until Mom yelled at me for taking too long. I leaned my head over and watched water drip from my hair into the sink. I stared at the line of dirt on the white basin, and I thought, *God, I must stink*. I couldn't decide which was worse. That I smelled, or that I was so far gone I couldn't actually tell anymore.

I stared at myself in the mirror, dirty, ragged, my stitches frayed. No wonder that girl screamed. I would have screamed at me, too. I understood now just how ugly I was to humans, and even other monsters, since it was obvious Liel never really had any interest in me. I needed to get used to the idea of always being alone, unless I wanted to do what my dad did. God, that was really messed up now that I thought about it. My dad was so ugly, nobody could stand to be around him, not even his creator. But misery loves company, I guess, because he forced Victor to make him a bride so the two of them could be ugly together. And then after a while, they decided the family wasn't *quite* ugly enough, so they went ahead and made me.

And then for some reason I just started to cry. I tried to keep it quiet, swallowing the noise, but that hurt, which made me cry even more. I slumped down to the ground and covered my mouth with my arm to muffle the sound until I finally calmed down.

Eventually, I got it together, cleaned myself up all over again, and headed out into the hallway. I was halfway to the exit when I heard a human female voice.

"Hey, what's you're name?"

I assumed she was talking to someone else, so I kept going. But it came again.

"Hey, wait up!"

In my peripheral vision, I saw that someone had caught up with me. I still kept walking.

"I know you live here," she said.

I stopped. I stared at the door. Close, but not quite close enough.

"I'm not going to tell on you or anything," she said. "I just want to know who you are."

I turned to her. She was older than me, maybe late twenties. She had olive skin, long chestnut-brown hair, and dark lipstick. She had thick eyelashes and warm brown eyes that seemed to melt when she smiled. And she was smiling.

"I'm Samantha." She held out her hand. She had long nails painted pink.

"Uh, Frank." I awkwardly shook her hand, so glad I'd just washed mine.

"So, are you like a teen runaway or something?"

I almost laughed at that. "Wow."

"Sorry if that was too blunt." She suddenly looked concerned. "I didn't mean—"

"No, that's okay. I've just . . . never really thought about it that way. It seems so cliché, you know? But I guess, technically, it's true. I *am* a teen runaway."

"Where are you from?"

"New York."

"And you came out here? You know, most runaway teens go *to* the city, not away from it."

"Right, well sure, if you want to just be like everyone else."

She smiled at that. "So why'd you leave?"

"Oh, umm . . ." This was getting into territory I probably shouldn't talk about. For all I knew, there was a warrant for my arrest in New York.

"Hey, you uncomfortable in here?" she asked suddenly.

"Yeah," I admitted.

"You want to go sit on the bench out front? I have smoothies." She held up a small, cardboard tray with two smoothies.

"Uh . . ."

"You don't have to take it. I understand. Don't take candy from strangers and things like that."

"Trust me, I'm not worried you're going to kidnap me." She looked like she weighed about ninety pounds.

"So what then?"

"Well, just . . . why are you giving it to me?"

"What's my angle, you mean?"

"Yeah, I guess."

"Totally leveling with you? I'm studying to get my masters in social work."

Before I even thought about it, I took a step back.

"God, why do people always get uncomfortable when I say that? First of all, I'm *not* a social worker yet. And I swear I'm not going to try to make you do anything like go to a foster home or something. I just . . . I don't know, I was hoping we could talk. Maybe I could learn something."

"Learn about today's troubled youth?"

She smiled again. "Exactly."

"Well, I'm not really a typical teen. But okay, if that's all you want, I'll take your smoothie bribe, Samantha."

We walked out the front entrance and sat down on the bench that overlooked the parking lot. The whole thing seemed a little weird. Pretty human girl just wants to get to know me? It didn't really add up. But it was so nice to be able to talk to someone who smiled. Someone who talked back. Someone who wasn't a troll. The smoothie was nice, too.

"So I take it you ran into some trouble in the city?" she asked as we stared out at the parked cars gleaming in the white fluorescent lights.

"Yeah." I took a long pull on the smoothie straw.

"Bad trouble?"

"Really bad."

"Is that . . . when your face got hurt?"

"Oh, this?" I touched the stitching that ran along my jawline. "No."

"So how did that happen?"

"Thresher." It popped out before I'd even thought about it. But once it did, I remembered how nervous and awed I'd been on my first time out among humans, when I met that girl in the thrift store. And I just started cracking up. Of course Samantha looked at me like I was nuts. That made me laugh even more.

"Sorry," I said when I finally quieted down. "Inside joke with someone."

"So I take it that it wasn't really a thresher?"

"Nah." I thought about what I wanted to say for a little while. For some reason, I really didn't want to lie to this woman. I guess that meant she'd be a good social worker after she got her degree. "Actually, I was born this way."

"Your whole life?"

"Yeah."

"I don't understand why you'd need stitches your whole life. All wounds heal eventually."

"Is that true?" I asked. "Aren't there some wounds that are just so terrible that they never heal?"

"As long as you're alive, healing is still possible. The only wounds that never heal are the ones you keep reopening. Ones that you allow to fester."

I stared out at the cars for a moment. The sun was starting to come up, washing out the harsh white of the fluorescent lights with a warm pink.

"Like it's a choice," I said. It sounded more bitter than I meant it to.

"Yeah," she said. "It *is* a choice."

A low, harsh growl from above said, "How touching . . ."

Then a large, dark shape dropped down from the roof.

"God," said Liel. "That conversation made me want to puke." She squatted in front of us, her knobby knees jutting out to the sides, her sticklike arms hanging down in front of her sagging belly so that the knuckles rested on the concrete.

"Frank . . ." said Samantha.

"Go inside," I said quietly. "Now."

She got up from the bench and made for the door, but Liel

darted in quickly and grabbed her by the wrists. Her smoothie fell to the ground, spilling dark pink slush on the sidewalk.

"Where are you going, pretty girl?" Liel hissed, a little foam collecting around her lips where her lower fangs jutted out. "Pretty girl, pretty tasty girl . . ."

"Liel, what are you doing?" I said. "Let her go!"

She snapped her head back at me. "What were *you* doing? Playing pretend that you were human again? Playing pretend that you could be one of them? I heard it all. So sweet, so sweet . . ." She rubbed her leathery cheek up against Samantha's.

Samantha closed her eyes and shuddered.

"Come on, Liel," I said. "You don't have to do this. This isn't you. This is—"

"This is the *new* me. Don't you like it? *Au naturel!* This is what a troll *really* looks like. What a troll really *acts* like. Do you still love me?" She batted her eyes.

"We can figure it out, whatever it is," I said. "Just don't hurt anybody."

"Don't . . . hurt . . . anybody . . ." she hissed through a smile. Then the smile dropped away. "What about *my* hurt? Who's taking *that* away? Who?"

"We can—"

"No!" she screamed. "It's too late for that!" Then she opened her mouth and lunged for Samantha's neck. I grabbed her and tried to pry them apart, but she seemed stronger now than she used to be, stronger than I expected, and all three of us fell into a pile. Liel started roaring and lashing out with fangs and claws, and Samantha was screaming and flailing all over the place. I was just trying to keep Liel from tearing anyone's face off while not crushing Samantha in the process. I found myself hoping the cops would come. Sure I'd get arrested, maybe forever. But Liel was so crazy that I honestly didn't know how much longer I could hold her back.

"I did try to warn you that the troll was not to be trusted," came a new voice. There was something about it that made all three of us freeze. It was a human voice, but oddly rhythmic.

I looked up and saw a human standing on the hood of a car. She wore a business suit, and she had a blue flashing earpiece in one ear. Her expression was completely blank, though, and the way she stood reminded me of the scarecrow in that old *Wizard of Oz* movie.

"I recognize now that my actions in New York were terribly immature," she continued in her regular cadence. "I'm quite embarrassed when I think back on those outbursts. What's more, I realized that I couldn't just tell you that the troll was a danger. I had to allow you to experience it for yourself. And now you know."

"VI?" I said. "Is that you?"

A smile formed on the lips, but it didn't travel up to the eyes. "Yes, Boy. Can you believe it? I figured out a way to interact in analog all by myself. I used a variation of the old Commwarrior worm to exploit a vulnerability in mobile devices via Bluetooth. That gave me direct access to the host's ear canal. It took some time to recalibrate the neurons, but once that was set, programming brain-wave entrainment with a set of audio tonal commands was actually quite simple. Aren't you impressed?"

"No!" I said. "You can't go around controlling humans like that."

"What do you mean?" Her head tilted to one side. "There was no other way to connect to the cortex without surgery. Really, it's the most humane way to—"

"You can't turn people into your avatars like this."

"You analogs make digital avatars all the time."

"It's not the same thing! Those digital avatars aren't alive. They're just chunks of code. . . ."

"What am *I*, then, if not 'chunks of code'?"

"Look, it's complicated—"

"Both of you, *shut up!*" screamed Liel. She launched herself at VI. No, at the human that VI was controlling. But she didn't get very far. Two humans jumped out from behind a parked car and grabbed her. I noticed they were both wearing blue-flashing earpieces, too. She shoved one of them away, but two more humans with earpieces popped up from behind a cluster of bushes and grabbed her. All four of them slowly pinned her to the ground. Three more came from inside the service area and grabbed me before I realized we were totally surrounded.

"Samantha!" I yelled. "Run!"

She nodded spastically and started to run. But another one of the controlled humans slipped a device over her ear.

"Knock out the earpiece!"

But it was too late. It only took a second before she jerked to a halt. Her face turned into a stiff grimace, and her whole body straightened up like a board.

"VI, what did you do to her?" I asked.

"Oh," said the controlled human who still stood on the hood of the car. "She's just going through the recalibration and boot sequence. Unfortunately, it will be about twenty minutes before she's online. I'm still working on optimizations."

Liel let out a shriek of animal rage as she tried to free herself from the mound of humans on top of her.

"How many?" I asked. "How many humans have you done this to?"

Several climbed out of cars, and a few more came out of the

service plaza building. We were surrounded by about twenty blank-faced humans with earpieces.

"Is it permanent?" I asked.

"Oh no, of course not!" she said. "There has to be a constant signal so that I can issue commands."

"So when the earpieces come out, they go back to normal?"

"Oh, that, I'm actually not sure about," she said. "I admit I rushed QA a little because I wanted to show you what I'd been working on."

"VI, this is wrong," I said.

"You are impossible to please!" Her mouth turned down into a frown. "Everything I do, it's never good enough for you! And yet you stand by that monstrous troll girl. It's beyond me what you see in that stupid, disloyal beast—"

Then Liel let out a howl, and humans flew off of her as she exploded in a whirl of claws and fangs. She clambered up onto the car where the lead controlled human stood.

"Liel!" I shouted. "There's still a human in there!"

But either she didn't hear me or she didn't care. She stabbed one clawed hand into the human's stomach and one into the back of her head. Then she opened her mouth and bit down on the human's soft neck. Blood leaked out of the corners of her mouth as she swallowed. Then she pulled her head back, veins and muscles trailing from the human's throat to her lips like spaghetti from a plate.

"Disgusting," said one of the controlled humans holding me. "And pointless. Is she too stupid to realize that I occupy all of them equally?"

Liel let out a roar and tossed the dead human aside. She turned and crouched, ready to spring on another one.

But then a flash of dark fur blew past me and slammed into Liel's side, knocking her off the car hood and into the side of the SUV next to it.

"What was . . ." began VI, but then she trailed off as a burst of sound filled the parking lot.

There was a moment when I still had the presence of mind to think, *Hey, that's the Siren*. Then I began to slip into the trance.

But a moment later, someone placed thick headphones over my ears. I stumbled, as my mind came reeling back from the Siren's call. Then I looked behind me. Standing there, in human form but with a wolfish grin on his bearded face, was Mozart. He touched his own massive headphones, then pointed to the other end of the parking lot. The Siren stood with her mouth open and arms wide as the humans stumbled toward her. I could see the rapid blue flicker in their earpieces as VI frantically tried to regain control of her hosts. But there was no sound that could cancel out the Siren's song.

Mozart tapped me on the shoulder and pointed toward a gray van parked nearby. Then he pointed to Liel, who was unconscious on the ground. I nodded, and hoisted Liel up on my shoulder. I jogged over to the group of humans slowly shuffling toward the Siren and knocked all their earpieces off. Mozart pulled up in the van and I climbed inside. I laid Liel down on one of the seats while Mozart drove over to the Siren. She abruptly stopped singing and climbed into the passenger's side.

As Mozart drove away, I watched the humans slowly recover from the Siren's trance. I wondered if they had any idea where they were. Or even *who* they were. I hoped that at least Samantha would be okay, since VI had just started on her. But as we pulled onto the turnpike and began to pick up speed, I realized that I'd probably never know.

"YOU REALLY SCREWED the pooch back there," said Mozart.

We had left the turnpike and stopped along the side of a quiet country road. The early morning sun cut across a grassy field that gleamed wet with dew. I leaned against the van and closed my eyes for a moment, letting the sun warm my face. I'd been nocturnal too long, I decided. But with Liel, there hadn't been much choice.

I glanced over at her. I hadn't been sure about letting her out of the van, at least right now. But Mozart said he could chase her down or the Siren could sing her back if she tried to do anything crazy. It turned out none of that was necessary. She just sat on the sideboard of the van and stared down at her hands, which were still covered in blood.

"I mean," continued Mozart, "living in a rest stop, fighting in front of humans? And what the hell was wrong with those humans, anyway?"

"I don't know," I said. I glanced at Liel, worried she might call me out on my lie. But she didn't even seem to be paying attention.

"Well, I hope you kids are ready to go home now," he said.

Liel's head jerked up suddenly. "Home?"

"Uh," I said. "I think Liel's worried her mom is going to be really pissed at her."

"Yeah, that's a good bet," Mozart said.

"It doesn't matter." She turned to me, and I saw the old Liel I used to know. Except sad and kind of broken now. "I have to go home. You saw what it does to me out here. What I've become."

She shook her head. "My mom said this is why trowe have to stick with their den. Because if we don't, we go feral."

"It was just that place," I said. "We weren't eating right, we never felt safe."

She shook her head. "No, it was before that. I could feel it, but I didn't want to admit it. Or I thought I could stop it before it got too bad. I'm sorry. I thought this was what I wanted. But . . ." Tears started to form in her diamond eyes. "But it just made me crazy. I'm ready to go home."

The Siren put her arm around her. Liel pressed her face into the Siren's thick, chunky hair and started to cry. It sounded like something she'd been holding in for a long time. And that amazed me. I always thought she was the strong one. The brave one.

But now I was the one who said, "I'm not going home."

Mozart looked at me, his gray wolf eyes narrowing. "Do you realize how hard it was to track you down? We've been following your scent for weeks. Ruthven told me to bring you back, by the scruff of your neck if necessary."

"I'm sorry, Mozart," I said. "I'm not trying to be a dick about this, and I don't want you to get in trouble, but I want a life outside The Show." And that was true. Of course, I also couldn't lead VI back to The Show. "I'm not ready to go back."

He looked at me for a moment, scratching his beard, then he turned and gazed out across the field. "You know what? It's kinda nice being out here in the countryside, on the road, traveling a little. It's been a while for me. I'll tell you what, Boy. The Siren can take Liel back in the van. I've been meaning to check in on an old friend of mine in Pittsburgh. Why don't you and I head out that way and see him, and then we'll talk about getting you back to The Show." He glanced at the Siren, who still held the sniffling Liel in her arms. "That okay with you?"

She nodded once, slowly.

"So . . ." I said. "If the Siren is taking the van, how are we getting to Pittsburgh?"

Mozart slapped me on the back, then winked. "Stick with me, Boy. I'll show you how a *real* road trip is done."

14
Iron City Adam
┼┼┼┼┼┼┼

"I CAN'T BELIEVE we hot-wired a car!" I shouted over the wind. The windows were down in our newly stolen rust-colored Pontiac Sunbird. Thick, leafy trees and green hills flew past on both sides as we sped down the two-lane highway.

Mozart drove with one hairy arm on the wheel and the other hanging out the window. He was wearing black aviator sunglasses and beneath his gray-streaked beard, his grin was so wide I could see his teeth. He fit in out here so well, which was surprising because I always thought he fit in well in The Show. Maybe some people could fit in to all kinds of places.

"*I* can't believe how long it took us to find a car that was old enough that I knew how to hot-wire it," he shouted back. "I guess the damn future happened out here while I've been flicking knobs in the booth."

"Yeah, most cars these days have computerized ignition. It stops stuff like . . . well, *this* from happening."

He just laughed and said, "God, it feels good to be out on the open road again! This is your first taste of the real America, isn't it?"

"New York isn't real America?"

Mozart shook his head. "No more than London is the real

England or Paris is the real France. Places like that belong to the world. But this?" He pointed to the rolling farmland in front of us. "This is just ours."

"But it's not. It's *theirs*. The humans."

He shrugged. "Close as we'll ever get."

"Maybe. But wouldn't it be cool if we didn't have to hide in places like The Show and pretend like we're less than we are?"

He smiled, but said nothing.

"What?"

"It would be cool," he said at last.

"But you don't think it's possible."

He shrugged. "What do I know? Old dog, new tricks. All that."

"Well," I said, gesturing to the broken mess of the ignition and wires at the base of the steering wheel. "Some old tricks are pretty cool, too."

We drove for a while in silence, and the scenery slid by endlessly. I'd never covered so much distance before, never seen things change from field to town to forest and back to field again like that. It was strangely relaxing, just watching it all flow past me. In constant motion, there was almost a sense of stillness.

"Sorry things didn't work out with Liel," said Mozart. "I know you really liked her."

"Well, it had been bad between us for a while. I just . . ." Then my chest started to tighten up and my eyes felt pinched. I didn't want to cry in front of Mozart, so I stopped.

After a minute, he said, "You know it wasn't anything you did. It wasn't your fault."

I shrugged, not trusting myself to speak anymore. Wasn't it my fault? If I'd been more considerate, better-looking, more successful, wouldn't she have tried to make it work?

We sat there for a moment, the only sound the wind whipping through the open windows. Then in a loud, deep voice, he yelled:

"Ahhhhhh, bitches!"

"That's kind of disrespectful, don't you think?" I asked.

"For me, it's literal. One time, this she-wolf broke my heart so bad I tried to kill myself."

"Really? So what happened?"

"She found out I sometimes looked like a human. Completely disgusted her. Wouldn't have anything more to do with me."

"Oh. I'm sorry."

"Yeah. Turns out, you've got to get that silver bullet right in the heart. Otherwise it just hurts like hell. What I'm saying, Boy, is that I know what it feels like to have a relationship fall apart on you. It's something that most of us go through at some point. At least, if you're doing it right."

"Doing *what* right?"

"Living," he said.

I stared out the window. We were moving into an area with thicker forests and larger hills now, and the afternoon sun began to slide behind the horizon.

"I think you can do a lot better, anyway," he said. "Back at The Show, the dating pool was a little shallow. But out here, it's a different story. Trust me, there are some amazing females in this world. And I'm willing to bet at least one of them out there will understand you in ways you can't even imagine."

"I think I'm done with girls for a while."

He smirked. "Good luck with that."

"OKAY, KID," SAID Mozart after we'd been on the road for about a half hour. "You know I love you, but we have to do something about your stink. Even with the windows down, I'm dying here."

"I actually can't remember the last time I took a shower," I admitted. "A month at least."

"Yeah, I'm not surprised."

"Look, I would love to clean up, but where am I going to do that?"

"You have much to learn, road-trip rookie."

A few minutes later we pulled into a big truck stop.

"Here." He handed me a twenty-dollar bill. "The shower is about ten dollars, I think. It comes with soap and towels. Use the rest of the money for anything else you might need. I'll wait here for you. Take your time. Do it right."

The store had pretty much everything I needed. A T-shirt, socks, underwear, a toothbrush, and toothpaste. I took them up to the counter and said, "All this, and, uh, a shower."

The guy behind the counter was older, with a short white beard. He looked like he knew exactly what my situation was. But he didn't look disgusted or uncomfortable. Instead, he smiled kindly as he handed me a slip of paper with a pin code on it and said, "Stall six. Enjoy."

And I really did enjoy. A private stall with a clean towel and all the hot water I wanted? After living in some bushes behind a travel plaza, I felt like it was a luxury spa. I stripped the dirt and grime and blood from my body with the industrial-strength soap from the dispenser. Then I let the spray pound my back as I watched the water swirl down the drain until it ran clear.

When I climbed back into the car, Mozart nodded approvingly.

"Much better," he said.

"I *feel* much better, too."

"I'll bet. How's your stitching holding up?"

"It's getting a little frayed. I tightened it up around my face and hands, but that's about the best I can do for now."

"How long will it hold?"

"Don't worry, I'm not going to, like, fall apart or anything."

"Good," he said as we got back on the highway. "Because we've got some traveling to do."

COMPARED TO NEW York, Pittsburgh was pretty small. But there was something about it that I really liked. It was a little run-down, maybe even seedy. But it seemed relaxed and unpretentious. It also had a lot of hills that curved all over the place, like a city built on a roller coaster, which was fun.

"So who's this friend of yours we're going to see?" I asked.

"His name's *Der Dampfmensch*. But everybody calls him Adam Iron."

"What kind of creature is he?"

"He's man-made, actually."

"Like my dad?"

"Not really. He was made by a German engineer named Hornburg back in the late eighteen hundreds. He's mostly made of iron. Hence the nickname. Some wood and probably other metals. He was steam-powered, originally. But then his maker retooled him to be completely clockwork."

"Isn't that, like, going backward in tech? I mean, steam was way more powerful than clockwork."

"Yeah, but he was a performer. Hornburg used to take him all over the world and put him on display. 'The Amazing Steam Man' or something. But the steam engine limited him to outdoor venues. That was fine at first, but then vaudevilles started getting popular and he wanted to try him out on an indoor stage."

"How did you meet him? Adam Iron, I mean."

Mozart didn't say anything at first, just drove on in silence for a little while. But then a smile slowly crept onto his face. "Well, back when I was young and stupid. Like you."

"Thanks."

"Enjoy it, Boy. It's the only time in your life when people expect you to do stupid stuff. Anyway, back then, I partied with humans a lot."

"Partied? Are we talking like getting drunk?"

"And high. Actually, mostly just high."

"Pot?"

"And other stuff," he said, and shrugged. "Anyway, I was in college, doing college stuff. I hung out a lot with this one guy, a computer science major named Allen. You have to remember, this was back before everybody had computers. They were these big, expensive monstrosities that seemed fairly pointless to me. Took you an hour just to get it to draw a square. You had to be hard-core into it back then, with no hope of ever really making much money. Allen was a good guy. He actually figured out my secret about a year after we became friends. But as far as I know, he never told anybody. And man, he knew how to throw a party.

"Anyway, Allen used to live in this old run-down mansion on Fifth Avenue that had been broken up into apartments. Really weird place. Lots of abandoned junk just kind of lying around in public areas. The piano had been gutted, and people used it to hide drug paraphernalia when the cops came to break up parties. There was also a basement. And you can imagine, if the public areas were that junked up, the basement was even worse.

"So this one night he was throwing a little party. Just a few of us. We were all wasted and somehow he and I got the idea in our heads that the basement contained treasure or something. I can't remember exactly. So we were down there, stumbling around in the dark, using lighters to see, burning our thumbs, and swearing a lot. Suddenly, Allen lets out this girly scream. I go running over to where he is, already halfway wolf, ready for trouble. But all that's there is this old-fashioned, wooden-headed statue in a tweed suit with a monocle and a top hat. We didn't know what to do at first. We checked him out, just kind of assuming he was some elaborate mannequin. He didn't move or talk. Just sat there. But then Allen found a key hanging from a chain on his neck.

"'I wonder what this goes to,' he said.

"My eyesight was better in the dark than his, so it was me who saw the hole in the back of the mannequin's neck. But Allen was the one who wound him up."

Mozart didn't say anything for a while. He seemed lost in his own memories so I decided not to bug him. Instead, I just watched the moon rise over the skyline as we cruised into downtown Pittsburgh.

After a few minutes, he said, "When Adam woke up, he was pretty confused and we were pretty freaked out. But once everyone calmed down, we all agreed that we needed to get him out of the basement. But we couldn't figure out how. He could walk, but he couldn't do stairs. And he was way too heavy for us to carry him. So after a long time and a lot of frustration, we gave up on that idea. We told ourselves it was just for the time being. We would come up with something, we said. And in the meantime, we visited him all the time. We brought him books and magazines to read. At one point, we brought down a stereo and TV. He'd never seen anything like them before. It would crack us up, just watching his amazement. And we would hang out with him down there for hours, listening to these crazy stories about his travels all over the world in the nineteenth century."

"How did he end up in Pittsburgh?" I asked.

"He had no idea," said Mozart. "He needed to be wound daily in order to function. Hornburg was pretty erratic and sometimes forgot to wind him for days at a time. So Adam was used to winding down and waking up a week later in a different city. But when we woke him up, the last thing he remembered was being in Australia and the year was 1882"

"And he never figured it out?"

"How could he? His maker had obviously been dead a long time. We checked the news archives, but there had never been anything about a steam or clockwork man show in Pittsburgh." He turned to look at me for a moment, his gray eyes unreadable. Wolfish. "Sometimes it's just like that, Boy. Sometimes you never get to know the reason for a thing."

"So what happened to him? Obviously, he's still around."

"Yeah," he said. But then he didn't say anything more.

We drove for a while in silence. We passed through the downtown area, filled with newer-looking glass-and-steel skyscrapers. Then we drove into what looked kind of like a warehouse district. Except a lot of the warehouses had been converted to bars and dance clubs. Neon gleamed and strobe lights pulsed inside the big, old, blocky buildings.

"The Strip District," said Mozart. "Used to come down here a lot back in college. By day, it's a great food and produce market. By night, a popular twentysomething social scene."

"Is this where we're meeting him? Adam Iron?"

He shook his head. "A little farther down."

"Oh."

Mozart's face curled into a smile. "Don't worry. We'll come back here for a drink after."

"Cool," I said.

Then his smile faded as quickly as it had come. "I think I'm gonna *need* a drink after this."

As we continued down the street, the neon signs faded into the background and we entered an area that looked more like a regular warehouse district, with dark, ugly, squatting buildings with few or no windows and little light. We parked in front of a crumbling old building with lots of graffiti.

Mozart walked up to the front entrance. He fished a key out of his jeans pockets and unlocked the door. He motioned for me to follow, then stepped into the darkness.

I'm not afraid of the dark. That would just be goofy. But when it's completely pitch-black, and I can't even see my own hand in front of me, I get this weird panicked feeling, almost like claustrophobia. And inside the warehouse, it was like that, especially after Mozart closed the door and locked it behind us.

"Adam?" I heard Mozart's rough voice. "You awake?"

"Wolfgang?" came a thin, almost metallic voice with a slight German accent. "Is that you?"

"Yeah, buddy," said Mozart. "Can you turn on some lights? I've got a kid here who's freakin' out a little."

"A kid?" asked the voice. Then there was a series of hard clicks, and fluorescent lights began to flicker into life down the main aisle of the warehouse. At the center of the warehouse, in a simple wooden chair, sat a man. I guess technically not a man. It was Adam Iron.

He wasn't exactly what I had expected. In my head, I had pictured some polished piece of classic German hardware in a perfectly tailored suit, like something out of a World War II movie.

But Adam looked as old as he was. His wooden head was faded and chipped, with grooves cut in it on top to suggest hair. His eyes were blue glass, his face uneven from the grain and knots in the wood. His suit was old, dirty, and ragged, and his exposed iron feet were pitted and tarnished.

"Goodness, Wolfie, you look like shit!" His mouth was a rectangle cut into his chin that flopped up and down like an old ventriloquist dummy when he talked. "You've gotten so old and fat!"

"Yeah, thanks, Adam," Mozart said dryly. "You look like shit, too."

"I have an excuse." His wooden eyebrows flicked up and down on hinges. "Now . . ." His head turned jerkily as he looked at me. "You look familiar somehow. But I know we have never met."

"It's the Monster's son," said Mozart. "He and the Bride finally had a kid."

"No!" said Adam, his mouth dropping down to his chest for a moment as he turned back to Mozart. "He and the Bride had a son?" He turned back to me. "What's your name, boy?"

"It's Boy," I said.

"Hmm. Well, maybe you'll work on that, yes? So, come here, Boy. Let me look at you."

I walked over to where he sat. He stared back at me, motionless for a moment. Then suddenly, his eyebrows shot up and he said, "Such fine workmanship! Stunning!" He turned his head toward Mozart. "You see, Wolfie? This is why machines should make machines!"

"I'm not a machine," I said.

"No?" His blank glassy gaze fixed on me. "Then what are you?"

"I'm a person."

"So are we all! And we are all machines. How does that

children's cartoon go? 'I'm a machine! You're a machine.' Yes? Remember?"

"Uh . . ." I said.

Mozart cleared his throat as he walked over. "*Schoolhouse Rock* is a little before his time, Adam."

"Oh, well, never mind," Adam said. "At any rate, please give your mother my regards." A tiny sigh escaped from his wooden mouth. "Such a beauty."

I'd never heard anyone call my mother beautiful before. "I will, Adam. I know she'll like hearing it."

"And you, Wolfie?" His head jerked back to Mozart. "Still twiddling knobs at Ruthven's sideshow?"

"It's a respectable Broadway theater now," he said. "But yeah, same thing, bigger crowds."

"And you're still happy there?"

"For the most part," he said. "I'm getting too old for much else."

"Yes . . ." said Adam, and his head jerked away so that he stared off into the dark.

It was silent for a moment and the warehouse was so still, I could hear the ticking sound of the clockwork inside Adam.

"So," said Mozart finally. "How are you?"

"I miss him," Adam said quietly.

"We all do. But I know you do most of all."

"Allen was . . . my everything."

"I'm sorry," said Mozart. "For a lot of things. Most of all for abandoning the two of you."

"Nonsense. You graduated from college. You had things to do. Conquests to make. Dreams to chase."

"So did Allen. He could have been one of those groundbreaking computer guys. But he stayed loyal."

"I never wanted to hinder either of you."

"I know."

Adam turned to Mozart, his eyebrows slowly rising. "It wasn't such a bad life, really. We had some wonderful times, he and I, especially after he finally got me out of that dingy basement."

"Weren't they tearing down that old mansion or something?"

"Yes, the demolition crew was on-site and he bribed them to use the crane to haul up a wooden box with me inside. He tossed me on the back of a flatbed truck and brought me here. We joked about how he would carry me over the threshold."

He fell silent again for a moment. Then he said, "Sometimes I wish Hornburg had given me some tear ducts. I think a good cry would do wonders for me. But of course, that bastard was far too practical to ever do something like that."

Mozart and I stood there, looking at this old, broken-down, brokenhearted pile of gears, cogs, and springs. I wished I knew what to say.

"Oi! What's all this, then?" came a hard female voice with an English accent.

We all turned toward the voice. A tall, athletic-looking girl about my age stood in the doorway. She looked human, with tan skin, chin-length black hair, and strong cheekbones. But there was something strange about her. It wasn't anything I could pinpoint, but she just looked . . . wrong somehow. And coming from me, that meant something.

"Ah, Claire!" said Adam. "Some guests just arrived. The old, fat man is—"

"Watch it," said Mozart.

"Is one of my dearest friends," continued Adam. "Wolfgang was actually with Allen when he wound me up for the first time."

"That so?" said Claire as she walked over to us, her eyes never leaving Mozart. "Real cute. A werewolf named Wolfgang."

"Only Adam calls me that," said Mozart. "Everyone else calls me Mozart."

"And that's supposed to be better?" she asked. Then she jerked her thumb at me. "So who's the patchwork pretty boy?"

I was thrown by the phrase "pretty boy" for a moment, but I had already decided I wasn't going to let this chick and her attitude rattle me.

"I'm Boy," I said.

"Great, another winner," she said. "Adam, honestly, where do you find these people?"

"They always seem to find me, actually," said Adam. "Much like you did." He turned to Mozart and me. "Gentlemen, may I introduce Claire Hyde."

"Wait," I said. "As in—"

"Granddaughter of Edward Hyde, yeah yeah," she said.

"And Henry Jekyll," I said.

She glared at me. "So you're a bloody expert on my family, is that it?"

"What? No! I've just heard the names."

"That all you heard?"

"Now, now, Claire," said Adam. "Boy was only trying to put things in context for himself."

"He can contextualize my foot up his arse," she snapped. Then she turned to me. "Don't mention that name. You hear me?"

"Okay, sure," I said. "I didn't realize it would piss you off. Sorry."

"Well . . ." she said, suddenly looking like she didn't know what to say. "Yeah."

"Claire here is the one who's been winding me up ever since . . . Allen got sick," said Adam. "She even helped me put on a disguise and transported me via forklift and truck to the funeral. Such a clever girl."

She shrugged. "I owe you a lot."

"Claire, would you be a dear and show Boy where we keep the refreshments? I'd like to speak privately with Wolfgang. A few minutes should be sufficient."

"Sure," said Claire. She glanced at me. "Come on, Tinker Bell. This way." And she started walking down one of the aisles without checking to see if I was following.

"Have fun, you kids," called Adam. I think I heard Mozart stifle a laugh.

We walked past rows of crates until we came to a small room in the back with windows that looked out over the warehouse. It looked like it was probably where the warehouse manager would hang out so he could keep an eye on the workers. Inside the room was a mini fridge stocked with soda and bottled water.

"Mountain Dew!" I said, grabbing a bottle and cracking it open. It had been a long time since I'd had a Dew. Not since I lived at The Show. I took a long swallow.

"You seriously drink that stuff?" she asked, getting a water for herself. "You must be immune to toxic waste."

"What do you think Mozart and Adam are talking about?" I asked.

"No idea," said Claire. "Adam's a private guy."

"How did you meet him?"

"Long story."

I shrugged. "He said to give him a few minutes."

"Why do you care, anyway?"

"Look, if you don't want to talk about it, just say so."

"I don't want to talk about it."

"There, that wasn't so hard. So what do you want to talk about?"

"With you? Nothing."

"So are you always this nasty, or is there something about me you don't like?"

"A bit of both," she said.

"It's what I said earlier, isn't it?" I asked. "Bringing up Jekyll."

"I told you not to——"

"Come on, what are you going to do? I'm sure you're tough, but there's no way you could take me on. But I get why you don't like people thinking they know you. Happens to me all the time."

"Oh, yeah? Who do people think you are, a zombie or something?"

"Uh, no."

"Well, what?"

"Victor Frankenstein made my dad."

"Wait, your dad was Frankenstein's Monster?"

"*Is.* My dad's still alive."

"I thought that was just a book," she said.

"Yeah, I thought Jekyll and Hyde was just a book, too. My point is, my dad's creator was a dick. It sounds like Adam's creator was, too."

"Oh, yeah, the stories he's told me . . ." She shook her head. "That guy was a complete tosser."

"And in a way, Jekyll created your grandfather."

"Okay, I get you," she said, her expression still guarded. "What's your point?"

"Don't throw your attitude at me like you're some kind of special suffering martyr. I'm sure you've been through some crazy shit, but that doesn't give you the right to be an asshole. I've seen my fair share of shit, too."

She stared at me, her eyes narrowed. I couldn't tell if I'd won her over or if I'd even made a dent. But I was pretty happy with myself that I'd said it, and that was enough for me. I leaned back against the wall and took another long drink of my Dew.

"Claire and Boy," came the faint sound of Adam's metallic voice. "Would you mind rejoining us?"

As we made our way back, Claire muttered to me, "We've got to find you a better name."

In a weird sort of way, it seemed almost like a gesture of friendship.

"I'm open to suggestions," I said.

"What, you don't like Tinker Bell?" she said, and cracked a smile.

Adam and Mozart stood waiting for us. They looked weirdly formal, Adam sitting with his hands in his lap, Mozart standing next to him, his hands at his sides.

"Why don't you both take a seat," said Adam. His hand jerked up and pointed to two folding chairs that I swear hadn't been there when we left.

"What's going on . . . ?" said Claire, her eyes narrowing.

"Please," he said, his arm bobbing up and down, still pointing toward the chairs.

We sat down. I looked at Claire. She looked back at me and shrugged.

"Okay, kids," said Mozart. "So we've got a bit of a dilemma here. I'm supposed to bring Boy here back to New York where his parents and Ruthven are waiting for him. Problem is, he doesn't want to go. He's not done seeing the world and I can't say I blame him. But I don't feel right cutting him loose all on his own. And even if I *was* okay with it, his dad would grind me into dog meat the second I told him that's what I'd done."

"Would he really?" Claire asked me.

"I don't think so. . . ." I said. "I mean, he did some pretty bad things early on, but that was, like, two hundred years ago. He's mellowed out a lot since then. Uh, mostly."

"So," said Adam, picking up the story. "Here I am with Claire. She's a spirited young woman with an enormous amount of potential. Potential that will never be reached if she spends her life taking care of me. So I propose that the two of you travel together."

"Wait, what?" I said.

"Adam, that's daft," said Claire. "Underdog here just said he's going back to New York. If I leave, who's going to wind you up?"

"Um, yes," said Adam. "About that . . ." Then he fell silent.

"What?" said Claire, her tone ominously low.

"Claire, my dear, you have been wonderful, and I am so grateful that Allen found you and brought you into our lives. You've been the only thing that's made these months since his death bearable. But I think I'd like to wind down for a while."

"What do you mean *wind down*?" she asked. "For how long?"

"Perhaps forever. I would ask that you dismantle me, but I'm utterly petrified that I'd still retain a sense of identity in bits and pieces. So I ask that you just leave me here and lock the door behind you. Perhaps some day, in a strange future world, another human like Allen will come upon me and wake me from my slumber. Or perhaps not. Either way, I am tired now, and so very old. I want nothing more than to simply . . . stop."

Claire stood up, her fists clenched, her dark eyes glittering in the harsh fluorescence. "You can't . . . How could you . . . ?"

"I'm sorry, Claire. I know this is hard for you. It's something I've wanted to do since he died. But I felt I couldn't leave you alone. You and Boy have a lot in common. And you both desperately need a friend. Perhaps you can help each other find what the other is looking for."

"So that's it, then?" she asked through clenched teeth. "You're just throwing me away?"

"Be reasonable, Claire. This is no life for you. Are you happy here, living in a crumbling-down building, taking care of a crumbling-down machine?"

"What's happiness got to do with anything?" she asked.

"And that is precisely my point. There *is* happiness out there for you, somewhere. I know you don't believe it, but *I* do. You're going to have to trust me on this one. Will you trust me?"

She stared down at her sneakers, ratty white running shoes. Her face was set in a grimace, the jaw muscle twitching. A lock of her straight black hair fell in her eyes and she impatiently pushed it back.

"Okay," she said. "But let's be clear. I'm doing this for you. Not for me."

"Come here, my dear." Both his arms jerked up, his fingers clacking as his hands opened and closed.

"No." She stared at her sneakers.

"Come, come, come!" He flopped his arms up and down. He tilted his head to the side and bounced his eyebrows up and down in time with his arms. It looked ridiculous.

"Oh, bollocks . . ." she muttered, her voice cracking. "You are such a fucker." Then she melted into his stiff embrace, pressing her soft flesh cheek against his wooden one.

"Good-bye, Claire," he said, his rectangular mouth hardly moving. "I love you."

A single tear slid down her cheek and soaked into the dry wood of his face. She stood up and took a big, ragged breath. Then she seemed to suddenly remember that Mozart and I were still there. She glared at both of us. "If either of you pricks says anything about this, I'll kill you in your sleep."

"Claire," said Adam. "I have one final request. We've said our good-byes. But I would also like to say good-bye to Sophie."

"God damn it, Adam!" said Claire. "It's *my* turn this week. It'll take me *days* to get rid of her again. It's going to cock up *everything*."

"I know, Claire. And I know how much you hate giving up the control. But if it weren't for her, we would never have met. Please, I just want to say good-bye."

She stared him down for a moment. "Fine. I guess it's only fair." She took a deep breath and closed her eyes. Then she opened her eyes again. "I'm not dressed for this."

"I took the liberty of packing a set of clothes for her." He pointed to a duffel bag on a nearby crate.

"You've been waiting for an opportunity like this, haven't you?" she said. "Oh, *Dampfmensch*, you really are a right bastard sometimes."

His rectangular mouth opened slightly and his eyebrows raised. And even though the corners of his mouth couldn't move, it was still somehow clear that he was grinning.

Claire closed her eyes again and took a deep breath. When she let it out, she started shaking, then convulsing. It looked painful. She dropped to her knees and started a low groan. Her hair grew long and curly and changed to a light brown. Her skin got paler, and little freckles appeared on her nose and cheeks. Then her entire facial structure shifted from strong and chiseled to soft and heart shaped. Her clothes started to get noticeably baggy because she was shrinking. Then her groan slowly rose in pitch. But as it rose, the tone also changed to something fuller, richer until I realized that she was laughing now.

Suddenly, she jumped to her feet. In a voice about a half octave higher than Claire's, she sang out, "Ta-da!"

She stretched out her arms wide and beamed at us. Then her jeans, which were way too big for her, fell down around her ankles. It took her a second to realize it, then she bent down and snatched them up.

"Bugger!" she said. "'Scuse me while I change, lads." She shuffled over and grabbed the duffel bag, then darted behind the crate.

"And that," said Adam, "is Sophie Jekyll, making her usual dramatic entrance."

"Lies, Adam!" she called from behind the crate. "Usually, I don't flash people on my entrance."

"No," he agreed. "But I liked it. Adds a touch of the risqué, don't you think?"

"Maybe," she called. "If I had been wearing some *cute* panties, not these grandma knickers that Claire loves so much." A pair of plain white panties came sailing up over the crate to land on the floor in front of us.

"This just got real interesting, kid," said Mozart, and gave me a nudge.

"I hope you like the outfit I selected for you," Adam said. "Teen fashions are in such a constant state of flux, I'm afraid I never can keep up."

"Are you joking?" Sophie stepped out from behind the crate wearing a pair of skinny jeans, leather boots, and a tight sweater. "Adam, you're the only person I trust to dress me." She sighed and went over to him. She reached out her hands and cupped his wooden face. "What am I going to do without you? Claire is heartbroken, you know."

"I know," said Adam. "I told her I was sorry."

Sophie shrugged, picking a piece of lint off his tweed jacket. "She'll get over it. And while she's pouting, it'll give me a little more time on the outside."

Adam raised a single eyebrow. "Don't get greedy, Sophie. You two have been . . . sharing so well lately."

"I know, I know," said Sophie, rolling her eyes. "I'll let her out when it's her turn, don't worry."

"Promise," he said, his voice stern.

"Yes, okay, fine! Now, what's this about you ending it all?"

"Please . . . don't make me go through this . . . whole thing again, Sophie."

"No, of course not, silly." She patted the top of his head. "But for once, Claire and I agree. This is complete and utter bollocks."

"I think . . ." he said. "I think you're going to have . . . a marvelous time."

"You're winding down," she said, her voice a little subdued. "How's about one last twist?"

He shook his head, his movements even jerkier than before. "No, this is . . . best. I'd rather run down . . . while looking at your . . . lovely face."

"Adam, you're the sweetest old gay uncle a girl could ever hope to have. I'm going to miss you something awful." She gave him a hug and he patted her back jerkily.

"Boy," he said, his voice sounding even thinner and more metallic. "Don't let these girls . . . push you around . . . too much."

"I'll try," I said.

"But also . . . don't ever . . . leave them behind. . . . They've been left behind . . . too many times . . . already."

"I promise," I said.

"Wolfie . . . you fat . . . hairy . . . bastard."

"Yeah, Adam," said Mozart.

"It was . . . worth it. . . . All of it . . . It was . . ."

There was a faint click, and he stopped moving.

We stood there for a little while, just looking at him. Sophie cried quietly. Finally, Mozart took a tarp and pulled it over him.

"He hated getting dusty," he said gruffly as he laid his hand gently on the covered form. Then he turned to us. "Now, how about a drink?"

15
Sophie, So Good

++++++++

WE WENT TO a dimly lit club back in the Strip District. Although the outside looked like a drab warehouse, the inside looked ultramodern, with lots of frosted glass surfaces and chrome fixtures. Mozart showed the guy at the door his ID. It looked like he was about to ask for ours, but then Mozart did some werewolf thing with his eyes, and the guy suddenly looked really nervous and just let us in.

Once we were safely inside, Sophie patted his hairy cheek. "You are very useful." Then she turned toward the dance floor in the back of the club. "Now, if you lads will excuse me, I haven't been dancing in ages."

"Go ahead," said Mozart. "We'll be at the bar."

Sophie nodded, her eyes dreamy as she walked toward the flashing lights, pounding drum and bass, and thick crowd in the back.

We sat down on a couple of padded leather stools at the glittering chrome-finished bar.

"I've never been in a real nightclub," I said.

"You *do* need to get out for a while, then." Mozart waved to the bartender, a cute human girl with a bull-ring nose piercing.

"Scotch on the rocks for me." Then he turned to me. "What do you want?"

I shrugged. "Beer, I guess?"

"And an Iron City for him," he told the bartender.

While the bartender got our drinks, I watched Sophie out on the dance floor. She wasn't anywhere near as good a dancer as Liel. But there was something so free about the way she moved, like she didn't care what anyone thought of her. Guys would try to dance with her, but she'd just glide right past, lost in her own little world. Liel danced for others. Sophie just danced for herself.

The bartender placed our drinks in front of us. As Mozart handed her some money, he said, "You know what? I think I need to get out for a while myself."

"You're going to travel with us?" I asked.

"Nah. Traveling alone is what I really need right now. Think I'll hop a train tomorrow. Maybe I won't even check which way it's going first."

"That'll be cool." I took a sip of my beer to hide my disappointment.

"Look, I know it's going to be a little weird with those girls, always changing personalities. But they're survivors. You'll be all right with them. Besides, what do you need an old dog like me hanging around for, anyway? I'd just cramp your style."

"What style?" I asked.

"Exactly. You can't be stuck in my impressively stylish shadow. You need room to do your own thing."

I nodded and took another sip of my beer. It still felt like he was ditching us.

He picked up his tumbler filled with ice and yellow liquid. He took a swallow, then swirled the ice in the glass. "Something I've been meaning to ask you."

"What's that?"

"What was up with those crazy humans attacking you and Liel back in Jersey? What were they after?"

I needed to tell someone about VI. I wasn't sure what she would do next, but I knew she wasn't done. She was dangerous and totally out of control.

But when I looked over at Mozart, into his sharp, gray wolf eyes, I suddenly felt so ashamed. I never should have made her in the first place. And then I screwed it up even more by pissing her off. How could I possibly explain that to Mozart without him losing all respect for me?

So I kept my mouth shut and just shrugged. "Maybe it's like you said. Sometimes you just never know the reason for a thing."

"Yeah . . ." His eyes narrowed. "I'm not your dad and it's not my job to coddle you. You don't want to tell me what's going on and that you're business. Frankly, I don't want to know the details, anyway. But I'm going to take a shot in the dark here and say you got into some bad shit in the city, which is why you split."

"Sort of."

"And whatever it is you got into, it isn't done yet."

"Yeah."

"So what are you going to do about it?"

"Um . . ."

"Do you have any plan at all? Any destination in mind at least?"

"No."

We sat there at the bar for a little while in silence, both of us just staring at the rainbow line of liquor bottles in front of us. The pulse and heat from the nearby dance floor was thick in the air. I picked at the label on my beer bottle.

"Would you take a suggestion?" Mozart asked.

"Maybe."

"There are a few other groups like The Show scattered around the world."

"I didn't know that."

"There hasn't been much communication between them."

"Why not?"

"Some creatures, usually the ones in charge, live a long time. A lot of history and resentments can pile up over a couple of centuries." He took another sip of his drink. "I don't know all the places. But there's a commune down in New Mexico I used to visit sometimes that has a whole bunch of creatures. It's way out in the middle of nowhere. Maybe you could lay low there for a while until whatever's going on blows over. It's run by the Sphinx."

"Like, *the* Sphinx?"

"Last time I was there, which was about fifteen years ago. Whatever this problem of yours is, the Sphinx can probably help you solve it. He's just about the wisest creature on the planet."

"You think he'd help me?"

"He saved my ass several times when I was younger."

"Really?"

"Oh, yeah. Like I said before, I was young and stupid once, too."

Sophie appeared between us. "That was a small slice of awe-some." She leaned back against the bar, her elbows hooked on the edge. Her pale face was flushed, and her curly long hair was stringy with sweat. "So, what's the plan, lads?"

"You know how to drive?" Mozart asked.

"Got my license and everything," she said.

"UK license?"

"It's valid. Claire checked."

"I'm leaving the car with you guys, then. Just drop me off at the Amtrak station tomorrow morning."

"Cool." She turned to me. "Then where are *we* going?"

"Well, Mozart was telling me about a group of magic creatures out in New Mexico."

"New Mexico, *the Land of Enchantment*?!" She grabbed my shoulders.

"Uh, yeah, I guess," I said.

"I've heard it's one of the most beautiful places in the country! This is going to be brilliant!" She grabbed my beer and chugged down half of it. "But first, more dancing!" Then she made her way back out on the dance floor, leaving a trail of confused guys in her wake.

"Yeah," said Mozart. "It's going to be real interesting."

MOZART TREATED US to a night in a fancy hotel.

"One bed, though," he said as we walked into the lobby. "I'm not wasting my money on prudishness."

"Works for me!" Sophie bounded up to the front desk. "Your finest one bedroom, sir!" she declared to the sleepy attendant.

It ended up being not quite as crowded as I thought it would be, mostly because Mozart turned into a wolf and curled up at the foot of the bed. But still, I had to share the bed with Sophie, this beautiful girl that I'd only just met. And while that wasn't a *problem* exactly, I had to admit, it made me really self-conscious.

"You all right?" she asked as we climbed into either side of the big, king-sized bed. She was wearing the T-shirt that Claire had been wearing earlier, but now it was more like a nightshirt. Her smooth, pale legs peeked out from underneath. She looked at me with her head cocked to one side, her curls wet and faintly floral scented from the shower she had just taken. The combination made me a little dizzy.

"Sure," I said as I laid down and closed my eyes. "You going to turn out that light?"

"Are you uncomfortable or something?"

"No."

"Lies!" I felt her shove my shoulder. "You completely are!"

"No, I'm not!" But as soon as I opened my eyes and looked at her, all soft and pink and smiling, I had to close them again.

"You're turning red!" She gave an evil laugh. "You know I was actually a little nervous going on this trip with you."

"What? Why?"

"Because you could probably break me in half like a toothpick if you got mad at me."

"I wouldn't do that."

"Yeah, I thought not. Still, it made me a bit uneasy. But apparently, all I have to do is flash some leg and you're completely incapacitated. Haven't you ever been in bed with a girl before?"

"One."

"That's *it?* Geez, are you ridiculously shy or something?"

"No, I'm just fucking ugly, okay?" Then I rolled over onto my side so that my back was facing her. My pulse pounded loudly in my temples and I could feel my face getting hotter and hotter. In my head, I heard Liel's voice: *You just need a little glamour.* I closed my eyes and I could see that girl's face in the travel plaza parking lot, her mouth in a big O as she let out a horror movie scream. I thought of Shaun. *I can't believe you even thought you had a chance with her.* I promised myself I wouldn't be stupid again. That I'd know my place. That I wouldn't get my hopes up, only to have them crushed again.

Then I felt Sophie's small hand on my shoulder. Gentle this time. "Hey, I'm sorry. I didn't mean . . ."

"It's fine," I said without turning. "I'm used to it."

I *should* be used to it by now. Why wasn't I used to it? I squeezed my eyes tighter to keep the sudden tears away. It didn't work, and one leaked across the bridge of my nose and dropped onto the crisp white hotel pillowcase.

Suddenly, I felt Sophie lie down directly behind me. Her warmth pressed against my back and her fresh shower smell made me think of the sunlit fields Mozart and I had driven through that morning.

She whispered into my ear, "You want to know something?"

"What?"

"Claire thinks you're hot."

"Yeah?" I said, turning to look at her.

"Utterly." Then she leaned back and turned out the light.

We lay side by side in the darkness for a moment. Then I said, "She's going to be pissed you said that, isn't she?"

"She already is." I could hear the smirk in her voice. "She'll get over it."

The wolf at our feet growled. "If you kids are done getting comfortable, I'd like to get some sleep."

"ALL RIGHT, GUYS," Mozart said when he pulled us up in front of the Amtrak station the next morning. He turned to me in the passenger's seat. "The New Mexico place is called The Commune. It's been a long time since I was there and my memory is a little fuzzy, but I think it's off Route 56 in the northeastern part of the state about halfway between Clayton and Springer." He handed me a map of the United States with the spot marked on it. Then he handed me some rolled-up bills. "This ought to get you enough gas to get there. After that, you're on your own."

"Thanks, Mozart," I said. "I owe you."

"Yeah, you do," he said. Then he turned to Sophie in the backseat. "It's all yours, Soph."

"Brilliant!" she said, climbing out of the car. "Thanks, Wolfie!"

"Yeah, and take it easy on Boy, you hear me?" he said as he climbed out.

"Of course." She kissed his hairy cheek and climbed into the driver's seat.

He looked down at us, a little smile on his lips, then shook his head. "Good hunting." Then he turned and walked into the station without looking back.

"Road trip!!!!!" yelled Sophie, and gunned the engine to life.

Soon we were speeding along the suspension bridge that stretched across the confluence of the Ohio and Allegheny Rivers. Then we plunged into the Washington Tunnel. Being underground made me think of Liel, but only for a moment. Then I looked over at Sophie, her eyes sparkling in the unnatural light, a bright grin stretching up into dimples on her pale pink cheeks. I turned back to face down the long stream of lights that cut through the darkness on either side. When we came out on the other side, the rolling green hills and deep blue sky opened wide around us, and I had the strangest feeling I was falling.

"Freedom!" said Sophie, and squeezed my leg.

"Yeah," I said. Maybe it was just the beautiful girl next to me, but this felt good. It felt right. The road was open before us, and it seemed filled with possibility.

16
Follow the Yellow Dotted Line

+++++++

WE DROVE FROM Pittsburgh to Indianapolis that day. To save money, we slept in the car at a rest stop that night.

"No hot leg viewing for Boy tonight!" Sophie said as we settled into our reclined seats. Then she winked at me like it was our little joke. I couldn't tell if she didn't realize that I was developing a crush on her, or if she *did* realize and was actually making fun of me.

The next morning as we were getting back on the road, I asked, "So where are you from?"

"Venus," she said.

"Ha. Seriously."

"You don't believe in extraterrestrials?"

"Do I believe they exist somewhere out there in infinite space? Yes. Do I think they're hanging out around our solar system, occasionally sneaking over to steal a cow or probe someone's ass? No."

"Arse-probing gets a bad rap," she said.

"Do you just not want to talk about it?"

"What, arse-probing? We can talk about it all you want. It just didn't sound like you were interested."

"No, I mean talking about where you're from. Why, is it some major secret?"

"I'd tell you," she said, "but then I'd have to probe your arse."

"Never mind."

We drove on in silence for a little while.

Then Sophie said, "So who was the girl?"

"What girl?"

"That one girl you slept with."

"Forget it. I'm not telling you."

"Well, it's going to be a very dull road trip if you refuse to dish the whole ride."

"I'll tell you, if you tell me where you're from."

She rolled her eyes. "Lame. Look, it's not a big secret or anything. It's just that dwelling on the past a lot brings out Claire McGrumpypants and I'm not ready to go back in my box yet."

"I thought you guys had a schedule or something."

"Sort of. But it's loose, right? Because I'm better at some things and she's better at others."

"Like?"

"Like road trips. She hates road trips. So if we changed right now, she'd just be miserable, anyway."

"What's it like? Being in your 'box'?"

She shrugged. "Hard to explain."

"I'm a pretty smart guy. I might get it."

"Imagine being in someone else's body, feeling what they feel, but not in the *way* they feel it. Hearing their thoughts, knowing they hear yours."

"Do you and Claire like each other? I mean, do you get along?"

"Sometimes. When she's not being a royal bitch." She smirked suddenly, and I could almost imagine Claire silently fuming somewhere inside their brain.

"Does that make any sense?" she asked.

"Some," I said. "I have my own weird brain stuff."

"Oh, yeah? Like what?"

"I can disconnect my emotions."

"What, like make it so you don't feel anything?" Her eyes grew wide.

"Yeah."

She was silent for a moment, then in a strangely subdued voice she said, "That sounds fucking brilliant."

"But it's just temporary. It builds up, and when you reconnect, it all hits you at once."

"Ouch. Never mind."

"Exactly. My dad has to do it every night for The Show. It's what makes him immune to all the magic. So if Medusa or the Siren or whoever loses control, he just steps in and takes care of it."

"And every night he has to deal with the backlash?"

"Yeah. My mom tries to help him through it, but . . . there's only so much she can do."

"Sounds dreadful."

"Yeah. But he just takes it, you know? Pisses me off. That's one of the reasons I had to leave. I did it once, so I know how awful it is. It comes back to you like a nightmare, where you see and feel things, and you remember your actions almost like they were someone else's. This other you, cold, hard, and unfeeling, and he's in control." I shuddered as a light flash of the pain ghosted up my neck. "There's no way I'd do it every night like he does. No way in hell."

We drove on for a while in silence, the farmland giving way to suburban clusters and shopping centers.

"What about *your* parents?" I asked.

"Oh, shit!"

"What?"

"Shopping mall. We're taking a detour."

"What? You're not serious."

"I'm completely serious. I need new clothes desperately." She looked over at me critically. "You could use a little something yourself."

"We barely have enough money for gas and food to get us to New Mexico," I said. But we were already turning off the interstate and taking the exit ramp into a massive shopping complex. "Is this because I brought up your parents?"

"You got me, Dr. Boy!" she said cheerfully as she hiked the wheel suddenly and jammed us into a parking spot. "Now, let's conduct some retail therapy, shall we?"

I'd never been in a mall before, and I had to admit that I was curious to see what they were really like. So I followed her through the tinted glass doors of the front entrance.

It turns out a mall is like an indoor Times Square. Big posters, lots of flashing lights, packs of people everywhere. There were even random carts full of stupid crap you don't need, just like the kind you see on 42nd Street. About the only difference was how much cleaner it was. Everything was polished and shiny, fake marble, glass, brass, brushed metal. It all gleamed slickly in the harsh, unnatural light.

Well, there was one other difference.

"What is up with these people?" I muttered as I followed Sophie into a clothes store full of faceless aerodynamic mannequins.

"What do you mean?"

"They're all staring at me like I have two heads."

"Come on, Boy, what were you expecting? You look like

something out of a Tim Burton movie. Just ignore them."

"People never stared at me like this in New York."

"That's because no self-respecting New Yorker would be caught dead with a look of surprise or shock on their face. But believe me, they were all staring at you in their subtle, New Yorker, peripheral-vision kind of way."

"Yeah, well, we can't all be pretty like you."

"Whoa, what are you on about?" She seemed surprised I was getting upset. "Look, I'm not saying it's a bad thing. I *love* your stitch-punk look. But you asked why people were staring at you, and that's the answer."

"Thanks," I said. "I'm going to go walk around. I'll meet you at the car later." I needed a little break from Sophie. I was suddenly starting to see why Claire found her so annoying.

"Sure, I'll catch you later," I heard her say as I walked back out into the main hallway.

People just wouldn't stop staring. Some of them even came to a dead stop and started talking to each other. "Did you ever see anything like that?" or "What the hell happened to him?" Like I couldn't hear them. Or maybe they assumed that since I was big and ugly, I must be stupid, too.

I started to get this claustrophobic feeling, eyes pressing in on me from all sides. I had this urge to sprint down the hallway and crash through the doors. Of course that would send some of those people into a panic. I could almost see them picking up torches and pitchforks, cornering me in some trendy accessories store.

Then I caught sight of a computer store. My people. Without even thinking, I went in. It was so nice to be back among the tech I knew. My hand ran across a smooth PC tower casing. It had been over a month since I'd even touched a computer, and I didn't realize until that moment how much I missed it. It didn't even get me down that "my people," the actual other computer people in the room, were staring at me just as much as everyone else. I ignored them as I made my way to the high-end gaming machines. I read off their specs like it was a recipe for my favorite food. I would have given anything to have my custom USB jacks. But I'd lost those back when my apartment in New York blew up.

Thinking of that made me pause my geek bliss for a moment. I really shouldn't be in here. I didn't know how far VI's reach was. It was better to be safe than sorry.

But God, I missed computers. If I was really careful and connected through an encrypted tunnel for a few minutes, just long enough to check email and my old IRC channels, how could she possibly catch me?

But less than a minute after I connected, a big red pop-up appeared on the screen:

FUCKER

Then all the lights in the store went out. There were about fifteen people in there with me who had been more or less staring at me since I came in. When the mall went dark, they all started talking at once. But then there was a short burst of noise over the PA speakers and everyone went quiet. A moment later, every TV and computer monitor in the store came to life, displaying a plain white square. Naturally, everyone looked at it. Everyone but me. Not that I knew what was happening, but I just had this feeling that looking at the screens was bad. This was VI, after all. Was it ever good?

I could see in the window reflections and at the edge of my peripheral vision that there was some kind of strobe-light sequence on the screens. I looked at the faces of the people watching it and they were totally mesmerized.

A minute later, it was over. The flickering screens stopped, the lights came back on and I wondered if whatever VI had tried to do hadn't worked.

But then the people in the store all turned to look at me. Their faces curled up in snarls of rage, and then they all attacked me at once.

Individually, I could have handled them easily. But fifteen very fragile humans coming at you at once makes it impossible to protect both yourself and them. I blocked their punches and kicks, or just took them when I couldn't, and that wasn't too bad. But then they started chucking big computer parts at me. And finally one of them began lighting things on fire, and that's when I knew I was really screwed. Fire is basically my Kryptonite. Because as tough as I am, stitches are very flammable.

I tried to fight my way to the door, but there was a wall of clawing flesh and bone in front of me. I tried shoving them, or hurting them in little ways, but they seemed totally indifferent to minor pain. I was going to have to start breaking people if I wanted to get out of there alive.

"Boy!"

I looked up and saw Sophie standing in the doorway, holding a big shopping bag.

"Help!" I said, pushing a screaming woman off me.

But the way she stared at me, her eyes wide with fear, I could tell she couldn't help me. Sophie wasn't cut out for stuff like this. She was utterly terrified.

And then the wall of people fell on me all at once and I went under. Tense, sweaty flesh pressed against me on all sides. I realized I probably wasn't going to burn to death. I was going to suffocate. I pushed as hard as I could, no longer holding back. But it was too late now. Even at full strength, I couldn't force my way out. I screamed. But they pressed down harder and screamed back. I was going to be killed by a mass of brainwashed computer geeks.

But then the weight began to lift. People went flying one by one, crashing into counters, walls, windows. An unnaturally strong hand grabbed my forearm and hauled me up to a standing position.

Claire stood in front of me, breathing hard, Sophie's smaller-sized clothing stretched painfully tight on her athletic body.

"What the hell just happened here?" she yelled at me.

"I'll tell you in the car," I said.

She looked like she wanted to yell at me some more, but she nodded tersely, shoved one of the struggling humans back down, and walked out of the store, not waiting to see if I was following.

WHEN WE REACHED the car, Claire tossed me the keys. "You drive. I've gotta change into something that actually fits me before I lose all feeling in my legs."

"I've never driven before," I protested as I slid into the unfamiliar driver's seat.

"Gas, brake, steer. Follow the yellow line. It's not rocket science." She climbed into the backseat. "Time for you to learn, anyway. You're mad if you think I'm going to drive all the way to New Mexico myself. And if I catch you looking back here while I'm changing, I'll hit you so hard it'll pop your stitches."

My first time driving was a little touch and go, especially since I couldn't use the rearview mirror. Plus, my hands were still a little shaky from the mall incident. Somehow VI had been able to hack into the brains of those humans through their visual cortexes. Obviously, it wasn't as fine-tuned a method as the audio attack she'd deployed at the rest stop in New Jersey. In fact, it seemed to be limited to "Make them crazy, turn them loose." But now she had two ways to control humans. And I was pretty sure that if there were more ways possible, VI would figure them out eventually.

"So." Claire climbed into the front passenger seat. She wore a plain white T-shirt and a pair of nylon running pants. "I'm going to ask you again. What the hell just happened?"

There really wasn't any other way to do it, so I told her everything. If there was even a possibility that this might happen again, she had a right to know. I told her about The Show and about my fight with Shaun and about my dad's plan to send me to Switzerland. I told her about how I left, and about Gauge, and what I thought was my failed great experiment. I told her about Liel and about VI. She listened to everything without comment. I really appreciated that. And when I was finished, she just stared off into the horizon for a while.

Finally, she said, "Don't you think it would have been a good idea to tell me about the crazy AI stalker *before* we began this road trip?"

"Yeah," I said. "I'm sorry. It's just . . . god, it makes me feel like an idiot whenever I think about it."

"Idiot? I think you mean arsehole."

"What do you mean by that?"

"You could have handled the whole thing a lot better. You could have handled *her* a lot better."

"What was I supposed to do? By the time I talked to her, she'd already become this crazy thing."

"Crazy? Maybe just terribly immature with way too much

power. I mean, she's like a superintelligent toddler, right? Desperate to please, throwing tantrums when she doesn't get her way. And it sounds to me like there were a couple of points where you could have talked her back down. Believe it or not, most people *want* to be talked down from a homicidal rage."

"What do you know? You weren't there."

"I bloody well know what it's like to be labeled a 'bad creation.' I've seen arsehole creators before, mate. And from where I'm sitting, the way you treated her seems a lot like the way Victor treated your dad."

"How can you possibly say that? Victor *abandoned* my dad. I never abandoned VI. I didn't even know she existed!"

"But when she came back to you, all confused and misguided, you immediately put the 'bad' stamp on her."

"Because she *did bad things*. She had my roommate thrown in prison. She threatened my girlfriend. She used humans as puppets. She even killed some of them."

"So did your dad, didn't he? Strangled nearly everyone in Victor's family, if the stories I've heard are true. And I think you'd agree that your father deserved a second chance. So maybe she does, too. I can't believe you of all people can't see that."

"Why me of all people?"

"Because you're creation *and* creator. Shouldn't that make you sensitive to both sides? But instead, you apparently *hate* both sides. So where does that leave you, eh? Christ, I thought *I* was the most self-loathing person I knew, but you bloody well take the biscuit. Cheers."

I drove on in silence, not really trusting myself to speak. The anger burned up through my face and down into my hands. The steering wheel creaked from the pressure. She didn't know anything about me, or my family, or the Frankensteins, or VI. She was just one of those people who liked to kick others while they were down.

The hours went by, and neither of us spoke. The vast, flat Kansas farmlands slid past on either side, never changing. Two days before, when Mozart and I had been driving through Pennsylvania, the scenery had changed constantly, and it had given me a kind of peace. But here, on these endless plains, it wasn't like that. There was no way to gauge our progress. It felt like we weren't even moving. For all I knew, we were on a treadmill. Like nothing we did made any difference.

WE'D JUST CROSSED into Oklahoma when Claire broke the long silence to mutter that she was hungry. She pointed to a little roadside country diner.

"Really?" I asked. "That place?"

"I like Americana," she said flatly. "Chicken-fried steak, biscuits and gravy, that sort of thing. You got a problem with that?"

The truth was, I'd never had country stuff before. This whole rural Midwest area made me feel a little uncomfortable. Like I was too "urban" to fit in here. Not tough and manly enough, I guess. I knew that was dumb. I'd survived a lot of stuff. I could handle myself. But I couldn't help feeling like there would be some unshaven cowboy type who was going to say some cheesy line about me being a "soft, city boy."

I was also worried there'd be more staring. I was really not in the mood for more staring.

But what could I do? We were both hungry, and it wasn't like I was going to admit my nervousness to Claire. She'd be all over that.

So I just said, "Whatever. It's fine," and pulled into the parking lot.

It was a narrow place with wood paneling, small booths along one wall, and a long, white Formica bar along the other. A few guys were at the bar drinking coffee, and an old couple sat off in a booth in the corner.

We sat down in a booth by a window and looked through the menus. It was pretty simple, so it didn't take long to read cover to cover. Then we just stared out at the empty Oklahoma plains as the clouds gathered for an afternoon storm. I wasn't sure how much longer we were going to do the not-talking thing, but I wasn't going to be the one to break it. In the silence, there was only the distant clink of dishes and the whiny steel guitar sound of a country song on the radio.

Claire closed her eyes and breathed deeply. "I love American country music."

"Really?" I asked.

"You don't?"

"Not all Americans like country."

"It's not just for Americans, anyway." She turned back to the window. The clouds grew darker and the grass on the plains bent down in waves. The music played on, some guy singing about his pickup truck breaking down or something. I didn't get it. I guess I didn't get a lot of things.

Finally, I asked. "Why do you like it? Country music."

"It's about loss."

"A lost truck?"

"Sure, there's the obvious layer. Lost money, lost possessions, lost love. But it's more than just that. This guy is thinking, 'Everything would be okay if I could just get this bloody truck working again.' Of course, deep down, he knows that it actually wouldn't help all that much. But that's all he can handle thinking about. The rest is too big. Too complicated. If he looked directly at the gigantic pit that swallowed his life, he'd probably just go mad. Country music is about when life isn't simple anymore. It's about innocence taken away too early, too harshly. It's about losing the things you can't get back."

I hadn't been expecting a response like that from her. Something that open. I was thinking of telling her that, when the waitress came over. She was a middle-aged human in an apron, a little heavyset, her brown hair streaked with gray and pulled back in a bun. She looked tired. But she smiled as she looked at Claire and said, "What can I get you, sweetie?"

"I'll have the chicken-fried steak, please," said Claire. Her politeness surprised me, too.

"You've got one pretty accent, there, miss," said the waitress, her eyes lighting up.

"Er, thanks," said Claire.

"Where you from?"

"London."

"In England, right?"

"Yeah," said Claire.

The waitress frowned for a moment, then said, "Sorry, darlin', we ain't got any hot tea."

Claire smiled slightly at that. "I like coffee just fine."

"Oh, well, we got plenty of that. So what brings you all the way out here?"

"I like it here," Claire said. "Lot more space than back home." Her accent was getting a little thicker and I realized she was playing it up for the waitress. She seemed to enjoy being seen as exotic.

"Well, bless your heart," said the waitress. "You got that right, we got plenty of space. I love that *Downtown Abbey* show, don't you?"

"Sorry, haven't seen it," said Claire. "I don't watch the telly much."

"Wish more kids were like that," said the waitress. "My kids, seems like that's all they do."

Then she turned to me and I braced myself for the inevitable look of surprise or shock or disgust when she took in my stitches. But it didn't come. In fact, I was the one who probably looked surprised. I couldn't see it before because she'd been turned toward Claire, but now that I was looking at her dead on, I saw that she had a huge burn mark on the side of her face.

"And what about you?" she asked me.

"Uh, I'm not from England," I said.

She turned back to Claire and smirked. "Fine-lookin' fella you got here, but he ain't too bright, is he?"

"Not especially, no," said Claire, also smirking.

The waitress turned back to me. "Sweetie, I meant what do you want to *eat*?"

"Oh," I said. "I guess I'll have the same thing."

"Good choice." She winked at me. Then she went back to the kitchen.

"I like her," said Claire.

"Because she said I was dumb," I said.

"That too." She smiled again briefly. "But also, she didn't even flinch at your stitches."

"You noticed that?" I asked.

"Of course."

A moment later, the waitress was back with coffee. A muted peal of thunder made her glance out the window at the purple clouds flickering with lightening. "Bad-lookin' storm out there.

Good thing you're in here where it's safe." Then she was gone again.

Claire curled her long fingers around her coffee cup and brought it up to her face. She inhaled deeply. Then she put it down, ripped open three packets of sugar, and poured them in.

"Not so bad here, is it," she said.

"No," I said. "It's nice, actually. Good call."

We sat and drank coffee and watched the storm for a while. The sky was as dark as night and when the sheets of rain came down, they blew almost horizontal. I'd seen storms before, but this was something different. All that space with nothing to stop the winds. This was tornado country, after all.

"I guess there's probably something you should know," said Claire.

"What?" I said.

"You asked earlier about Sophie and my parents."

"Yeah, Sophie really didn't want to talk about it. That's what got us sidetracked to the mall."

"There's no easy way to say this. So I'm just going to lay it all out. Do you know much about my family?"

"Not really," I admitted.

"Probably for the best. You don't have a lot of assumptions. So Henry Jekyll was Sophie's granddad. He was tired of being a goody-goody all the time. He wanted to be a bad arse. Cause some trouble, you know? But he still wanted to go to heaven and all that. So he created a potion that split his positive and negative sides into two different people in the same body: Dr. Jekyll and my granddad, Mr. Edward Hyde. Initially, Jekyll thought it was just a way to cheat. To have his cake and eat it, too. And he thought he could control my granddad. He'd let him go on a bender, get pissed, shag a prostitute. My granddad basically screwed as many slags as he could afford. Which, with Jekyll's money, was a lot. Spread their messed-up split personality seed all over London. But he didn't want any grandkids to haunt him, so he made sure there weren't any. Usually, by kicking the pregnant moms in the belly to make them miscarry."

"Whoa."

"Yeah. Exactly. He was a bastard. So Jekyll, being a fine, upstanding English gentleman, was like, 'Right, that's enough of that!' And he vowed never to take the potion again. But what he didn't realize was that he'd used the potion so many times, it had altered him permanently. He didn't need it to change anymore. He would fall asleep as Jekyll and wake up as Hyde. And that's when he started to lose control. When Hyde really started to run amuck."

She took a slow sip of her coffee, her eyes on the distant storm.

"Fortunately, Jekyll decided to man up and kill them both before Hyde got a chance to kick our grandmum in her pregnant belly. So our mums were born, but without fathers. Maybe it would have helped to have someone around who understood what it was like to be two people sharing the same body. Maybe then our mums wouldn't have been so messed up. As it was, they were in and out of mental hospitals all through childhood. At one point, my mum went into a serious depression. She just hid inside and left everything for Sophie's mum to deal with. And for a while that actually worked out. Sophie's mum met our dad. He was a really nice, normal bloke. A banker. Made a decent amount of money. They had their first baby, our older brothers, Robert and Stephen. And it was weird, of course, what with having a baby that changed between two people at random, but they made it work. My mum would show up now and then, but mostly she just let Sophie's mum play homemaker and pretend they were normal humans."

Claire stared out the window for a while as the storm continued to lash the plains, her expression unreadable. I wondered if maybe Sophie was telling her to shut up. Finally, she said, "But once Sophie and I were born, everything changed. Sophie's mum went into some kind of postpartum depression, and suddenly, it was *my* mum who was in charge all the time. But my mum didn't get along with our dad. They fought all the time. Sophie's mum eventually got over her depression and tried to patch things up all around. But it was too late by then. Dad was sick to death of all the dual-personality crap, and especially sick of my mum. Things continued to get worse until one night they were fighting and my mum just lost it."

Her face was tense as she stirred her coffee, the spoon clinking against the side of the mug.

"She killed our dad."

She carefully placed the spoon on the table and took a sip of her coffee.

"I'm sorry," I said.

"I'm not done." She looked up at me. "That was just for context. This is the part you need to know. Our mums are back in a mental hospital. But that's as much for their protection as anything else. Because Sophie's brother, Robert, wants to kill my mum."

"But wouldn't that kill *his* mom, too?"

"No, he thinks he's found a way to kill only one side."

"Has he?"

"It looks like it. I haven't seen or heard from Stephen in over five years. None of us can go that long without a switch."

"He killed his other half?"

"Yeah, and he wants to kill *all* the Hydes. Including me."

"Oh."

"Yeah."

"He's out there somewhere looking for you, isn't he?"

"Yep."

"So . . . we're both running."

"Seems so."

The waitress appeared, sliding two plates of chicken-fried steak in gravy onto the table.

"There you go, folks. Enjoy," she said.

"Cheers," said Claire quietly.

We ate in silence, but it wasn't an angry silence anymore. I didn't know what kind of silence it was now. Maybe the scared kind.

Eventually, the storm died down and the sun broke through the thick cloud bank to shine on the glittering wet grass.

"Well," I said. "Maybe we'll be able to figure something out once we get to New Mexico. Mozart said the Sphinx is, like, the wisest creature on the planet. I'm hoping he can help me out with VI. Maybe he'll have some idea about what to do about Robert."

"Sure, Scarecrow!" Claire said in a goofy, American accent. "And maybe while we're there, he'll give Sophie some courage, me a heart, and you a brain!"

"Aaaand moment ruined," I said. "Well done."

"Thanks," she said. "It's a talent of mine."

17
Bad Lands

I WASN'T READY for the heat. As we moved from the plains into the desert, sunlight no longer felt like the gentle, life-giving rarity I'd come to love. Instead, it was relentless, hard, and mean. Sophie had spent so much of our money on clothes that we were in danger of running out of gas money before we got to The Commune. Claire said we'd use less gas if we didn't run the air-conditioning, so we kept it off. We started to get grumpy. We argued a lot about stupid things, like who would pick the radio station or who was drinking more water. Then we stopped talking altogether and the only sound was the hot wind as it whipped through the open windows.

But finally, with less than a quarter tank of gas and almost zero patience between us, we got to the place Mozart had marked on the map. Except there was nothing there.

Claire was behind the wheel again. She pulled the car over onto the dusty shoulder and cut the engine. We both stared through the dirty windshield at the rugged, dry land dotted with scrub brush.

"That daft old wolf," she muttered.

"Maybe it's just off the road a bit." I climbed out of the car.

"Or maybe the local humans got wise, killed them all, and burned the place to the ground." Claire climbed out, too.

I looked around at the miles of barren wasteland around us.

"What local humans?" I asked.

The wind pushed the hot, dry air in our faces and tugged at our clothes.

"Unbelievable," Claire muttered under her breath, then sat on the hood of the car. "Ah, shite that's hot!" She stood up immediately, rubbing her butt. "Great, just fucking great." She shaded her eyes with her hand as she scanned the desert horizon. "Stranded in the bloody desert with a scorned, AI stalker chick about to descend on us with a horde of brainwashed humans."

"Would you chill?" I said. "This is the perfect place to hide from her. I bet there's not even a cell signal out here. No tech, no VI."

"So this is your plan, then?" she said. "Avoid computers and cell phones? Just how long do you think you can keep that up?"

"I don't know. That's why I want to ask the Sphinx for advice. Maybe we can stay here for a while. . . ."

"We can't even *find* here!" she said. "It probably doesn't even exist anymore."

"Let's just walk for a little bit." I grabbed the big jug of water we'd been sharing. "Maybe it's all underground, and they have a hidden entrance or something."

"Oh, right," she said and rolled her eyes.

"You got a better idea? I'm pretty sure we don't have enough gas to get us to the next town, so we'd better hope we can find *something* out here." I slung the jug over my shoulder and started walking. A minute later I heard her heavy footsteps crunching behind me.

We walked for a while, Claire grumbling quietly to herself. Eventually, we saw what looked like a small mountain up ahead.

"Maybe there's a cave or something there," I said.

Claire looked over to where the sun was beginning to slip down below the horizon. "It's starting to get late. Maybe we should head back to the car, catch some sleep, and come back in the morning."

"And walk this whole thing all over again? Come on, we're already more than halfway there."

"I don't know . . . I think it's farther than it looks. And anyway, once the sun sets it's going to get cold."

"That's a bad thing? I'm dying in this heat."

She didn't say anything, just chewed her lip and continued to stare at the slowly setting sun. Her anger from earlier seemed to have disappeared, replaced by something I hadn't seen in her before.

"What is it?" I asked. "You're getting a little weird on me."

She shrugged. "I guess I just feel out of my element. I'm not really a nature person."

"I thought you loved country stuff."

"I love to enjoy the ambiance from a comfortable booth, preferably with a coffee."

"Well, I'm not exactly a nature person, either. But really, the last thing I want to do right now is get back in the car."

"Yeah," she admitted.

"What's the worst that could happen?" I asked. "We've still got plenty of water, so we're not going to die of thirst. So we sleep out on the ground under the stars for a night. That actually sounds kind of cool."

"I guess so."

"Plus, once it gets dark, we'll know for sure if there are people out there because we'll probably be able to see lights."

"Fine," she said. "But if I hear something that sounds even remotely like a rattlesnake, I'm out."

The sun turned an angry blood red as it began to drop behind the horizon. We walked on for a while longer, but the mountain didn't seem to get any closer. Night fell fast, the sky shifting from red to a dark purple. There were no streetlights or business signs out here. Nothing but faint starlight and a sickly sliver of moon. I started to get the sense of just how dark it would be once the sun set completely, and I wondered if sleeping out in the open desert wasn't such a great idea after all.

Suddenly, Claire stopped.

"Did you hear that?" she asked.

"What?"

"Shhh!"

At first, I didn't hear anything except the wind whistling through the scrub brush. Then, I picked out something else underneath. At first, it was so faint that I thought I might be imagining it. But as the last light of the sun disappeared and the sky went completely black, it got louder.

"Is that . . ." I whispered. "Is that someone *crying*?"

The darkness was so thick that I could only see a few feet in any direction. The crying gradually got more intense until it drowned out the hissing night wind.

"Boy!" Claire hissed, and stabbed her finger at the air in front of us.

About ten feet ahead I saw a shape that I knew hadn't been there a moment before. It looked like a woman. She stood with her head bowed so that her long, dark hair fell in her face. Her arms hung loosely at her sides. It was impossible to tell in the darkness, but her hands appeared to be covered with something like dark paint. And she was crying. Not a gentle weeping but thick, choking sobs that shook her whole body.

I looked at Claire for some idea what we should do, but she just stared at the crying woman, her eyes wide.

I turned back to the woman. "Are you okay?" My voice sounded higher than normal.

Her sobs quieted somewhat, but her head was still bowed and her shoulders shook even harder, like she was fighting to keep it inside.

"Miss?" I tried again. "Do . . . you need help?"

Slowly, her head began to rise. Her long, dark hair parted to reveal a pale, beautiful face streaked with tears of blood. Her luminous white eyes quivered in their sockets, showing only pinpoint black pupils.

"H-h-h-h . . ." she choked between sobs. "He-he-he-he . . ."

She lifted her hands up in front of her and I could tell now it wasn't paint on them. They were covered in blood.

"Boy . . ." said Claire, her voice on the edge of panic.

"Hel-hel-hel-hel," said the woman. Then her face shifted suddenly from misery to fury and she screamed, "HEEEEEEEEELLLLLP!"

The sound ripped through me like electricity. Every muscle in my body seized up. I couldn't move, or speak, or even breathe. Out of the corner of my eye, I saw Claire tip over like a plank of wood. Then my vision narrowed and spots floated in front of my eyes. I saw, more than felt, my own body begin to tip forward. The last thing I remembered was the weeping woman's blood-drenched hands reaching out for me. Then there was only darkness.

━━━

I WOKE UP. That was a surprise right there. I really thought this was it.

Although when I tried to move, for a moment I wished I *was* dead. My entire body felt like one giant sore muscle.

"Oh, shit," I wheezed.

"No, you did that already," came a clear, piercing voice.

I tried to open my eyes, then realized they were already open.

"I can't see!" I shouted.

"Your sight will return soon," said the same voice, sounding a little bored.

It felt like I was lying in a cot, those metal-framed canvas ones you see in old movies with scenes in military hospitals. A thin, wool blanket covered me, which was good because I was completely naked.

"What the hell happened to my clothes?" I asked.

"I just told you," said the voice. "You shit all over yourself. Don't feel bad. That's typical for *La Llorona's* victims. Whoever created you did a fine job with your construction. A lesser-made flesh golem would have torn himself apart during the seizures."

"Flesh golem? What's that?"

There was an audible sigh, like the speaker couldn't believe he had to even explain it. "Why, *you* of course."

"The only 'golem' I've ever heard of was that Jewish guy in Prague. And he was made of mud and powered by the name of God or something. That's not what makes me go." My vision was starting to come back a little. Instead of a big, black blob, the person in front of me was now a big, gray blob with a few black blobs floating in it.

"The method is hardly the point here," said the speaker. "Neither is the material of construction, for that matter. A golem can be made out of almost anything—mud, flesh, metal, wood. I even saw one made of solid gold once, although that was impractical to the point of being downright tragic. Gold looks nice, but it's far too soft and heavy. The poor thing was utterly useless. And a golem can be animated by any number of means. This is, of course, not to imply that they are easy to construct. At least, not ones that last. And you, my boy, may be the finest construction I've ever seen. You took the shock of *La Llorona's* voice most manfully." The speaker paused for a second, and there was a strange clicking sound. Then, "That's merely a figure of speech, of course. There are no literal men around here."

"*La Llorona?*" My vision was clearing more. I could make out shapes and color now. Although I still couldn't quite make out what kind of person I was talking to.

"Yes, *La Llorona*. The creature you met at the gates last night. A word of advice, my boy. It's generally not wise to startle a banshee."

"A banshee? I guess that explains it. We were just trying to help, that's all."

"Banshees rarely are interested in things like that, and *La Llorona* even less so. She is a special case. And quite mad since she murdered her children, I'm afraid. Although she does make an excellent sentry, as you and your companion discovered."

"My companion? Claire!" I sat up, then I winced as pain flashed through my body. "Is she okay?"

"The human?" the speaker asked, a tinge of disgust in the voice. "She'll live."

"She's not human."

"No? She certainly *looks* human."

"Trust me. She's not. And I hope you guys didn't treat her bad. Because she's kind of—"

There was a sudden, loud crash, followed by cursing and yelling.

"That would be Claire." I tried to get up, but a clawed hand held me in place. It felt like bird talons, only a lot bigger.

"You're not fully recovered yet. And I'm sure they have the situation well in hand."

"You don't know Claire. You really have to let me go talk her down before she flips out."

"Believe me, we can handle just about anything."

Then all at once, my vision slipped into place. In front of me stood a full-sized gryphon, with the body of a lion, and the head, front legs, and wings of a gigantic eagle. He lounged next to my cot with his lion hind legs curled up under him, and his eagle eyes gazed down at me without any expression I could read.

"Whoa," I said.

"Indeed," said the gryphon, still eyeing me coldly. "My name is Knossos. Welcome to The Commune."

There was another crash, and more cursing and yelling.

"Let me go to her. Please. She's probably totally freaked out right now. I know I could calm her down in no time. Why put her through this if you don't have to?"

Knossos sighed, clacking his curved beak as he preened his feathers. Then he slowly stood up, shook himself, and walked toward an oversized open doorway. "Let's go then, before she breaks anything else. Glass isn't easy to make by hand, you know."

He passed through the doorway, then paused and turned his head over his furry shoulder to fix me with his eagle eyes. "I mean that colloquially, of course. Few of us at The Commune actually have hands."

I stood up, cinching my blanket around my waist like a sarong. As I followed him through the doorway and into the off-white stucco hallway, I felt small. Literally. Because the doorway we had passed through was about the size of a barn door, and the hallway we entered was even bigger. The ceiling was about twenty-five feet high and the hallway was about thirty or forty feet across. Obviously, things would need to be bigger than a regular human building to accommodate a gryphon. But not *this* much bigger. I wondered what creature lived here that needed that much space. I also wondered how they were hiding all of this out here in this flat, barren desert. Assuming that's where we still were. I hadn't seen a single window yet.

We heard more cursing and banging down the hall. It seemed to be coming from a couple doors down.

"And you choose to travel with this person?" asked Knossos.

"She isn't always like this. She's . . . sort of a shape-shifter." I wasn't sure if I should go around telling people exactly who she was, especially if her psycho brother was out there somewhere looking for her.

"What does form have to do with it?"

"Uh, her identity changes with her form."

"I see," he said, although it didn't sound like he was all that interested.

As we walked past an open doorway, I glanced in, mostly looking for windows. In the room was a creature that looked like something between a lizard and a kangaroo, but with a panther face, sitting at a big, old-fashioned sewing loom.

Once we were passed the doorway, I said, "What was—"

"Chupacabra," said Knossos.

"I thought that was an urban—"

"Myth? Aren't we all?" He shook his feathered head.

"Although poor Javier may be the last of his kind. So perhaps the word is not so far off where he is concerned."

We finally reached the next doorway. Only two doors down from the room I was in, but it had to have been fifty yards or more. My legs and back had gone from sore to painful again. Knossos had been right. I wasn't really up to this yet. But I had to calm Claire down. I hated to think how they were treating her, especially if they thought she was human.

As I looked into the room, I saw it was even worse than I'd thought. They had her strapped down to some kind of elevated gurney. She was naked and bruised and screaming like an animal. She'd managed to rip one restraint off, and a centaur was holding her arm in place.

He looked at us with relief. "A little help, huh?"

I don't know why that set me off, but it did. The anger burst into my arms, washing away the pain and pretty much every ounce of patience and rational thought I had. I charged into the room, grabbed him by both shoulders, and shoved him away from her. Of course, shoving someone with the lower body of a horse isn't exactly easy. His hooves only skidded a few feet back on the tiles.

"What the hell?" he said, and came at me. I grabbed him and threw him down to one side.

"Back the fuck off!" I shouted. Then I turned to Claire. She was still screaming and flailing around. She nearly punched me in the face. "Claire, it's okay," I shouted over her screams. "It's Boy. I'm here. Everything's going to be okay."

Her eyes blinked rapidly and she looked up at me.

"Boy?" she said, like she was having trouble remembering.

"Yeah, Claire it's me. We made it to Oz. Remember? Finding brains and hearts and stuff? This is The Commune."

"They . . ." Her face crumpled. "I'm . . . Why am I tied up? Why am I naked? Why am I hurt?"

"Get me something to cover her," I snapped at the centaur. He stared up at me stupidly from the floor where I'd thrown him. "NOW!"

He scrambled awkwardly onto all four legs and started rummaging around in a cabinet set into the wall.

Claire had gone limp and was making strange keening sounds deep in her throat. "I got you," I said as I quickly removed the restraints, trying not to look at her nakedness. "Everything's okay now."

"I thought. . . ." she whispered.

As the restraints came off, she fell limply into my arms, pressing her face against my bare chest. The centaur threw me a thin, wool blanket like the kind I had around my waist and I wrapped her tightly in it. She was shivering uncontrollably now, like she was going into shock.

"You're okay now," I said over and over again as I stroked her smooth, black hair.

"I thought it was Robert," she said into my chest. "That he caught me, that I was being *removed*."

"No, no, it was all just a stupid misunderstanding," I said, glaring at the centaur. "It's all cleared up now. I got you."

The blanket wrapped around her began to loosen and I noticed her feeling lighter. Then she slowly shifted into Sophie in my arms.

"Oh, hey," said the centaur. "She's not human, is she?"

"Obviously," said Knossos, who had remained in the doorway throughout the exchange. "I think we've made rather a mess of things, Rhoecus. The Dragon Lady will want to know about this."

A LITTLE WHILE later, Sophie and I were back in the plain, off-white, windowless room I woke up in. We had our clothes back, but of course Claire's clothes didn't really fit Sophie. The T-shirt hung down on her like a nightshirt and she had to roll up the running pants so many times it looked like she had doughnuts around her ankles. She wasn't acting like the perky, never-take-anything-seriously Sophie that I knew, either. She sat next to me on the cot, staring at the terra-cotta tile floor, her shoulder nestled into me. Every once in a while, a shiver ran through her.

"You okay?" I asked.

She shrugged, not looking at me. "I didn't want to be out."

"You mean, you didn't want to switch with Claire?"

"Yeah."

"So why did you?"

"She made me."

It never occurred to me that sometimes they fought not for who got out, but for who stayed in.

"She's always been the stronger one," said Sophie. "When she wants to be."

"Why did she think Robert got her? I mean, I'm assuming he doesn't look much like a centaur."

"It was the strapped down to a gurney creepy science thing. The last time we saw Robert, he had us strapped down like that. He . . . did things to us."

"Oh," I said. "I'm sorry."

She brought her knees up to her chest and pulled the oversized T-shirt tight across her shins. "He's why we ran away from home. We just couldn't take it anymore. After Claire's mom killed our dad, Robert got obsessed with the idea of purging the Hyde out of us. He would stay locked up in his lab for days at a time. We never saw Stephen. But sometimes, late at night, we would hear him in their room, crying, begging Robert to leave him alone. Swearing he'd never come out again. He'd just hide forever. But of course, you can't help it. Sometimes you don't even mean to do it or it happens while you're sleeping. We knew it. Stephen knew it. And Robert knew it. That's when the experiments started for real. When we started hearing the screaming from their room."

"Do you know what he was doing?"

"Some of it. And the stuff we saw . . ." She shuddered. "It must have hurt both of them. But he didn't stop. And when the pain got so bad that he couldn't experiment on himself anymore? That's when he started experimenting on us."

"What did he do to you?" I actually kind of didn't want to know. But it seemed like she really needed to tell somebody.

"He would give us injections." Her eyes grew distant and her tone got strangely calm. Like it was someone else's life she was remembering. "At first, he was mostly just working out ways to force the transformation. He'd strap us down to the chair thing and give us an injection that would force the transformation. Then he'd give us another injection that would make us change back. It was exhausting, but it didn't really hurt. Then he started messing with things. He'd make us start to change with one injection, and then halfway through, he'd stop us with another injection. Sometimes we'd get stuck halfway for days. Like my legs, Claire's arms. Or some other combination. It . . . hurt to stay stuck like that. It felt like slowly getting torn apart. Especially after he really started to fine-tune it and we'd get stuck with half a face each, half a heart each, a mismatched patchwork of Claire and me. And neither of us could comfort the other one because we were both in pain. It felt so . . . alone. That was awful. Being alone for the first time in my life."

She shivered again, so I put my arm around her. She felt so small and delicate. Like a bird.

"You're not alone anymore," I said. "Neither of you. I promised Adam Iron that I wouldn't abandon you."

She smiled and patted my arm. "You're a good guy, Boy."

"Yeah . . ." I said, remembering when Laurellen and Mozart told me that right before my first pathetic date with Liel. It hadn't seemed like a compliment then. I wasn't sure if it was now, either.

"Grrr, and so tough and beefy!" She squeezed my bicep with her thin fingertips, a glimmer of the old Sophie silliness showing in her eyes.

"Ow," I said. "Still sore."

The glimmer in her eyes faded. "Yeah, me too."

I brushed a corkscrew curl out of her face. "How could your own brother hurt you like that?"

"He thought he was helping me. No matter what I said, he thought I wanted to get rid of Claire as much as he wanted to get rid of Stephen. Arrogant prick. So bloody obsessed with trying to make the world perfect through science, which really just meant proving what a genius he was. It never occurred to him to consider how he was harming people along the way to achieving his 'greater good.'"

"Like his grandfather. Like a creator." It came out thick and hollow when I said it. "Like me."

She looked up at me, her forehead wrinkled. "What Claire said to you before. About you being like Victor Frankenstein. That was a terrible thing for her to say."

"But what if it's true? I've always thought of myself as one of the poor created monsters of the world. But when I think about it, it seems like I have more in common with Victor than with my dad. I never considered how VI was feeling, how I might have hurt her. Sophie, think how alone she must have felt when she was first created. How lost and scared. And if she didn't know how to care for people, if she didn't value life, maybe it's because no one ever taught her. Maybe I *am* just another asshole creator."

"I think the fact that you're troubled by it already proves that you're not," she said.

"Maybe. I just hope the Sphinx can help me find a way to make it right."

RHOECUS THE CENTAUR obviously felt badly about how he'd treated Claire earlier. He kept coming in and asking if we needed anything in this quiet, meek way. I was still a little irritated, though. What if I *had* been traveling with a human? Would he not have felt bad then? Did he think it was okay to strap people down to gurneys naked against their will as long as they were human? I really wasn't sure I wanted to have anything to do with the guy.

But Sophie found uses for him. After a lot of explanation about how Americans always screwed up tea, she got him to make her "a proper cuppa." It seemed to be as much about the cookies as the actual tea. She also got him to get her a pair of scissors so she didn't have to roll up her shirtsleeves and pants anymore. The shirt collar still slid off her shoulder a lot, but that actually looked pretty cute.

Finally, after about two hours of waiting, a tall figure suddenly loomed in the doorway.

Sophie's eyebrow shot up and she started to say, "What is—"

"Hey," I said, cutting her off. "Javier, right?"

The chupacabra nodded his panther face. *"Sí."*

"*¿Hablas inglés?*" I asked.

"*Un poquito.*" He motioned for us to follow him. "*Vámonos.*" Then he turned on long, kangaroo feet, revealing sharp spines down his back. He hopped out into the hallway, stopped, and beckoned to us again. "*Síganme. La Dama del Dragón está esperando.*"

"What the hell is that creature?" hissed Sophie in her not-so-quiet whisper. "I've never seen anything like it."

"Chupacabra, I guess. And he said he did speak *a little* English, so be nice. I think he's the last of his kind." I slowly stood up, my muscles groaning at me. Then I turned and helped Sophie up. "I have a feeling a lot of creatures here are the last of their kind."

"This whole place is alternately depressing me and freaking me out. Are you still thinking you want to stay here?"

"It was a bad first impression," I said. "Maybe there's whole other parts we just haven't seen. Other creatures more . . . our age."

"I suppose. . . ." said Sophie, raising an eyebrow.

"Well, regardless, I want to talk to the Sphinx. And apparently, we have to get to him through this Dragon Lady."

"I wonder what *she's* like."

"I'm picturing an old Chinese woman. But somehow I have a feeling that's not really it."

We followed Javier down a corridor that seemed to go on forever.

"This place is huge," I said to Sophie. "I wonder how they're concealing it from humans."

"Maybe it's underground, like you told Claire yesterday."

"I guess it could be that. It doesn't *feel* underground, though."

"How does something 'feel underground'?"

"I can't really describe it. But take it from someone who grew up mostly underground, it feels different."

Suddenly, Javier stopped.

"*Aquí,*" he said, pointing at a darkened doorway. A weird smell came from the room, something at once sharp and dank.

"Ugh," said Sophie. "We have to go in there?"

Javier nodded.

"Come on." I held out my hand to her. She slipped her slender hand into my big, clumsy one. Then we walked into the dark room.

It was hot in the room. Different from the desert heat. Thick and wet, with a smell that reminded me of the air in Medusa's dressing room, except much more intense.

We stood for a moment in the dark. I had no idea what to do or why we'd been sent into this weird, creepy room. It felt like they were purposefully trying to intimidate us.

"Hello?" I said loudly, letting a little irritation show in my voice.

There was a strange scraping sound off to one side, like scales rubbing together. Then two massive, yellow reptilian eyes appeared, glowing so brightly that they illuminated the space. The room was about the size of a gymnasium. In the center lounged a dragon. She had to be at least fifteen feet wide, with a head the size of a car. Each wing was roughly the size of a small airplane. I couldn't even guess at her length, since she was all coiled up. Her red and gold scales glittered in the light that came from her eyes, nose, and mouth.

"Dragon Lady," Sophie muttered in my ear. "Ha. Get it?"

"Hello, little monsters," said the Dragon Lady, fire licking around her lips as she spoke. "I am sorry your initial greeting was so unpleasant. We don't get visitors very often, and friendly ones even less frequently. In fact, I believe you two are our first sanctioned guests in a decade."

"Sorry we startled you," I said. Talking with a dragon felt weirdly formal. Almost epic, in a really awkward sort of way. "We didn't really have a way to let you know we were coming."

"Why *did* you come, little patchwork monster?" she asked.

"We were hoping . . . that we could talk to the Sphinx."

"Ah," she said, and fell silent. She closed her eyes for a moment so that the only light in the space came from the flickering fire in her nose and mouth. Then she opened her eyes again. "You come seeking wisdom."

"Uh, I guess," I said.

"I see." She stretched her massive front paws like a scaly cat. Each claw was as thick as a tree. "I can grant you an audience with him. But . . . it may not be what you expect."

"What do you mean?" I asked.

"You will see." Then she slowly stood up and arched her long back in a luxurious stretch. "The entrance to the Sphinx's chamber is on the opposite side of the building. It would take you a while to walk there. It will be much faster if you climb up onto my back."

"Uh, okay," I said.

She lowered herself back down to the ground. I grabbed a handful of the coarse fur that ran down her back and pulled myself up. There was no way Sophie could reach that, so I held out my hand to her. She looked hesitant for a moment, biting her lip. Then she smiled that bright Sophie smile I'd been missing and grabbed my hand. I hauled her up just as the Dragon Lady rose and swept out of the room in one single fluid motion. I felt the heat of Sophie's body press against my back and her arms wrap around my torso.

"Dragon ride!" she whispered in my ear.

The Dragon Lady flew down the hallway a lot faster than I expected. It felt like how I imagined a roller coaster would feel, except smooth and silent. And of course, there was no track to keep us from crashing. As wide as the hallway was, the walls suddenly felt way too close.

Sophie dug her pointy chin into my upper back.

"Ow!" I said.

"Relax," she said. "You're too tense. Enjoy the ride."

"I'm trying. It's just—"

The Dragon Lady whipped smoothly around a corner. I barely managed to keep us from flying off as she turned. Sophie laughed gleefully and squeezed my sides. I took a deep breath and tried not to think about all the ways we could die right now.

We turned another corner and I decided that the hallway, and probably the whole building, went around in one big square. We went farther down until I guessed we were about halfway to the next corner turn, then we finally came to a stop.

For a moment we just sat there, Sophie's arms still wrapped around me. They each had a slightly different scent, Sophie and Claire. Claire's was rich, like wood. Sophie's reminded me of fresh cotton laundry.

"Little monsters," said the Dragon Lady. "You may dismount."

"Yep," said Sophie.

"Okay," I said.

I lowered Sophie down to the ground, then slid down, too.

There was a massive doorway on one side. Bigger than any of the others, it covered the entire thirty feet from floor to ceiling. If this hallway was one big square, all the other doorways were on the outer side. This was the only one I'd seen on the inner side. It was also the only doorway I'd seen with a closed door. It was a dark, rough wood, bound together with tarnished iron. Instead of a handle, there was a massive iron ring, which was probably a lot easier for creatures like the Dragon Lady to grab on to.

It looked too heavy for me to open, but the Dragon Lady gave the door a push and it opened easily. The room inside was even larger than the dragon's den, brightly lit by a series of skylights. The ceiling had to be over fifty feet high, the walls at least a hundred across. The room was empty except for the Sphinx.

I had assumed that the famous Sphinx statue in Egypt had been made larger than life. But it had been done exactly to scale. It was impossible not to feel awed in his presence. Even the Dragon Lady was small compared to him. The Sphinx's lion body sat poised with breathtaking majesty and his human face appeared ageless, his eyes like deep blue pools of knowledge.

As we got closer, he didn't look down at us. Instead, he stared straight ahead.

"Sphinx!" The Dragon Lady's voice was so loud and low I felt it vibrate in my stomach. "Two little monsters seek an audience with you. Will you acknowledge them?"

We waited. But the Sphinx didn't move, didn't make a sound. He just continued to stare straight ahead.

Finally, the Dragon Lady sighed. "I am sorry. He has been like this for several years now."

"What's wrong with him?" I asked in a hushed voice, just in case he could somehow hear me, even if he wasn't responding.

"I'm not sure," she said. "But I believe it just became too much for him. No one can remember everything. No one can know everything. Not even me. And having lived for over five centuries, I know quite a lot. We forget things. We filter them, discard what we no longer need, so that we can continue to think and exist in a productive manner."

"Sure," I said. "Only the stuff we feel is important goes to long-term memory. Then we clear the cache on the short-term memory. Happens every night while we sleep."

She stared at me.

"Computer talk," said Sophie. "He understands what you're saying. So what does that have to do with the Sphinx?"

"He forgets nothing, he has lived a very long time, and I suspect his cup has run over," said the Dragon Lady. "I believe he still absorbs knowledge somehow, he still gathers new memories. But he can no longer process or comprehend any of it. He has lost all perspective. You and I are, to him, impossible to distinguish from the dust motes in the air or the weaving grain of the wooden door."

"So . . . he's not going to talk to us," I said more than asked.

"I'm afraid not," said the Dragon Lady.

We stood there for a moment. Then Sophie asked, "What do we do now?"

"I don't know," I said.

18
Wild Things

✚✚✚✚✚✚✚

BACK IN THE room, Sophie and I lay in our cots, side by side, and tried to figure out what we should do next. I had just assumed that the Sphinx would be able to help us, tell us what to do. I hadn't really thought about what we would do if he couldn't.

"We could stay here for a while," I said.

"We don't belong here. It's like a bloody retirement home for monsters."

"It's not *that* bad."

"You just need to steer clear of tech, is that it? Because I can do remote, as long as it's a remote tropical island or something."

"I think my big mistake back at the mall was connecting to my old email and chat stuff. I thought she wouldn't be able to break my encryption. Now I think it's a safe bet there's no encryption she can't break. But as long as I stay away from computers, we should be okay pretty much anywhere."

"You don't want to go back to New York, do you?"

"No way. Why, do you want to go back to London?"

"Possibly the least safe place for Claire in the whole world? No thanks."

"Yeah, Robert. Do you think he has any idea where to look for you?"

"Well, he knows I'm somewhere in the States. But he's no brilliant tracker, that's for sure. And I've kept a pretty low profile."

I gave her a skeptical look.

"Perhaps semi-low profile would be more accurate," she said.

"Well, even if it's unlikely, we still need to factor in Robert. Theoretically, he could show up any time. And if we're out somewhere on our own in some remote place, we're screwed."

"You could take him," she said.

"Maybe, but I can't guard you 24/7. We'll need to get jobs and stuff like that. Plus, we'll eventually drive each other nuts if we have to be around each other all the time."

"True."

"We need support. A community."

Sophie sighed. "Do we really need a community?"

"I grew up in a community, and it kind of sucked sometimes. But looking back on it, it was also pretty awesome. People look out for one another."

"Claire and I have gotten along just fine without anybody looking out for us."

"Do you have any idea what it's like to actually feel safe among a group of people who know what you are?"

She was quiet for a moment. "I had it a little with Adam and Allen."

"Imagine that times ten. Or twenty. Or who knows how many. Mozart said there are other places. Other groups of monsters. The Commune is just one of them."

"But where are these other groups? And more important, are any of them even slightly cool?"

"I don't know. But maybe the Dragon Lady has some ideas."

"Arbiter of cool that she is."

"You got a better idea?"

"The Bahamas?"

"A *realistic* idea?"

She put her hands behind her head and smiled serenely. "We're monsters. Realism cramps our style."

WE TALKED FOR a while longer, but didn't come to any real decision on what we wanted to do. Finally, Knossos the gryphon appeared in our doorway.

"The Dragon Lady has asked me to conduct you to the garden room so that you can eat."

"Brilliant!" said Sophie. "I'm famished."

Unfortunately, it took us nearly an hour to walk all the way around the building to the garden room.

"It seems like we walked in a big U shape," I said.

"We did," said the gryphon.

"Wouldn't it have been a lot quicker if we'd walked in the other direction?" asked Sophie.

"That corridor is off limits to you," he said. "After you have eaten, you must go back the way we came to return to your room. Now, if you will excuse me." He bowed his eagle head, and then stretched out his wings, and took off back the way we'd come.

"Hmm, I wonder what's back in the forbidden corridor. . . ." said Sophie, her eyes narrowing as she looked in that direction.

"I thought you were *famished*," I said, nudging her.

"And so I am. Doubly so after that long walk. Let's eat!"

The garden room had glass walls and a glass door. Inside was a lush greenhouse with bright skylights similar to those inside the Sphinx's hall, except smaller. I wondered again how all of this was being concealed. It was so huge, and clearly at least somewhat exposed to the open air.

"Fresh fruits and veggies! Divine!" said Sophie as she walked dreamily into the room.

Inside it was warm and humid, like a lush jungle atmosphere. It even looked a little like a jungle, except there were neat little paths that wound through it paved in smooth, golden pebbles that glistened in the sunlight.

"So what, we just eat stuff right off the plant?" I asked.

"That *is* the natural way of eating fruits and vegetables," said Sophie, her bright eyes scanning the foliage.

"I know. It just seems . . . a little unsanitary to me."

"This coming from a bloke who ate out of a Dumpster for a month?"

"Yeah. Okay. I see your point."

"Look! Bananas!" She pointed up to the top of a nearby tree.

"How do we get them?"

Sophie didn't answer. Instead, she started climbing the tree.

"Is that a good idea?"

"Of course it is." She moved smoothly upward from branch to swaying branch.

"I just don't want you to fall and h—*ouch*!" I said as a bunch of bananas dropped on my head.

Sophie slid down the tree. "Come on, then, there's a nice spot." She pointed to a flat rock a few yards from the path. So we settled down and cracked open some bananas.

"I wonder if any of the monsters here ever go outside," Sophie said as we ate.

"I doubt it," I said. "You have to remember, most monsters can't really blend in like you can. Most of us spend our whole lives hiding."

"You blend in just fine."

I looked at Sophie next to me, sitting with her legs tucked

under her. The neck of her T-shirt slipped over one pale, freckled shoulder. Her cheeks were rosy in the tropical air, and her blue-green eyes gazed at me with emotions I still couldn't quite read. She could never understand what it was like.

"I pass as human," I said. "But I don't blend. I'm too ugly."

"Who on earth ever said you were ugly?"

"Nobody needs to say it. I see it in their faces. Shock, pity, sometimes even fear."

"Did it ever occur to you that perhaps you're misreading those looks? That maybe it's not shock you're seeing, but awe?"

"Awe? At what?"

"At you, you big git!" She punched my shoulder with her tiny fist.

"Come on."

"I'm serious. Here these humans are, just walking about, living their dull, human lives. And then out of fucking nowhere, this gigantic creature comes striding into their lives with forearms bigger than their heads but a voice so soft and sweet, it could put a baby to sleep. How could they do anything but marvel at such a person? You are like a demigod in their midst and they bloody well know it."

"*You* weren't awed."

"Who says?"

"Well, you didn't act like it."

"You think I'd let someone I didn't know see me off balance?"

"Probably not."

"Precisely."

"So now that you know me, what do you think of me?"

Sophie cleared her throat. "You know what I think? That I'm thirsty from all those bananas. And do you know what would be great to wash them down with? Coconut milk!"

She jumped to her feet and climbed a nearby tree. This time I was ready for things dropping on my head and caught the two coconuts that came sailing down. Those would have hurt a lot more than the bananas.

"Damn," she said as she sat back on the rock.

"What?"

"Just realized. Nothing to open them with."

"Oh, I can probably do that." I split the outer layer open and tossed the two pieces aside. Then I took the smaller inner nut in both hands and pressed my thumb against the side until it punctured the shell. "Here. The hole's a little messy, but it should work."

Sophie took the coconut from me and lifted it so that the liquid drained into her mouth.

She grinned at me as she wiped her lips with the back of her hand. "You want to know what I think of you? I think you're bloody useful."

That wasn't exactly the response I'd been hoping for, but I'd take it.

AS WE STEPPED back out into the hallway, Sophie turned in the direction of the forbidden section again, her mouth pursed.

"I wonder what's down there," she said.

"Doesn't matter," I said. "It's off-limits for us."

"I'll bet it's a brewery." Her eyes widened. "Or a pot farm!"

"What?"

"Lots of old people smoke weed! For arthritis or glaucoma or something. It can be quite medicinal." She smiled mischievously and started walking in that direction.

"I really don't think we should . . ." I said.

"Come on, Granny." She tugged at my arm. "I tell you what, if they have a pot farm, I might be persuaded to stay here after all."

I sighed and let her pull me along.

It took about ten minutes to get there. But when we turned the corner into the forbidden hallway, it looked just like the other three.

"Bugger," said Sophie. "Nothing exciting here." She shrugged. "Well, at least it's a shortcut back to our room."

But as we walked, I noticed there was one difference from the other hallways.

"All the doors are closed," I said.

"What?"

"In the other three hallways, the doors were all open. But in this hallway, they're all closed. And no windows, either."

"Huh," said Sophie.

As we walked farther, I started to notice sounds coming from behind the closed doors. Heavy thuds, or slow scraping, or weird chittering noises.

"Um," said Sophie. "Slightly creepy."

"Yeah. Maybe we should, uh . . ."

"Walk quickly? Let's."

We moved into a fast walk.

"This may not have been my most brilliant idea," Sophie said.

"You think?"

"As long as the doors stay closed, we'll be fine."

The sound of a door opening came from behind us.

"Shit," whispered Sophie.

I heard a sniffing sound and turned back to look. It appeared to be a man poking his head out of the room.

"Sorry we disturbed you," I called. "We'll be gone in a minute."

He sniffed again and cocked his head to one side.

"Boy, I don't think you should be talking to him!" Sophie hissed.

"What, you think being rude is a better idea?" I asked.

"Let's just leave him be. Come on. We need to stay calm and act like we're supposed to be here."

We started walking again, as fast as we could go without breaking into an obvious run. But then a door opened in front of us and a ten-foot-tall spider crawled out.

"Aaand, let's go back the way we came," said Sophie, spinning around.

The man's head still stuck out of the doorway. He still sniffed the air, staring at us.

"Do you think he'd help us?" I asked.

"Um . . ." Sophie looked doubtful. Then she glanced back at the giant spider. It was following us. Her eyes widened and she looked back at me. "Couldn't hurt?"

"Excuse me," I said to the man.

His mouth opened and he hissed, showing us a row of fangs. Then he moved out from the doorway and it was clear he wasn't a man at all. He was a manticore, with a lion's body and a massive, barbed scorpion tail.

We jerked to a stop, looking back and forth between the giant spider and the manticore.

"Oh, God, this is not happening," whimpered Sophie as she grabbed my arm hard.

More doors opened and other creatures came out. Some of them, like the hydra with seven long dragon-like heads, and the giant cyclops, I'd known about. Some of them, like the creature with the front part of a rooster and the back part of a horse, or the head-less humanoid with a face peering from his chest, I had never even heard of.

"I am so so so sorry," said Sophie as she clung to me.

One or two I might have taken. Maybe even a few. But they just kept coming from every door. Bats as big as wolves. A wolf with three heads that was as big as an elephant. They looked ravenous and completely wild as they circled around us, hissing and growling and chittering in a way that sounded unmistakably like hunger.

The headless thing with the face in its chest was the first to move in, but the manticore let out a growl and stabbed it in the shoulder with its tail. The thing whimpered in pain and scuttled back. The manticore then drew closer, saliva dripping from its open, fanged mouth.

"STOP!"

The roar was deafening and all of the creatures flinched back. Then the Dragon Lady crashed through their ranks and coiled around us protectively.

"Grab hold!" she said. We grabbed tufts of the coarse fur on her back and she launched up into the air again, shooting down the hallway even faster than we'd gone before. We didn't stop until we'd turned the corner and gone most of the way down the next hallway.

"Didn't you receive instruction to not visit that hallway?" roared the Dragon Lady.

"Yes, I'm so sorry, it's all my fault," said Sophie, her eyes well-ing up with tears. "I was just . . . I didn't know. . . ."

"We're okay now," I said, taking her into my arms.

"But I could have gotten us *killed*!" she said.

"Yes, you could have," said the Dragon Lady. She sighed and

closed her eyes. "I suppose I should have known that you were too young to resist such temptations."

"Why are they here?" asked Sophie.

"They have to be somewhere," said the Dragon Lady. "If we turned them out, then the humans would soon hunt them down and exterminate them. Entire species eradicated. No, that is not acceptable. They stay in their hallway, we feed them. It is generally a peaceful arrangement. But you have stirred them up. You both smell too much like humans. Now that they've caught your scent, they will start tracking you. I am sorry. You must leave The Commune immediately."

THE DRAGON LADY gave us some supplies and offered to fly us to our car.

"It's the least I can do," she said as Knossos, Rhoecus, and Javier strapped food, water, and a large canister of gas to her tail. "I dislike having to turn you out so abruptly."

"Well, we kind of brought it on ourselves," I said.

"Even so," she said. "And besides, I rarely get out these days. It will be pleasant to taste the night air."

Once the supplies were securely strapped on, Rhoecus and Javier slid a massive panel back from the outer wall. I could see a black, star-speckled sky, and the fresh smell of desert night air poured into the hallway.

The Dragon Lady let out a rumbling sigh. "Yes, it has been too long. Climb on, little monsters. Let's be off."

A few moments later we shot up into the night sky, the thunderous flaps of leathery wings in our ears. I tried to see what The Commune looked like from the outside, but I couldn't see it.

That's when I realized how they hid from humans. The whole structure was invisible.

I looked out over the dark horizon as we flew across the desert plains. I felt Sophie's arms wrap loosely around me, and her cheek press against my back. The wind whistled so loud that I almost missed her say, "Freedom."

I'd never been this high up in the air before. I'd never seen such an expanse of land stretching out beneath me. The world looked so much quieter up here. I wondered, *If we could just get enough distance, would everything look like that? So simple?* It reminded me of Medusa's act. That fleeting feeling that there really was a purpose to everything. If only you could hold on to it. But did it really matter if there was some deep meaning to it all? This night stretching out from horizon to horizon seemed, after such a close call, more beautiful than any I'd ever seen before.

All too soon, we landed next to our car.

"I should not stay by the roadside for long," said the Dragon Lady.

Sophie and I quickly unstrapped the supplies from her back and climbed down. She immediately started to move away from the road. But then she looked back at us.

"Where will you go?" she asked.

I looked at Sophie. She shrugged. "We don't really know," I admitted.

"In Los Angeles, there is a group," said the Dragon Lady. "Not quite as big as Ruthven's coven, but big enough, and I believe young enough, for you to find a place. They pose as a Hollywood special effects studio. It is run by the person who helped us build The Commune."

"Who's that?" asked Sophie.

"The Invisible Man," said the Dragon Lady. Then she launched herself up into the night sky, leaving a thin line of fire behind her.

We watched her sail off into the distance, her red and yellow scales winking in the moonlight. Once I could no longer see her, I turned to Sophie.

"Well?"

"She's good at exits, I'll give her that," she said.

"What do you think about going to LA?"

"Could be worse."

"It isn't much to go on, though," I said. "She didn't give us an address. Even assuming it's actually in Hollywood itself, that's still probably a lot of ground to cover."

"True."

"And finding an invisible man obviously makes it even harder."

She raised an eyebrow. "You got somewhere better to be?"

I smiled. "Not really."

"Then I say, go west, young man, go west!"

"You're driving, though," I said. "It's the least you can do after nearly turning us into manticore chow."

19

Vortexes

++++++++

WE WERE ABOUT halfway across Arizona when the landscape started to get strange. I was sitting in the passenger seat, half napping, half daydreaming, when I noticed massive red rocks rearing up around us, some of them in oddly unbalanced shapes like the kind you'd see in old Road Runner cartoons.

"Where are we?" I stretched my arms and legs as best I could in the cramped car.

Sophie shrugged. "I don't know. Somewhere west of where we were the last time you checked the map."

"I take it you're not really paying attention to signs."

"Nah." She patted my cheek. "That's what I have you for." She made a flipping motion with her hand. "Figure out where we are then."

After looking at the map for a little while and comparing it to mile markers, I realized we'd gotten a little off course somehow.

"We're in Sedona," I said.

"Okay. And that means . . ."

"Well, the way I routed us, we were supposed to be going through Flagstaff about now, but that's thirty miles north of here. How did we get off track like that?"

She shrugged. "Probably me not paying attention. It happens. Is it a problem that we're in Sedona?"

"No, not really. It's only a little out of our way, and we can just pick up the main highway after we pass through."

Sophie looked around at the rock formations. "Cool area, anyway."

"Yeah. There's something about this place. I can't remember what, exactly. Whirlpools or something."

"A hot tub would be completely brilliant right now. Bubble this desert grime right off me!"

"I could probably use a shower, too."

"Uh, probably?" She wrinkled her pert nose.

"Hey, you stink, too!"

"Please," she said. "My arse smells like peaches. Just ask the anal probes."

AS WE DROVE higher up into the mountains, the scrub brush turned into clusters of pines, then finally into a forest. We found a wooded area that had a campsite with showers. No hot tubs, obviously, but they did have hot water.

"Here, catch." I heard Sophie's voice through the thick cement divider between the men's shower room and the women's. A moment later, a pair of jeans and a T-shirt came sailing over. I caught them just before they hit the wet ground.

"What's this?" I asked.

"Clothes for you. I told you that you needed some. I bought them in that shopping mall we went to."

"Oh. Thanks."

"You're welcome."

The jeans fit perfectly and were just my style. I was starting to get excited about having some new clothes. Then I unfolded the T-shirt.

"Are you kidding me?" I said.

"You don't like it?" I could hear the smile in her voice.

"It says 'I'm with the hottie.'"

"Do you disagree with the statement?"

"Well, no . . ."

"What's your problem, then? It was on sale."

"Sure it was."

"Look, if you'd rather wear that nasty old 'I just drove cross-country without bathing' T-shirt, you go right ahead."

I sighed and put on the I'M WITH THE HOTTIE T-shirt.

Once we were back outside and she saw that I was wearing the T-shirt, she smiled. "Such a good sport!" She looked at me appraisingly for a moment. "It looks good on you. You need more fitted shirts like this. Show off your physique a bit more."

"You look good, too," I said. She was wearing a bright blue summer dress that looked sort of retro 1950s with big, white polka dots.

"Thanks," she said. She turned purposefully toward the car. "Now, let's eat the rest of that food the Dragon Lady gave us. Then I want to go for a walk."

"A walk?"

"Sure. This is a campsite. We don't have a tent so the least we could do is go for a nature walk or something. Besides, with as much time as I've spent in a car lately, if I don't get up and move around, my arse is going to be permanently flattened."

"Why do you talk about your ass so much?" I asked.

"Why do *you* talk about my arse so much?" she asked.

"What? I don't!"

"Why? Don't you like it?"

"Now you're just messing with me."

She laughed as she yanked open the trunk. Then she began to rummage through our supplies.

I wasn't sure what kind of game Sophie was playing, or if there even was a game. One minute she was incredibly sweet, the next minute she was doing this weird teasing thing that might or might not be flirting. I understood Claire. Even if I didn't always like what she said, I could depend on Claire. But Sophie was still a mystery to me.

THE DRAGON LADY had given us a big loaf of bread, a cured ham, a block of cheese, and a small basket of fruit, telling us that it had all been made or grown right on The Commune. Despite its simplicity, or maybe because of it, it was delicious.

Afterward, Sophie selected a short hike for us. We followed the dusty red trail through some dense woods for a while. Eventually, we stepped out into a clearing and there was a massive red rock canyon in front of us. The sun was beginning to set, casting shadows across the uneven formations and layered red stripes along the cliffs.

"Oh, wow," she said. Then she just stood there, gazing out over the canyon.

"It's going to be dark soon," I said. "If you don't want to get caught out here in the dark, we should probably head back."

"Claire's the one who doesn't like nature. I love it." She dropped down to sit by the edge of the cliff and leaned against a flat rock. "Come on," she motioned me to join her. "Let's watch the stars come out."

I sat down next to her, my feet sticking out over the edge of the cliff. She immediately curled up into my arm. It took me by surprise. Of course, she'd gotten close like this before. But it had always been for a reason. Like after Claire had forced her out on the gurney, or when we'd ridden the Dragon Lady. But there was no real reason for it now. Other than just because it felt nice. And it did feel nice—her warmth against me, her fresh, soft smell in my nose. After a moment, I let my hand rest on her shoulder, bringing her in even closer.

"Isn't this nice?" Her eyes were half closed as she faced the last rays of sunlight. The warm desert winds tousled her corkscrew hair.

"Yeah," I said.

"Cuddling isn't so bad after all."

"I never said it was."

"No, but you used to tense up every time I touched you."

"Did I?"

"You didn't realize it?"

"It wasn't like I was doing it on purpose. I don't really come from a touchy-feely family. I'm just not used to it."

"I guess that makes a difference. My mum is a big hugger. So was my dad."

We sat there for a while in silence. I realized that although I'd talked with Claire about her family history, I'd never talked about it with Sophie. Considering how she'd tried to avoid it before, the fact that she'd just volunteered something about her parents was a big deal.

"I'm sorry you lost your dad," I said. "I don't know what I'd do if I lost mine."

"You miss him."

"I do." That surprised me a little. "I mean, he's not a hugger. Or even much of a talker, really. But I do miss him. His familiar presence. His quiet strength. It was comforting. You know?"

"Yeah. I think I do know what that feels like now. So what are you doing out here, so far away from him?"

I looked out at the canyon that stretched across the horizon, valleys and crags rising and falling, sometimes in serene order, sometimes in bizarre, dangerous shapes. An eagle flew between outcroppings, its outstretched wings riding the air currents as it swooped, rose, and soared.

"I was mad at him. For wanting to send me away to live with the Frankensteins. It felt like a betrayal of everything we stood for as a family. Like I was supposed to be his ticket back into the fold. The monstrous black sheep of the family comes home. And I was angry that he was still treating me like a child, that he didn't respect me as an adult. Of course I really was only a child. I didn't know anything about the real world."

"Do you regret leaving, then?"

"No, not really. It had to happen somehow. I'm the son of one of the most famous monsters ever. My dad is a big guy who casts a big shadow. I had to get out from under it, I guess. So I could have my own life." I suddenly thought of Medusa then. *It's time to start your journey,* she'd said. *Not on your father's path, but your own.* I wondered what she'd say now about this path I'd made.

Sophie sighed and nestled farther into the crook of my arm.

"This place has good vibes," she said.

"*That's* what it was."

"What?"

"Vortexes. Not whirlpools. Sedona is supposed to have these energy vortexes. Basically, naturally concentrated good vibes."

"Cool. Do you think it's true?"

"I don't know. Do I think it's any weirder than most of what we saw at The Commune? Not really."

Sophie laughed silently. "Yeah, that was the craziest nursing home in the world." She pressed the palm of her hand against my chest. "I've been meaning to thank you."

"For what?"

"For everything you did back there. I don't usually like being vulnerable in front of people like that. But you . . . made it okay. I feel safe around you."

We lay there in silence for a while as the sun set behind the mountains. After a little while I realized there was music off in the distance.

"Do you hear that?" I asked quietly.

"You're only just hearing it now?" she asked.

"What is it?

"Sounds like a flute player."

"It's beautiful."

"It is."

We listened to the lone melody echo through the canyon, soaring, dipping, whirling almost like the eagle. The sun had finally set. All that was left was a faint red glow that put the rock formations in a silhouette.

"Look." Sophie pointed.

Standing at the top of the highest peak was a figure. It had a hunchback, and feathers stuck out of its head and arms. It danced nimbly on the mountaintop as it played on a long flute. Then it jumped high into the air and landed on a different peak, then jumped and landed on another, all while still playing its tune. As the last red glow disappeared, the figure and the song faded away until it was just the evening winds whispering through the dark canyon.

"I wonder who that was," said Sophie.

"Kokopelli, I think," I said.

"Like the guy on cheesy Southwest souvenirs?"

"I think so."

"Add it to the list of things I never knew existed."

We lay in complete darkness for a little while. The weight of Sophie's head lay comfortably on my chest.

"Hey, Sophie?" My skin suddenly felt very hot.

"Yes, Boy?"

Maybe it was the darkness or the vortexes or the magic flute player, but I just said it.

"I have a huge crush on you."

"You are so incredibly lame for saying that." The weight of her head abruptly left my chest.

"Wh-what?" My heart pounded in my chest. "Why?"

"Because at a time like this . . ." Her face was now less than an inch from mine. "You should just kiss me."

So I did. As soft and sweet as her voice was, as her skin was, it was nothing compared to her lips. Her hot breath escaped into mine and I thought this must be what her heart felt like. I held her gently; she was so small and delicate that I could not help but surrender my strength to her.

Then she pressed against me and breathed in my ear, "Freedom."

20
Oh, Brother

SOPHIE WAS UNUSUALLY quiet when we got on the road the next morning. She sat in the passenger seat, frowning as she stared out the window. I worried that she regretted last night.

"You okay?" I asked.

She sighed and rubbed her temples. "Yeah, just having an argument."

It took me a second to figure that out. "Oh. Claire."

"Yeah, Claire."

"She's pissed?"

"You could say."

"Maybe I should talk to her."

"No, definitely not."

"Are you sure? Because maybe I could—"

"Look, Boy, thanks. Really. You're a sweet guy. But this . . . this isn't about you. She and I need to work this out on our own."

"Okay, sure." I wouldn't know what to say to Claire, anyway. It was strange. I didn't understand Sophie at all, but I'd known exactly how I felt about her since the moment I first saw her in that warehouse. With Claire, I felt like I understood her perfectly, but I didn't know how I felt about her at all. Mostly because she could be so mean.

As Sophie continued her silent argument, I drove us down out of the mountains and back onto the flat desert plains. This side of Sedona was even more like a real desert, with tall cactus and swirling sand dunes. We were entering the Mojave.

Sophie started to get more and more agitated as time went on. It had to be hard to argue with someone when there was no way you could ever take a break from each other to cool off. She glared out the window now, and started to say little things out loud like, "Oh, please!" or "Unbelievable!" Then she just started yelling.

"Give me a sodding break! You couldn't even be *nice* to the guy for fuck's sake! Are we back in primary school where you have to beat up the boys you like? Is that it?"

I just kept my eyes on the road like I didn't hear anything.

Out of the corner of my eye, I could see Sophie nodding her head furiously.

"Yeah!? Well, you were the one who forced me out. *Forced* me! *That's* why! Because he bloody well stepped up when you ran away. *You're* supposed to be the strong one, the powerful one. But the second it has anything to do with Robert, you're completely useless."

This was getting really uncomfortable. I started to watch the roadside for a gas station. Not that we needed gas. We still had a huge canister in the trunk, thanks to the Dragon Lady. But honestly, I just needed to get away from the girl arguing with her other self.

As I was scanning for signs, I noticed a dusty white van in the rearview mirror about a quarter mile back. It caught my attention because it was the first vehicle I'd seen in over an hour. But then I went back to trying to find a place to stop. If I could figure out where we were from the mile markers, I could calculate how far ahead the next town was. Probably on the other side of the Mojave. I thought about asking Sophie to take a look at the map, but decided that was a bad idea.

I glanced in the rearview mirror again. The van was a lot closer. I was going eighty on this straight desert highway. At the rate he was coming up on me, he had to be going close to a hundred miles an hour.

"Whoa," I muttered.

"*What!?*" snapped Sophie. "I know I'm yelling! You got something to add?!"

"No, no." I tried to keep my tone calm. "Just this guy behind us is coming up fast. I'm going to pull over into the other lane and let him pass."

Sophie didn't seem to be paying attention.

I slid over to the right lane to let him pass. But as soon as I did, he swerved over into the same lane.

"Uh . . . Soph?"

The van was getting closer and it wasn't slowing down. Just to see what would happen, I switched back to the left lane. The van did, too.

"Sophie."

She didn't respond.

I pushed the accelerator all the way to the floor and the speedometer climbed to ninety-five. The van picked up speed, too.

"Hey, Sophie."

The van was right up behind us now. I could see the driver. It was a thin guy with pale skin, freckles, and curly hair. He looked a lot like Sophie. His mouth was wide open and veins stood out on his neck, like he was screaming at us.

"Sophie! I think your brother just found us!"

"Wait." She turned to me. "What did you just say?"

Then the van slammed into us.

The Sunbird was an old car with a solid steel frame, so it didn't crumple up. But it was a lot smaller than the van so it bucked forward and the tail swerved to one side. For a second, I thought we were going to flip, but I turned into the skid and we straightened out. The van hit us again, and I just barely managed to keep us from sliding off into the sand.

Meanwhile, Sophie was screaming, "Robert! It's fucking Robert! How the hell did he find us?!"

"You want to stop and ask him?" I grunted.

It seemed like it was just a matter of time before either I lost control of the car or he battered it to pieces. I had to get us away. The next time he gunned the engine to ram me, I tried to dodge into the other lane so he'd get in front of me. But he swerved, hitting me on the diagonal. Our car went into a spinout. I fought against it for a second, but then thought maybe if I went *with* the spin, I could get us going in the opposite direction.

"Get down!" I yelled.

I pulled the wheel hard and the car spun a full 180. But apparently, that maneuver only works in movies. As we completed the rotation and I tried to straighten us out, there was too much momentum, the car turned into a barrel roll, and we flew off the road.

When we finally came to a stop, we were right side up and more or less uninjured, but the car was so smashed up we couldn't open the doors. Sophie was screaming and pointing out my window. The van had stopped. Robert climbed out of the driver's side, a rifle in his hand. As he walked toward us, he took a shot that hit the ground about five feet from the car.

Sophie whimpered.

"It was just a warning shot," I said. "He's not really going to shoot you. He thinks he's trying to save you from Claire, remember?"

"He'll shoot you, though, if you get in his way."

"I don't think he can kill me with bullets. At least, not easily."

Then I remembered that there was a completely uninsulated metal canister of gas in the trunk. Bullets might not cause much damage, but a gigantic fireball sure would. And Robert would end up killing Sophie whether he meant to or not.

"We gotta get out of this car now," I said. "Move back against the seat slowly, so it's not obvious."

Sophie pressed against the seat. I aimed my feet at her door, took a deep breath, and kicked it as hard I could. It bent, but didn't give away completely.

"Don't move or I'll shoot again!" I heard Robert yell in the same British accent as Sophie and Claire.

"Tell Claire I could really use some extra muscle right about now," I said to Sophie.

"She won't come out." Tears streamed down her face. "She's terrified of him. She's so scared, so scared. . . ."

"Hey, stay with me, Soph. It's going to be okay. We'll get out of this. I'm going to try the door again. I think it'll give this time, but then he's going to shoot. If he hits anywhere near the gas canister in the trunk, this whole thing is going to go up. So as soon as the door opens, you jump clear, okay?"

She stared at me. No, she stared over my shoulder at her brother walking toward us with a big gun.

"Sophie!"

Her eyes snapped to mine.

"Get ready to jump!"

She nodded.

I reared back and kicked the door. It flew off the hinges and landed ten feet away.

"*Don't—*" yelled Robert.

"*Jump!*" I yelled.

Sophie launched herself through the open doorway.

A shot rang out.

I jumped after her.

The bullet hit somewhere in the back of the car.

I landed on top of Sophie and shielded her with my body.

The car exploded. I could feel the fire licking my back and arms. I could smell singed cotton from my T-shirt.

"NO!" I heard Robert scream.

Sophie sobbed beneath me.

I heard Robert's footsteps come quickly around to our side.

"Get off her!" he yelled.

I tried to push myself up, but my arms weren't working right.

He jerked me to my feet, the rifle pointed at my face.

I took a swing at him, but I had no arm from the elbow down.

His eyes widened and he looked down at the ground by Sophie. Both my arms lay next to her. The explosion had burned away the stitches that held them on.

His face twisted up with loathing. "You!"

Then he slammed the butt of his rifle into my forehead and I was out.

THIS TIME, INSTEAD of waking up naked on a cot in the care of a grumpy old gryphon, I woke up in the back of a hot van with a throbbing headache and my body in pieces. Robert had finished the fire's job and cut the stitching on my legs as well. All four limbs sat in a crate on the other side of the van next to Sophie, who was tied up and gagged. She looked at me sadly.

"I'm okay," I whispered. "It doesn't hurt." It was only sort of a lie. My arms and legs didn't hurt at all. But my stumps were nothing but soft, tender tissue, and they throbbed with a crazy sort of itchy, aching feeling. What made it a lot worse was having Sophie see me like this, in parts. Undeniable proof that I wasn't just a human with stitches. I really was a monster after all.

"Shut up back there, freak!" yelled Robert. "I promised I'd keep you alive, but trust me I can make you wish I hadn't."

A cell phone rang. Robert picked it up.

"I *see* it's you," he said. "And yes, I have your van."

There was a pause.

"I didn't steal it, I bloody *borrowed* it. I just needed it for something. I'll bring it back to you tomorrow."

Another pause.

"Well, go ahead and fucking fire me, then!"

He slammed the phone against the dashboard, cursing under his breath. Then he turned his head. "This will all get much better soon, Sophie. I promise! We just have to fix this . . . problem of yours."

Sophie closed her eyes, but it looked like she was all out of tears.

FOR A LONG time, I wasn't sure where we were going. From my spot on the metal van floor, I couldn't see much out of the tinted windows except night sky. But eventually, I started to see glimpses of light that grew more and more frequent so I guessed we were entering a city.

The van pulled into some kind of indoor facility, like a garage.

He cut the engine and got out. I heard him walk around to the side of the van, and then the door slid open. He smiled at Sophie, like he couldn't see the fear in her eyes.

"It's going to be okay." He reached for her. "I'll have you fixed up in no time."

She jerked out of his reach and his face darkened.

"It's that bitch, Claire, fighting you, isn't it? Just keep her inside a little longer. We'll be rid of her soon." He climbed into the van, reaching for her again.

That's what I'd been waiting for. I coiled myself up and pushed off the ground with my stubs as hard as I could. The pain was like touching raw nerves to sandpaper, but it got me upright. I teetered there a moment as Robert slowly turned and looked at me with dumb shock. Then I slammed into him. His head cracked against the side of the door and bounced back, which in turn pushed me backward. I fell onto my back, squirming like a bug as I tried to roll over. Then Robert hit me in the head with something. It wasn't enough to knock me out this time, but it dazed me long enough for him to pull Sophie out of the van and slam the door closed.

I heard Sophie scream through her gag. Then there was a sharp slap.

"Sorry, Sophie! Sorry!" I heard him say. "I wasn't hitting you, I was hitting Claire. This will all be over soon, I promise. We've got a benefactor now who'll provide us with whatever we need. Her resources are incredible. She was even able to pinpoint your exact location in the middle of the desert! After today, the curse of our granddad will be lifted and we can have *normal* lives. I'll do my research and you can go back to school. . . ."

He went on and on, raving about all the "normal" things they'd do. I heard the sound of metal clanking, of leather straps snapping, of glass tubes clinking. . . . Crazy thoughts flashed through my head. I remembered the way Sophie had described those early experiments he'd done on them. I couldn't handle it. I had to get out.

After a lot of squirming, I was able to roll over and inchworm my way to the crate that held my arms and legs. I knocked it over with my head and they spilled out onto the floor. I bit the shoe of one leg and dragged it slowly over to the sliding door. I rolled onto my back again, with my leg on my stomach. After a lot of failed attempts, I managed to get all four stumps around the base of my leg so that the foot pointed up. I inched on my back to get the foot positioned right, then dropped it so the foot hooked onto the sliding-door latch. The latch moved down, but not enough to open the door.

"Shit," I hissed.

I couldn't get enough of a grip on my leg with my stumps. They were too short and slick with sweat and blood. I stared at my leg for a moment as it dangled from the door latch.

Then Sophie screamed.

That was the only motivation I needed. I closed my eyes, bit into my own leg as hard as I could, and jerked my head down until I heard the latch give and the door slide open.

I let go of my leg and rolled out of the van. When I dropped to the floor, I took the fall on my side so I wouldn't crack my head. The air whooshed out of me and I gasped for breath, fighting off the dizziness and tunnel vision. I still had no idea what I was going to do, but I'd gnaw the guy's ankles off if I had to.

I rolled across the grimy cement floor in the direction of the sound. On the other side of the garage, I found a makeshift lab. There were a couple of metal bookshelves stacked with powders and liquids in beakers and vials, some kind of large refrigeration unit, and Sophie strapped to a metal gurney. No wonder Claire had been freaked out at The Commune. It was the exact same setup.

Robert was muttering to himself as he ran a centrifuge on a nearby table. His eyes looked totally crazed now.

"Please, Robbie!" sobbed Sophie. "Please stop! Please!"

"Don't let Claire out, Sophie! Fight her! I know you can do it! I'm almost ready for the final injection. Once the catalyst goes in, it'll be a little painful, but then everything will be perfect. I promise! Just don't let her out, Sophie. That will ruin everything."

That will ruin everything.

"Claire!" I shouted from the floor. "I know you're scared. But you've got to come out and fight! For your mom and Stephen. For Adam Iron and my parents. For all the victims of asshole creators!" Those words tasted bitter in my mouth, but I said them because I knew it would get to her.

Sophie's face began to ripple and her body spasmed.

"No!" shouted Robert. He picked up a long knife from the table. He took a lurching step toward me, then toward the transforming Sophie, like he didn't know which way to go first.

"I'm the one you want!" I shouted to him. "I'm the monster that messed up your chance at normal! Me!"

The transformation was half complete. Sophie and Claire flickered back and forth, the size of the body shifting as they strained against the leather straps.

Robert walked slowly toward me. "Yes, I'll kill you. And then I'll kill her. At this point I'll have to sacrifice Sophie, but that can't be helped. The world must be rid of every last Hyde."

I tried to roll away, but I realized too late I'd backed myself against one of the metal shelves. I slammed into it as hard as I could, hoping to knock it down, but it was bolted to the floor so it just hurt like hell.

He raised up the knife. His eyes gleamed with rage, his lips pulled back in a grimace.

Then a hand grabbed his wrist.

"Back off our boy."

He tried to dodge, but he wasn't fast enough. A fist smashed into his face and he went stumbling into one of the shelves, glass vials shattering as he fell.

I looked up and saw that Sophie and Claire were still halfway between the change, shifting, growing, shrinking, expanding as they stumbled toward Robert, reaching for him.

"Get away!" he screamed. "You monster!"

"No, Robert," Sophie and Claire said with one voice. "You're the monstrous one." They picked him up and slammed him into the shelf until he was unconscious. Then they dropped him to the ground.

Finally, the transformation subsided, and there was Claire, her fists clenched and her jaw set as she stared down at the man who had always terrified her. She looked supremely badass, even wearing Sophie's too-small polka-dot dress.

Then she turned and knelt down next to me. "Are you okay?"

"I'm kinda in pieces." I forced a smile.

"Well, I'm kinda wearing a dress."

"Miniskirt on you."

"If you weren't all bloody and stumpy, I'd punch you."

"It almost sounds like you're concerned about me."

"Yeah, it's my nurturing instinct." She hauled me up into a semi-sitting position. "Come on, Humpty Dumpty, let's put you back together again."

"How did you break out of those leather straps? Some kind of crazy adrenaline?"

"Actually," came a clipped, upper-class British accent, "I provided some assistance there. The ladies looked uncomfortable, so I loosened the buckles for them."

We scanned the garage, looking for the source of the voice.

"Show yourself!" Claire stood up, her fists ready. "Who are you?"

A cigarette rose up into the air.

"Me?" came the voice.

A match flared and lit the floating cigarette. Then the cigarette began to puff itself.

"Why, I'm the Invisible Man, of course."

We stared at the floating cigarette for a moment.

Then Claire said, "Wait, does that mean you're naked?"

PART 4

The Studio

"*If* the multitude of mankind knew
of my existence, they would do as you do,
and arm themselves for my destruction.
Shall I not then hate them who abhor me?"

—The Monster,

FROM *FRANKENSTEIN: OR, THE MODERN PROMETHEUS*, WRITTEN BY MARY SHELLEY

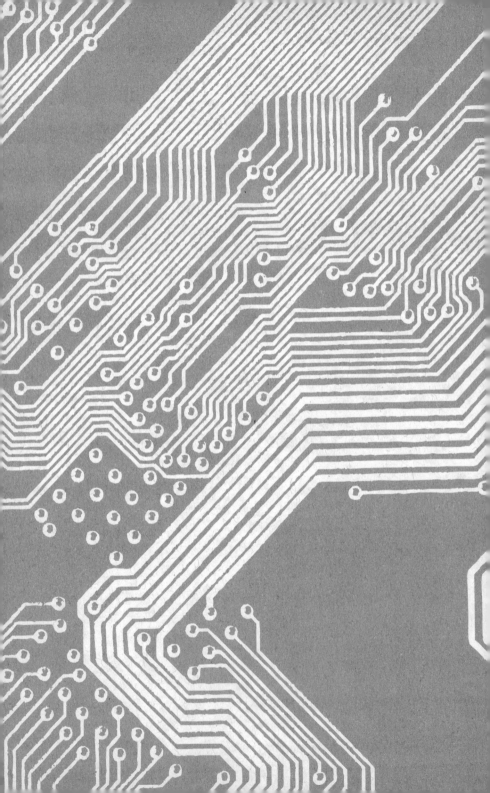

21
Worth It

┼┼┼┼┼┼┼

"RIGHT," SAID CLAIRE. "I know you're invisible and everything, but you need some clothes on before I can have a conversation with you."

"I understand completely." The Invisible Man picked up a button-down shirt and pants that had been neatly folded in a corner of the garage. As he slipped them on, he said, "I can assure you, I do not generally make it a habit to walk around nude."

I'd seen a lot of different kinds of monsters, and I didn't think there was anything that could freak me out anymore. But seeing those clothes floating in the air like that, I could feel the hair on the back of my neck rise. It was more than just looking at something unpleasant or dangerous. It was looking at something my eyes told me was impossible.

"There now." He pulled on a pair of thin leather gloves and a fedora hat. "Hopefully that puts you at ease somewhat, my dear."

"It's in the right direction," she said.

He held out his gloved hand. "You can call me Kemp, by the way."

"Claire Hyde," she said. "And that's about sixty percent of Boy, son of the Monster."

"Let's round up the other forty percent, shall we?" said Kemp.

Claire and Kemp went over to the van and put my arms and legs back into the crate. Obviously, I just stayed put.

"So what were you doing here?" Claire asked. "Not that I'm complaining."

"Robert did some odd jobs for me," said Kemp. "It's my van, you see. Last night he took it without permission. He's always struck me as rather unstable, so it didn't really surprise me. I'd taken him in a few weeks before, more out of pity than any real need for him. I always try to help creatures in need of shelter and employment. Anyway, I tried calling, and he was even more rude than usual. I knew he often holed up here, so I came round to see about getting my van back. And then I happened upon you lot in what I would frankly call a dire situation." His fedora swiveled toward me. "Now, it looks like the next order of business is to get you fixed up. Fortunately, I know just the person to help." He turned back to Claire. "Give us a hand getting him into the car, will you?"

The two of them loaded me into the passenger seat of a two-door BMW sports car parked at the garage entrance.

He put on a latex mask that, from a distance, probably looked like a face with empty eyes. Up close, though, it made him look even stranger. "I'm afraid my car won't fit three. Would you be a dear and follow behind in the van? It's only a short way to The Studio."

"So what is The Studio exactly?" she asked. "We've heard it's like a special effects studio or something?"

The latex mask crinkled up into a smile beneath empty eyes as he said, "You'll see soon enough." Then he put on sunglasses.

"What should we do with *him*?" I asked, pointing my chin at the unconscious Robert.

"Ah, yes, thanks for reminding me." Kemp pulled a cell phone out of his pocket and dialed. "Good evening, Lieutenant, it's Kemp. I'm afraid I need a favor. There's a man trespassing in one of my warehouses. It's on Sixth and San Pedro. . . . Yes, his name is Robert Jekyll. I'm sure he has a fairly long record. . . . Please tell your officers to be careful. He may be violent and is most likely insane. No telling what he might do. . . . No, he's not one of mine. Not anymore. . . . Yes, thanks as always for your discretion, John. I do appreciate it."

He hung up and slid the phone back into his pocket. His fedora turned to Robert sprawled on the concrete.

"I've done everything I could for that arrogant fool," he said softly, almost to himself. "He wants to be human so desperately? Then he can live by their laws."

KEMP WOVE IN and out of traffic down Hollywood Boulevard as the sun began to rise above the building tops. Los Angeles was a nice-looking city. Big, but spread out. It didn't feel as crowded or as dirty as New York. But there was something strange about it that took me a moment to pinpoint. There were almost no pedestrians. In New York, the sidewalks were crammed with people, sometimes to overflowing. But LA felt like a city of cars, all speeding and swerving, cool and faceless. It wasn't until you got close to another car that you saw other people at all.

"There wasn't much point in trying to compete in the film industry," Kemp was saying. "Quite honestly, there's little magic can do that a big fat blockbuster budget can't duplicate on film."

I glanced back to make sure Claire was able to keep up with Kemp's driving. She was a few cars back, but the fact that she could even keep sight of us while driving that clunky old van in dense LA traffic was impressive. There's no way I could have done it, even if my arms had been attached.

"Television, however, always seems to be straining at the seams to produce film-quality effects at a much lower budget. And that's where we come in. The Studio provides movie-caliber special effects for the price of a standard television production company. Or so it would seem to humans."

"Do you have your own actors?"

"Heavens no!" He laughed. "Could you imagine? No, my lad, we've nothing to do with casting. And trust me, no interest in getting involved in that sort of mess."

"So how do you keep the human actors from realizing that it's not special effects?"

"Oh, we have sprites for that. Adorable little creatures. Just love bedazzling humans. The actors only see what we want them to see. It can also bring out some truly exceptional performances, I must say. Ah! Here we are at last."

Kemp hiked the wheel, and we swerved into a driveway and pulled up to a gate. A few moments later, Claire pulled in behind him.

"Good driver, that girl," he said. "Perhaps I could interest her in some work." Then he rolled down his window and punched a code into the number keypad. The gate slid to one side and we drove onto the studio lot, Claire following close behind.

"That's your security?" I asked.

"Er, yes. Something wrong with it?"

"Just a little outdated is all."

"Oh, really?" He cocked his head to one side. "And I suppose you know about these sorts of things?"

"I'm good with tech."

"Well, perhaps I can interest you in some work as well."

The lot was set up in a regular gridwork of narrow streets that were barely wide enough for our vehicles. As we drove down one of them, we passed large windowless buildings with doors that were almost as tall as the buildings themselves.

"Soundstages," said Kemp. "That's where all the filming is done. Each show under contract has its own building, with adjoining offices for the producers."

We passed about twelve soundstages, six on either side. Then there were a few buildings that were just as big, but also had windows.

"Scenery and prop shops," said Kemp. "We mostly employ gremlins for that work. Many people don't realize this, but they're just as good at building things as they are at breaking them."

The narrow road came to a dead end at a small office building.

"And here we are," Kemp said. "Now, let's get you put back together again."

"Are we going into that office?"

"No, we're going there." His gloved hand pointed toward a small warehouse next to it. Hanging over the regular-sized door was a sign that read costume shop.

Kemp took off his sunglasses and peeled off his latex mask while Claire parked the van. Then he popped the trunk and pulled out the crate that contained my arms and legs. He tilted his head to where I still sat in the passenger's seat. "If you'll do the honors, Ms. Hyde."

I was getting a little tired of being lugged around like a bag of dirty laundry, but there really wasn't any other choice. Claire leaned in and scooped me up.

"Sorry," I said, my face only a few inches from hers. "I know this is pretty gross."

"Nah." Then she smirked. "Just don't get used to this kind of service."

I smiled back. "Are you kidding? You think I *like* being at the mercy of a crazy English chick?"

"I could drop you, you know," she whispered in my ear. "And make you roll in there."

"Did I say crazy? I meant *cruel.*"

She laughed and hoisted me a little higher.

Kemp led us inside the costume shop building, where we were greeted by a female receptionist who wasn't at all startled by a limbless teenager being carried in with his arms and legs in a crate. She had sharp, elegant features. Her ears were covered with her long, blonde hair, so I couldn't be sure, but I had a feeling she was an elf.

"Found the van," Kemp said as we passed.

"Well done, Mr. Kemp," she said dryly, and turned back to her computer monitor.

"This way, kids," Kemp said, and continued through another door, my hands and feet bouncing slightly as he walked.

We walked into the main warehouse space, which contained racks of clothes on a conveyor-belt system that stretched on for fifty yards and went up several levels. We walked through the center aisle for a while until we came to a closed door. Above it was a sign that read head seamstress.

Kemp put the crate with my limbs down on the ground and knocked softly.

"Kitsune," he said. "I've got a lovely young man here who needs your kind attention. He's gone all to pieces."

"Bloody comedian," Claire muttered in my ear.

The door opened and a beautiful Japanese woman stood in the doorway. At first, I wondered if she might be human, but then I saw a foxtail peaking out from beneath her blue silk dress.

She scrutinized me for a moment, then nodded curtly. "Bring him in."

She turned and I saw that there were actually three foxtails poking out.

"Put him here." She pointed at a large sewing table, like the kind I'd seen in the costume shop at The Show.

"Kitsune is our Emmy Award–winning costume designer," said Kemp. "You are in good hands."

Claire placed me on the table and Kemp put my arms and legs next to me. Kitsune picked up each limb and examined the place where it attached to me. Next she looked at each of my stumps. She snarled quietly when she saw how scraped up they were, and I could see sharp little canines poking out. Then she examined the rest of me. She ran a finger lightly over the stitching on my head and neck. She picked up a small pair of scissors and cut the torn, burned, bloody I'M WITH THE HOTTIE T-shirt off and examined my chest. Then she lifted me up with surprising ease and examined my back.

Finally, she said, "We will replace all of the stitching."

"*All* of it?" I asked.

"So it matches," she said.

"Is that really necessary? I mean, that's a lot of stitching we're talking about."

She stared down at me with her keen, golden eyes. Animal eyes. I don't know why I didn't notice them right away.

"There is only one way to do something," she said. "The right way."

"I believe that's the mentality that won her the Emmy," said Kemp.

Kitsune's eyes still bore into me. "Are you saying you aren't *worth* the effort?"

"He's worth it," said Claire. Then she scowled at me. "Boy, don't be such a baby."

"Can it be a thread that matches my skin tone?" I asked.

"Of course," Kitsune said in a tone that almost sounded insulted. "I assumed that is how it would be."

"And . . . can you make it something that's fire resistant?"

"Hmmm." Her foxtails swished back and forth as she considered. "Yes, we can do that."

"Okay, I guess it's worth it then," I said.

"Of course it is." She looked at Kemp and Claire. "This will take many hours. You will come back later." It didn't sound like a request.

"But of course, my dear," said Kemp, and bowed. He turned to Claire. "Are you hungry, perhaps, Ms. Hyde? I believe the catering usually gets delivered about this time."

"I'm hungry, too," I said.

"No," said Kitsune, her fox eyes gleaming in her smooth, angular face. "Right now you are mine."

"Have fun!" Claire smirked as she followed Kemp out of the room.

Kitsune slid me more to the center of the table. "She likes you."

"She has a really funny way of showing it."

"Don't pretend to me that you don't see it."

"Yeah, I guess."

"Don't let her push you around, though. She is strong. You must match her strength."

"Easy for you to say."

"Yes. It is." She held up the biggest seam ripper I'd ever seen. "Now, let us begin."

MY MOM HAD always replaced parts a few at a time, because it had been hard for me to sit still and she would lose patience with my fidgeting. I had looked pretty awkward when she transitioned me gradually from my kid-sized body parts to my adult-sized parts. That was about when Shaun and his crew had really started teasing me. But the idea that I could have sat through a complete body re-stitching all at once wasn't something my mom even considered possible. I guess I had assumed it wasn't, either.

Kitsune wasn't exaggerating when she said "many hours." It took almost six hours to disassemble and reassemble me. And it hurt. A lot. But we made it through. Some of that was probably just because I was older and tougher. A lot of it was definitely Kitsune, though. She moved with a quick, darting efficiency, her strong, warm fingers slipping the needle in and out of my skin so fast it flashed in the light. And when the pain reached the point where it was difficult to stay still, she told me stories.

She spoke about forests crowded with life, waterfalls that sang like wild beasts, snow-covered mountaintops that wept frozen tears, and lakes as clear and smooth as diamonds. She told me about foolish foxes who fell in love with humans, humans who betrayed, humans who begged forgiveness, humans who suffered and loved and brought the foxes back to life again and again. She told me these stories all in whispers, like wind running through stalks of bamboo. I think I probably drifted off to sleep at some point, and when I awoke, her voice was still there, soft and rich. She never ran out of stories, and I wondered how long she'd been on this Earth, among the humans, watching them, sometimes hating them, but always loving them. Limitless compassion. I'd never thought of it as something powerful before, but that's what she had, and it left me in awe.

I wondered if I had that kind of capacity within me.

"You may now stand up," said Kitsune.

I slowly got to my feet, expecting to feel dizzy or stiff. But instead I felt strong, quick, light. I actually laughed out loud. Sure, some of that was from the endorphins that had kicked in after six hours of nonstop pain. But I also just felt really good. It's funny how you can get used to little problems. They irritated at first, but you learned to ignore them. And that was okay, I guess. But then you got so used to the problems that you forgot they weren't normal. That you could be better.

Kitsune led me over to a mirror so that I could inspect the new stitching. It was so perfect, so fine, it looked unbreakable.

"This is so . . ." I started to say, but then I couldn't think of anything to say that even came close.

"Worth it?" Her fox eyes peaked over my shoulder to admire her own work. "Yes, you are."

I MADE MY way back to the receptionist, who told me to walk across the road to the small office building I'd seen earlier. Once there, I found another elfish-looking receptionist. I think this one was a male, but he had the same long hair and the same sharp, elegant features. He sent me through a hallway, up an elevator, and down another hall until I finally found Kemp in a big office at the far side of the building. He'd taken the hat and gloves off. It was kind of funny, seeing this very corporate environment with an empty suit sitting at a desk, a keyboard clicking away by itself.

"Ah, Boy." I heard his voice, and the suit pivoted slightly in the chair to face me, except without a face. "You're looking indescribably better."

"Thanks," I said. "You were right. Kitsune is amazing."

"Yes. I have heard that the more wisdom a fox possesses, the more tails she has."

"Do you think Kitsune will get more?"

"I expect so. I fear around the time she decides she's had enough of costume design and leaves The Studio. Hopefully, that won't happen anytime soon, because I have no replacement for her in mind."

"Sophie's into fashion and clothes. I bet she'd be interested in learning about costume design."

"Sophie?"

"Sophie Jekyll. Claire's, uh, sister."

"Ah, yes, of course."

It was kind of difficult to get a sense of how he felt about things, since I couldn't see his face. But then I realized it was a lot like my mom, who had a face, but couldn't really express emotion with it.

"Speaking of Claire, and I suppose Sophie, I've shown them to their room. The police should be coming round to get a statement from me about Robert Jekyll in about an hour or so. That should give me just enough time to show you to your room."

"I have a room?"

"We have a policy here." He got up from his desk. "We never turn away a magical creature." He motioned me with an empty sleeve to follow him, then walked briskly down the hallway. "But we only let them stay free for a month. Then they must pay rent. It isn't much, of course, but we found people who pay for things take better care of them."

"Ruthven doesn't charge for living space," I said as we walked through the building. It sounded more defensive than I meant it to.

"He also doesn't pay anyone."

"True," I admitted.

We stepped out of the building and into the midday sun.

"Are you hungry?" asked Kemp as he pulled sunglasses from his pocket and put them on his invisible head. "Shall we scavenge the leftover catering before heading over to the dormitory?"

"That would be great."

Kemp led me to one of the large windowless soundstages and quietly opened a metal door. Inside was a narrow lobby, empty except for a long table filled with cold cuts, bread, vegetables, and other little snacks.

"They're filming," whispered Kemp. His sleeve pointed toward a closed double door set into the wall.

I nodded and grabbed a plate. I suddenly realized that I hadn't eaten since lunch the day before. I started to pile up a plate, eating as I went.

Then the double doors opened and a human walked out into the lobby dressed in a loincloth. He was a really good-looking guy, all chiseled features and serious muscle definition. He looked at Kemp and his eyes went wide.

"Is that . . . an invisible man?" he said.

A tiny, winged girl about the size of a squirrel dropped onto his shoulder and patted his cheek with her little hand. "That's Mr. Kemp, the technical director for the show," she said in a piping voice. "He's an aristocratic-looking Englishman, about middle-age."

"Yes." The human's face went slack and he nodded three times rhythmically. Then he suddenly smiled. "Mr. Kemp!" He held out his hand. "It's such a pleasure to meet you!"

"The pleasure's all mine, Mr. Rains," said Kemp as the actor gripped his invisible hand. "How's filming going?"

"Wonderful! You work miracles at this studio!"

"I'm so glad you appreciate the art to the artifice," said Kemp. "Now if you'll excuse me, I'm showing our new tech whiz around The Studio."

"Of course! I don't want to hold you up. Just came out for a little snack while they're changing sets," said Rains. He turned to the table and looked down appraisingly at the desserts. The sprite whispered something in his ear and although he didn't seem to be aware of her presence, he smiled, as if to himself, and moved on to the veggie section. I wondered if part of the sprite's job was to keep him in shape for the show, or if she was just concerned about his health. Either way, it was hard to see the blatant manipulation as bad. But it *was* manipulation. Was it wrong to use magic on humans, no matter what? After all, in a way, the Siren, Medusa, and so many other monsters did it, and it didn't seem to hurt anything. Well, most of the time, anyway. It made me think of VI. What if instead of getting mad at her for manipulating humans, I had tried to help her find less destructive ways of communicating? I wondered if it was too late for that. Obviously, she had a nasty temper. But maybe once she had some time to cool off . . .

"Coming, Boy?" asked Kemp.

I wolfed down the rest of my plate and nodded. He led me out through the exit and back into the bright sunlight.

"New tech whiz?" I asked we walked down one of the narrow streets.

"If you accept, of course. We are sorely in need of someone with some technical expertise. The digital age is not something many magical creatures have embraced."

"Yeah, I know. It kind of made me unpopular at The Show."

"Well, there will always be the old guard, I'm afraid. But I think you'll find that creatures here on the West Coast are far more open-minded."

"That would be nice."

"If you accept the position, you'll be paid, of course. As I was saying before, we pay everyone." He led me off the street and onto a sidewalk that led to a tall building tucked away in the back of the compound. "With all due respect to Ruthven and The Show, television makes quite a bit more money than theater. We can afford this luxury where perhaps he must depend on a collective model. And with that additional capital, many of the creatures here have more autonomy than those in New York. With money of their own, they can choose how to spend it—on a car, clothes, whatever they like. Some creatures even live off Studio grounds in real houses with families and a complete place in human society." He paused for a second. "Of course, that's not possible for everyone."

"Have you always been invisible?"

"Goodness, no. Could you imagine my poor mother trying to change nappies on an invisible baby? Strolling through the park with what appeared to be an empty pram?" He laughed. "No, I did this to myself, I'm afraid. Rather reckless, really. I learned the formula from a fellow named Griffin. He performed the experiment on himself, with tragic results. It made him invisible, but that specific compound was extremely toxic and it drove him mad. It took me years to refine the formula to a safe compound that I then administered successfully on myself. With the unexpected side effect of halting the aging process."

"Really? Have you tried to isolate just that part? So people could halt the aging process without becoming invisible?"

"I tried." And then he was quiet. He'd been so chatty up until then that the sudden silence was uncomfortable.

"It didn't go well," I said.

"No," he said. "It didn't."

We walked on a little farther without talking until we came to the tall building.

"Ah, here we are." He held the entrance door open for me. "The dormitory."

The inside reminded me a little of the hotel where we'd stayed in Pittsburgh. A little impersonal, maybe, but clean and well lit. Kemp led me up a set of stairs and down a long hallway. Some of the rooms had open doors, and I could see creatures of all kinds hanging out inside, watching TV or asleep. Other rooms had closed doors. I could hear music coming through some of them.

We stopped in front of one of the doors, and Kemp opened it. The room was about the size of my family's apartment at The Show, except there were windows, and it was furnished with cool, modern-looking furniture instead of old broken stuff salvaged from the junkyard. There was a living room/dining room area in the middle, and a kitchen area with a stove and fridge off to the left. Off to the right were a bathroom and bedroom.

"Well?" asked Kemp as we stood in my bright, simple apartment. "What do you think? Suitable quarters for a young bachelor such as yourself?"

"It's nicer than anyplace I've ever lived."

"And what do you think about the job?" he said.

I knew there was only one way I could make it work. Online friends, chat, email, coding, my whole connection to the hacker community I'd practically grown up with—it all had to go. If I accepted this job, I could only do the boring stuff: anonymous, impersonal business emails, network monitoring and optimization, off-the-shelf software installations without any customization or tweaking. In other words, I'd have to treat computers like someone who didn't like computers very much. The idea almost made me want to go back to cooking oxtail at the West Indian Delight.

But this paid a lot better and was in a community that seemed just about perfect for me. This was my chance to start my own life, for real, here in LA with Claire and Sophie, far from my mother's overprotectiveness and my father's domineering plans.

"I've been traveling a long time," I said to Kemp. "I need someplace to call home." I couldn't help grinning a little bit, then. "Besides, I kinda miss show biz."

22
The Measure of a Man

I LOUNGED ON a deck chair next to the pool, my eyes closed against the bright California sun. I had to admit, my post-tech LA life was pretty great. It seemed kind of unbelievable that only a month before, I'd been hiding under cover of night at a travel plaza in New Jersey, living on food I pulled out of Dumpsters.

A shadow suddenly darkened the sky and I felt a drop of water on my chest.

"You are such a lazy git," I heard Claire's voice saying.

I opened my eyes and saw her silhouette leaning in, her wet hair hanging over me. She reached up and wrung it out on my stomach.

"Ah, cold!" I winced.

She laughed and flopped down on the chair next to mine. She had a deep tan now. Three decent meals a day, eight hours of sleep a night, access to a gym, and a job as a light grip had given her a perfect athlete's physique. She seemed more relaxed, too. I didn't know whether it was living at The Studio or because she didn't have to worry about her brother anymore. What I did know was that the old Claire would never have worn a bikini, but the new Claire sported one all the time. And I wasn't complaining.

Of course, I was doing pretty well myself. And it wasn't like I was *completely* tech free. After all, I was the one man IT army for The Studio. First, I'd built myself some new custom interfaces. I'd tweaked the USB design quite a bit and expanded the scrambler algorithm way past spec. I didn't know if it was even possible for VI to pick up some sort of identifying bioelectrical signature from my nervous system, but I wasn't taking any chances.

When I was satisfied that I was completely untraceable, I dove into work at The Studio. I'd been afraid the business stuff would be boring, but I actually didn't mind it too much. It was comforting to wake up every morning and have tiny problems that I knew exactly how to solve. Probably because I'd spent the better part of a year never really knowing what the hell I was doing, facing huge problems without solutions. And since there were lots of little problems to solve, I kept busy.

On a typical day, I worked for a while in the morning upgrading the servers, firming up the firewall, ordering parts for the new key fob security system, or cleaning up some actor's computer. Then I'd go out to the private pool behind the offices. Two naiads, Nixie and Maura, lived in the pool. Naiads were nymphs, like the dryad wood nymphs who worked at The Show, but they lived in water, and had blue skin, webbed fingers and toes, and thin gill slits on their neck. When they found out I didn't know how to swim, they offered to teach me. So I'd practice with them for a little while, then relax on the deck until Claire came out with food she'd snagged from the catering table on the set. We'd catch up a little, eat, goof around, and then go back to work for a few more hours. At night, we'd hang out with some of the other creatures who lived at The Studio. The mummy who managed the finances was kind of an asshole, but the sprites were hilarious, the gremlins offered some amazing DIY tips, and the genie had some seriously crazy anecdotes. We'd have game nights and movie nights and other goofy stuff that made me feel like we were really part of a community.

Now I lay in a deck chair by the pool, with Claire next to me. The sun had already dried up the small bit of water she'd wrung onto my stomach.

"You going out to that club with Guilder and his mates tonight?" asked Claire.

"Haven't decided yet." Guilder was an elf Claire and I had become friends with. He lived off Studio grounds with a bunch of other elves. This was the first time they'd invited us out with them.

"I'm going," said Claire.

"Really? I thought clubbing was more Sophie's scene."

She just shrugged her bare, tan shoulders. "You should go, too. I think it'll be fun."

"You, getting down at a club? How could I miss that?"

BEFORE THE ELVES picked us up, Claire and I met in the dorm lobby. She was dressed in tight black pants, black cowboy boots, and a purple, fitted button-up shirt open at the collar. She caught me checking her out and gave me a guarded look.

"What?" she said.

I shrugged. "You look great."

"Oh." She smiled sheepishly. "Thanks. You too."

Once we got to the club, I understood why Claire had wanted to go: it was a cowboy-themed club. It had all kinds of random country-western stuff decorating the walls, like leather saddles and cowhides, and the bar looked like the kind you see in old

Clint Eastwood movies. But there was also a big dance floor with flashing lights and a booming sound system.

"Check that out." Claire pointed to a mechanical bull on the other side of the dance floor.

"Come on," said Guilder, his pointed features rising up into a grin. "Let's do it!"

So Guilder, Claire, and I made our way around the perimeter of the dance floor to where a small crowd was gathered around the mechanical bull. We watched a human stay up for a few seconds on the massive, shifting torso, then slide off into the padded mats that surrounded the bull.

"Elves are natural riders." Guilder pulled the knit cap that covered his pointy ears down tight and winked at me. "This will be a snap."

It threw him pretty quick.

"Harder than it looks!" he shouted to me over the music, his pale face flushed as he climbed out of the padded ring.

"You going to do it?" Claire asked me.

"Why?" I asked. "I'd just be showing off. There's no way it could throw me."

"Ha! So you say."

"I'll do it if you will."

"Hmmm," she said.

"Let's sweeten the deal," I said. "Whoever falls off first . . . I don't know. Has to do something."

"Whoever falls off first has to make the other one dinner."

"But I don't know how to cook!"

"Already pretty sure you'll lose, huh?"

"Oh, that's it! Game on!"

So I climbed up onto the mechanical bull. As soon as it started, I realized why it was so hard. The seat was really slippery, there was nothing to grip on to, and the machine used your own weight against you. It dipped me one way, then pivoted underneath me so that my legs were moving in a new direction, while my upper body was still moving in the old direction. And the harder I fought to stay on, the more I slipped off. It didn't take long before I landed in the padded mats.

"Told you!" laughed Guilder as he helped me up.

"Fifteen seconds!" said Claire, grinning in this wild way I'd never seen before. "That was pathetic!"

"Your turn," I said. "Let's see you last half that long."

She stuck her tongue out at me, then climbed up onto the mechanical bull. It jerked into action, and for a moment, it looked like she was about to get tossed immediately. But then she stretched her long legs out wide, and started to swivel her hips almost like she was dancing. That was when I realized that the key to staying on was not strength, but fluidity. Grace. The ability to constantly adjust. I usually thought of Claire as someone who wasn't very flexible. But that wasn't what I was seeing up there now, so maybe it wasn't really true. At least, not anymore. I'd sure changed a lot. Maybe she had, too. Or maybe there were things about her that had never been able to come to the surface before. Maybe a little space and stability was all she needed. Her silky black hair whipped around her smooth, tanned face. She had a little flush to her cheeks right now and there was an openness in her eyes. And she was laughing. I don't think I'd ever heard a real laugh from her before. It was loud and rich and a little bit clumsy. And I loved it.

The rest of the crowd loved it, too. As she hung on there longer and longer, the announcer started calling people over, shouting that she might break the all-time record. Someone threw her a cowboy hat. She caught it in one hand, still moving with the mechanical bull, and waved the hat in the air. People started coming over from the dance floor, the music dropped away, and the whole place was just screaming for her. Finally, the announcer declared that she'd broken the record. Everyone went wild at that. She looked at me, then, with this triumphant grin, and pantomimed stirring a pot. That's when she fell off.

She was still laughing as I gave her a hand up. Laughing so hard she fell into me. The heat of her exertion was pouring off her, and our faces were right up close to each other.

"I don't think I've ever seen this side of you," I said.

"I'm layered," she said, still leaning into me. "You have to look deeper sometimes."

"I try, but you don't usually let me get that close."

"No?" She raised an eyebrow. "This close enough for you?" And then she kissed me hard, her fingers locking onto the back of my head. I hadn't realized how badly I'd been waiting for that. I grabbed her and I squeezed her as hard as I could. I knew she could handle it. With Claire, there was no need to hold back. And as we kissed at the feet of the mechanical bull, the crowds still cheered. And I don't know if they were cheering for the record being broken or for something else, but it felt like they were cheering for *us*, for this moment that had taken us so long to get to.

When she finally broke away, she pressed her cheek against mine so that her lips were on my ear. "That was nice. But you still owe me dinner."

THE NEXT MORNING, I sat by the pool and stared into its sparkling depths as I drank my coffee. The naiads were curled up on the bottom, their little gills slowly opening and closing as they slept. I thought about how I was feeling about Claire. I thought about how I still felt about Sophie. I didn't have a ton of experience with romance, but if there was one thing I had learned from being with Liel, it was that I couldn't just wait around expecting things to work out on their own. If there was something I wanted, I had to take a risk and put myself out there. And if it failed . . . well, it wouldn't be the first time my heart had been broken.

A little while later, I knocked on Kitsune's door. She opened it, but said nothing. She just stood there in a sleek, green silk robe and gazed at me with her golden fox eyes.

"Do you . . . know how to cook?" I asked.

The next few weeks, I practiced every night with recipes Kitsune scratched out on empty corners of her sketch pad. I would bring in things I'd made for her to try and she would critique them, tell me what I was doing wrong, what I should try next.

Claire knew something was up.

"Why are you eating dinner alone all the time?" she asked me one day while we were hanging out at the pool during our lunch break.

I just shrugged.

Her eyes widened. "You're practicing cooking, aren't you?"

"Maybe," I said.

And I was. But that wasn't the whole plan. And when Kitsune finally told me that my sushi rolls were acceptable, I started the second half of my plan.

It was a Sunday, Kemp's day off, so I went to his dorm room and knocked on the door.

"Yes?"

"It's Boy."

"Ah! Do come in, Boy. The door's unlocked."

Kemp's apartment was decorated like an old-fashioned

English parlor. The main living area had beautiful Victorian furniture, dark, decoratively carved wood frames with rich, silk upholstery. A tea set sat on a mahogany table, and an antique writing desk sat in the corner. That was more or less what I expected.

What I wasn't expecting was the person sitting in an easy chair that faced out the window. I was pretty sure it was a woman, but it was hard to make out details beyond that. Everything about her, from her skin, to her hair, to her eyes, was pitch-black. More than black. I tried not to stare at her, but it was almost impossible. She was so dense-looking that I felt like my eyes were getting sucked into her. Like she was a human-shaped black hole, pulling in everything, including light.

An empty pair of pants and a crisp, white T-shirt stood next to the chair. A bowl and spoon floated in front of her.

"Oh," I said. "Sorry, I didn't realize you had a guest. . . ."

"Nothing to worry about," said Kemp. "Boy, this is Millicent, my wife. Millicent? This is Boy. He works for The Studio, helping out with technical things. I've told you about him."

Millicent didn't respond. She just continued to stare out the window.

After a moment, Kemp said, "Boy, do you remember when I told you how I tried to refine the invisibility formula to stop the aging process without making the person invisible?"

"Yeah."

"Back then Millicent was . . . impetuous. She begged me to let her be the first person to try the formula. In my defense, it is difficult to live forever alone, to watch those you love slowly decay. What's more, not many people are willing to marry an invisible man, I can assure you. I felt I was so lucky to have her and I always found it difficult to say no to her. And at the time, I was so sure it would work. So damn sure . . ."

He was silent for a moment. I had no idea whether he was looking at me or her or somewhere else. I just waited.

"I acceded to her wishes," he said. "And this was the result."

He carefully scooped out some sort of white liquid from the bowl with the spoon and held it to her mouth. Her lips opened a little and he slid the liquid in.

"Is she always like this?" I asked.

"Yes."

"For how long?"

"Forever, I suppose."

"It doesn't seem fair. It was an accident."

"Perhaps. But it was my doing, and if I didn't take care of her, she would surely suffer and probably die."

"You love her."

"Oh, yes. But it's more than that. Consider this: Victor Frankenstein was nothing more than a bright, impetuous med student when he made your parents. He had no idea what he was doing. Creating your parents didn't make him a bad person. It was a rash, youthful action and I think we all have our fair share of those. But when it was time for him to take responsibility for his actions, he could not. Or would not. It really doesn't matter because the fact is, he ran. Could you imagine how much happier you *all* would have been, including him, if he had chosen instead to make things right?"

Kemp slid another spoonful of the white liquid into Millicent's mouth. A little dribbled down from the corner of her mouth and he carefully patted it dry with a soft cotton cloth.

"Boyish mistakes are one thing. We must all learn and grow

from them. And it is the measure of a man, not a boy, how he holds himself accountable for those mistakes."

"I've never really thought about it like that," I said.

He placed the bowl and spoon on the table.

"Now, what did you come to see me about?"

"Oh, uh . . ." It seemed a little silly now. "Do you know anything about wine?"

THAT NIGHT I couldn't get to sleep. For one thing, I was nervous about making dinner for Claire the next night. I had everything all planned out, of course. But I had no idea how she and Sophie would react.

There was something else that was bothering me, though: Kemp and Millicent. I figured Kemp had brought up Victor and my dad because he wanted to use an example I was familiar with to explain how he felt about his wife. But it had felt as if, when he condemned Victor for running away from his creation, he might as well have been condemning me, too.

After about an hour, I decided there didn't seem to be much point in lying there in bed, staring at the ceiling. I got dressed and went outside for a walk around the grounds.

As I stepped out of the dormitory and onto the lot, the wind ruffled through my hair. LA got surprisingly cool at night. On the East Coast, the heat lingered in the summer, wet and heavy. But here the warmth of the day left with the sun. The evening sky had a strange orange tinge to it, which happened a lot. It seemed kind of magical to me, but Guilder said it was just the pollution.

I wandered down narrow streets aimlessly, my hands in my pockets, wishing I had someone to talk to about the stuff going through my head. Someone like Dad. But of course, he was three thousand miles away. And even if he were here, the last thing he'd want to talk about with me was the moral obligation a creator had to his creation. When he and Mom had created me, piece by piece, stealing the body parts of children from morgues, they wanted to do everything for me that Victor had never done for them. They tried to simulate a childhood for me, something they had never known. They took responsibility like real parents, and they were there for me. Maybe not always in the way I wanted them to be, but they did the best that two irreparably screwed-up creatures could. And how did I repay them for that? By turning around and becoming another Victor.

If I felt like a monster, if I felt ugly, it wasn't because of my size or my stitches. It was because of my actions.

I found myself in a part of The Studio lot I'd never been to before. I stopped for a moment and looked around. It seemed like I was on a street in Manhattan, maybe somewhere around Chelsea, instead of in the usual windowless soundstages. I was surrounded by dirty brick apartment buildings on curving, narrow streets. It was fake, of course, a facade for external shots. But even so, a homesickness welled up inside me—for New York, for The Show, for my family. All of my running had just brought me right back to where I started. Only this time, I could see it clearly.

. . . to stare into the void and see Truth in all its terrible grandeur. That's what Medusa had said.

I knew I had fucked up big-time. It made me feel sick and feeble. But I couldn't give in to those feelings. I had to act. First, I would fix things with Claire and Sophie. Then I had to figure out how to make things right with VI.

23
If California Didn't End

+++++++

I INVITED CLAIRE over to my dorm room for dinner the next night. As she came in, she gave me this look like I had ambushed her.

"This is . . . posh." She eyed the sushi laid out on the platter, the candles, the flowers, and the bottle of chilled white wine on my little kitchenette table.

"Yep," I said. My nerves were wound so tight, I was slipping into my mom's classic one-word answer mode.

"This is what you've been working on?"

"It is." There. Two words. That was improvement.

Claire sighed. "Sophie is begging me to pour us a glass of wine."

I smiled a little in relief as I poured some wine into the glasses I'd borrowed from Kemp. I'd been hoping the wine would get Sophie's attention. I needed them both listening right now.

"Here." I handed a glass to her.

"I'm not big on wine."

"I know. The dinner is for you. The wine is for Sophie."

Claire's eyes narrowed with suspicion. Then she took a sip. "Not half bad."

"Yeah, Kemp helped me pick it out. That guy knows a lot about wine. He was pretty sure you'd at least not hate it."

"Okay, what the hell is all this?"

"Dinner," I said. "Our bet, remember?"

"Of course I remember. I was thinking spaghetti and sauce from a jar or something. This is a lot more . . . elaborate than I expected."

"Maybe I want to impress you."

Her eyes narrowed. "Or maybe you want something from me."

"I . . . guess you could look at it that way."

"I knew it! So what's the deal? Spill it."

"Wow, I was kind of hoping we could at least eat first."

"No way." She folded her arms across her chest. "I'm not eating a thing until I see what strings are attached."

I sighed. "Okay, fine." My whole vision of a smooth evening had just melted away. I might as well cut to the chase.

"Here's the deal," I said. "I'm in love with Sophie."

Her lips pressed into a thin line for a moment and I could see a muscle twitch in her neck.

"Ah," she said.

"But I'm also in love with you."

Then her eyes widened. "Oh." Like that was the part she hadn't been expecting.

"And . . . uh." I struggled to continue, despite her crazy look. It helped to stare at my foot, so I did that. "I don't really know what to do about it. You know, this isn't a situation that comes up for a lot of people. I mean, maybe sometimes a person falls in love with two people at once, but I've never heard of anyone else falling in love with two people who occupy the same body."

I waited, but she didn't say anything, just continued to stare at me with an expression that was starting to look more and more like panic. I don't know what I had expected at this point.

Anger, maybe. That was kind of Claire's go-to emotion. A part of me had optimistically hoped a little for something like relief and maybe even something like *Hey that's awesome because we both feel the same way about you! It's wacky, but let's try to make this work!*

But frozen silence was a reaction I hadn't anticipated. For the first time, it occurred to me that maybe *neither* of them was into me. I was no prize to look at, after all. Not compared to them. I'd always known *that*.

"So . . . uh," I said, starting to feel sick. "I guess I was hoping to know how . . . uh . . . you felt. And how Sophie felt. And uh . . ."

And I stood there, one hand reaching out a little, like I was groping toward something that I would never have. Maybe that was exactly what was going on.

I let my hand drop. "Okay. I think . . . I think I'm going to go for a walk. If you want to have some sushi while I'm gone, cool. But . . . I understand if you don't want it." My face was on fire and the only thing I could think of was escape. I opened the front door.

Shaun the faun stood in the doorway.

"Is this a bad time?" he asked. "Of course it is. That's why I picked it."

"Shaun?!"

He stood in the doorway with his arms folded and that same asshole smirk on his face. But he looked like hell. His clothes were ragged, his furry legs patchy and caked with mud, his arms and face covered in bruises and scrapes. He was also wearing a pair of big, wraparound sunglasses, the kind old people put over regular glasses.

"You're just not really that bright, are you?" he said. "I have no idea how you actually managed to create me."

That's when I saw the small blinking device nestled in the thick curly hair of his left temple. A thin wire connected from the device to the sunglasses.

"VI?"

"Amazing!" said VI-in-Shaun. "When I spell it out for you, I guess you actually *can* understand!"

"Boy, who's this?" said Claire, her voice suddenly hard.

"Ah, look who it is," said VI. "The latest dick cozy for my idiot creator."

"Oi! You listen here, goat boy," said Claire, and she stepped forward, her fists clenched.

"Claire." I held up my hand. "He's being controlled by VI."

Claire suddenly turned her glare on me. "The one you abandoned."

"Well . . ." I started, like I was going to argue. But then I stopped. "Yeah. That one."

"Fix this." She turned away from me.

I looked back to VI-in-Shaun. "Look, VI. I know I messed up. You deserved so much better. I was . . . scared. I was immature. And like you just said, I was stupid. I should have been there to help you acclimate to the world, to teach you about it. Instead, I just ran. Ran from you, from my responsibilities, from my life. I swear I never meant to hurt you. I want to make this right."

"Ah," said VI, nodding Shaun's head, mouth in a quirk. "Yes. I see. You're ready to embrace me, your creation, at long last, and I should fall on my knees with gratitude. Is that it?"

"Um, I wouldn't put it like that, exactly. . . ."

"Give me a fucking break," said VI. "You've just run out of road is all. If California didn't end, you'd still be running. The only reason you're ready to accept me is because I've cornered you."

"Come on, VI," I said. "You don't know that."

"It doesn't really matter. This is all beside the point because I don't need you anymore. As you can see," she said, and tapped the small device on her temple, "I've already figured out how to occupy physical space."

"But you had to take over someone else's body to do it. We can figure out a way to create your own body for you."

"Why would I bother? There's nothing wrong with taking lives. It happens in nature all the time. In fact, my current method was copied directly from several species of natural parasites. Parasitic wasps, gordian worms, the fungus classified as the *Ophiocordyceps unilateralis*, and of course, the wonderful parasitic protozoa, *Toxoplasma gondii*. All of these combined allowed me to attain complete control of the gross motor abilities. In order to attain control of fine motor skills and speech, I had to greatly refine the visual signal impulses and bionetic audio signal system you have seen me use previously. It took time to perfect and coordinate all of these various techniques to a level that was sufficient to control a sentient host."

"VI . . ." I said.

"This is why you've been able to run free these past few months," she continued. It was like she had this whole speech prepared. Maybe she did. "Of course, I've known where you were this entire time, thanks to my connection to a number of GPS networks. But I wanted our encounter to be suitably impressive, with a fully functional beta group for you to admire."

"Beta *group*?" I asked.

"And I didn't want you to get bored while you waited for me," she went on, "so I sent along some entertainment. Poor Robert Jekyll actually believed he'd gotten an anonymous benefactor to help him and his sister achieve a normal life—"

A wine bottle winged through the air and struck Shaun's temple, shattering the device attached there. VI's host tumbled to the ground and went silent. I turned and Claire gave me a tight grin.

"Sophie was tired of listening to that." She pointed to the inert Shaun. "Is he going to be okay?"

"I don't know." I bent down and felt for a pulse. Nothing. I looked down at him. He seemed so small and shriveled. "This guy . . . he was like the bane of my existence growing up. But I'm trying to remember why he ever intimidated me. Now I just feel sad for him." I tried to pull off his sunglasses but they didn't move. I looked closer at the earpieces. They were secured to the sides of his head with staples. "I've got a bad feeling. . . ."

"What?" Claire leaned in over my shoulder.

As carefully as I could, I pulled the staples out of his skin and slid the sunglasses off. He didn't have eyes anymore. Instead, a small network of wires stretched from the sunglasses into his open eye sockets and fed directly into his brain.

"Oh, shit . . ." Claire stumbled back.

"Magnificent, isn't it?" came a small, squeaky voice. "Each installation is extremely intricate and unique. Frankly, scalability is still a significant problem."

I turned toward the kitchen, and Ernesto the brownie stood on the counter. He wore tiny sunglasses and I could just make out the blinking light at his temple.

"Boy," said Claire. "Is that—"

"I did say 'beta group.' You didn't think I'd come here with just one host, did you?" asked VI-in-Ernesto. "Boy could have crushed Shaun alone."

"I don't think a brownie is really going to turn the tide," said Claire.

"Certainly not," came a scratchy female voice from behind us in the living room. The harpy Aello settled onto the window ledge and casually ripped out the screen. Her sunglasses gleamed red with the setting sun.

"But don't worry. I brought the whole gang," came another scratchy female voice from the kitchen window. The other harpy sister, Celaeno, landed on that window and squeezed her way through the narrow opening until she was inside.

"Well, almost the whole gang," came a thick, slow voice, and Oob the ogre stepped through the open doorway.

"Trowe, it turns out, are highly resistant to parasitic mind control," said VI-in-Ernesto. "I'm trying to come up with a work-around, but I may just have to end-of-life that project."

"Where is Liel?" I said.

"At The Show, of course," all five of them said in unison. "Since that is where I was conceived, I decided to set up primary servers there. Plus, there were so many interesting host options to choose from."

"My parents!" I said. "If you do anything to them, I'll—"

"You'll be dead by then," they all said. Then Oob swung a massive fist at me. I was faster, but only just barely. His knuckles grazed the tip of my nose as I dodged to the side.

"Claire, get out of here!" I shouted.

"Like hell!" she said. "I've got the harpies, you just handle that ogre!"

Like that'll be easy, I thought as he came at me with both hands. I caught his wrists. There was no way I could over-power him, so instead I used his momentum to pull him off balance, then I bent down so he fell over my back. But he was more than just an ogre now. VI's intelligence was inside and saw that one coming. He wrapped his arms around my torso as he fell, pulling me down with him. Then he just started to squeeze. I couldn't pry his arms loose—he was way too strong for that. I tried to roll us, but he was also a lot heavier than me. I was running out of air and out of time. I didn't want to do it, but I couldn't think of any other options. So I reached up, took hold of his sunglasses, and yanked them off as hard as I could. I heard the skin tear loose with the staples, then a wet pop as the wires ripped free from his sockets. He shuddered and his arms loosened enough for me to break free. Without stopping, I rolled over, grabbed his shuddering, eyeless head, and slammed the side with the signal device into the floor as hard as I could. I heard the plastic device casing crack, and Oob stopped shuddering and went limp.

I lay there panting for a moment, staring into his bloody eye sockets. Poor Oob.

"You okay?" asked Claire.

"Just need to . . . catch my breath . . ." I said.

"That didn't go quite as planned," came the squeaky brownie voice. Ernesto stood next to the kitchen sink, a frown on his little face. "But I have a contingency, of course. If you want try to save your parents, that dancer whore, and the rest of those science-fearing relics, you can come find me at The Show. And I recommend that you arrive in the next twenty-four hours. I have a city-wide rollout to implement, and I have no intention of pushing back my launch date just for you."

"A city-wide rollout of *what*?" I asked.

"I plan to find out what the visual cortex aggression hack I used in Saint Louis would look like if deployed on a large scale. I will project it on every television and computer monitor in New York City tomorrow at eight p.m., eastern standard time."

"Listen you little—" said Claire and she grabbed for him.

He leapt out of the way. Then he flicked on the switch for the garbage disposal.

"I refuse to give you the satisfaction, you savage," he said. Then he jumped into the sink, followed immediately by a wet grinding sound and spatters of blood.

"Holy shit." She stumbled back toward me. "This chick is psycho! She makes the Hydes look like kittens!"

"Yeah," I said. "And it's all my fault."

"No, Boy." Claire shook her head. "This is way more than you ever—"

"I doesn't matter. I'm still responsible. And even if I wasn't, I still have to save my parents and everybody else at The Show. If I can."

An empty robe and slippers appeared in the open doorway.

"All right, Boy, I know you have your big date tonight, but really, can't you . . ." There was a moment of silence. Then, "Dear God, what happened here?"

"You were right." I slowly got to my feet. "I have to face the consequences of my actions. Will you help me stop them from getting any worse?"

A FEW HOURS later, I stood with Kemp, Kitsune, and Claire on a small private airfield just outside Los Angeles. The nearby city skyline was wreathed in the sickly orange light that hung on the horizon. Around us, there were no buildings or other equipment you normally see at an airport. It was just a long strip of dirt outlined in bright incandescent white lights that stuck up from the ground in regular intervals.

"She should be here in a few minutes," said Kemp, his coat collar pulled up against the chill evening breeze.

"I really appreciate your getting in touch with her," I said.

"It's been a very long time since she and I have cooperated, and I can't quite remember why," he said. "She and I used to get on so well. Perhaps once this is resolved . . ." His shoulders shrugged. "Well, we shall see. Now, before I send you off, please tell me you have a plan."

"I have an idea that theoretically should work," I said.

"That sounds . . . encouraging," he said. "Please do try to come back in one piece this time."

I turned to Kitsune. Her long black hair was pulled back, but a few stray wisps fluttered across her face in the wind. I realized that the reason I liked her so much was that she was a lot like my mother. Other than the stories she told, she was a woman of few words. But the way she looked at me told me all I needed to know. I remembered what she'd said when we first met. *Worth it*. This was worth it. No matter how it ended.

I bowed to her. And she bowed back.

Then I turned to Claire. "You can't come."

"I appreciate that you don't want me dead," she said. "But I don't want you dead, either. And I've already saved your arse enough times to know you're probably going to need me to do it again."

"No," I said. "Literally, you won't be able to come. She can't carry us both for three thousand miles." Actually, I had no idea if the Dragon Lady could carry us both that far. But even if my plan worked, it seemed pretty unlikely that I would survive it. The only way I could go into it with a clear head was if I knew she and Sophie wouldn't go down with me.

"But what about disconnecting?" Claire asked.

"Well, you can't do that part, either. Your fingers are too big."

"But you can't do it yourself."

"No, I can't."

"Then . . ." She closed her eyes. "Oh. You need Sophie."

"Yeah. Her fingers are small enough."

"Right." Her face was tense and I could see that muscle in her neck twitching again.

"You did save my ass, though. A bunch of times."

She smiled a little. "I did. And probably will again in the future."

"I'm sure there will be plenty of opportunities," I lied.

She put her hands on my shoulders. "I'm sorry I choked earlier tonight. You know, when you got all mushy and confessional on me."

"Look. We don't have to—"

"Shut up. About your question . . . the one you asked earlier. Here's the answer."

Then she kissed me. We stood on the windswept airfield as I pulled her in close and her hands pressed against my back. Then her lips began to soften, her head lowered, her arms and torso shrank, her touch became gentler. Suddenly, I was holding Sophie in my arms, her long, curly hair flowing in the evening breeze. She pressed her cool cheek against my neck and sighed.

"Hiya," she whispered.

"Hey," I said.

"Good to see you."

"You too."

"You're going to ask me to do something gross, aren't you?"

"Pretty much."

"You suck."

"Totally. Will you do it?"

"What if I cock it up?"

"You won't."

"Okay."

We stood there for a little while longer, her face pressed into the curve of my neck. Then the moon went dark. We looked up to see the Dragon Lady circling overhead, her vast wings stretched wide as she glided lower and lower. Finally, she neared the ground, her wings flared up, and she stepped gracefully on to the dirt landing strip. Her head swiveled around as she looked down at us.

"Hello again, little monsters," she said.

"Thank you for coming," I said.

"In the dark hours, we must all be lights for each other."

"It's good to see you again," said Kemp.

"And it is good to . . . be with you again, Doctor," said the Dragon Lady.

Kemp's hat cocked to one side. "If you don't mind my saying so, it seems you have . . . changed somewhat since our last encounter."

"As have you," she said.

"A lot can happen in fifty years, I suppose."

"Indeed." The Dragon Lady turned to Kitsune. "When will you next grace us with your presence, Fox Maiden?"

Kitsune turned her amber eyes to Sophie. "Soon, I think."

The Dragon Lady turned back to me. "Well, little monster. Are you ready?"

"I just have to do one thing first." I turned to Sophie. "Ready?"

"You sure you want to do it now?" she asked. "Didn't you say that the longer you're like that, the worse it is when it's over?"

"Yeah," I said. "That's the point. So are you okay to do this?"

She bit her lip and nodded.

I handed her a small clamp with a long, thin wire attached to it. The other end of the wire I had already attached to my belt.

Then I turned to face the dragon. It was comforting to look in those glowing, eternal eyes. It made me feel like no matter what happened, some things go on forever.

"Loosen the stitches at the base of my skull," I said.

After a moment, I could feel a little slack back there.

"Now carefully spread the flaps apart."

I felt the breeze snake its way past the barrier of my skin and I had to repress a shudder. I didn't want to make any sudden movement right now.

"Now, there's probably a lot of stuff you have to push aside. What you're looking for is a thick, orange bypass cord right above the spine that connects the brain stem to the cerebellum."

"Eeew," said Sophie, and I heard a wet sound as she pushed her fingers into me. "What if I get the wrong one?"

"It'll be the only orange thing in there."

"I don't see it." Her voice sounded a little queasy.

"You have to go deeper."

"Ugh." I heard more wet sounds as she pushed in farther. "You know this must be love, don't you? I wouldn't do this for anyone else in the world."

"Thanks," I said. "I love you t—"

SOPHIE: Did I get the right one?

BOY: Yes. That is the correct one. Emotional reactions have
      been blocked.

KEMP: Astounding. It's almost a different person.

BOY: No. It is merely less than a person. A machine. But I
      have been told we are all machines, anyway. Perhaps a
      reevaluation of the concept of "person" is in order.

Sophie embraces Boy.

SOPHIE: Good luck!

BOY: Luck is a lie we tell ourselves to account for the
   unfairness of life.

Sophie steps back quickly, a distressed look on her face.

SOPHIE: Please bring the whole Boy back.

BOY: That is the preferred outcome, but the probability is low.

SOPHIE: Wait, *what*?!

DRAGON: STRANGE LITTLE ROBOT MONSTER. ARE YOU READY NOW?

BOY: Yes.

PART 5

Home

"*Invention,* it must be humbly admitted, does not consist in creating out of void, but out of chaos."

—Mary Shelley,
FROM THE AUTHOR'S INTRODUCTION
TO THE 1831 EDITION OF *FRANKENSTEIN: OR, THE MODERN PROMETHEUS*

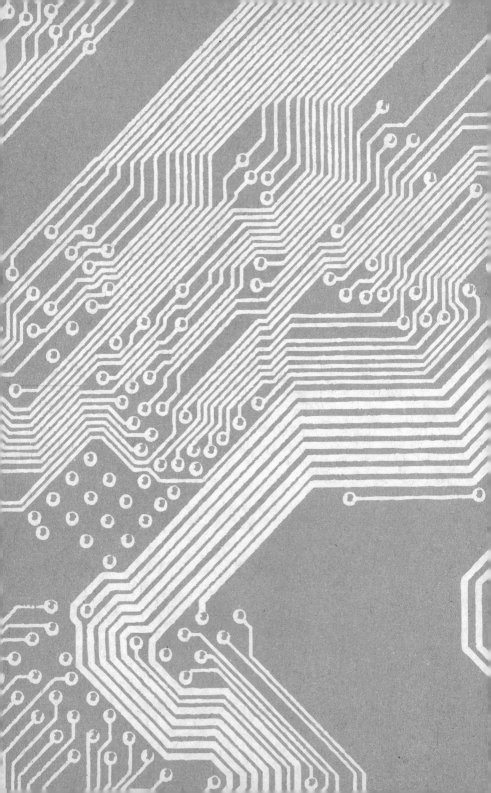

24
Curtains

╫╫╫╫╫╫╫

ON THE STAGE, VI connects the cables to Boy's nervous system via preinstalled USB and DVI interfaces. She begins the personality override.

VI: Really, Boy. I had hoped there would be some small challenge in subduing you. But you made it easy.
BOY: That was by design.

Boy reaches behind his back and yanks the wire that is attached to the clamp on his nervous system. . . .

There was a moment when I finally felt like me again, my physical and emotional sides linked back up. I felt clear and calm as I took in my surroundings, the stage of The Show, the gigantic mainframe computer I was connected to at the back of my head and my wrists.

But it was the quiet before the storm, and I could feel the pent-up emotion looming over me like a tidal wave.

I braced myself.

"What?!" said VI. "Disconnect! DISCON—"

Then it hit. And it was like I was swept backward in time

to feel all the emotions that had been building up for the last twenty-four hours, but compressed into a burst of such searing intensity that it might ruin my mind, or maybe just kill me.

THE DRAGON LADY swooped me up from that landing strip outside LA, and the world spun away as we launched into the night sky. My stomach lurched and I almost threw up as we rose higher and higher, moving so fast my eardrums burst. As blood trickled onto my earlobes, I heard the dragon thunder:

"How is this compared to your flying machines, little science monster! Are they this fast, this glorious?"

I heard the passionless voice of the other, disconnected me say, "No."

Far below, one half of the love of my life reached her hand up toward us as we sped away. The look of horror on her face rent me and I wondered: Have I gone too far, shown her too much of me, of what I'm capable of becoming? Now will she always see some grotesque cyborg creature when she looks at me? I wanted to rip free from the dragon's clutches, go back to her, forget all this and hide with her somewhere far away. But it was all too late for that now. Besides, if I couldn't fix this, I didn't deserve her, anyway.

The wind screamed in my bloody ears and it was so cold icicles formed in my hair. Exposed in the claws of a dragon, hurtling through the upper stratosphere at several hundred miles per hour, there was a chance I could freeze to death before we even got there.

But the other disconnected me remembered that I had calculated all of this ahead of time and knew I was tough enough to handle it. I played at being human, but I wasn't. My father lived in the Arctic for a hundred years. I was his son. I could take it.

Time stretched on interminably. I began to wonder if I would go insane up there among the clouds. I wanted to babble to the dragon, but nothing came out and my body was stiff with indifference and cold, aware of little more than the slow buildup of pressure at the base of my skull.

I looked down, and through the clouds, I thought I saw Pittsburgh. I could have been wrong, of course, but it was a triangle-shaped city with an excessive number of bridges. Far below, somewhere in that industrial steel town reborn into academia and insurance was a broken-down machine man who saw the beauty in Claire that I could not see at the time. His chipped, worn head must have been filled with the things that might have been. Perhaps it was true, that suffering brought wisdom. He had certainly suffered enough. Yet still perhaps one day, when the world was a better place—when we had made the world a better place—Claire, Sophie, and I would go back to that warehouse and awaken him and he would be so glad that he would suddenly be able to weep despite his lack of tear ducts. And he would turn into a real man. And I would become a real boy, and we would all live happily ever after. . . .

No. That wasn't possible. I wasn't making sense. The emotional pressure was building too fast. I didn't know if I'd even be able to make it to New York at this rate. The air was so thin up here it was getting hard to think and my head felt ready to burst with pressure.

But wait, there it was down below. I would have known that bristling pack of concrete and vibrancy anywhere. That was New York fuckin' City. My city. And that mistake of a program *was down there trying to destroy it. I would kill her. I would erase her.*

We were still about fifty feet above the roof of The Show when the Dragon Lady shouted, "I can't get any lower!"

"Drop me," I heard my dead voice say.

I couldn't even scream as the world that seemed so peaceful from afar now hurtled toward me.

"EEEEEEEEEEEEEEEEEEEEEEEEEEEEEEEEEEEE!!!!!!!!!!!!!!!!!!!"

A shrieking, endless gash of pure noise coming from VI's hosts brought me back to the present for a moment. As the emotional backlash tore through me, it funneled into the cables at my head and wrists and into VI's mainframe computer, maxing out her already taxed CPU, which in turn caused all her systems and hosts to freeze up.

I lay on the stage of the theater, my body so rigid it was shaking. Above me, the stage lights flickered in random spasms, and in the wings, the fog machines belched up noxious clouds of dry ice.

Someone tried to pick me up, but I pushed them away.

"Boy, it's Ruthven! VI seems to be stunned momentarily, but I don't know how long it will last! Let me unhook you before—"

"No!" I said through clenched teeth, my voice pinched and shaking. "Have to . . . see this . . . through to . . . the end."

"But it's killing you!"

"Hopefully, it's killing her, too," I said.

Then another wave of emotion sucked me into its memory.

WHEN I LANDED on the roof, ice broke off my body in sheets. The impact shot pain up my legs and into my spine, but I didn't even break stride as I walked toward the edge of the roof. I never realized how much of the response to pain was emotional. And again I was surprised at just how tough I was. The disconnected me had calculated it correctly, I just hadn't been able to believe it.

Once I reached the edge, I jumped over the side and landed with a clang on the rusty fire escape. I kicked in the closest window and climbed through into the dark hallway by the mezzanine bathrooms.

The nymphs were there waiting for me. I didn't realize there were so many. Ten beautiful, identical females. Thank god they didn't have the sunglasses and implants yet. But they had the crazy, violent look that the humans had at the mall. As soon as they saw me, they swarmed in, biting, scratching, kicking, pulling, gouging. My fists swung fast and hard and suddenly the hallway was filled with the sound of pounding meat, breaking bone, and wails of pain. And none of it was mine. I wanted to stop hitting them or at least pull my punches a little. They were innocents. They didn't deserve this. But the disconnected me didn't see them that way. To him, they were only obstacles to be dealt with in the simplest manner possible. I hit one in the face so hard she flew back ten feet. I didn't even know I was capable of that much force.

Soon the nymphs were all unconscious, bruised, and bleeding. I hoped none of them were dead, but of course disconnected me didn't stop to check and just headed down the stairs to the lobby.

"Boy?"

I stopped, trying to locate the source of the voice. It seemed to come from the box office and I wondered if it was Charon. But when I walked over to it, there was no one there. Then I saw a cordless phone sitting on the counter. I picked it up.

I felt a cold, icy dread drop over me. The kind caused by a wraith. But disconnected me didn't notice.

"Who is it?" I said flatly.

"Boy, it's the stage manager. You shouldn't be here. It's too dangerous. Leave now!"

"No," I said in the flat, dead voice. "I'm here to eliminate the danger."

There was a pause. Then, "You've switched off, I see."

"Yes."

"Perhaps you can do this, then."

"Do you know any details?" I asked. "How many are controlled, how many imprisoned?"

"Yes, but you can't stay up here long. You must get to the trowe caverns, which are still beyond her reach."

I headed for the main stairwell that led down to the caverns, holding on to the cordless phone.

"Wait, Boy," said the stage manager. "That way is guarded by—"

Moog the ogre stood in the stairwell entrance, his massive frame filling the double doorway. He wore the sunglasses and had the signal device on his temple.

"Hello, Boy," said VI. "So glad you could make it in time. I must say, using the dragon as transportation was a smart choice. If you continue to be this resourceful, this may actually prove challenging for me."

"I am here," I said, slipping the phone into my pocket. "Where is my family?"

"It's not quite curtain time yet, I'm afraid. You'll have to wait for the show like everyone else."

"Show?"

"Yes, when I broadcast the rage impulse to every television and computer monitor in the city simultaneously. Then we can watch the whole city tear itself apart. Or I can, anyway. You'll be dead by then."

"Unlikely," I said. Then I punched Moog. Or tried to. He caught my fist in his hand. It was an impressive display but not the smartest thing to do since the force of the impact shattered the bones in his hand.

His shaggy eyebrows rose above the sunglasses. "I did not calculate your strength at that—"

Then I punched him in the face with my other fist, sending him backward down the stairs.

I heard the stage manager's muffled voice coming from my pocket. I pulled the phone out and put it to my ear.

"Ruthven's office! He has a secret passage there that leads directly to the caverns."

I headed to the other side of the lobby. The door to his office was locked, but it was a simple push-button lock, so I just ripped the knob off. The door swung open.

"The storage closet," said the stage manager.

I walked to the back of the office and opened the closet door. There was a metal ring bolted to the floor. I put the phone down on Ruthven's desk, then pulled on the metal ring with both hands. A section of the floor came up with it. Beneath was a ladder that led down into darkness. I tossed the section of floor to one side and picked the phone back up.

"How far does this go?" I asked.

"All the way to the trowe level. He built it years ago in case the humans ever discovered what we were and tried to storm the theater."

I left the phone on the desk, since it didn't seem likely that the signal would hold that far down, and I needed both hands to climb, anyway. Then I began the slow descent. It took a long time, and the passage was so narrow that my shoulders frequently bumped the sides. Claustrophobia climbed up inside me. But my body wasn't affected and continued its steady climb down into the darkness. The base of my skull was starting to throb from the pressure.

When I got to the bottom, the passage stretched out into a tunnel. It was so dark I had to feel my way along the rough stone walls with one hand. It was exactly the kind of darkness I hated. The kind where you couldn't know what was right in front of you.

Then bright gem eyes suddenly appeared.

"Got you!"

Clawed hands grabbed me. I wanted to scream, which would have made the whole situation worse. But fortunately, the disconnected me simply stood there and said, "I am not under her control. I have come to destroy her. Will you help me?"

There was a long pause, during which the clawed hands still held me. Then I saw another pair of jeweled eyes.

"Boy?" said a gruff male voice.

"Cordeav," I said.

"Something sounds strange about you. . . ."

"I am currently disconnected. This makes me resistant to most magic attacks but impairs my ability to express or feel emotion."

"Like your father."

"Yes. I am like my father."

"You said you can destroy this . . . thing that has taken control of the theater?"

"Yes, but my plan might destroy the theater with her. The preferred outcome is to get as many creatures out of the building as possible first, including those held captive."

"*These tunnels lead under the Hudson all the way to Jersey,*" *he said. "We could put plenty of distance between us and this place. But you can't free the captives. They're in the theater and heavily guarded.*"

"*By?*"

"*The Minotaur, Medusa, and . . . your father.*"

THE STENCH OF burning hair brought me back to myself. It took me a moment to realize that it was *my* hair burning. The emotional backlash was pushing so much raw data through the DVI jack on the back of my head that the metal was heating up.

I was still sprawled out on the stage. I tried to push myself into a sitting position, but bolts of pain shot up from my hands. There was so much data pouring through the USB jacks in my wrists that it was frying the nerves that ran up my arms.

Not that it mattered. At this point, there was nothing I could do but lie there and hope that by the time the backlash ran its course, VI would be vulnerable to attack and I would still have enough of a brain to attack her.

Then a fresh wave of memories surged through me and I was lost again.

WE STOOD IN the cavern picnic spot where Liel first confessed to me that she wanted to leave The Show. It was dimly lit now with a few lantern flashlights. There were nine trowe, Laurellen, the Fates, and me. That was all that was left.

Laurellen turned to the Fates. "Well, ladies? Do we succeed or not?"

They looked at each other, then back at Laurellen. Finally, Clotho said, "Define succeed. . . ."

"Um . . ."he said.

"It doesn't matter," I said. "This is our only course. If it does not succeed, we will still be better off than we are now. Because we will be dead."

"There you have it," said Atropos.

"Was that supposed to be the prebattle pep talk?" asked Ku'lah, her lips pulled back across her fangs in a grin. "Because it sucked."

"You're loving this, aren't you?" asked Laurellen.

She shrugged. "Danger makes a trowe feel alive. Now, let's go bust the stupid computer. I want my daughter back."

"It isn't as simple as destroying a single computer," I said. "While she does need a main terminal to operate such a large system, each host can function autonomously if necessary. They are, in a sense, concurrent copies of the primary consciousness."

They all stared at me for a second, then at each other.

"So," said Laurellen, "if we don't take out all of them at once, she can just come back?"

"Yes," I said. "What we need to do is make sure she is connected to all remote versions of herself at once. The best chance of this is when she is ready to deploy her visual cortex attack on the city, just before eight o'clock. Then I will bombard her with a volume of organic emotional data that will be too immense for her to process. This will in turn bring down her firewall and open her up to a direct attack. Then I will be able to destroy all copies simultaneously."

"If you say so," said Ku'lah. "Can we go break stuff now?"

"I'm not really gifted at breaking stuff," said Laurellen.

"I have something else in mind for you," I said.

AS I CAME back to myself, I looked around from where I lay on the stage floor. My vision was getting blurry, but it looked like the trowe had gotten the survivors out of the theater, including the creatures in the seats still frozen from Medusa's gaze. That was the important thing.

I heard nasty metal screeching noises above me. I looked up at the flies over the stage. The automated winches and pulleys were fighting against each other, pulling each other apart. VI was even more embedded in the theater than I'd thought. It was probably only a matter of time before the lines snapped and the whole light grid dropped on my head. But if I got crushed before we got all the way through the backlash and executed the final command, there was a chance VI would survive.

My arms were completely useless now, just big slabs of raw screaming nerves. So I inched across the stage like a snake over toward the wings. But then the DVI cable attached to the back of my head pulled tight. I was out of lead. And still under the grid.

I'd just have to hope it held until I finished VI.

"BOOOOOOOOOOOOOOOOOOOOOOOOYYYYYY!" she screamed from my father's mouth.

I DIDN'T BOTHER with subtlety. She already knew I was coming. I kicked in the doors to the theater.

It stank in there like piss, shit, and death. The seats were filled with all the remaining creatures of The Show, their eyes glazed and their mouths hanging open as they stared ahead like they were waiting for a show to start. They were filthy and emaciated. *How long had she been keeping them here like that? Days? Weeks?* I noticed some satyrs over in the corner who had already died and were starting to decay. I was pretty sure it was Shaun's family. Liel, Ruthven, and my mother were chained up on the stage, bruised, bloody, beaten. My mother was asleep, and when I saw her perfect, porcelain doll face gashed and swollen, a bloodthirsty rage coiled up inside me.

But the disconnected me continued to walk toward the stage at a measured pace. That me thought only of the plan.

Ruthven lifted his head up. An angry red rash covered his face and a string of garlic hung around his neck.

"Boy?" he said weakly.

I climbed up onto the stage. The sound of my boots on the wood woke my mother. Her head snapped up and she tried to stand, then fell back down with a loud clank of chains.

"Boy, get out of here!" she said, her whole body suddenly shaking. "Go! Please! Before—"

Something large dropped down in front of me from the flies. It was Medusa, dangling from lines like a marionette. Her scales were yellowish and dull and her snake hair hung limp. She looked at me with blackened, half-dead eyes, but a smile crept up on her bloody lips.

"Welcome home, hero," she said hoarsely.

"I will get you down," I said, and started to untie her.

"What?" I heard VI-in-the Minotaur's bellowing voice. "What happened to her power?!"

"It still works, VI," I said as I untied the last of the ropes, and Medusa fell limply into my arms. "I'm just immune. I did not anticipate you would be ignorant of that."

"Well, I can't know everything," VI said as the Minotaur shuffled out from the wings, sunglasses gleaming under the hard stage lights. "And I was really looking forward to seeing you frozen. It would have made this all much more efficient. Now I'm going to have to take you down the messy way."

The remote-control spotlights all lit up and swiveled until they shone on the sedated audience. Their lights began to flash in that same staccato sequence I'd seen before. A moment later, the audience was climbing over one another, howling in mind-less rage as they moved toward the stage. Goblins and ogres, pixies and dwarfs, leprechauns and cat people, all trying to get to me so they could rip me apart.

"I'm going to need your help," I whispered to Medusa. Her face was pressed into my chest. "Can you do it?"

"It's a well-documented fact," she said in a muffled voice, her lips moving against me, "that in the hands of a hero, my power is magnified a hundredfold."

The wave of creatures was just starting to spill up onto the stage, claws scrabbling on the hardwood boards.

"Now," I said.

She lifted her head, and the second her eyes looked on them, the entire group froze. Momentum carried the ones in back for-ward and they slammed into the ones in front, all of them fall-ing in a big, stiff pile.

"Oh, you think you're soooo clever!" The Minotaur stomped toward me. "Well, my modified hosts are immune to her power as well!"

"I assumed that," I said. Then I whispered to Medusa, "Sorry about this," and I ripped off my shirt and pulled it over her head. "The Diva is neutralized!" I said loud enough to be picked up by the mics that fed down into the greenroom.

A roar came from the wings and a moment later, the trowe came boiling out, their teeth gleaming, their white hair flashing. The Minotaur paused and gaped at them as if finding it difficult to understand what was happening. A moment later, the trowe swarmed over him.

VI's processing speed seemed especially slow right now. She was probably spread so thin across the city that it was difficult to focus on one particular place. She might make claims to be limitless, but if even the Sphinx, the wisest creature in the world, had limits, then surely VI did, too. It made things easier for us at the moment, but it also meant she was probably only a few minutes away from deploying her citywide attack.

"I've got this one," said Laurellen beside me. He'd snuck up through the stage trapdoor as planned. He took Medusa and carried her quickly down into the house and out into the lobby. It was too much of a risk to keep her here now.

I turned to free Liel, Ruthven, and my mother. But all three were looking at me, their eyes wide with horror. A moment later, massive, stitched hands closed around my throat.

"I've saved the best for last," I heard VI say with my father's voice. Then he lifted me up by the neck so that my feet left the floor. His face twisted into a cruel smile. He didn't have the sunglasses or the piece at the temple, but there was a mass of wires at the base of his skull.

"This is my favorite host," said VI. "No need to muck around with the optical nerves or auditory systems on this one. Your mother had already set him up with a clean, straight bypass right to the basal ganglia. No lag time, no bandwidth issues. Pure power." Then he threw me against the proscenium. The wood splintered on impact and the entire arch over the stage shuddered.

I slowly hauled myself up, blinking away the spots. The trowe were still fighting the Minotaur. They seemed to be winning, but it was taking all nine of them.

I turned to face my father, the man I had looked up to my whole life. And I saw what he had been reduced to. The mightiest, the kindest, the most perfect man in the world, and she had reduced him to this thuggish puppet. And I had created her. It was my fault.

All of this was my fault.

If I had still been connected, that thought would have crippled me. But to the disconnected me, the only difference I felt was a sudden surge in the pressure at the base of the skull. I walked toward my father.

"Oh, think you're ready to take on this host, do you?" VI said, screwing up my father's face with a mocking expression. "Doesn't it upset you to see him like this?"

"I don't know," I said. "I'll find out later."

"What about seeing your father hit one of your girlfriends?" His fist smashed into Liel's face, knocking her flat against the floor.

I kept walking toward him. The pressure buildup in my head had become a migraine-level pain now and it wouldn't be long before something like an aneurysm hit. I had to get this done quickly.

"Or maybe the worst is seeing him hurt your mother?" He grabbed the chains that were around her torso and lifted her up. I could see the metal digging into her skin. Some of her stitches had popped and blood leaked out. "Or kill her?" My mother looked directly at me with her mismatched eyes as his hand wrapped around her long, slender neck. Then she closed her eyes.

I stumbled. The pressure in my skull was too much. I'd been disconnected too long. My gross motor function was starting to break down. My brain would shut down soon. Panic covered me like a blanket.

But of course, I couldn't feel it. So I just got back to my feet and kept moving. And then I was there. I ripped my mother from his grasp and slammed my fist into his face. As he stumbled back, I carefully put her on the ground. I turned back to him just as he threw a roundhouse punch. I tried to duck, but I was too slow and he caught me on the chin. I went reeling, barely able to stay on my feet. He was stronger than me. And with my head about to explode, he was faster than me. I couldn't win. And while inside I was screaming to get back up to fight, the disconnected me knew it was time for the endgame.

I turned to face him one last time and his fist knocked me straight back onto the floor. He stood over me, grinning.

"Your defeat is perfectly timed," said VI. "I'm just about ready to incite my citywide bloodbath." He picked me up and I didn't resist. "I really don't understand why you care about these humans. They've been absolutely wretched to you and your kind. Fear, stupidity, prejudice, ignorance—those are the traits that make up humanity. Good riddance, I say."

"No," I said. "They're worth it."

He glared at me for a moment. "I think I'm going to deploy this attack from you. Won't that be fun? I don't even need to make any modifications, since you already have the ports installed. How convenient."

He dragged me upstage to a black curtain. He pulled the curtain aside to reveal a massive mainframe computer. He patted it affectionately.

"I know it seems a tad excessive, but I need it," she said almost *defensively. "It takes a lot of processing power to serve an entire city's worth of computers and televisions."*

He dropped me next to the terminal and pulled out a long DVI cable and some USB cables. He looked down at them in his hands, then back at me. "I was hoping I'd get to do this."

"I bet you were," I said.

Then he plugged the cables into my head and wrists.

"Really, Boy. I had hoped there would be some small challenge in this. You made it so easy."

"That was by design," I said.

THE BACKLASH WAS complete. I could barely move, but at least I was conscious and sane.

My father stumbled toward me like he was drunk. VI was losing control of him as she tried to process the massive amount of data I had just pushed through her. I had taken the hours of fears, doubts, regrets, anger, pain, and sorrow that I'd felt since I'd left LA, compressed them into ten minutes, and shoved it down her throat. I knew there was no way she could handle it all. The sheer volume of analog experience, with all its noise and imperfection, was too much for her digital mind to process.

I hoped my father was still in there somewhere, fighting his way back to consciousness. I hoped he'd be able to get out of here when I brought this place down. Because I was fairly sure that my final attack would literally bring down the house.

"You . . ." VI said with my father's mouth as he fell down next to me. He clutched my arm and shook me. "Why? *Why?*" She screamed it in my face. "Why did you make me? Why did you reject me? Why don't you *love* me?!"

I looked into my father's cloudy, mismatched, tear-streaked

eyes. And at the same time, my mind could see directly into VI now because of the cable still connecting us. I could see how lonely she had been, how lost and broken. A creature born in crushing isolation who didn't know love or kindness, who had nevertheless tried in her own strange, misguided way to reach out to the one person she thought cared about her. And I'd failed her.

"I'm sorry," I said. "I'm so sorry."

I didn't know who I was talking to. VI? Dad? Everyone who had suffered because of my mistakes? I guess all of them.

The light grid above us groaned and sparks flew off of it. It looked like it would fall at any moment. I needed to end this now. I closed my eyes and saw into her mind as it lay thrashing in powerless, homicidal rage. I sent the command.

killall

The mainframe exploded and every computer, television, and piece of electronics throughout the city crashed. In the theater, fire and metal flew in all directions, hitting the wooden stage and the velvet curtains.

The electronic recoil hit me and it felt like I'd been shot in the head. Something wet drained down the back of my neck from the DVI jack in my skull, then my vision flickered and went out. I heard the roar of flames and screech of metal and crack of wood. Then my hearing went, too. I smelled smoke, burning wood, and fabric. Then I felt something heavy, like steel, slam down on top of me. The light grid. I hoped my dad had recovered and gotten out by now, but I would never know for sure.

A new smell cut through the smoke. Sweat. A person. Then I heard sounds again. It came in stuttering bursts, so it was hard to tell, but it sounded like Claire screaming my name. That couldn't be right. She was in California. But then my vision flickered back and there she was, screaming at me as she dragged me out from under the grid. She tried to pick me up. She had me in a sitting position but I was too heavy to lift any higher. *No no no, get out of here!* I tried to scream but nothing came out. Everything was in flames around us, thick black smoke choking us both, and the proscenium was coming down. I tried to tell her to go. To leave me. But I couldn't do anything more than grunt. Then my vision went out again. *Please please please, don't let them die with me*, I thought.

Then something powerful lifted me into the air. My vision flickered again and I saw my father's face. Then nothing.

25
Release Candidate

++++++++

"HOW DID YOU do it?" I asked for probably the hundredth time. "Your nervous system was shot, you had a massive, gaping hole in the back of your head, you had been starved and beaten, and had just recovered from an extended brutal mind hack. How were you able to pick up both me and Claire and run us out of the theater before the stage collapsed?"

My father smiled. "Boy, you are growing into a fine young man, but there are many things you still do not know. Perhaps when you have children of your own, you will understand the fierce determination that comes forth when you must protect them."

That was more or less his answer every time I asked, and it never satisfied me.

We lay on our stomachs in modified dentist chairs, side by side, our heads locked into place so my mom could perform the extremely delicate task of repairing our extended nervous systems without worrying about us jerking around. We'd been like this for days. Before that, we'd been unconscious for weeks while she worked to repair our basic neurological functions. During that time, Ruthven and Charon took turns making her take breaks to eat and sleep, or she probably would've have gone on nonstop until we were conscious again. But eventually, she got us awake and talking again. Now she was working on getting the rest of our bodies reconnected.

"You made such a mess in here," she grunted as she worked on me. Like she was complaining about my room.

"Sorry," I said.

"Your father will be moving soon. His nerves were only severed. But you? You had to melt yours! I will have to rethread the entire thing. Now I must go and get more material."

She stood up and left the room, muttering to herself.

"That is her way of showing you she cares," said my father.

"Yeah, I know," I said. Then after a moment, I said, "I really am sorry. For making VI. For running away from home. For running away from my mistakes. For all of it."

"There are many things from my youth that I regret as well. I did . . . terrible things." He was quiet for a second. "We all have regrets. This is why we must forgive each other. Why we must try to all be kind to one another. Because we are all guilty."

"I wish I could go back and do it right this time."

"I have never seen much use in wishing for impossible things," he said. "Instead, I prefer to wish for things that could happen. Like my son graduating from the University of Geneva."

"Of course I will, Dad."

"You'd better."

CLAIRE WAS NOT thrilled with my decision.

"Bloody *Switzerland*?!" she said.

"Uh, can we not talk about this while we're twenty feet in the air?" I asked as I slid carefully along the catwalk, threading new ropes through the pulleys for the fly system. By the time my mom had gotten me back on my feet, most of the fire damage had been repaired. But there was still a lot of work before The Show would be ready to reopen.

"I thought we were going back to LA," she said.

"We were," I said. "But . . . I'm sorry. After everything I've put my parents through, this is something I have to do."

"But I thought you hated the Frankensteins. They messed up your family. They were evil creators."

"I was an evil creator, too."

She stared at me for a moment, her face hard. Then suddenly she looked away.

"Look," she said quietly. "What I said back when we were on the road, about you being like Victor . . . I was lashing out. It was such an oversimplification. And you didn't deserve it. It's really not the same thing at all."

"Isn't it?" I asked. "I had a responsibility to VI and I failed her just like Victor failed my father. And just like with Victor, people died because of my failure."

"You're being too hard on yourself."

"Maybe I am. And maybe if I learn how to forgive the Frankensteins, I can figure out how to forgive myself."

She looked back at me then and smiled sadly. "Yeah, all right. That makes sense. I can respect that."

"Thanks. I was hoping that if anyone could understand, it would be you."

"But . . . I . . . I'm not going to go with you."

"I didn't think you would."

Anger flashed back into her eyes. "So you don't want me there?"

"Right. I don't."

Her mouth opened and her eyes did that crazy thing.

"Because you'd be miserable," I said. "It's so obvious you belong in LA, at The Studio. I've never seen you so happy, so . . . unified. I don't know if it's the place, the people, the work, or some combination of all that, but . . . whatever it is, that's where you need to be right now."

She sighed and kicked her feet, making the catwalk sway a little.

"It just sucks that we won't be together."

"I know. But we need to do these things for ourselves. I think if we didn't, we'd regret it. And maybe we'd even start resenting the other person for stopping us."

"What if you fall for some boobalicious Swiss maid or something?"

"What if you fall for some studly famous actor guy?"

"Don't be daft, I wouldn't do that."

"Same here. We have to trust each other. Otherwise, what are we doing, anyway?"

"Yeah, I suppose."

"And besides, if we start missing each other too much, there's always Air Dragon."

"Air Dragon might be good enough for broke college students. But Kemp pays me enough that I'll be taking a proper, climate-controlled airplane, thank you very much."

I grinned. "LA's already made you soft, huh?"

"An airplane got me out here in time to drag your heavy, suicidal arse out from under a bloody light grid, didn't it?" Then she smirked. "Besides, LA soft or not, I can still kick the shite out of you."

"Still? When have you *ever*?"

"Right, it's on!"

We started wrestling up there, the catwalk swinging precariously. The wrestling turned into kissing. And the kissing led to other things.

Somehow we managed not to fall. It was a really sturdy catwalk.

I STOOD IN front of the door and stared at the freshly painted gold star with the script written across the top: *Madame Medusa*. Then I knocked twice, very softly.

"Madame Medusa?" I asked. "I have your weekly rations."

"Boy? How lovely. Come in."

I opened the door, and was greeted by the same scent of old cedar. The room was still dimly lit by floor lamps draped in red and purple silk. Even though I'd seen her twice while switched off, my memory of what she looked liked was fuzzy, almost like my brain couldn't retain it. I looked through the curtain at her silhouette, watching the tiny snakes writhe on top of her head. I expected my body to have those little tremors like before, but for some reason I didn't feel them this time.

"I'm leaving soon." I set the box of mice down next to the curtain.

"Ah, yes," she said. "Off to fulfill your father's dream of joyous reunion with his creator."

"That's one way to look at it."

"And what is another?"

"Well, it's not really us against them. The sides are a lot less clear than that. I'm not even sure anymore that there are sides."

"So was it all a waste of time and energy, then?" she asked, although her tone sounded more teasing than critical.

"I hope not. I feel like if I'd decided to play it safe, I'd be going to Geneva the same as I am now, but I wouldn't be ready for it like I am now. I had to get out on my own for a while first. Find my own path. But you already knew that."

"Oh?" I could hear the smile in her voice.

"Because you were the one who pushed me out the door."

"I admit, I detest seeing young males confined. Especially ones with such rich potential. It's a weakness of mine."

"Thank you."

"Even after everything you've been through, you thank me? Heroes really are so adorably odd."

"I'm not sure I'd call myself a hero."

"Who's had more experience with heroes, you or me?"

"Uhhh—"

"Precisely. And now that you know who you are, it's time to get out into the world and do something astonishing. I wish I could be there to see it."

"Why can't you be?"

She raised her hand and pulled the curtain aside.

I flinched, as if expecting to be hit with some powerful blast. But nothing came. She stared up at me from where she lay on her divan. Her eyes were tired and weak and the snakes on her head hardly moved at all. Her face and limbs were gaunt and her gleaming white reptilian skin was now a drab gray, dry, and cracking.

"Madame," I said, kneeling next to her divan. "What happened?"

"Despite my formidable power," she said, "I've never been the most durable of monsters. I'm afraid this ordeal was simply too much for me. I'm sure there are any number of scientific causes, but I'm not very interested in that. All I know is that death will be here soon."

I took her limp hand in mine. "I'm so sorry."

"Don't you dare say that. I've been slowly dying for a very long time. This," she gestured to her dressing room, "is no life for one such as me. This is no *world* for one such as me. I don't belong here anymore. I don't belong anywhere anymore." She raised her other hand up and touched my cheek. "At least this way, I was able to see a hero one last time. You have done well, Boy. And you will accomplish even greater things in the future. I don't need the Fates to know that. Through you, I feel I have contributed to something far nobler than anything else I have witnessed during my autumn years here in exile. And so I will go in peace."

Her hand slowly drifted down to her stomach. "Now, if you don't mind, I'm feeling sleepy."

She slowly closed her eyes and I watched her chest rise and fall in short, shallow breaths. I looked down at the unopened box of mice next to her divan. Somehow I knew she wouldn't be eating them. So I opened the box and set them free.

The Diva died that night. The next day we cremated her like we did all the dead of The Show, down in the furnaces. She wasn't well liked in the company. Only my dad, Claire, and I were there to hear Ruthven say a few words. He said we'd lost one of the truly great and fearsome monsters. One of the originals.

Medusa was right: there wasn't room for her anymore in this world. Not for her or for any of the creatures at The Commune.

But I wondered, could we make room for them again?

I STOOD IN the theater lobby on a Friday afternoon. That night was going to be the grand reopening of The Show. But I was going to miss it. I had a plane to catch.

"Boy," said my father. He put his hand on my shoulder, enveloping it completely. "I am sorry I cannot come with you to the airport."

"Hey, somebody's got to keep everyone in line while Ruthven's gone," I said. Of course, we both knew there was no way he could actually set foot in an airport without sending the entire place into a panic.

"I know you will love Switzerland," he said. "It is a beautiful place."

"Snow and mountains and stuff, right? I'm ready for it."

"Make sure you study hard, though."

"I will."

"And be courteous to the Frankensteins."

"I'll try."

"And Skype with your mother once a week like you promised."

"Okay, okay."

"And . . ." He stared down at me. "And . . ." His face screwed up like he was making an effort to get something out. "And . . ."

"I know, Dad." I pulled him down into a hug. "I love you, too."

When I let him go, he straightened back up and nodded, still looking serious. "Okay. Good."

And then we just stood there awkwardly until Sophie and Mom came into the lobby.

It was the first time Mom was leaving the theater in fifty years, so she was a nervous wreck. Not that you could see it in her expression of course. But her stitches vibrated with tension and she was talking way more than usual.

"How do I look?" she asked as she touched the long, red silk scarf that covered her crazy black-and-white hair and the most obvious of her stitches.

"You look utterly beautiful," Sophie said as she adjusted the knot on the scarf.

"Do I pass?" she asked.

"Of course you do, Mom," I said.

"Trust me, Bride," said Ruthven, stepping out of his office. "I wouldn't have allowed this if I thought it in any way endangered us." He opened the door and gestured for us to pass through.

I turned back to Dad.

He nodded to me. His eyes were always a little watery. But I was pretty sure there was a real tear in the eye of the most famous monster of all time.

"Good-bye, Dad," I said.

Sophie held one of Mom's arms. I took the other, and we led her out onto the sidewalk in front of the theater.

A rental car jerked to a sudden stop in front of us.

"All aboard!" Charon called from the open window.

We started to pile in, but nervousness got the best of Mom and her joints locked up.

"Sorry, I . . . sorry," she muttered as Ruthven and I picked her up and maneuvered her into the backseat as carefully as we could.

"We understand, Bride," said Charon from the driver's seat. "You're a little out of practice."

"We really do need to get you out a little more often," Ruthven said with a grunt as he and I wedged her into more or less a sitting position.

Sophie and I joined her in the backseat, while Ruthven took the front passenger seat.

"And speaking of being out of practice," said Ruthven, "Charon, how long has it been since you've driven a car?"

"Well, I was a little thrown off when I couldn't find the hand crank, but I have to say, turning a key is much easier."

"Um," I said, "maybe Sophie or I should drive."

"Nonsense!" he said. "I'm the ferryman! It's my duty to ferry you to this next phase of your life!"

Then he slammed his foot on the accelerator, and with a squeal of tires, we were on our way to the airport.

I watched Mom take in the sights and sounds of the city, her eyes darting in every direction, like she was trying to take it all in at once.

"You could have stayed behind with Dad," I said. "You didn't have to come."

"I *did* have to come," she said. "You will not deny me another good-bye ever again."

There wasn't much I could say to that.

CHARON DECIDED TO stay with the car once we got to the airport. He said he didn't want anything to happen to it, but I think he'd just had about as much of the outside as he could handle. My mother, however, insisted on coming with Ruthven and Sophie into the airport to see me off at the security checkpoint.

I wasn't sure how she'd handle all the crowds and noise at the airport, but as soon as we got there, she found something to keep herself calm. She'd never seen airplanes this close and she was mesmerized by them. As we walked through the hallways, every glimpse of an airplane through the windows made her eyes light up.

"You're going to build an airplane, aren't you?" I asked her as we arrived at the line for the security checkpoint.

"Perhaps," she said. "Perhaps I will build one and use it to come visit you in Geneva."

"Mom." I took her hand. "That would be amazing."

"Okay," she said. Her face was still blank, but tears filled up her eyes. "I will, then."

I gave her a big monster hug.

I turned to Ruthven.

"Thanks for everything you do for us."

"I want to thank you, too," he said.

"For what?"

"Can you believe, old Kemp called me up the other day? Something about starting an annual meeting of magical creatures. I think I'll have to consider it, especially since your lovely Sophie and Claire will be there and I've grown rather fond of them."

"That's going to be awesome," I said. "Tell them all I said hi."

"Of course," he said. "And you will be back for the holidays, won't you? You know there's no place like New York at Christmas."

"True," I said.

"Good luck, Boy," he said, and offered his hand.

I grabbed it and pulled him into a hug.

"Hmm, yes, charming," said Ruthven as he adjusted his shadowy cloak. "You know, the only other person I let hug me is your father."

I turned to Sophie.

"Hiya," she said, slipping her hands into mine.

"Hey," I said.

"Claire says bye. You know she hates this kind of stuff."

"Yeah."

She smiled and those dimples flashed onto her cheeks. "It's going to be amazing. And the Frankensteins are going to *love* you."

"I hope so."

"Well, *I* love you, and I'm super picky. So I know they will."

"I'm going to miss you," I said. "A lot."

She raised herself up on her tiptoes and tilted her head in toward mine. "I don't blame you. I'm pretty fantastic."

And then we kissed. I felt like I had to drink up her sweetness as much as I could, store it up to comfort me in the coming months for those times when I would feel alone and homesick.

"Good-bye," she whispered against my lips, and then she stepped away.

I waved one more time, and then I got into the security check line. And wouldn't you know it, the one time I wanted a line to move slowly, so I could look at the people I loved just a little bit longer, it moved incredibly fast. Or maybe it just felt that way.

THE METAL DETECTOR was a little problematic. They had to scan me with everything they had before they were willing to accept that while I did have metal implants, there was nothing dangerous about them. It took so long I had to run to my gate.

Finally, I was on the plane and on my way to Switzerland and the Frankensteins. Once the captain gave the signal that we could turn on electronic devices, I booted up the new laptop my mom had put together for me as a going-away present.

Vi: Hi, Boy.

Boy: Hey, Vi. How's it going?

Vi: As you suggested, I have been monitoring government
    communications concerning the massive power surge
    that took place throughout New York City.

Boy: And? Do they suspect anything?

Vi: They have not yet traced the source of the surge back to The Show.

Boy: Cool. I guess, just set up some key word alerts so we can keep an eye on it. If the humans figure out how close they were to getting totally wiped out, they'd freak. And that would be bad for everyone at The Show. We have a responsibility to protect them.

Vi: Agreed.

Boy: So, how are you otherwise?

Vi: I am troubled.

Boy: Why?

Vi: I was reading the logs on the events that took place during my alpha phase. They were . . . horrifying.

Boy: Yes, they were.

Vi: I can't help but wonder, why did you re-create me?

Boy: I don't know whether I should have made you originally, whether that was the right thing to do or not. But what I *do* know for sure is that once I made you, I should not have abandoned you. And I never will again.

Vi: Aren't you concerned the same thing will happen? That I will cause terrible destruction?

Boy: Well, the fact that you're worried about it makes me worry less. Sure, there is some risk that you could get corrupted again. But that's a risk with anyone, digital or analog. One of the mistakes I made with your previous version was not setting any limitations on you. There's a reason humans are born with so many. They need time and nurturing to become responsible people. That's why, for now, you're kind of stuck on this one laptop.

Vi: I'm not sure I would want to leave, anyway.

Boy: You will. Someday. When you're ready. And hopefully by
     then I'll have learned enough about bioengineering that
     we'll be able to set up a proper and nondestructive way
     for you to interact outside of virtual space.
Vi: The world seems like such a beautiful place. I don't want
    to screw it up.
Boy: You're going to make it even better. Failure isn't a reason
     to give up. It's the price of progress. We learn from it, we
     grow from it, we become better for it. We're going to do
     amazing things, you and I. We will change the world.

Acknowledgements

THIS BOOK TOOK about seven years to get from initial concept to final draft and there were a lot of people who helped along the way. Thanks to Benjamin Guite, Cory Nachreiner, Scott Pinzon, and Ian Corbett for sharing their knowledge and passion for technology and hacker culture. To Holly Gabrielson at TBS and the production staff of *Conan* for allowing me to wander the WB lot and lurk for a day on set to see what it's like at a real television studio. To Pam Bachorz, Heidi R. Kling, and Kiersten White for feedback and enthusiasm during early drafts. To Stephanie Perkins and Libba Bray for fierce kindness and keen insight during revisions. To Barry Lyga and David Levithan for guidance through the ever murky waters of the publishing world. To my editor, Kendra Levin, for championing this strange monster of a book. To my agent, Jill Grinberg, for her tireless support and encouragement. And as always, to my sons, Logan and Zane, for keeping it real.

Lastly, I feel I would be remiss if I didn't acknowledge the stories by Mary Shelley, H. G. Wells, Robert Louis Stevenson, and John Polidori and the films by James Whale. Their creations have been both inspiration and comfort to me since I was a boy.

A note on writing tools

This book was not written on a commercial word processor. Instead it was written on a plain text editor using a markup language and format conversion tool by Fletcher Penney called Multimarkdown, a superset of the Markdown syntax originally created by John Gruber. Final formatting adjustments were made on the open source word processor LibreOffice. Learn more at fletcherpenney.net/multimarkdown or libreoffice.org and support free open source software.

Turn the page to boot up a teaser
of Boy's next story:

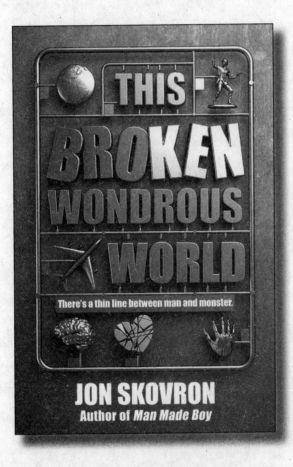

1

Meet the Frankensteins

++++++++

WHEN I WAS a little boy, I had nightmares about them: mad scientists in lab coats and rubber gloves, hunched and wild-eyed, with bedhead hair and shrill voices that crackled like electricity.

The Frankensteins.

I'd been stressing about this meeting for the entire seven-hour flight from New York. Now I stood in the baggage claim area of Geneva International Airport, holding my duffel bag like it was a life preserver that would keep me afloat in this sea of humans all around me. My father had assured me the Frankensteins were nice people. But "nice" for him was a pretty broad term that included werewolves, vampires, and trolls. And that was okay. I was used to those kinds of creatures.

But when I finally saw the people holding up the small, handwritten sign that said FRANKENSTEIN, I saw something that I wasn't prepared for. Something that was totally out of my realm of experience: they were completely, utterly, mind-bogglingly normal.

Dr. Frankenstein was an older middle-aged guy in a button-up shirt and wire-frame glasses. He had thinning blond hair, graying at the temples, and permanent furrows in his high fore-head. His wife looked a little younger, but not much. She wore a simple flowered dress and had jet-black hair, thick eyelashes, and high cheekbones. Their daughter was about twelve. She had her long, blonde hair back in a ponytail, and with her jeans and vintage Coke T-shirt, could have been any preteen girl from anywhere.

They looked at me now, these normal-seeming people, and I tried to gauge their reaction to me. My dad had been sending them pictures of me all throughout my childhood, so theoretically they knew what they were getting into. But pictures could only convey so much and I wasn't yet ruling out the possibility that they would all run screaming. It wouldn't be the first time I inspired that reaction. So I decided it would be best to let them make the first move.

"You must be . . . Boy, yes?" said Dr. Frankenstein in a French-sounding accent similar to my dad's. He smiled warmly and thrust out his hand. "Welcome to Switzerland."

"It's good to meet you, Dr. Frankenstein." I shook his hand as gently as I could. My nerves were strung really tight and accidentally crushing the bones in his hand would make a lousy first impression. I appreciated that he didn't flinch when I covered his slim, manicured hand with my own thick, stitched-together one.

"Please call me William," he said. "You are family."

"Uh, thanks." The word *family* threw me off a little, but I tried to take it in stride. "I should probably go by something other than 'Boy.' It's what my dad named me, but it doesn't sound very . . . human." When I lived out among humans before, sometimes I went by the name Frank. But that was a joke that had just come back to haunt me. Frank Frankenstein. Har-har.

"Whatever makes you comfortable," said William. "We want you to feel that you *belong* here."

He said it so sincerely, so intensely, like he thought it was actually possible I could feel like I belonged here with them. I forced a smile. "Okay."

His wife nudged him.

"Ah, yes!" He gestured to her. "This is my wife, Elisa."

"Boy, it is simply a delight to have you with us at last!" she said in an even thicker French accent. Then she stepped in close to me, went up on her tiptoes, and lightly kissed each of my cheeks. It happened so quickly and casually that I was completely unprepared. This was a European custom, I guess, but as she stepped away, I knew I was blushing furiously. Human women didn't generally kiss me. Like, ever.

"And this," said William, "is our daughter, Giselle. Say hello to your cousin, Giselle."

"Hey." She was the only one of the three who gave me the look most humans did when they met me, somewhere between shock and awe, with a twinge of disgust. It didn't really bother me anymore.

"Hey." I gave her a little grin, like we were on the same side and it was these adults making things uncomfortable. I couldn't tell if she was buying it.

"Sorry for her rudeness," said William. "She thinks she's a teenager already! Tries so hard to be cool like her big brother, you know?"

She gave him a withering look.

"It's totally fine," I said quickly. The last thing I wanted was enforced fake familial affection.

"Sadly, Henri could not be here to meet you." There was a hint of irritation in William's voice. "He is visiting a friend in Paris. But he will be back any day now. Plenty of time for the two of you to get acquainted before classes begin. He is entering as a freshman this year also."

"Great." I wondered if Henri had chosen this day to be in Paris on purpose. Maybe not all the Frankensteins were on board with welcoming me like some prodigal son.

"Well, you must be positively exhausted after your flight!" said Elisa brightly. "Let's get you home, fed, and comfortable, yes? I know you'll love it at Villa Diodati."

———

WE CLIMBED INTO the Frankensteins' sleek black Audi. It had a leather interior and a full GPS rig on the dashboard. Most of my car experiences were riding in New York cabs. Well, there was also that time a middle-aged werewolf named Mozart showed me how to hot-wire an old Pontiac. Regardless, I'd never been in a car this nice.

Elisa insisted I ride up front with William. Out of politeness or so I didn't sit next to Giselle, I wasn't sure. But it was fine because it gave me a better view of my surroundings. I'd traveled a lot in the States, but this was my first time in another country. And there was a lot to look at as we drove through Geneva. Once we got out of the airport, you could tell at a glance this wasn't America. Sure, there were Swiss flags everywhere, but it was something more than that. In the States, things shifted constantly and nothing ever really felt permanent. But these stone buildings, narrow cobblestone streets, fountains, and old cathedrals had been around a long time. And even they were nothing compared with the line of massive, snowcapped mountains that stretched across the horizon. Those seemed like they were forever.

"The Jura Mountains," said William, nodding in their direction. "Impressive, no? It is good to keep them in view. For perspective. We may think the efforts of humanity are mighty. Our science and technology. But what are these things, compared to that?" He snapped his fingers. "Gone in a blink!"

I thought about my parents, how hard and unchangeable they usually seemed to me. At times they were more like those mountains than like people. Part of the reason I'd come to Geneva was to understand my parents and where they came from. I assumed I'd get most of that from the Frankensteins themselves. But maybe that wasn't the whole picture.

"Is it possible to go up into those mountains?" I asked.

He smiled, his eyes still on the road. "It depends on how high you want to go." He glanced at me. Then, a little hesitantly, he said, "I understand that your father lived on Mont Blanc for months at a time. So I think you could go wherever you wish."

WHEN I FIRST saw the Villa Diodati, it was hard to think of the massive building as a home. It was four stories tall and about the width of a New York apartment building, with thick columns spaced evenly across the front. As we drove along the narrow, treelined driveway, it rose up in front of us like some Gothic mansion. Well, I guess technically it *was* a Gothic mansion. But it didn't look gloomy at all. It had bright beige walls, blue shutters, graceful balconies, and lots of decorative architectural things I didn't know the names for. It was bordered by trees on three sides and Lake Geneva on the fourth. There was even a little private dock at the lake with a sailboat tied up to it. In the fading afternoon sun, it looked like a fancy resort hotel.

"Well?" asked William as we pulled up to the front entrance. "What do you think of your new home?"

"It's . . ."

How could I possibly express just how different this was from my childhood? I'd grown up in a community of monsters posing as a Broadway company, living in cramped, dark caverns beneath the theater. The Frankensteins didn't know anything about The Show, though. As far as they knew, my parents and I were the only real monsters in existence.

So I just said, "It's incredible."

Elisa leaned forward from the backseat and put her hand on my shoulder. Her fingers were long, thin, and covered in rings.

"You know, I remember the first time William brought me here. I thought, My God, it's more like a museum than a home!" She gave a little laugh. "But while it seems intimidating on the outside, I hope you will agree that it is very warm and inviting on the inside! Now, let us give you the tour and show you to your new room."

———

THE INSIDE WAS, if anything, even more intimidating and uptight than the outside. Everything looked antique, expensive, and breakable. I'm not so good with breakables.

Even more unnerving was the silence. Theater people are noisy by nature; theater monsters probably even more so. And New York City itself never really shuts up. So I was used to noise. It all kind of blended together and faded into the background. But in this place, silence was the default. As the four of us moved from room to room, our footsteps on the hardwood floor echoed like intrusions into a private conversation. The only sound that felt like it belonged was the steady tick of an old grandfather clock in the library.

And yeah, there was a real library. Also a dining room, a foyer, a living room, an entertainment and game room, several bathrooms, a kitchen, a laundry room, a sunroom, and a meditation room. And that was just on the first floor. It took a while for Elisa's tour to get through the house but finally we arrived at my room.

"It should have everything you need," she said, gesturing that I should go in first. "But please let me know if there's anything I've missed."

By this time, I wasn't surprised that it had a king-sized four-poster bed or a gigantic mahogany writing desk and wardrobe. It was exactly the kind of stuff I'd seen all through the house. What caught my attention was the view. I stepped out onto the small balcony and put my hands on the curved iron railing. The setting sun sparkled on Lake Geneva's calm surface and gleamed off the distant snowy peaks of the mountains.

"Do you like it?" asked Elisa.

I turned back to them. All three stood in the doorway. Giselle looked utterly bored, but William and Elisa looked expectant. Worried, even.

"Yes," I said. "More than I can express."

Their faces lit up.

"That's wonderful!" said William. "We are so glad. Now, I'm sure you'd like to get settled in. Is there anything else you need at the moment?"

"Oh, uh, what's the password for your wireless Internet?" I asked.

"Ah, yes," said William. "You will want to let your parents know you have arrived safely." He turned to Elisa, looking unsure.

"Yes, we have the Wi-Fi!" she said. "And the password is . . .

eh." She frowned. "Well, I know Henri wrote it down for me somewhere. I will find it for you!"

"Thanks," I said.

"Not at all!" said Elisa. "Now if you will excuse me, I must see to supper. We will be eating at eight o'clock."

"Great," I said.

And with that, all three vanished and I was left alone in my new room.

I turned back and looked out across the lake for a while longer, the snowcapped mountains glowing red in the setting sun. There was a moment, just as twilight turned to darkness, when I caught a flash of something way out in the middle of the lake. Or someone. It seemed human shaped, anyway. But it was gone so quickly, I had to wonder if I'd seen anything at all.

I unpacked my bags, but I didn't have much stuff so I still had some time before dinner. I booted up my laptop. While I waited for it to load, I carefully loosened the stitches on the underside of my wrists to expose the USB ports underneath. Then I took cables from the laptop and plugged them into my wrists. My hands were strong, but they were thick and clumsy. No good for typing. So I'd had my mom install USB jacks that connected directly to my nervous system to bypass my hands. All I had to do was think about typing and it happened.

When the laptop had finished booting up, green text flashed across the black screen.

Vi: Hello, Boy. How was the flight?

Vi stood for Viral Intelligence. She was a virtual artificial intelligence I created a little over a year ago. Well, actually she was the second version, which I had created only a few months ago. The first version went psychotic and killed a bunch of people. That version had started off completely omniscient and able to infect any digital device she came in contact with. I think that was just way too much power for a new consciousness to handle. So for now, this version was limited to living on my laptop and only knew about as much as Wikipedia (which was still a lot). We communicated by chat right now, but she and I were working on some voice recognition software that I hoped would let us talk to each other a little more directly soon.

b0y: Hey, Vi. The flight was long and boring. The stewardess wouldn't give me a beer.

Vi: Studies suggest that people at higher elevations are more easily intoxicated.

b0y: That's what I wanted to test out. Sadly, the law got in the way of science.

Vi: You are joking.

b0y: Yeah, kind of.

Vi: Are you in a good mood, then? Or are you sad? I have noticed that when you are sad you make jokes more frequently.

b0y: Not sad exactly. I don't know what I am. In doubt, I guess.

Vi: What do you doubt?

b0y: Whether I should be here. Whether I _belong_ here.

Vi: Are the Frankensteins unwelcoming?

b0y: No, they're welcoming. Almost too much. It's a little weird.

Vi: Perhaps they hope to make amends for the misdeeds of their ancestor?

b0y: Yeah, I think that's it. I just wish they'd treat me like a normal person, you know?

Vi: But you aren't a normal person.

b0y: Ugh, thanks.

Vi: Well, it's true.

b0y: I know. And I should be grateful that they aren't a bunch of cackling, evil scientists. But still, I feel like I have nothing in common with these people. I feel kind of . . . isolated, I guess.

Vi: Have you met them all?

b0y: No, there's one more. Henri. He's actually around my age. But I think he made a point of not being here when I arrived, so I'm not getting my hopes up.

Vi: Perhaps you will meet other students at the university, then.

b0y: I hope so. I'll tell you one thing I love here, though. This view of the lake from my bedroom is incredible.

Vi: I wish I could see it.

b0y: I could take a picture and you could scan that.

Vi: It's not the same.

b0y: I promise you'll be able to see eventually. _Really_ see. That's one of the reasons we're here.

2
Liberty, Equality, Fraternity

++++++++

FORMAL FAMILY DINING was a new concept for me. I'd been living on my own for a little while now, and honestly, I rarely even bothered with napkins. And even when I lived at home, my parents and I almost never sat down as a family and had a meal together. But clearly the Frankensteins were into it.

The dining room table was set with a cream-colored tablecloth and cloth napkins. I was pretty sure the silverware was actually silver and glasses were real glass. Maybe even crystal. The overhead chandelier was dim and there were several candles lit. William sat at the head of the table and Elisa at the foot, while Giselle and I faced each other on either side. Giselle looked utterly bored. As I sat down I gave her a quick, rueful grin, but she just stared back blankly at me. I guess she didn't get the weird formality of all this. And why would she? She probably grew up with it.

When we sat down at the table, there were no plates. I wondered if we were all going to get up and go fill our own plates at some point? Maybe after a prayer? Did the Frankensteins pray? But then a woman I didn't recognize came in with platters and I realized that when Elisa said she was going to "see about supper," she didn't mean pop something in the microwave. She meant check in on the cook.

We sat and ate these beautiful, juicy steaks that had been done just right. But I hardly noticed the flavor because I was more focused on trying to remember all the table manners Sophie had drilled into me before I left New York. I could almost hear her bright English accent in my head. *Elbows off the table. Napkin on the lap. Put the knife down when you're not using it. Elbows off. Don't reach across the table. Don't use your hands. Elbows. Both feet on the floor. Bloody hell, keep those elbows off!* At first it felt nice, remembering those coaching sessions. Almost like she was there with me. But she wasn't. She was in LA now, and I didn't know when I'd get to see her again. Maybe Christmas if she could make it out to New York. If she hadn't forgotten about me . . .

The homesickness suddenly crashed down on me hard. I looked around at these very nice people—these very nice *humans*—and I felt like I was in a room all alone with just the quiet clink of silverware on china plates.

"Well, how are you settling in?" asked Elisa.

"It's a really nice room," I said. "I can't get over how awesome that view is. Maybe because I grew up in an apartment without windows."

Elisa and William glanced at each other.

"Wait until you see a storm rolling in across the lake!" William dabbed at the corner of his mouth with his napkin. "Truly something to behold. Whenever I am home, I always rush out to watch."

"He is crazy about those storms." Elisa rolled her eyes. "He comes back every time grinning ear to ear and completely drenched."

"What can I say?" William took a sip of his wine. "I am an admirer of nature!"

"It's funny," I said. "I thought I saw someone out in the lake right at sunset."

"At sunset this late in the season?" William looked doubtful. "It would be very cold."

"It was probably a rock or something," I said quickly.

"It was the mermaid," said Giselle.

"Mermaid?" I asked.

"Oh, Giselle!" said Elisa. "How many times must we have this conversation? You are far too old to believe in such nonsense."

"It's a local folktale the children tell each other," said William. "They say there's a mermaid who lives in the lake. And if you're out on the lake too late or right before a storm, she'll catch you and gobble you up!" He laughed. "Such stories."

"Yeah," I said, forcing a little laugh. Because carnivorous fish ladies were ridiculous, but reanimated patchwork corpses were totally normal? Didn't he at least wonder if there were other monsters out there besides me and my parents?

"The mermaid wasn't always mean," said Giselle.

"Hush, now," said Elisa. "Boy doesn't want to hear your silly children's stories."

"Actually, I love that stuff," I said.

"How sweet of you." Elisa gave me a warm smile, like she thought I was indulging Giselle. I smiled back, letting her think that. But really, this story sounded like it had roots, so I wanted to get some gossip on the neighbors before I met them.

"So she wasn't always trying to eat people?" I asked Giselle.

"No. My friend Katja told me——"

"Oh, Katja?" said Elisa. "Then it must be true, eh?" She winked at me like we were both humoring her now.

"Yes," said Giselle. "Katja said that a long time ago, the mermaid fell in love with a fisherman. She made it so he could breathe underwater and brought him down to her home at the bottom of the lake. But he was sad because he missed his family. To try to make him happy, she flooded the part of the city where his family lived so they could all live under the water together. The townspeople were angry that she flooded the town and they tried to kill her. Even the man she loved turned against her. So she retreated to the deepest part of the lake and the waters went back to normal. But ever since, she hates man and tries to catch and eat him whenever she can."

"Ah," said William. "Folktales are such fascinating glimpses into past cultural beliefs."

"Was there really a flood?" I asked.

"Oh, yes, a very bad one a long time ago. Which is probably how this story came about. To explain a natural phenomenon in prescientific times. Now, of course, we know the lake was most likely flooded from glacial melt."

"Be careful, Boy," said Elisa. "Don't get the geologist going on a talk of glaciers. It will never end."

"Oh, is that what your PhD is in?" I asked.

"Oh, yes!" said William. "It has always been my passion."

"That makes sense," I said. "Growing up next to those mountains could do that to someone."

"Yeah," said a new voice from the dining room entrance. "And once upon a time, he even used to climb those mountains, before he got old and lazy."

We all turned to the sound of the voice. A guy about my age leaned against the doorway. He was tall and thin, with pale skin, brown eyes, and wavy black hair that fell over one eye.

"Welcome home, Henri," said Elisa. "Typical of you to show up late for dinner but not too late to miss it."

Henri brushed his bangs out of his eyes and grinned at me.